Gaston Boissier, D. Havelock Fisher

The Country of Horace and Virgil

Gaston Boissier, D. Havelock Fisher

The Country of Horace and Virgil

ISBN/EAN: 9783337227685

Printed in Europe, USA, Canada, Australia, Japan

Cover: Foto ©Andreas Hilbeck / pixelio.de

More available books at **www.hansebooks.com**

THE
COUNTRY OF HORACE AND VIRGIL

BY

GASTON BOISSIER

OF THE FRENCH ACADEMY

TRANSLATED BY

D. HAVELOCK FISHER

WITH MAPS AND PLANS

LONDON
T. FISHER UNWIN
PATERNOSTER SQUARE
1896

CONTENTS.

CHAPTER I.

THE COUNTRY OF HORACE AND VIRGIL.

CHAPTER I.

HORACE'S COUNTRY HOUSE.

ONE cannot read Horace without longing to be acquainted with that country house in which he was so happy. Can we know exactly where it was? Is it possible to find again, not the very stones of his villa, which time has doubtless scattered, but the charming spot he has so oft described—those lofty mountains which "sheltered his goats from the summer fires;" that spring by which he was wont to stretch himself in the day's hot hours; those woods, those rivulets, those valleys—in fine, that landscape which he had before his eyes during the longer and better portion of his life? People have been asking themselves this question ever since the Renaissance, and its solution might have been early foreseen. Towards the end of the sixteenth century some learned men, who had started in search of Horace's house, surmised the place where it should be looked for, but their indications being vague, and not always based on solid proofs, they failed to produce a general conviction. Besides, there was no lack of persons who did not wish to be convinced. In every corner of the Sabine Hills some village sage vociferously claimed for his district the honour of having sheltered Horace, and would not hear of its being bereft of it. And this is how his house came to be located at Tibur, at Cures, at Reate—everywhere, in short, but where it ought to be.

The problem was definitely solved in the second half of the last century by a Frenchman, Abbé Capmartin de Chaupy. He was one of those who go to Rome to spend a few months, and remain there all their lives. When he had once resolved to find the site of Horace's house, he did not spare himself trouble.[1] He went over nearly the whole of Italy, studying monuments, reading inscriptions, questioning the people of the country, and personally investigating the sites which best answered to the descriptions of the poet. He travelled by short stages on a horse, which, if we are to believe him, by dint of being taken to so many antiquities had almost become an antiquarian itself. This animal, he tells us, went to ruins of his own accord, and his fatigue seemed to vanish directly he found himself on the pavement of some ancient way. Capmartin de Chaupy wrote three large volumes of nearly five hundred pages each [2] about

---

[1] It must be mentioned that Capmartin de Chaupy was passionately fond of Horace, and found reasons for everything in his favourite author. He lived long enough to witness the French Revolution, and it is said that it did not take him by surprise. Horace had taught him to foresee it, and he willingly pointed out the places in his works where it was predicted in express terms.

[2] *Découverte de la maison de campagne d'Horace*, par L'Abbé Capmartin de Chaupy, Rome, 1767-1769.

his journeys, and the results to which his indefatigable labours had led him. His subject—the site of Horace's house—could not be expected to fill so many pages, and the author often turns aside to speak on other matters. He writes how he travelled, stopping at each step, and often leaving the highroad in order to plunge into byways. He spares us nothing, but elucidates, in passing, obscure points of geography and history, notices inscriptions, finds lost towns again, and fixes the direction of ancient roads. This manner of proceeding, then much in vogue among the learned, nearly deprived Chaupy of the honour of his discovery. De Sanctis, a Roman *savant*, who had heard his labours spoken of, started on the same track, and easily out-stripping him, published a little dissertation on the same subject which was favourably received.[1] This was a great grief to the poor Abbé, who complained bitterly. Happily, his three volumes, which appeared almost immediately afterwards, brought over public opinion to his side, and few now deny him the glory of having found Horace's country house, of which he was so proud.

Roughly speaking, this is how he sets to work to prove to the most incredulous that he is not mistaken. He first establishes the fact that Horace had not a plurality of domains, since he himself tells us that he possesses only the Sabine estate, and that this estate is enough for him: *satis beatus unicis Sabinis*.[2] It follows therefore that all his descriptions must refer to this estate and be applicable

---

[1] *Dissertazione sopra la villa di Orazzio Flacco*, dell' abbate Dominico de Sanctis.   [2] *Carm.*, II. 18, 14.

to it. This basis fixed, Chaupy visits in turn every spot on which it has been sought to place the poet's house, and has no difficulty in showing that not one of them quite agrees with the pictures he has drawn of it. It can only be to the east of Tivoli and near Vicovaro, as this district alone corresponds exactly with the lines of Horace. More striking and more conclusively convincing still is the fact that all the modern names here have kept their likeness to the ancient ones. We know from Horace that the most important town in the vicinity of his house, whither his farmers repaired on every market-day, was called Varia. The table of Pentinger also speaks of Varia, placing it eight miles from Tibur. Well, eight miles from Tivoli, the ancient Tibur, we to-day find Vicovaro, which has kept its ancient name (*Vicus Varia*) nearly unaltered. Again, at the foot of Vicovaro flows a little brook called the Licenza : it is, with very slight change, the *Digentia* of Horace. He tells us also that this brook waters the small town of Mandela. To-day Mandela has become *Bardela*, which is almost the same, and to make assurance doubly sure, an inscription found there completely restores to it its ancient name.[1] Lastly, the high Mount Lucretalis, which shaded the poet's house, is the Corgnaleto, called *Mons Lucretii* in the charts of the Middle Ages.[2] It cannot be chance alone that has brought together in the same locality all the names of places mentioned by the poet; neither is it chance that has made this canton of the Sabine Hills to

----

[1] Orelli, *Inscr. lat.*, 104.

[2] "Vie d'Horace," par Noel des Vergers, p. 27, in Didot's *Horace*.

correspond so perfectly with all his descriptions. It is certain, then, that his house was in this region, watered by the Licenza, on the slopes of the Corgnaleto, not far from Vicovaro and Bardela. It is thither we must send the worshippers of Horace (if any yet remain) if they would make a pious pilgrimage to his villa.

I.

HOW HORACE CAME TO KNOW MÆCENAS — CHARACTER OF MÆCENAS—LIFE IN HIS HOUSE—THE PALACE OF THE ESQUILINE.

Before taking them there, let us briefly recall how he became its owner; for this is an interesting chapter of his history.

We know that after having fought at Philippi as a military tribune in the Republican army, he returned to Rome, where the gates were opened to him during an amnesty. This return must have been most sad. He had lost his father, whom he tenderly loved, and had been deprived of his estate. The great hopes he cherished when, at twenty years of age he had seen himself distinguished by Brutus and put at the head of a legion, were rudely dissipated. He said "they had cut his wings."[1]   He fell from all his ambitious aims into the miseries of an embarrassed existence, and, in order to live, the late military tribune had to buy himself a government clerkship. Yet poverty was not without its use, if, as he asserts, it gave him the courage to write

---

[1] *Decisis humilem pennis—Epist.*, II. 2, 50.

verses.[1] These verses met with great success; he had adopted the right way to attract public notice: he spoke ill of persons of credit. His *Satires*, in which he expressed himself freely in an age when nobody dared to speak, having made a noise, Mæcenas, who was curious, wanted to see him, and had him introduced by Varius and by Virgil. These facts are known to all: it is needless to insist on them.

Mæcenas was then one of the most important personages of the Empire, and shared with Agrippa the favour of Octavius. But their behaviour was very different. While Agrippa, a soldier of fortune, born in an obscure family, loved to adorn himself with the first dignities of the State, Mæcenas, who belonged to the highest nobility of Etruria, remained in the shade. Only twice in his life was he officially charged with the exercise of public authority: in 717, during the embarrassments caused by the war in Sicily against Sextus Pompeius; and in 723, when Octavius went to fight Antony. But he bore a new title which left him outside the hierarchy of ancient functionaries.[2] But he would accept no more honours. He obstinately refused to enter the Senate, and remained to the end a simple knight, humbly taking a place below all those sons of great lords, who were quickly raised to the highest offices through family influence. It is not easy to understand this disinterestedness, as rare then as it is now. His contem-

---

[1] *Paupertas impulit audax Ut versus facerem—Epist.* II, 2, 51.

[2] It is generally thought that he was named by Octavius Prefect of Rome (*præfectus urbi*), but a commentator of Virgil, discovered at Verona, calls him præfect of the prætorium, and M. Mommsen thinks this was really the title he bore, and that it was created for him.

poraries, while loading him with praises, have omitted to tell us the reason of it. Perhaps they themselves found it difficult to fathom it. So refined a politician does not readily reveal the motives for his conduct. It has usually been attributed to a kind of natural idleness or indolence, which made him dread the stir of business, and this explanation is near enough to the mark if not exaggerated. An impartial historian tells us that he knew how to shake off his torpor when action was necessary: *Ubi res vigilantiam exigeret, sane exsomnis, providens atque agendi sciens.*[1] But he kept himself in reserve for certain occasions, and did not deem everything in human affairs worthy to occupy him. He had indeed both talent and taste for politics, and that he never entirely weaned himself from them is proved by the circumstance that Horace one day felt it necessary to say to him: "Cease to let thy repose be troubled by the cares of public business. Since thou hast the happiness to be a simple private person like ourselves, do not concern thyself too much with the dangers that may threaten the Empire."[2] He busied himself with them, then, too zealously to please his Epicurean friends. Although without a political office, he had his eyes open to the manœuvres of political parties, to the preparations of Parthia, of Cantabria, and of Dacia. He liked to speak his mind touching the great questions on which depended the peace of the world ; but his opinion once given, he withdrew, and left to others the care of putting it into execution. He reserved himself for things that asked but a single effort of thought. To prepare, to com-

---

[1] Velleius Paterculus, II. 87, 2. [2] *Carm.*, III. 8.

bine, to reflect, to foresee the consequence of events, to surprise the intentions of men, to direct towards a single end contrary wills and opposed interests; to create circumstances and turn them to account—this, assuredly, is one of the highest applications of the intelligence, one of the most pleasurable exercises of the mind. The charm of this speculative statecraft is so great that, in passing from counsel to action, one seems to lower oneself. The execution of great projects calls for tedious precautions, and bears in its train a crowd of commonplace cares. Yet a statesman is only complete when he knows both how to conceive and how to act; when he is capable of realising what he has imagined ; when he is not content with taking broad views of things, but can descend to details. It seems to me then that the friends of Mæcenas, who praised him for avoiding all these petty troubles and choosing only to be the most important adviser of Augustus, honoured him for being, in reality, merely an imperfection.

They are mistaken, too, I think, when they represent him as a sage who fears turmoil, who loves silence, and who seeks to escape from applause and glory. There was, perhaps, less modesty than pride in his resolve. He disliked the crowd, and took a kind of insolent pleasure in setting himself at variance with general opinion and in not thinking as everybody else thought. Horace tells us that he braved the prejudice of birth, which was so strong around him, and that he never asked his friends of what family they came.[1] He feared death, and, what is more common, he dared to own it.[2] But, on the other

---

[1] *Sat.*, I. 6, 7.

[2] The lines in which Mæcenas owned that he feared death are

hand, he felt but little dread for that which follows death. The cares of sepulture, the torment of so many, left him quite indifferent. "I don't bother about a tomb," said he, "if you neglect to bury anyone, nature sees to it."

"*Nec tumulum curo : sepelit natura relictos.*"[1]

This line is certainly the finest he has left us. It is in the same spirit of haughty contrariety that he affected to disdain all those honours which his friends used to run after. He well knew that this contempt of opinion was not a thing to mar his renown. The crowd is so constituted that it does not love, but cannot help admiring, those who differ from it; hence there are people who hide themselves in order to be sought, and who think that one is sometimes more conspicuous in retirement than in power. Mæcenas was perhaps of the number, and it may be suspected that his attitude was not entirely devoid of coquettish calculation. Not only did he suffer little loss from the voluntary obscurity to which he condemned himself—he might even think that it conduced to his glory more than the most brilliant dignities. When nothing remains of statesmen but a great name, and one thinks they have done much without knowing exactly what it is they have done, one is often tempted to attribute to them

---

known to all, thanks to the translation which La Fontaine has made of them in his Fables :—

> "*Mecenas fut un galant homme :*
> *Il a dit quelque part : ' Qu'on me rend impotent,*
> *Cul-de-jatte, goutteux, manchot, pourvu, qu'en somme,*
> *Je vive, c'est assez ; je suis plus que content.'*"

[1] Sen., *Epist.*, 92, 35.

that which does not belong to them, and to believe them to be more important than they are. This is precisely what has happened in the case of Mæcenas. Two centuries afterwards, Dion Cassius, an historian of the Empire, attributed to him a long speech, in which he is supposed to suggest to Augustus all the reforms which that prince afterwards carried out. According to this, the honour of those institutions, which through so many centuries have governed the world, is due, not to the Emperor, but to the Roman knight. We see then, that if Mæcenas remained in the shade from calculation, this calculation was completely successful, and that his clever conduct at the same time assured his tranquillity during life, and has increased his reputation after death.

Whatever might have been the reasons which led him to shun public life, it is sure that, while refusing honours, he did not mean to doom himself to solitude. He certainly was not one of those philosophers who, like the sage of Lucretius, have no other distraction than to look from "the height of their austere retreat upon men groping along the road of life." He intended to lead a joyous existence, and, above all, to gather round him a society of choice spirits. But he would not have found this so easy had he busied himself more with public affairs. A politician is not free to choose his friends as he pleases. He cannot shut his doors to important personages, bores though they sometimes are. The position which Mæcenas had made for himself allowed of his receiving only clever people. At his house he gathered round him poets and great men. The poets came from all ranks of society; the great lords were gleaned from every political party. Side by side with Aristius Fuscus and the two Viscus, friends of Octavius, were seen Servius Sulpicius, son of the great jurist so highly praised by Cicero, and Bibulus, who was probably the grandson of Cato. It may be asked whether that fusion of parties, which brought about the oblivion of past hatreds, that union of politicians of every shade of opinion upon a new ground, which made the honour and strength of the rule of Augustus, did not begin at Mæcenas' house? Among the poets whom he had drawn to him are found the two greatest of that age. He did not wait to attach them to him until they had produced their masterpieces; but foretold their future greatness by their maiden efforts. This does honour to his taste. Certain details of the *Bucolics* of Virgil had caused him to foresee the great touches of the *Georgics* and the *Æneid*, and through the imperfections of Horace's *Epodes* he forecast the *Odes*. And thus it was that this house, so obstinately closed to so many great personages, was early opened to the Mantuan peasant and to the son of the Venusian slave.

These men of letters and great lords passed a very pleasant time together. Mæcenas' fortune allowed him to gratify all his tastes, and give those who surrounded him a liberal existence. The Roman quidnuncs would have dearly liked to know what went on in that distinguished but exclusive company. So should we, and we often long to imitate the bore who, to Horace's great annoyance, one day followed him all along the Sacred Way, to make him talk a little. We should like to get from him some particulars about those clever men with whom he used to foregather, and we search his works to see whether they will not tell us something about life in Mæcenas' house. Unfortunately for us, Horace is discreet, and only lets fall from time to time a few confidences, which we hasten to gather. One of his shortest and weakest *Satires*, the eighth of the First Book, offers us a sample of this kind, because it was composed when Mæcenas took possession of his house on the Esquiline. This was an event of importance both to the master and his friends. He desired to build a house worthy of his new fortune without paying too dearly for it. The problem was difficult, yet he solved it admirably. The Esquiline was then a wild desert hill where slaves were buried and capital punishment carried out. No one in Rome would have consented to dwell there. Mæcenas' who, as we have just seen, took pleasure in doing nothing like anybody else, bought large grounds there, getting them very cheap, planted magnificent gardens, whose reputation lasted nearly as long as the Empire, and had a large tower built, commanding all the horizon. It was doubtless a great surprise for Rome when these sumptuous buildings were seen rising in the worst-famed spot of the city; but here the spirit of contradiction, already remarked in Mæcenas, served him well. The Esquiline, rid of its filth, turned out to be healthier than the other quarters; and we are told that when Augustus caught a fever on the Palatine he went to live for a few days in Mæcenas' tower, in order to treat and cure it. This afforded the poet an opportunity to compose his eighth *Satire*. In it he celebrates this marvellous change, which has turned the cut-throat Esquiline into one of the most beautiful spots in Rome :—

" Nunc licet Esquiliis habitare salubribus, atque
Aggere in aprico spatiari."

And that the charm of these gardens and the magnificence of these terraces may be the better appreciated by contrast, he recalls the scenes that used to take place in the same spot, when it was the trysting-place of robbers and witches. I suppose this little work must have been read during the feasts given by Mæcenas to his friends when he inaugurated his new house, and as it had at least the merit of timeliness, it was probably much appreciated by them. It may therefore give us some idea of what was liked and applauded in that elegant society. Perhaps those who read the *Satire* to the end, bearing in mind the occasion for which it was composed and the people who were to listen to it, will feel some surprise. It ends with a rather strong pleasantry, which it would be difficult for me to translate. Here then is what amused the guests at the table of Mæcenas. Here then is what those clever men liked to listen to at Mæcenas' feasts.[1] Do not let us be too much astonished. The great classic ages we admire are generally the outcome of rude epochs, and often in their first years they retain something of their origin. Beneath all their delicacy there remains a substratum of brutal vigour which easily mounts to the surface again. What broad things were said in the conversation of people of the seventeenth

---

[1] Let us not forget that it is the same society who, in the journey to Brindisi (*Sat.*, I. 5) took so much pleasure in the insipid dispute of two buffoons. It is very difficult to understand how, after listening to these gross pleasantries, Horace can tell us, " We passed quite a charming evening."

century, nobody feeling alarmed, which could not be heard to-day without a-certain embarrassment! How many customs there were which to us seem coarse, but which then appeared the most natural things in the world! It was later on that manners acquired their final polish, and language became scrupulous and refined. Unfortunately this progress is often paid for by decadence, and the mind, during the process of polishing, risks becoming enfeebled and savourless. Let us then not complain of these few outbreaks of a nature not yet entirely reduced to rule. They are witnesses at least to the energy abiding at the root of characters by which art and letters profit. The age of Ovid always comes soon enough.

We see that at the moment in question Horace held an important place in this society. That he did not attain to it immediately we know from himself. He tells us that when Virgil took him to Mæcenas for the first time, he lost countenance, and could only say a few disconnected words to him.[1] The reason is that he was not like those fine talkers who have always something to say. He was only clever with people whom he knew. As for Mæcenas, he was one of those silent ones " to whom belongs the world." He answered but a few words, and it is probable that they parted not very well pleased with each other, since they remained nine months without wanting to meet again. But this first coolness over, the poet showed what he was. Once intimate, he made his protector admire all the resources of his mind, made him love all

---

[1] *Sat.*, I. 6, 56.

the delicacy of his character. So Mæcenas loaded him with kindness and benefits. In 707, a year after he became acquainted with him, he took him on that journey to Brindisi, whither he was going to conclude peace between Antony and Octavius. A few years later, probably about 720, he gave him the estate in the Sabine Hills.

II.

WAS HORACE REALLY A LOVER OF NATURE—THE SECOND *EPODE*—HOW RESIDENCE IN ROME BECAME UNBEARABLE TO HIM—THE CONSEQUENCES FOR HIM OF HIS INTIMACY WITH MÆCENAS—BEGGARS AND BORES— THE JOY HE MUST HAVE FELT WHEN MÆCENAS GAVE HIM THE ESTATE IN THE SABINE HILLS.

The circumstances which led Mæcenas to make his friend this handsome present are not well known to us; but a clever man like him doubtless possessed that quality which Seneca required before all in an intelligent benefactor—he knew how to give seasonably. He thought, then, that this estate would please Horace very much, and he certainly was not mistaken. Does this mean that Horace was altogether like his friend Virgil, and that he was only happy when among the fields? I do not believe it. Without doubt Horace also liked to be in the country; he liked the fields and knew how to portray them. Nature, discreetly drawn, holds a great place in his poetry. He uses it, like Lucretius, to give more force and clearness to the exposition of his philosophical ideas. The recurrence of the seasons shows him that one must neither cherish hopes too vast, nor too enduring sorrows.[1] The great trees bowed by the winds of winter, the lightning-smitten mountains, teach him that the highest fortunes are not safe from unforeseen accidents.[2] The return of spring, "trembling in the zephyr-shaken leaves,"[3] serves him to restore courage to the desperate by showing them that evil days do not last. When he desires to counsel some sad spirit to forget the miseries of life, in order to teach his little moral he leads him to the fields, near the source of a sacred fount, at the spot "where the pine and the poplar mingle together their hospitable shade."[4] These pictures are charming and the memory of all men of letters has preserved them, yet they have not the depth of those offered to us by Virgil and Lucretius. Horace will never pass for one of those great lovers of Nature whose happiness is to lose themselves in her. He was too witty, too indifferent, too rational for that. I add that up to a certain point his philosophy turned him from it. He several times rebelled against the madness of those morbid minds who are forever running about the world in search of internal peace. Peace is neither in the repose of the fields nor in the bustle of travelling. It may be found everywhere when the mind is calm and the heart healthy. The legitimate conclusion of this moral is that we carry our happiness within us, and that when one lives in town it is not necessary to leave it in order to be happy.

It seemed to him then that those people who pre-

---

[1] *Carm.*, II. 9, 1.

[2] *Ibid.*, II. 10, 9.

[3] *Ibid.*, I. 23, 5.

[4] *Ibid.*, II. 3, 6.

tended to be passionately fond of the country, and who affected to say that there alone one can live, went much too far, and on one occasion he very slyly laughs at them. One of his most charming *Epodes*, the work of his youth, contains the liveliest and perhaps the most complete eulogy of rustic life that was ever penned. "Happy," he tells us, "he who, far from affairs, like the men of old, ploughs with his own oxen the field his fathers tilled:" and once launched, he never stops. All the pleasures of the country are reviewed one after another. Nothing is wanting; neither the chase, nor fishing, nor seed-time, nor harvest, nor the pleasure of seeing one's flocks graze, nor of slumbering on the grass, "while the water murmurs in the brook and the birds moan in the trees." One would think he meant to reconstruct in his own manner and with the same sincerity the beautiful passage of Virgil:

> " *O fortunatos nimium, sua si bona norint.*
> *Agricolas !* "

But let us wait till the end: the last lines have a surprise in store for us; they teach us, to our amazement, that it is not Horace we have been listening to. "Thus spoke the usurer Alfius," he tells us; "immediately resolved to become a countryman, he gets in all his money at the Ides. Then he changes his mind, and seeks a new investment at the Kalends."[1] The poet, then, has been laughing at us, and what adds cruelty to his pleasantry, the reader only perceives it at the end, and remains a dupe down to the last line. Of all the reasons that have been given in explanation

---

[1] *Epode* 2.

B

of this *Epode*, only one seems to me natural and probable. He was irritated at seeing so many people frigidly admiring the country. He wanted to laugh at the expense of those who, having no personal opinion, thought themselves obliged to assume every fashionable taste and exaggerate it.[1] And we too have to suffer these empty enconiums on the beauties of Nature from those who go to visit the glaciers and the mountains solely because it is "the thing" to have seen them, and we can understand the ill-temper these conventional enthusiasms must have aroused in an honest and accurate mind that cared only for the truth.

But if Horace did not possess all the ardour of the Banker Alfius for the country, if he lived willingly in Rome, it was because he did not remain there always. Then, as now, people took good care not to stay there during those burning months "which made so much work for the undertaker of funeral pomps and his black lictors."[2] From the moment *Auster*, "heavy as lead,"[3] began to blow, all who could do so went away. So did Horace. While the rich dragged a numerous attendance in their train, were preceded by Numidian courtiers, and accompanied by gladiators to defend and philosophers to amuse them, he, being poor, jumped upon the back of a short-tailed mule, put his scanty baggage behind him, and went gaily on his way.[4] The goal of his journeys was probably not always the same. In the mountains of Latium and the

---

[1] Some critics would see in this *Epode* a parody of the *Georgics*. I do not believe it. At most, Horace's raillery could only reach those who thought themselves obliged to exaggerate the ideas of Virgil.

[2] *Epist.*, I. 7, 5.   [3] *Sat.*, II. 6, 18.   [4] *Ibid.*, I. 6, 105.

Sabina, "along the slopes of the Appenines, by the borders of the sea, there is no lack of pleasant and healthy spots. Thither go the Romans of to-day, to pass the time of the malaria."[1] Horace doubtless visited them also; but he had his preferences, which he expresses with great vivacity, putting before all the rest Tibur and Tarentum, two places very distant and very different from each other, but which seem to have had an equal share of his affection. He probably often returned to them, and although tastes change with age, we have proof that he remained faithful to the last to this affection of his youth.

Despite these yearly rovings, which sometimes took him to the extremities of Italy, I cannot help thinking that Horace long remained but a lukewarm friend of the country. He had not yet a villa of his own, and perhaps he was not sorry. He took a willing part in the distractions of the great town, and, as we have seen, only left it during the months when it is unwise to stop there. Yet a moment came when these journeys, from being a mere amusement, a passing pleasure, became for him an imperious necessity; when Roman life was so wearisome and hateful, that, like his friend Bullatius, he felt a craving to hide himself in some lonely townlet, and there "forget everybody and make himself forgotten."

This feeling is very apparent in some parts of his works, and it is very easy to see how it arose.

A wise man, instead of uselessly bewailing the mischances that happen to him, seeks to turn them

---

[1] *Epist.*, I. 2, 9.

to good account, and his past troubles serve him as a
lesson for the future.   So I think it was with Horace.
The years first following his return from Philippi must
have been for him very fruitful in reflections and
resolutions of every kind.   He has represented himself
at this epoch upon his little couch, musing on the
things of life, and asking himself, "How must I
conduct myself?   What had I best do?"   The best
thing for a man to do who had just suffered so sad a
disillusion was surely not to expose himself to a fresh
one.   The disaster of Philippi had taught him much.
Henceforth he was cured of ambition.   He had come
to know that honours cost dear, that in undertaking to
bring about the happiness of one's fellow-citizens one
risked one's own, and that there is no lot more happy
than his who keeps aloof from public life.   This is what
he resolved to do himself, this is what he recommended
without ceasing to others.   Doubtless his great friends
could not quite renounce politics or abandon the Forum.
He counselled them to take occasional distraction from
them.   To Quintius, to Mæcenas, to Torquatus, he said :
" Give yourselves then some leisure ; let your client dance
attendance in the ante-chamber and get away by some
back door.   Forget Cantabria and Dacia : don't always be
thinking of the affairs of the Empire."   As for him, he
promised himself faithfully *never* to think of them.
Far from complaining that he no longer had any part
in them, he was happy that their cares had been taken
from him.   Others accused Augustus of having deprived
the Romans of their liberty ; he found that in freeing
them from the worry of public affairs he had restored it
to them.   To belong entirely to himself, to study him-

self, to know himself, to make for himself, as it were, an inward retreat in the midst of the crowd—in short, to live for himself; such for the future was his only thought.

But one seldom regulates one's life as one would. In this as elsewhere, chance rules supreme. Events delight to play havoc with the best-concerted resolutions. The friendship of Mæcenas, of course a very happy thing for Horace, was not long in causing him much embarrassment. It brought him into contact with great personages whom he was obliged to treat affably, although he often found it difficult to esteem them. He was forced to associate with a Dallius, called "the acrobat of the civil wars" (*desultor bellorum civilium*), because of his skill in playing from one party to another; with Lucinius Muræna, who was levity itself, and who finished by conspiring against Augustus; with Munatius Plaucus, the former flatterer of Antony and the buffoon of Cleopatra, said to be a traitor by temperament (*morbo proditor*). All wanted to be thought intimate with him. They asked him to address to them one of those little pieces which did honour to him who received them. They wished their names to be found in the collection of those works which men thought predestined to immortality. Horace did not like it; it was doubtless repugnant to him to appear the vulgar singer of the court and the prince. So, even when obliged to yield, he did not always do so with a good grace. For instance, he only writes once to Agrippa, and it is to tell him that he will not sing his praises, and to pass him on to Varius, the successor of Homer, and alone worthy to handle so fine a subject. He does not wish to busy himself with Augustus either. He pretends to be afraid of compromising his hero's glory by singing his praises badly, and does not claim to have genius enough for so great a work. But Augustus was not to be put off with this excuse; he pressed and prayed the too modest poet again and again. "Know," he wrote to him, "that I am angered at thy not yet having thought to address one of thy epistles to me. Dost thou fear that in the after-time it will be shameful for thee to seem to have been my friend?"[1] After these amiable words, Horace could no longer resist, and from compliance to compliance he found himself led against his inclination to become the official poet of the dynasty.

Being seen allied with so many important men, the familiar of Mæcenas, the friend of the Emperor, he could scarcely fail to be considered as a sort of personage. He did not, it is true, fill any public office; the most they had left him was his knight's ring, won in the civil wars;[2] but, in order to have authority, it was not necessary to wear the *pretexta.* Mæcenas, who was nothing to him, passed for the counsellor of Augustus: might not Horace be suspected of being the confidant of Mæcenas? Seeing him drive out with him, and sit in the theatre beside him, everybody said: "What a happy man!"[3] If the two talked it was imagined they were debating the fate of the world. In vain Horace affirmed upon his honour that Mæcenas had only said to him: " What o'clock is it? It is very cold this morning;" and other secrets

---

[1] Suetonius, *Vita Horatii*, p. 46 (Reifferscheid).

[2] *Sat.*, II. 7, 53.

[3] All the following details are taken from the sixth *Satire* of the Second Book, and the ninth of the last.

of the like importance; people wouldn't believe it. He could no longer walk as formerly in the Forum and the Field of Mars, listening to the quacks and fortune-tellers, and asking the dealers the prices of their wares; he was watched, followed, approached at every step by the unfortunate and the inquisitive. A newsmonger wanted to know the situation of the armies; a politician asked him for information concerning the projects of Augustus, and when he answered that he did not know anything about these matters, they congratulated him on his statesmanlike reserve and admired his diplomatic discretion. He met on the Sacred Way an intriguer, who begged him to introduce him to Mæcenas: they brought him petitions, they requested his support, they put themselves under his protection. Envious people accused him of being an egotist who wished to keep for himself alone the favour he enjoyed, and enemies re-called the story of his birth, triumphantly repeating everywhere that he was only the son of a slave. It is true that this reproach did not affect him, and what they threw in his face as a disgrace, he boasted of as a title of honour; but meanwhile the days were passing. He was no longer his own master, he could no longer live as he liked, his dear liberty was being stolen from him every moment. Of what use was it to have kept aloof from public functions if he had all its plagues without en-joying its advantages? These worries maddened him, Rome became unbearable, and he doubless sought in his mind some means of escaping from the bores who beset him, and of regaining the peace and liberty he had lost.

It was then that Mæcenas gave him the estate in the Sabina—that is to say, a safe asylum to shelter him from the troublesome, where he was to live for himself alone. Never was liberality more seasonably bestowed or welcomed with such joy. The timeliness of the benefit explains the warmth of his gratitude.

III.

JOURNEY TO THE HOUSE IN THE SABINA—THE TEMPLE OF VACUNA—ROCCAGIOVINE—*FONTE DELL' ORATINI*—PROBABLE POSITION OF THE HOUSE—EXTENT OF HORACE'S DOMAIN—PLEASANTNESS OF THE SITE.

We now know how Horace became possessed of his country house; it remains for us to become acquainted with its neighbourhood, and to ascertain whether it deserves what the poet has said about it, and why it pleased him.

It was, as we have seen, near Tivoli. The road thither is the ancient Via Valeria, one of the most important Roman routes to Italy, leading into the territory of the Marsians. It follows the Anio and traverses a fertile country surrounded by high mountains, on whose summits stand some villages, true eagles' nests, that from afar seem unapproachable. Now and again one meets with ancient monuments, and one treads beneath one's feet fragments of that Roman pavement, o'er which so many nations have passed without being able to destroy it. In three or four hours we reach Vicovaro, which, as I have already said, was formerly *Varia*, the important town of the neighbourhood. There we must leave the main road,

VALLEY OF THE LICENZA
Horace's Country House.

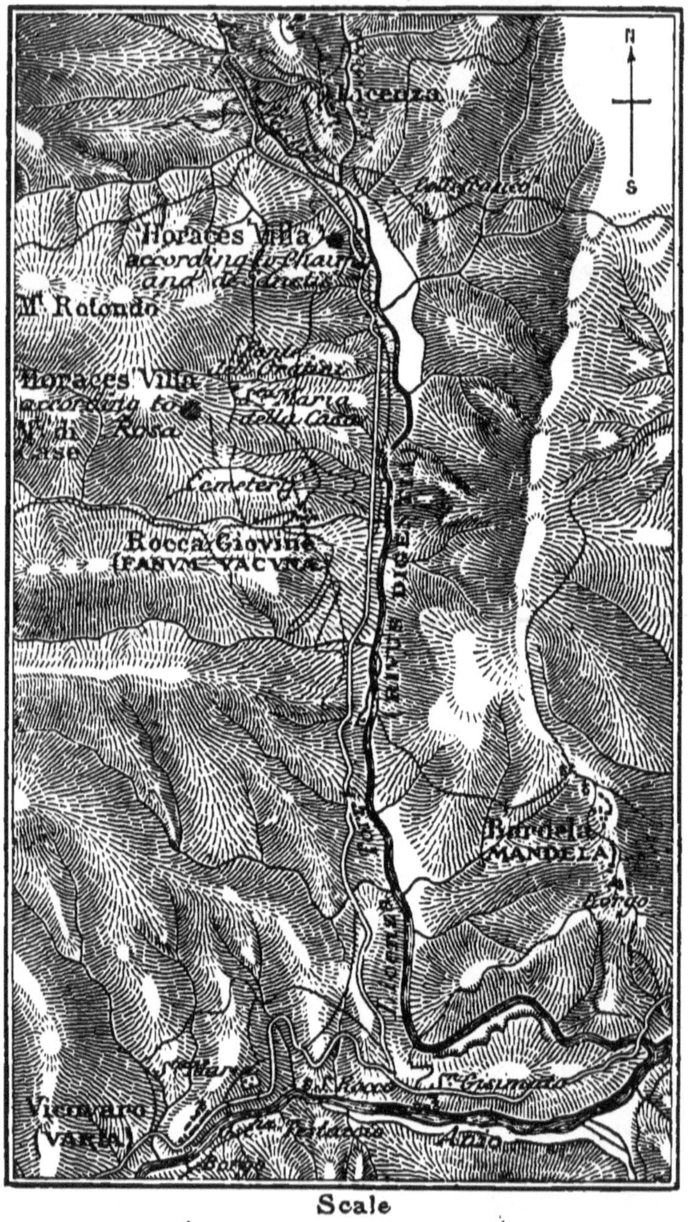

and take to the left one which follows the banks of the Licenza.[1] On the other side of the torrent, a little higher than Vicovaro, we see Bardela, a large village, with a castle that from a distance looks very welL It was a village where Horace tells us one shivered with cold: *rugosus frigore pagus*.[2] Abbé Capmartin de Chaupy remarked that the place really is sometimes invaded by cold fogs descending from the adjacent mountains. He tells us that one day when drawing, "he felt himself seized from behind by a cold as piercing as it was sudden," but as he is accused of partiality to Horace, and wants all the assertions of his dear poet to be verified to the letter, he may be suspected of having put just a little goodwill into his shiver! I went that way in the month of April, about noon, and found it very hot. After passing Bardela, at a turn of the road, Roccagiovine is seen to the left. It is one of the most picturesque villages in the neighbourhood, being perched upon a pointed rock that seems to have become detached from the mass of the mountain. The way up to it is rough, and while fatiguing myself in the ascent, the expression used by Horace came home to me ; he tells us that to get home again he has to "scale his citadel."[3]

There occurs a landmark which will serve to direct us. In a charming epistle addressed by Horace to one of his best friends to tell him how much he loves the country, and that of all the good things of Rome he only

---

[1] The map of the Licenza valley here given was designed from a very detailed and exact topographical plan kindly furnished me by M. Tito Berti.

[2] *Epist.*, I. 18, 105.   [3] *Sat.*, II. 6, 15.

regrets to have no longer the pleasure of seeing him, he ends his letter by saying that he has written it behind the ruined temple of Vacuna: *Hæc tibi dictabam fanum post putre Vacunæ.*[1]

Vacuna was a goddess much honoured among the Sabines, and Varro tells us that she was the same as the one called "Victory" in Rome. Near the village a fine inscription has been found, from which we learn that Vespasian has rebuilt at his own expense the Temple of Victory, which was almost destroyed by age : *Ædem Victoriæ vetustate dilapsam sua impensa restituit.* The coincidence has led it to be thought that the edifice rebuilt by Vespasian was the same that was falling into ruin in the time of Horace. In restoring the temple the Emperor gave the goddess her Roman name, in lieu of the other, which was no longer understood. To-day the inscription is set in the walls of the old castle, and the square hard by has been named by the inhabitants *Piazza Vacuna.* Horace, then, is not quite forgotten in the place he lived in eighteen centuries ago.

If you want to know to the life what Sabine villages are like, you must climb up to Roccagiovine. Nothing is more picturesque so long as one is content to look at them from a distance. Catching sight of them from the valley, crowning some high mountain and pressing round the church or the castle, one is delighted with them. But all changes as soon as one gets inside. The houses now are only tumbledown hovels, the streets infected alleys paved with dung. One cannot take a step without meeting pigs walking about. In all

---

[1] *Epist.*, I. 10, 49.

the Sabina the pigs are the masters of the land. They
are aware of their importance and do not disturb themselves for anybody. The streets belong to them, and
sometimes the houses. It must have been just the same
in the time of the Romans. Then also they formed the
chief wealth of the country, and Varro never speaks of
them but with the greatest respect. I saw one there in
the piazza, wallowing with an air of delight in a black
stagnant pool, and immediately called to mind this
charming passage of the great farmer: "They roll in
the filth, which for them is a way of refreshing themselves, as for men to take a bath." But one finds
antiquity again everywhere. The women we meet are
nearly all beautiful, but with a vigorous masculine
beauty. We recognise those sturdy Sabine women of
old, burnt by the sun, accustomed to the heaviest
tasks.[1] At the end of the valley I see a railway in
course of construction; women are mingled with the
workmen, and, like them, carry stones upon their heads.
There are scarcely any men in the village at the hour
we pass through it, but we are surrounded by a crowd
of robust children with eyes full of fire and intelligence.
They are curious and troublesome—their usual fault, but
at least they do not hold out their hands, as at Tivoli,
where there are so many beggars. In this out-of-the-
way spot, the blood has been kept pure. These are the
remains of a strong proud race that bore a good part in
the fortunes of Rome.

If, as we may believe, Roccagiovine is built on the
site of the *Fanum Vacunæ*, here Horace's estate must

---

[1] *Carm.*, III. 6, 37.

have begun.   So, bearing to the right, we continue the ascent by a stony road shaded here and there by walnut trees and oaks.   Before us, on the mountain sides, cultivated fields are spread out, with a few rustic dwellings.   Nothing appears on the horizon like the ruins of an ancient house, and at first we are in doubt as to whither we ought to wend our steps.   But we remember that Horace tells us there was close to his house a spring which never dried up, an uncommon quality in southern countries, and which was important enough to give its name to the rivulet into which it fell.   If the house has disappeared, the spring, at least, must still be there; and when we have found it, it will be easy to fix the place of the rest.   We follow a little path skirting an old church in ruins—the *Madonna della Casa*—and a little lower we come upon the spring we are seeking.   The country people call it *Fonte dell 'Oratini* or *Fonte de' Ratini;* is it by chance that it has kept a name so near akin to that of the poet ?[1]   In any case it is very difficult not to believe it to be the one of which he has spoken to us.   There is not a more important one in the vicinity; it gushes abundantly from the hollow rock, and an old fig-tree covers it with its shade.   I know not whether, as Horace asserts,[2] "its waters are good

---

[1] *Fons etiam rivo dare nomen idoneus.—Epist.*, I. 16, 12.   M. Pietro Rosa bids us remark that to-day the Licenza still only takes its name from the moment it receives the waters of the little fountain. Till then it is only called *il Rivo* (the brook).   See the notice which Noël des Vergers has put at the beginning of Didot's *Horace*.

[2] This is quite how Horace has described the fount of Bandusia (*Carm.*, III. 13, 1).   He speaks of this " oak placed above the hollow rock from which gushed the prattling wave."   It is known to-day that Bandusia was situated in Aquilia, near Venusia.   But it is quite

for the stomach and relieve the head,"[1] but they are fresh and limpid. The spot round about them is charming, quite fitted for reverie, and I can understand how the poet counted among the happiest moments of his day, those when he came to take a little rest here: *prope rivum somnus in herba.*[2]

The position of the spring found again, that of the house may be guessed. Since Horace tells us they were near each other,[3] we need only seek in the vicinity. Capmartin de Chaupy placed the house much lower, near the bottom of the valley, in a place where some remains of ancient walls and pavement still were to be found. But these remains seem to be of later date than the time of Augustus. Besides, we know from Horace himself that he lived on a steep plateau, and he speaks of his house as of a sort of fortress. I believe then that M. Pietro Rosa was right in placing it a little higher. He supposed it must be a little above the *Madonna della Casa.* Just there an artificial terrace is remarked, apparently arranged in order to serve as the placement of a house. The soil has long since been under cultivation ; but the plough often turns up bits of brick and broken tiles that seem to have formed part of an ancient building. Is it here that the house of Horace really stood ? M. Rosa

---

possible that Horace may have given to the little spring that flowed near his house the name of the one where he had so often slaked his thirst in his youth, ere he quitted his birthplace. The resemblance between the landscape described in the Ode of Horace and the real site of the fountain *dell' Oratini* renders this hypothesis very probable.

[1] *Epist.*, I. 16, 14 : *Infirmo capiti fluit utilis, utili alvo.*

[2] *Ibid.*, I. 14, 35.

believes so.   It is certain, in any case, that it could not have been far distant.[1]

From this elevated spot let us cast our eyes over the surrounding country.   Below us we have a long, narrow valley, at whose bottom flows the torrent of the Licenza. It is dominated by mountains which seem to meet on every side.   To the left the Licenza turns so sharply that one cannot perceive the gorge into which it plunges ; to the right the cliff on which Roccagiovine sits perched seems to have rolled into the valley to close its ingress, so that no issue is seen on any side.   I recognise the landscape as it is described by Horace :—

> " *Continui montes, nisi dissocientur opaca.*
> *Valle.*"[2]

Having glanced over this fine assemblage of mountains, I return to what must interest us above all. I ask myself, in the extent of grounds which my eyes take in, what could have belonged to the poet ?   He has never expressed himself clearly as to the true limits of his domain.   Occasionally he seems desirous to diminish its importance—his house is only a cottage (*villula*),[3] surrounded by a tiny little field (*agellus*),[4] of

---

[1] I must say, however, that the opinion of Capmartin de Chaupy and of De Sanctis is that which prevails in the neighbourhood.   It has lately been taken up again and strongly maintained by M. Tito Berti (see the *Fanfulla della domenica*, 1st November 1885).   In spite of the reasons given by M. Berti, however, the site pointed out by De Chaupy appears to me somewhat too near the Licenza and rather too low. But there certainly was the house of a rich Roman in this spot.   M. Berti has found interesting mosaic pavements there, and perhaps it would be useful to push the excavations a little further.   Care has been taken to mark on the site where Chaupy and M. Rosa respectively place the house of Horace.

[2] *Epist.*, I. 16, 5.   [3] *Sat.*, II. 3, 10.   [4] *Epist.*, I. 14, 1.

which even his farmer speaks with contempt. But
Horace is a prudent man who willingly depreciates himself in order to escape envy. I think that in reality
his estate in the Sabina must have been pretty extensive.
" Thou hast made me rich," [1] he one day told Mæcenas
—doubtless not rich like those great lords and knights
who possessed immense fortunes, but surely much more
so than he had ever wished to become or dreamt of becoming. However moderate by nature, few deny themselves
an occasional excess in their dreams. Horace tells us
that these ideal excesses, these dreams which he formed
in his youth without hoping ever to see them accomplished, were far surpassed by the reality :

" Auctius atque
Di melius facere." [2]

We possess information which will give us a very
correct idea of Horace's estate. He did not keep all
the ground on his own account. The trouble of farm-
ing on a large scale would not have suited him at all.
So he let out a part to five freemen, who had each his
house, and who went on the *nundinæ* or market days
to Varia, either on their own business or that of the
little community. [3] Five farmers presuppose a pretty
large estate, and it must be added that what he kept
for himself was not without some importance, since
eight slaves were required to cultivate it. [4] It seems to
me then that a great part of the grounds around me,
from the top of the mountain to the Licenza, must have
been his. This extensive space contained, so to speak,
different zones, which admitted of varied species of

---

[1] *Tu me fecisti ocupletem. —Epist.*, I. 7, 15.

[2] *Sat.*, II. 6, 3.   [3] *Epist.*, I. 14, 2.   [4] *Sat.*, II. 7, 118.

husbandry, afforded the owner various temperatures, and consequently offered him distractions and pleasures of more than one kind. In the middle, half-way up the hill, was the house with its dependencies. All we know of the house is that it was simple, neither gilded wainscoting, ivory ornaments, nor marbles of Hymettus and Africa being seen in it.[1] This luxury was not suitable for the depths of the Sabina. Near the house there was a garden which must have contained fine regular quincunxes and straight alleys shut in by hedges of hornbeam, as was then the fashion. Horace somewhere speaks against the mania affected by people of his time for changing the elm, which unites with the vine, for the plane-tree—the bachelor tree, as he calls it; and he attacks those who are lavish in violet beds and myrtle fields, "vain olfactory riches,"[2] as he calls them. Did he remain faithful to his principles and allow himself no pleasure? and was his garden quite like Cato's, where only useful trees and plants were found? I should not like to say so too positively. More than once it has happened to him not to apply to himself the precepts he gives to others, and to be more rigorous in his verse than in his life. Below the house and the garden the ground was fertile. It is here those crops grew, which, as Horace says, never deceived his expectations.[3] Here, too, perhaps, he culled that wine which he served at his table in coarse amphoræ, and which he does not praise to Mæcenas.[4] Yet a

---

[1] *Carm.*, II. 18, 1.   [2] *Ibid.*, II. 15, 6.

[3] *Ibid.*, III. 3, 16, 30: *Segetis certa fides meæ.*

[4] There is some uncertainty as to whether Horace's estate produced wine. The poet seems to contradict himself on this point. In the

little further down, towards the banks of the Licenza, the soil became damper, and meads took the place of cultivated fields. Then as now the torrent, swollen by storm rains, sometimes left its bed, and spread over the surrounding ground, causing Horace's farmer to grumble, since he dolefully foresaw that he would have to make a dyke to protect the land from the flood.[1] But if the country was smiling towards the bottom of the valley, above the house it became more and more wild. Here were brambles " rich in sloes and red cornel," [2] with oaks and holms covering the slopes of the mountain. In his youthful dreams of which I spoke just now, the poet asked nothing of the gods but a clump of trees to crown his little field.[3] Mæcenas had done things better; Horace's wood covered several *jugera*. There was enough of it " to feed the flock with acorns, and furnish the master a thick shade."

Horace, then, had not received from his patron merely a little scribbler's corner of a garden, "a lizard's hole," as Juvenal says; it was a real estate, with pasture lands, fields, woods, and a complete rustic equipment, at the same time a pleasure and a fortune. How had this estate fallen into the hands of Mæcenas? It is not known. Some scandal-mongers have suggested that

---

epistle to his *villicus*, he says, "This corner of ground would rather grow incense and pepper than a bunch of grapes." Elsewhere he invites Mæcenas to dinner, and tells him he can only give him a middling Sabine wine of his own bottling, which seems to show that he gathered it himself (*Carm.*, I. 20). But vines certainly grow in the Licenza valley, and at Roccagiovine one drinks a wine now that is not bad.

[1] *Epist.*, I. 14, 29.   [2] *Ibid.*, I. 16, 9.

[3] *Et paulum silvæ super his foret.—Sat.*, II. 6, 3.

it might very well have been confiscated from political enemies, and that probably Mæcenas gave his friend lands not his own.   These inexpensive liberalities were not uncommon at that time.   It is said that Augustus one day offered Virgil the fortune of an exile, and that the poet refused it.[1]   I hope that Horace was not less delicate than his friend.   But these are mere hypotheses, which must not stop us.   All we know about Horace's estate is that it was in a very bad condition when given to him.   The ground was covered with thorns and brambles, and it was long since the plough had passed over it.[2]   When he took possession, he was so unwise as to bring to direct the works one of those town slaves, who, according to Columella, are only a lazy, sleepy race (*socors et somniculosum genus*).[3]   All the wretch knew about the country was doubtless from the well-kept gardens round about Rome.   When he got to the Sabina, and saw those untilled fields that had been given him to cultivate, he thought that he had fallen into a wilderness, and begged to be allowed to go away again at once.   Horace himself, in spite of his love for his property, has not exaggerated its merits.   The soil, he tells us, is far from being so fertile as that of Calabria, and above all, the vines here are much inferior to those of Campania.[4]   What he praises without reserve is the temperature,[5] equal in all seasons; being neither too cold in winter nor too hot in summer.   He is inexhaustible in his praises on this point, and one understands that he should be keenly alive to it.   Is there a

---

[1] Donat., *Vita Virg.*, 5.   [2] *Epist.*, I. 14, 27.   [3] Colum., I. 8, 1.
[4] *Carm.*, III. 16, 33.   [5] *Epist.*, I. 16, 8 ; see also I. 10, 15.

greater pleasure, on leaving the Roman furnace behind one, than to take refuge in a charming retreat where the shade of the great trees and the fresh wind of the mountains allows one at least to breathe?

I remark also that he has never exaggerated the beauty of the scenery round about his country house. An owner's partiality does not mislead him to compare it to the famous sites of Italy—to Baia, to Tibur, to Præneste. Baia, he tells us, is one of the wonders of the world; nothing so beautiful is elsewhere seen:

"*Nullus in orbe sinus Baiis prælucit amœnis.*" [1]

Præneste also is an admirable spot, whence one enjoys one of the most varied and extensive views imaginable. Horace enjoyed being there very much, and returned again and again. It must be owned that the Licenza valley has nothing like it, and it would not surprise me if a traveller coming from Palestrina or Tivoli were to feel disappointed. That would be his fault and not Horace's, who has not tried to deceive us. If at first our expectation is not quite satisfied, we should only blame ourselves. He has nowhere asserted that this little solitary valley is the most beautiful spot in the world, as he has of Baia; he simply tells us he was happy here. Can one not be happy without always having an immense horizon before one, and living in a perpetual ecstasy? One must exaggerate nothing, in any direction. If the Sabine valley is not comparable to the beautiful sites I have just spoken of, it is still, in its small proportions, very pleasant. Let me add that many things must have changed since

---

[1] *Epist.*, I. 1, 83.

ancient times. Now the mountains are bare; they were formerly covered with trees. To realise what they must have been like, I deck them in thought with that admirable little wood of green oaks you pass through on your way to the *sacro speco* of Subiaco. The valley is no longer like what it used to be; it has lost the shades which Horace loved so well, and which reminded him of Tarentum :

" Credas adduction propius frondere Tarentum." [1]

But what has not changed, what used to be and still is the characteristic of this charming valley, is its calm, its tranquillity, its silence. At noon, from the *Madonna della Casa* one hears only the subdued sound of the torrent rising from the bottom of the valley. Here is just what Horace came in search of. Extraordinary sights cast the mind into a kind of ravishment that excites and troubles it. It is a fatigue which in the long run he would have ill borne. He did not wish Nature to draw him too much to her, and prevent him from belonging to himself. So nothing suited him better than this tranquil landscape where all is repose and meditation. Athough he was here near Rome, and as a rule his docked mule could take him thither in a day, he might think himself a thousand leagues off. [2]

---

[1] *Epist.*, I. 16, 11.

[2] Horace tells us, in the *Satire* descriptive of his journey to Brindisi, that active people pressed for time could cover 43 Roman miles (about 33 English miles) in a day. He, who liked his ease, took two days for the journey. The second day he went 27 miles. The distance from Rome to the villa in the Sabina must have been from 31 to 32 miles (about 28 English miles). The journey then could be done in a day. It is probable, however, that Horace, not wishing to tire himself, often slept at Tibur. It has been thought that in order to avoid going to

This is what he did not find elsewhere. At Præneste, when he went to sit and read Homer on the steps of the temple of Fortune, he perceived the walls of the great town in the haze. At Baia he met young folk intent on their noisy jollities. It was Rome again, seen from a distance or elbowed in the streets. Rome did not come into the valley of the Sabina, for who among these young *elegants* would have dared to venture into the mountains beyond Tibur? Horace, then, was really at home there. He could say, when he put his foot into his domain, " Here I no longer belong to the importunate; I have left the cares and worries of the town; at length I live and am my own master, *vivo et regno*."

IV.

RENOWN OF HORACE'S COUNTRY HOUSE AMONG THE POETS OF ROME—SITUATION OF POETS IN ROME—RELATIONS OF HORACE AND MÆCENAS TO EACH OTHER—HOW THE POET MADE THE GREAT LORD RESPECT HIM.

The villa in the Sabine hills, which holds so great a

---

the inn, he bought or hired a little house there, as was the custom of rich Romans. Suetonius even assures us that in his time they used to show at Tibur a house said to have belonged to him. In reality this assertion is not based on any precise text of the poet. When he tells us that he returns to Tibur, or that he likes to live there, the name of the town is probably taken for that of its territory. M. Camille Jullian has shown, in the *Mélanges d'archéologie et d'histoire*, published by the École Française of Rome, that Tibur, although of Latin origin, was the chief town of a Sabine district, and that the territory of Varia was dependent on it. It may then be understood that when Horace speaks of Tibur he means his house in the Sabina.

place in Horace's life, occupies no less a one in the history of literature. From the day when Mæcenas presented it to his friend, this quiet house with its garden, its spring hard by, and its little wood, has become an ideal towards which poets of all times have had their eyes directed. Those of Rome tried to attain it in the same way that Horace had done.[1] They applied to the generosity of rich people, and tried by their verses to arouse their self-love. I do not know any among them to whom this business seemed repugnant, and Juvenal himself, who passes for a fiery republican, has proclaimed that there is no future for poetry other than the protection of the prince.[2] This is also the opinion of his friend Martial, who has made a kind of general theory of it, which he sets forth with singular *naïveté*. There is, according to him, a sure recipe for the production of great poets; you have only to pay them well.

" Sint Mæcenates non deerunt Flacce, Marones." [3]

Had Virgil remained poor, he would have done nothing better than the *Bucolics*. Happily, he had a liberal protector, who said to him: "Here is fortune, here is the wherewithal to give you all the pleasures of life; tackle the Epic." And he at once composed the *Æneid*. The method is infallible, and the result assured. The poor poet would have very much liked the experiment to be made on him; and he would have asked nothing better than to become, for a fair consideration, a man of genius. So he wore out his life in offering

---

[1] *Epist.*, I. 10, 8.

[2] Juv., *Sat.*, VII. 1 : *Et spes et ratio studiorum in Cæsare tantum.*

[3] Martial, VIII. 56.

himself to every protector in turn;[1] none would agree to make the experiment; the time of the Mæcenates was past.

This baseness arouses the indignation of not a few persons, who feel called upon to expatiate on the subject. They begin by attacking Martial, and end by striking Horace. They have been answered more than once that what they call meanness was merely a necessity, and it has been shown that literature in those days did not give its followers enough to live on.[2] Until the invention of printing no clear idea of the rights of authorship could have existed. Once published, a book belonged to everybody. Nothing prevented those who got hold of it from having it copied as many times as they chose, and selling the copies they did not want. It was all very well for the bookseller to buy of the author the right to bring his book before the world; but as nothing assured him the durable property of the work, and as, when it had once appeared, all who possessed copyist slaves in their houses could reproduce and spread it, he paid very little for it, and what he gave did not suffice the author for his livelihood.[3] If, then, the author did not wish to

---

[1] Martial, I. 107, 3 : *Otia da nobis, sed qualia fecerat olim Mæcenas flacco Virgilioque suo.*

[2] See above all what Friedlænder says on this subject in his *Histoire des mœurs Romaines.* Curious particulars will be found in the fourth volume of the French translation.

[3] Martial regrets not being able to derive from his books sufficient profit to buy a little corner where he can sleep in peace (X. 84). He tells us elsewhere that his verses are sold and read in Britain. "But what boots it?" he adds; "my purse knows nothing about it" (XI. 3, 5), which proves that the booksellers of that country did not pay him.

die of hunger, he had no resource but to apply to some important personage and solicit his liberality.

It has also been remarked that what appears to us base and humiliating in this necessity was greatly diminished and almost cloaked by the institution of clientship. This was an ancient, honourable, national institution, protected by religion and the laws. The client was not dishonoured by the services which he rendered to his patron and the payment which he received from him; no one thought it strange that a great lord should pay with his money, aid with his influence, and feed in his house a crowd of people who came to greet him in the morning, formed his train when he walked abroad, supported his candidatures, applauded him in the tribune, and abused his opponents. Nor did anyone find fault with his including among these clients poets who sang his exploits, historians who celebrated his ancestors, and philologists who dedicated their works to him. This kind of dependence did not appear at all humiliating, and the clients profited by the popularity enjoyed by their principal. I may add that the writers who entered the house of a great lord in this way were usually a very humble kind of people, who had no right to be squeamish. Some, like Martial, had left a distant province where they had lived wretchedly in order to come and seek their fortune; the others were generally former slaves. At Rome slavery recruited literature and the arts. Among the masters of slaves it was a speculation to give some of them a good education in order to sell them dear. These often became distinguished men, who were made tutors and secretaries, and who were sometimes also writers and poets of merit. When they had won their liberty, which did not always endow them with means, they had nothing better to do than to attach themselves to an old master, or to some generous patron who offered them protection. For people of such an origin client-ship was not a decline. From servitude it was, on the contrary, a progress. This is how men of letters were so long the clients of the rich, without anybody appearing shocked or even surprised. Afterwards, when public instruction was organised in Rome and in the provinces, they became professors. During these centuries, the philologists, philosophers, and rhetoricians attached to the great schools of the Empire were at the same time historians and poets, and consecrated the leisure left them by their functions to literature. This position was assuredly better for their dignity and independence; but it had counterbalancing drawbacks of which this is not the place to speak.

It is conceivable that all these starvelings in search of a Mæcenas, whom it was not easy to find, should have imagined nothing more happy than the lot of Horace. They not only envied him the grant of the estate in the Sabina, but they could not get over their surprise when they saw him live on such familiar terms with his protector. They did not enjoy the same good fortune. When they came to greet the master in the morning, he scarcely vouchsafed them recognition and a smile. He left them talking with his steward, who took a good deal of asking before he would distribute to them the six or seven sesterces (about fifteen pence) composing the *sportula*. If the patron deigned to invite them to dinner, it was to humiliate them by all sorts of affronts.

They were made to sit at some table apart, where they were rudely treated by the slaves. While lobsters, murenas, and pullets large as geese passed before their eyes for the favoured guests, they were served with only a few crabs or gudgeon caught near the drains and fattened on the filth of the Tiber.[1] Being humble from necessity and proud by character, these outrages made them indignant, although they were always ready to expose themselves to them. Whenever they had endured them, they could not help thinking of Horace, a man of letters, the son of a slave, who not only sat at the table of a minister of state among the greatest personages, but was invited to his house and treated almost as an equal. This occasioned them as much admiration as astonishment. So in time a sort of legend came into being on the subject of this intimacy between the favourite of the Emperor and the poet. It seemed that nothing had ever troubled its serenity. There was, as it were, a perpetual combat of generosity and gratitude between the two friends, the one ever giving, the other ever thanking, while around them the society of Rome stood in ecstasy before the affecting picture.

The reality does not quite resemble the legend. It is less edifying perhaps, but more instructive, and above all it does greater honour to Horace. When his contemporaries congratulated him on having slipped into Mæcenas' friendship as on a happy chance, he proudly answered that chance had nothing to do with it.[2] He would have made the same reply to the men

---

[1] Juv., *Sat.*, V. 80, *et seq.*   [2] *Ibid.*, I. 6, 52.

of letters of the following century, who attributed the position which he made himself in a world for which he was not born solely to the good fortune he had of living in a favourable atmosphere, and the esteem then professed for literature and the lettered. They were mistaken. This position had cost him more than one battle. He had won it, had maintained it by the firmness of his character; he owed it to himself alone. He could apply to himself the famous saying of old Appius Claudius, for he alone was "the artisan of his fortune." I have often heard rigorous moralists treat Horace severely, and speak of him as of a mean and servile person. Beulé even declared one day that he should be banished from the schools, because he had only bad lessons to teach our youth. Does youth then no longer require to be taught how to come off well in delicate situations, to live with the greatest without abasing itself, to maintain its freedom with all while wounding the dignity of none,—in fine, to grasp, between the rudeness that loses all and the obsequiousness which dishonours, that degree of adroit honesty which no one can do without in life?

That the connection between Horace and Mæcenas was entirely free from storms cannot be admitted. The most tender and intimate friendships are also the most delicate, and those in which the least friction produces the most sensible effects. Minds, in approaching each other, clash. This is the law; the indifferent alone never quarrel. However great the sympathy which drew Horace to his friend, causes of disagreement were not wanting. First of all, Mæcenas was a poet, and a very bad poet. His verses—obscure, laboured, and full of mannered expressions—seemed made on purpose to drive a man of taste crazy. What must Horace think, and what could he say, when he was admitted to the honour of hearing them? What danger if he dared to express his sentiments! What a humiliation for him, and what a triumph for his enemies, if he were reduced to admire them! We do not know how Horace avoided this rock in intimate intercourse; but it at least is certain that in his works he never said a word about Mæcenas' verses. He calls him a learned man (*docte Mæcenas*), but of all his works he only speaks of a history in prose, not yet begun, and which was probably never finished. He might praise it without compromising himself. This prudent reserve seems not to have wounded Mæcenas, which proves him a clever man, devoid of the littleness of the professional author. It does honour to the two friends.

A thing of greater peril for Horace was the mixture of men of the world and men of letters found in the palace of the Esquiline. These two classes are not always in unison with each other, and when one tries to make them live together there is a risk of collision. In Mæcenas' house the men of the world belonged to the highest Roman aristocracy. They were persons of refined taste, who knew and respected all observances— slaves to the fashion of the day, and sometimes its creators. They could not help indulging in raillery when they saw their neighbours, the men of letters, fail in those sacred customs which are rigorous laws for some few months, and then suddenly become ridiculous anachronisms. Sometimes the poor poets committed this unpardonable crime without knowing it.

They did not always obey the rules which the master had set forth in his book concerning his toilette (*de Cultu suo*). They arrived ill - combed, ill - shod, ill-dressed; they wore old linen under a new tunic;[1] they had not taken time to adjust their toga properly. Seeing them thus accoutred, those present burst out laughing, and Mæcenas laughed like the rest. I do not think the victims of these railleries felt them much. Virgil, who was absent-minded, did not perceive them. Horace accepted them with a good grace; but, being malicious, sometimes took his revenge. Those great lords also were not without their oddities and absurdities, which could not escape so acute a wit. Fashionable life had then become very exigent and refined, and possessed its code and its laws. Dinners especially had assumed a great importance, and were regarded as a veritable affair of state. Varro, always pedantic and grave, even in trifles, undertook to set forth didactically all the conditions which a repast must fulfil in order to be perfect.[2] It was a very complicated science, and those who surrounded Mæcenas piqued themselves on practising it to perfection. Horace has laughed at this affectation in two of his *Satires*—the one in which he shows us the Epicurean Catius busied in collecting the precepts of the kitchen; the other where he describes the dinner of Nasidienus, one of those learned in the art of entertaining one's guests. The two pictures are very entertaining—the Epicurean amusing us by the gravity with which he expounds his precepts; while the other provokes our mirth by the fastidious

---

[1] *Epist.*, I. 1, 95. [2] *Aulu-Gelle*, XIII. 11.

pains he takes to maintain his reputation, and the comical mishaps which disconcert his plans. These railleries struck well-known personages, the friends of Mæcenas; and it may be suspected that something of them must have rebounded on Mæcenas himself. Did he not encourage the follies of Nasidienus by going to dine with him? Had he not, like Catius, invented new dishes, of which Pliny tells us that his authority made them fashionable while he lived, but that they could not survive him?[1]

These, I own, are little differences of but small importance. The real difficulties began somewhat later, and arose from the liberalities of Mæcenas themselves. The benefits of the great are chains. Horace knew this, but at least he tried to make his light. At first he would not take all that was offered him. In the ardour of his friendship Mæcenas wished to give him more and more every day. Horace only accepted the estate in the Sabina. "It is enough; it is even too much," he told him.

> "*Satis superque me benignitas tua.*
> *Ditavit.*"[2]

He made it also understood that he could, in case of need, even do without this estate which made him so happy, and did so at the moment when he was enjoying it with the greatest zest. "If Fortune stay true to me, I thank her; but when she shakes her wings to fly from me, I'll give her back her gifts; I will wrap me in my worth; I can content me with an honest poverty."[3]

---

[1] Pliny, *Hist. Nat.*, VIII. 43 (68). [2] *Epode*, I. 31.
[3] *Carm.*, III. 29, 53.

Here is Mæcenas well warned. His friend will not sacrifice his independence to his fortune; he will become poor again rather than cease to be free. A day came when he felt it necessary to say so still more clearly. He had left Rome at the beginning of August, promising to remain in the country only four or five days. But once arrived, he felt so comfortable there that he forgot to keep his promise. An entire month passed without his being able to tear himself away. Mæcenas, who could no longer live without him, complained with some bitterness; perhaps hinting in his letter that he had reckoned on more gratitude. We have in Horace's reply certainly one of his best productions.[1] It is impossible to clothe greater firmness in a gentler guise. Through agreeable narrations and pleasing apologues, his resolution shows itself as precisely and clearly as possible. He will not return in a few days, as is requested of him; so long as autumn lasts he will not expose himself to the fevers. Nay, more, if the winter promises to be severe, if the Alban mount is capped with snow, he will descend on the side of the sea, and shut himself in some warm retreat to work at his ease. It is only in spring, "with the first swallow," that he will be back. This term, as we see, is very indefinite. He purposely makes it so. One would think that he was resolved by a definitive trial both to make his liberty accepted by others and prove it to himself. In order to preserve it, he is ready to give back all that he has received (*cuncta resigno*). The house in the Sabina itself would seem to him too

---

[1] *Epist.*, I. 7.

dearly bought by the sacrifice of his repose and independence. " When one sees in an exchange that what one receives is worth less than what one gives, one must leave at once what one has taken and retake what one has relinquished." Mæcenas knew by this resolute tone that Horace had come to his decision, and did not renew his exigency. In a word, the conduct of the poet on this occasion was as clever as it was honourable. He knew that friendship demands a certain equality between the persons it unites. By avoiding exaggerated submissiveness, by safeguarding his liberty, and by upholding with jealous care the dignity of his character, he raised himself to the height of him who had loaded him with his benefits. It is thus that the nature of their connection was changed, and that instead of remaining his *protégé* he became his friend. It must be owned that the poets of the following age did not imitate this example. They were content to overwhelm the great personages who protected them with flattery and meanness. Can one be surprised that the latter, seeing themselves regarded as masters, treated them like servants ?

V.

HOW HORACE LIVED AT HIS COUNTRY HOUSE—HIS JOURNEYS—HE ACCUSTOMS HIMSELF TO REGRET ROME NO MORE—HIS LAST YEARS.

It is very annoying that Horace, who has described with so many details the employment of his days while he remained in Rome, should not have thought it necessary to tell us as clearly how he spent his life in the country. The only thing we know with certainty is that he was very happy there. He for the first time tasted the pleasure of being a proprietor. "I take my meals," said he, "before household gods that are mine own" (*Ante Larem proprium vescor*).[1] To have a hearth, domestic gods, to fix his life in a dwelling of which he was the master, was the greatest happiness that could befall a Roman. To enjoy it, Horace had waited until he was more than thirty years of age. We have seen that his domain, when he took possession of it, was very much neglected, and that the house was falling into ruins. He first had to build and plant. Do not let us pity him; these cares have their charms. One loves one's house when one has built or repaired it, and the very trouble our land costs us attaches us to it. He came to it as often as he could, and always with pleasure. Everything served him as a pretext to leave Rome. It was too hot there, or too cold; the Saturnalia were approaching—an unbearable time of the year, when all the town was out of doors; it was the moment to finish a work which Mæcenas had pressingly required. Well, how could anything good be done at Rome, where the noises of the street, the bustle of intercourse, the troublesome people one has to visit or receive, the bad verses one has to listen to, take up the best part of your time?[1] So he put Plato with Menander into his portmanteau, took with him the work he had begun, promising to do wonders, and started for Tibur. But when he was at home, his good resolutions did not hold out. He had something quite different to

---

[1] *Sat.*, II. 6, 66.

[2] *Ibid.*, II. 3, 11.

D

do than to shut himself up in his study. He had to
chat with his farmer, and superintend his labourers.
He went to see them at work, and sometimes lent a
hand himself. He dug the spade into the field, took
out the stones, etc., to the great amusement of the
neighbours, who marvelled both at his ardour and his
clumsiness :

"Rident vicini glebas et saxa moventem.'

In the evening he received at his table a few of the
neighbouring proprietors. They were honest folk, who
did not speak ill of their neighbours, and who, unlike
the fops of Rome, had not for sole topic of conversation
the races or the theatre. They handled most serious
questions, and their rustic wisdom found ready expression in proverbs and apologues. What pleased Horace
above all at these country dinners was that etiquette
was laughed at, that everything was simple and frugal,
that one did not feel constrained to obey those silly laws
which Varro had drawn up, and which had become
the code of good company. Nobody thought of electing
a king of the feast, to fix for the guests the number of
cups that must be drained. Every one ate according to
his hunger and drank according to his thirst. "They
were," said Horace, "divine repasts" (*O noctes cœnæque
Deum*).[2]

Yet he did not always stay at home, however great
the pleasure he felt in being there. This steady-going,
regular man thought it right from time to time to put
a little irregularity into one's life. Does not a Grecian
sage—Aristotle, I think—recommend that one excess

---

[1] *Epist.*, I. 14, 39.   [2] *Sat.*, II. 6, 65.

per month be indulged in, in the interest of health ? It serves, at least, to break the round of habit. Such also was the opinion of Horace. Although the most moderate of men, he found it pleasant to commit an occasional wildness (*dulce est desipere in loco*).[1] With age these outbursts had become less frequent, yet he still loved to break the sage uniformity of his existence by some pleasure jaunt. Then he returned to Præneste, to Baia, or to Tarentum, which he had loved so much in his youth. Once he was unfaithful to these old affections, and chose for the goal of his journey spots that were new to him. The occasion of the change was as follows : Antonius Musa, a Greek physician, had just cured Augustus of a very serious illness, which had been thought must prove fatal, by means of cold water. Hydrotherapeutics at once became fashionable. People fled the thermal springs, formerly so much sought after, to go off to Clusium, to Gabii, into the mountains, where springs of icy water were found. Horace did like the rest. In the winter of the year 730, instead of going as usual towards Baia, he turned his little steed towards Salerno and Velia. This was the affair of a season. Next year Marullus, the Emperor's son-in-law and heir, falling very ill, Antonius Musa was hastily sent for, and applied his usual remedy. But the remedy no longer healed, and hydrotherapeutics, which had saved Augustus, did not prevent Marullus from dying. They were at once forsaken, and the sick again began following the road to Baia. When Horace started on these extraordinary journeys, he took a

---

[1] *Carm.*, IV. 12, 28.

change of diet. " At home," said he, " I can put up with anything ; my Sabine table wine seems to me delicious ; and I regale myself with vegetables from my garden seasoned with a slice of bacon. But when I have once left my house, I become more particular, and beans, beloved though they be of Pythagoras, no longer suffice me."[1] So before starting in the direction of Salerno, where he did not often go, he takes the precaution to question one of his friends as to the resources of the country ; whether one can get fish, hares, and venison there, that he may come back home again as fat as a Phœacian. Above all, he is anxious to know what is drunk in those parts. He wants a generous wine to make him eloquent, and " which will give him strength, and rejuvenate him in the eyes of his young Lucanian sweetheart." We see he pushes precaution a considerable length. He was not rich enough to possess a house of his own at Baia, Præneste, or Salerno, the spots frequented by all the Roman fashionable world, but he had his wonted lodgings (*deversoria nota*), where he used to put up. When Seneca was at Baia, he lived above a public bath, and he has furnished us a very amusing account of the sounds of all kinds that troubled his rest. Horace, who liked his ease and wished to be quiet, could not make a very long stay in those noisy places. His whim gratified, he returned as soon as possible to his peaceful house amid the fields, and I can well imagine that those few fatiguing weeks made it seem more pleasant and more sweet to him.

One cannot read his works carefully without noticing

---

[1] *Epist.*, I. 15, 17.

that his affection for his country estate goes on constantly increasing. At first, when he had passed a few weeks there, the memory of Rome used to re-awaken in his thoughts. Those large towns, which we hate when we are forced to live in them, have only to be left in order to be regretted! When Horace's slave, taking an unfair advantage of the liberty of the Saturnalia, tells his master so many unpleasant things, he reproaches him with never being pleased where he is:

" Romæ rus optas, absentem villicus urbem
Tollis ad astra levis ? " [1]

He was himself very much vexed at his inconstancy, and accused himself " of only loving Rome when he was at Tibur, and only thinking of Tibur from the moment he found himself in Rome." [2] However he cured himself at last of this levity, which annoyed him so much. To this he bears witness in his own favour in the letter addressed to his farmer, where he strives to convince him that one may be happy without having a publichouse next door. " As for me," he tells him, " thou knowest that I am self-consistent, and that each time hated business recalls me to Rome I leave this spot with sadness." He doubtless arranged matters so as to live more and more at his country house. He looked forward to a time when it would be possible for him scarcely ever to leave it, and counted upon it to enable him to bear more lightly the weight of his closing years.

They *are* heavy, whatever one may do, and age never comes without bringing many griefs. Firstly, the long-

---

[1] *Sat.*, II. 7, 28.   [2] *Epist.*, I. 8, 12.

lived must needs leave many friends upon the way. Horace lost some to whom he was very tenderly attached —he had the misfortune to survive Virgil and Tibullus ten years. What regrets must he have felt on the death of the great poet of whom he said "he knew no soul more bright, and had no better friend!"[1] The great success of Virgil's posthumous work could only have half consoled him for his loss, for he regretted in him the man as much as the poet. He had also great cause to grieve for Mæcenas, whom he so dearly loved. This favourite of the Emperor, this king of fashion, whose fortune all men envied, finished by being very unhappy. It is all very well to take every kind of precaution in order to insure one's happiness—to fly from business, to seek pleasure, to amass wealth, to gather clever men about one, to surround oneself with all the charms of existence;[2] however one may try to shut the door on them, troubles and sorrows find a way in. The saddest of it all is that Mæcenas was first unhappy through his own fault. Somewhat late in life this prudent, wise man had been foolish enough to marry a coquette, and to fall deeply in love with her.[3] He had rivals, and among them the Emperor himself, of whom he dared not be jealous. He who had laughed so much at others afforded the Romans a comedy at his own expense. His time was passed in leaving Terentia, and taking her back again. "He has been married more than a hundred times," said Seneca, "although he has had but one wife."[4]

---

[1] *Epist.*, I. 14, 17.   [2] *Sat.*, I. 5, 42.

[3] "*Il avait eu le tort—un homme si prudent et si sage!—d'epouser sur le tard une coquette et d'en devenir très amoureux.*"

[4] Sen., *Epist.*, I. 14, 6.

To these domestic troubles illness was added. His health had never been good, and age and sorrows made it worse. Pliny tells us that he passed three whole years without being able to sleep.[1] Enduring pain badly, he grieved his friends beyond measure by his groans. Horace, with whom he continually conversed about his approaching end, answered him in beautiful verses : "Thou, Mæcenas, die first ! thou, stay of my fortune, adornment of my life ! The gods will not allow it, and I will not consent. Ah ! if Fate, hastening its blows, should tear from me part of myself in thee, what would betide the other ? What should I henceforth do, hateful unto myself, and but half of myself surviving ?"[2]

In the midst of these sorrows, Horace himself felt that he was growing old. The hour when one finds oneself face to face with age is a serious one. Cicero, when approaching it, tried to give himself courage in advance, and being accustomed to console himself for everything by writing, he composed his *de Senectute*, a charming book in which he tries to deck the closing years of life with certain beauties. He had not to make use of the consolations which he prepared for himself, so we do not know whether he would have found them sufficient when the moment came. That spirit, so young, so full of life, would, I fear, have resigned itself with difficulty to the inevitable decadencies of age. Nor did Horace love old age, and in his *Ars Poetica* he has drawn a somewhat gloomy picture of it. He had all the more reason to detest it because it came to him

---

[1] Pliny, *Nat. Hist.*, VII. 51 (52).   [2] *Carm.* II. 17, 3.

rather early. In one of those passages where he so willingly gives us the description of his person, he tells us that his hair whitened quickly.[1] As a climax of misfortune he had grown very fat, and being short, his corpulence was very unbecoming to him. Augustus, in a letter, compares him to one of those measures of liquids which are broader than they are high.[2] If, in spite of these too evident signs which warned him of his age, he had tried to deceive himself, there was no lack of persons to disabuse him. There was the porter of Neæra, who no longer allowed his slave to enter, an affront which Horace was obliged to put up with without complaining. "My hair whitening," said he, "warns me not to quarrel. I should not have been so patient in the time of my boiling youth, when Planeus was consul."[3] Then it was Neæra herself who declined to come when he summoned her, and again resigning himself with a good enough grace, the poor poet found that, after all, she was right, and that it was natural love should prefer youth to ripened age.

> "*Ahi,*
> *Quo blandæ juvenum te revocant preces.*"[4]

Fortunately he was not of a melancholy disposition, like his friends Tibullus and Virgil. He even had opinions on the subject of melancholy, which differ widely from ours. Whereas, since Lamartine, we have assumed the habit of regarding sadness as one of the essential elements of poetry, he thought, on the con-

---

[1] *Epist.*, I. 20, 24.
[2] Suet., *Vita Hor.*, p. 47 (Reiferscheid's edition).
[3] *Carm.*, III. 14, 25.　　　[4] *Ibid.*, IV. 7.

trary, that poetry has the privilege of preventing us from being sad. "A man protected by the Muses," said he, "flings cares and sorrows to the winds to bear away."[1] His philosophy had taught him not to revolt against inevitable ills. However painful they be, one makes them lighter by bearing them.[2] So he accepted old age because it cannot be eluded, and because no means have yet been found of living long without growing old. Death itself did not frighten him. He was not of those who reconcile themselves to it as well as they can by never thinking about it. On·the contrary, he counsels us to have it always in mind. "Think that the day which lights you is the last you have to live. The morrow will have more charm for you if you did not hope to see it":

> " *Omnem crede diem tibi diluxisse supremum ;*
> *Grata superveniet quæ non sperabitur hora.*"[3]

This is not, as might be supposed, one of those bravadoes of the timid, who shout before Death in order to deaden the sound of his footsteps. Horace was never more calm, more energetic, more master of his mind and of his soul, than in the works of his ripe age. The last lines of his that remain to us are the firmest and most serene he ever wrote.

Then, more than ever, must he have loved the little Sabine valley. When we visit these beautiful tranquil spots, we tell ourselves that they appear made to shelter the declining years of a sage. It seems as if with old servants, a few faithful friends, and a stock of well-

---

[1] *Carm.*, I. 26, 1.
[2] *Ibid.*, I. 24, 19.

chosen books, the time must pass there without sadness. But I must stop. Since Horace has not taken us into his confidence respecting his last years, and nobody after him has told us of them, we are reduced to form conjectures, and we should put as few of them as possible into the life of a man who loved truth so well.

CHAPTER II.

THE ETRUSCAN TOMBS AT CORNETO.

THERE is a famous saying of Tacitus, that imagination transfigures all that is unknown to us and makes it appear marvellous: "*Omne ignotum pro magnifico est.*" [1] Ovid, on the contrary, holds that we cannot desire the unknown: "*Ignoti nulla cupido;*" [2] and although they seem to contradict each other, I think they are both right. The unknown produces contrary effects upon us, according to the diversity of our natures; some it attracts, others it repels. We see this well by what happens in the case of the Etruscans. Many of the learned find a sort of provoking charm in the very obscurity which shrouds the origin of this people, in the little that is known of its history, in the hitherto existing impossibility of understanding its language. These are enigmas they fain would solve, and so passionate is their desire, that failure stimulates instead of disheartening them. The less they attain to knowledge, the more they seek to know. Others resign themselves to ignorance much more easily. They even suspect that in this civilization which so obstinately refuses to

---

[1] Agric., 30. [2] *Ars am.*, III. 397.

be guessed there was nothing worth knowing. So they
are inexhaustible in their sarcasms at the foolish curiosity of these poor pundits who delight to wander in
the dark, and lose their trouble and their time in trying
to solve the insolvable.[1]

I must own myself to be on the side of the curious.
Although their obstinacy has not always been fortunate,
I do not find it ridiculous. Reluctance to remain
ignorant of the past history of a race which held an
important place among ancient nations is a thing I
cannot understand. When I see in a museum the
beautiful works which the Etruscans have left us, I
am seized by an ardent desire to know who made
them. I cannot pass unmoved those great statues of
stone or terra-cotta lying stretched on their sarcophagi,
leaning upon their elbows, and seeming to look at the
visitors. They are so true, so living, that I always
want to question them about their history, and ask
them for their secret.

If this secret has been so well kept, if it is so difficult
to know this strange, mysterious people, it is not because,
like so many others, it has disappeared entirely. There
are few, indeed, of whom so many relics remain. The
amount of things that have been taken from their cities
of the dead during the last three centuries is incredible.
The museums of the entire world are full of their spoils;

---

[1] Mommsen is one of these scoffers, and the most pitiless. At
the beginning of his *Roman History* he rallies people who pile up
hypotheses about the Etruscans and their origin. "Archæologists,"
he says, "have a mania for foudly seeking to know what cannot be
known, and isn't worth knowing." Then he compares them to those
erudite fools of antiquity whom Tiberius jeeringly asked "Who was
Hecuba's mother?"

they have left us precious objects of every kind, and the harvest is far from being gathered. The Louvre already possesses many painted vases, due to the liberalities of Caylus, Forbin, and other enlightened amateurs, and to the acquisition of the collections of MM. Durand and Fochon ; and it might have been considered one of the museums richest in Etruscan antiquities even before 1862, when, through the intermediary of M. Léon Renier, the State acquired the Campana collection, which more than doubled its riches. It contained vases, pictures, jewels of the greatest value, together with a marvellous gathering of terra-cottas, mostly from Campania and Etruria. Three large rooms were filled with what had been found in the tombs of ancient Coere alone. So an idea of this little-known civilization may be found without leaving Paris, and by simply visiting the galleries of the Louvre. It is a journey within the reach of all, and from which all may derive great profit.

Yet the best way to study the Etruscans is to go and see them at home. The thousand objects we view with curiosity in the cases of a museum are much more curious still, and teach us more, when found in their natural place. One knows their purpose, and better understands their character. Among Etruscan cities, few have kept so many mementoes of their glorious past as Corneto, the ancient Tarquinii. It is thither we must go in order to study ancient Etruria on the spot. Not only does this town possess a larger number of ancient monuments than the rest, but we have the advantage here of their having been studied by distinguished *savants*, and, above all, by Dr Helbig, one of the directors of the Archæological Institution at Rome, who has already assisted us to a knowledge of the paintings at Pompeii.[1] I cannot perhaps do better than use his labours, and, following in his footsteps, visit with him the tombs of Corneto.

I.

HOW TARQUINII DISAPPEARED—CORNETO—RELICS OF THE MIDDLE AGES AND THE RENAISSANCE AT CORNETO— THE ETRUSCAN TOMBS—GENERAL ASPECT.

Travelling over maritime Etruria used to be troublesome work; and to risk oneself in these unhealthy, sparsely - populated regions presupposed considerable curiosity and no small amount of courage. To-day nothing is easier. A very interesting railway skirts the shores of the Mediterranean from Genoa to Palo, and being the shortest route from Turin to Rome, is very much used. One does not think of stopping at the intermediate stations, it is true, nor does what one sees of the Tuscan Maremma in this rapid flight make one wish to visit it more nearly. Yet it is wrong to do so; and a traveller stopping at Corneto, and remaining there at least an entire day, would not have reason to complain that the time was lost.

Corneto is situated between Orbetelli and Civita Vecchia. It is now a little town of some few thousand inhabitants, perched upon a verdant hill, and viewed

---

[1] See *Promenades Archéologiques*, p. 313 and following. The works of Dr Helbig on the paintings at Corneto are contained in the *Annales de l'Institut de Correspondance Archéologique*.

from below, strikes one by the number of its turrets. It is rather fatiguing work to get there, for the ascent of the hill-side is a rough one, but once on the summit, the view enjoyed repays us for our pains. Before us is the sea, with *Monte Argentaro* seeming from a distance to fling itself into the waves. Turning towards the land side, we see a little river, *la Marta*, plunging into the valley through the trees. Facing us, a hill rises opposite to that on which Corneto is built. They are only separated by a little smiling, fertile plain; and a few kilomètres further on they approach each other, and end by joining, so as to form a kind of low semicircle. Corneto occupies the extremity of the one nearest to the sea; Tarquinii was built on the other, just opposite to where Corneto now stands.

Tarquinii was one of the largest and most important cities of Etruria. Its wall was eight kilomètres round. There, it is said, in the first year of Rome, the Corinthian Demaratus came to settle, bringing with him all his riches, together with his family and his clients, some of whom were distinguished Grecian artists. When war broke out between Etruria and the Romans, Tarquinii chiefly bore the brunt of it. Its inhabitants defended their independence bravely, and Rome could only complete its subjection after a simultaneous massacre of all its aristocracy. In losing its liberty, it necessarily lost much of its importance. Yet Cicero still calls it "a very flourishing city."[1] How came it to disappear entirely later on, and to spring up again in another place and under a different name? We

---

[1] *De Rep.*, II. 18.

know but very imperfectly, but vicissitudes of this kind seem to have been inherent to the destinies of Etruscan cities. They had very checkered fortunes, and it was the fate of many to die and come to life again. This is explained, if one considers the surrounding country. It is at once attractive and terrible, fertile and plague-stricken. It is the Maremma—

" Dilettevole molto e poco sana,"

as a poet of the fourteenth century says. It has not the desolate look of the Roman Campagna, although as fearful to live in. In the plains vegetation is vigorous, and the hills are covered with cork oaks, mastic trees, and carobs. "How often," says M. Noël des Vergers, " while seeking under the luxuriant vegetation of the forests for traces of the mysterious nation that used to people these deserts, and finding so many proofs of its sojourn, have I begun to doubt that in these fragrant woods, these pasturages, this air, so soft, so mild, could lurk disease and death. To convince me there needed chance meetings with some of the rare inhabitants, whose shrunken features, dull eyes, yellow hue, and bulging stomach all speak of suffering better than the most eloquent narration could do."[1] To render the country habitable it was necessary to make it healthy, and this the Etruscans did. That they drained the marshes and gave a better flow to the rivers is beyond a doubt. Pliny the Elder admired the hydraulic works they had carried out in the valley of the Po while they were its masters ; they must have done still more for the very country which was their cradle and the centre

---

[1] Noël des Vergers, *l'Etrurie et les Etrusques*, I. p. 2.

of their domination. We may suppose that they dug there some of those great drains that are met with everywhere in the neighbourhood of Rome, and which, to use the expression of a sagacious observer, make all the Tiber basin and the slopes of the Alban Mount look like a gigantic warren.[1] But these works are, by their very nature, delicate and fragile. Nature can only be subdued at the cost of an endless struggle. If we relax a moment, she reassumes all her empire. A few years of negligence suffice to lose the fruits of many years of effort—the canals get choked, the ponds fill, and miasmas begin to infect the air again. In the eighteenth century the descendants of the great Medici having ceased to encourage the works undertaken by their ancestors for the purpose of rendering the environs of Lake Castiglione more healthy, and allowed the Fosso di Navigazione which joined this lake to a neighbouring river to become obstructed, it was remarked that in a few years the population of Grossetto fell from 3,000 souls to 700, and that the adjacent Campagna, instead of sowing 1,300 measures of corn every year as formerly, only sowed 300. The above example shows us how quickly things degenerate in this country,

---

[1] These small tunnels, generally 1 m. 50 high, and sometimes several kilomètres in extent, have long been known. They are so numerous in the Roman Campagna that it was difficult not to notice them ; but their purpose was not suspected. It is now generally agreed that they formed a kind of drainage destined to dry the soil and fight the malaria. On this subject the monks of M. Thomasi Crudeli, director of the Anatomical and Physiological Institution of Rome, may be consulted, and an article of M. de la Blanchère in the *Mélanges d'archéologie et d'histoire* (Vol. II.) published by the École Française.

and also explains how the depopulation and ruin of the
Etruscan cities proceeded so rapidly, and why, in some
cases, it was so complete.   Their decadence began
directly after their defeat by the Romans.   Towards
the end of the Republic several of them were already
desolate; the malaria, more feebly combated, had
resumed its power.   Virgil, speaking of Graviscæ, the
port of Tarquinii, which must have been near the
mouth of the Marta, calls it an unhealthy place.
Surely it could not have been so when the ships of
Greece and Carthage brought the merchandise of their
countries to these coasts.   It had become so since the
Etruscans, having lost their activity with their independence, no longer fought the terrible scourge with the
same energy.   But the evil could be repaired.   It was
possible, by an increase of effort, to render these lands
habitable again; and as they are fertile and smiling,
and attract the cultivator by their wealth, he returns
courageously, and sets to work again as soon as the
political situation improves, and he can hope to enjoy
the fruits of his labour in peace.   M. Noël des Vergers
bids us remark that Etruria, which seemed exhausted
towards the end of the Roman Republic, under the
Empire all at once revives.   The Campagna repeoples,
and the towns rise again.   Propertius tells us that in
his time, at the beginning of the reign of Augustus, the
shepherd led his flocks over the ruins of Veii.   Under
the successors of Augustus, Veii once more became an
important city, whose existence is revealed to us by
curious inscriptions.   Strabo mentions Fidenæ among
those ancient cities of Etruria destroyed by war, and
become simple private properties.   In the time of

Tiberius Fidenæ is once more an important city, giving games to which all its neighbours flock; and Tacitus relates that at one of these festivals more than 50,000 persons were killed or injured by the fall of an amphitheatre. There, indeed, we have very rapid resurrections. But some time after, when came the Empire's evil days, internal revolutions, and the disasters of invasion, the maritime coast of Etruria again became depopulated. The Gaul, Rutilius Namatianus, who passed along these shores when returning home from Rome, found them desolate. On his road he only saw the Campagna depopulated by the fever, and deserted towns. "Let not man complain of death," said he, surveying ancient Populonia, whose monuments lay strewn upon the ground; "here are examples which teach us that cities, too, may die."[1]

It is then that Tarquinii, in consequence of disasters of which we know but little, was abandoned by its inhabitants. To-day, vegetation has covered again the little that remains of the old city. From afar no vestige of it is seen. We must go about the hill where it was built, and carefully remove the grass, in order to discover the substructures of a few walls, or some fallen stones. How came the deserted city to remove to the other side of the plain? What reasons could it have for settling on the neighbouring hills? We do not know; but in this new site it shed a certain lustre during the Middle Ages. At Corneto some fine monuments of that epoch are shown, especially the church of Santa Maria in Castello, which has not been

---

[1] *Itiner.*, I. 413.

spoiled by clumsy restoration—a somewhat rare case in Italy. Being no longer used as a place of worship, it escapes the unenlightened zeal of the faithful and the bad taste of village priests, and remains as it was when consecrated in the twelfth century, with a few injuries of time that do not disfigure it. It preserves intact its *ciborium* ornamented with light columns; its marble ambo, just like that of St Clement's at Rome; and on the broken slabs of the old tombs which have served to mend its pavement, we read inscriptions reaching back to the first centuries of Christianity. At the Renaissance, Corneto still had a certain importance. A family rich and friendly to the Arts, of which there were so many at that time—the Vitelleschi—had a magnificent palace built there on the model of those at Florence, and equal to them in beauty and grandeur. As with them, the lower part is like a fortress, while in the upper part elegance holds sway ; so that strength and grace commingle in the most unexpected manner. Our surprise is great in going over Corneto to find, in a little town isolated on a rock in the midst of a desert, a church like St Clement's, and a palace recalling by its proportions and its architecture the most beautiful of Florence. But we are in Italy, where surprises of this sort are not uncommon. Elsewhere Art seems to have reserved itself for towns ; but in this privileged country it has grown with such vigour, has flowed in such abundance, that it sometimes overflowed into the very villages.

But one does not come to Corneto in order to study the Middle Ages of the Renaissance. They are found represented elsewhere by monuments more beautiful and more numerous yet. Here we are only looking for the Etruscans. So we must be content with a rapid glance at Santa Maria in Castello and the Vitelleschi palace, and hasten to see what remains of this lost people of ancient times.

Our expectation will not be deceived, and we shall be able to satisfy ourselves fully. Corneto gives a good example to other Italian towns by the care she takes of her antiquities. She is very proud of her past, and not only has she added the old name of Tarquinii to her own (*Corneto Tarquinia*)—a gratification of her vanity which cost her nothing—but she incurs great outlay in order to house her riches well and to increase them. These expenses are borne by the town and by a local Society, l'Universita Agraria, which has generously undertaken to bear half the burden. M. Luigi Dasti, the mayor, is a man of refinement, who loves his little town very much, and he sustains everybody's zeal. Thanks to him, it has been possible to carry on the excavations for the last ten years, although the Government has encouraged them but little. Fresh tombs have been discovered, others unearthed anew, and a museum has been founded destined soon to become one of the richest in Italy. This museum and these tombs are precisely what attract the stranger to Corneto.

He has not far to go to see the tombs; for the very hill on which Corneto stands was the Necropolis of Tarquinii. From their windows the inhabitants of the great city could see their family sepulchres rise one above another opposite to them. The spectacle of death did not then seem painful to them—a proof that they were not like their descendants, the Tuscans of to-day, who carefully hide their funerals, celebrate them at night, and carry off their dead at racing speed, as if to get rid of them as soon as possible. Tarquinii having existed during ten centuries, the hill which served it as a cemetery is pierced with tombs. Thousands have been discovered and there remain many more than have been found. Naturally, the simple sepulchres are the commonest; but there are also handsome ones that belonged to great families. Twenty-eight are known to-day ornamented with mural paintings, and it is with them we shall chiefly have to do.

All are cut in the rock, at depths varying from two to twelve mètres; and there must formerly have been some sign above the soil to indicate the existence of the tomb within. This was doubtless a more or less massy mound of turf, in one of whose sides was the door giving access to the vault. In the midst of the desolate plain of Vulci, in the plague-struck wilderness by which the great city has been replaced, rises a tumulus, fifteen mètres high and two hundred mètres in circumference. It is called in the neighbourhood "la Cucumella." It is a mass of accumulated earth covering two domes of masonry. Round towers, of which traces are still seen, rose above the monument. They were surmounted by symbolic animals, winged sphinxes, lions crouching or standing, destined to frighten away evil spirits. Although it has not yet been possible to pierce the stone arched roof, and the Cucumella obstinately keeps its secret, it may be affirmed to have been the top of a tomb. There is no longer anything of the kind at Corneto. The tumuli have all disappeared, and only the underground part, the sepulchres, have been preserved. These subterranean tombs are of very unequal size. The greater number consist of a square chamber three or four mètres in measurement. But some of them contain several rooms, while others are so vast that it has been necessary to have pillars to support the roof. The dead repose in large sarcophagi of stone or terra-cotta. When they have been burnt, their ashes are placed in urns of varied form. The same sepulchre sometimes contains both urns and sarcophagi, showing that both modes of burial were practised at the same epoch. In some ancient tombs, the dead, clad in his finest apparel and decked with his arms, lay stretched upon a bed of state. Those who had the good fortune to penetrate first, when all was still intact, have described to us the emotion with which they were seized on beholding these warriors in the very attitude in which they were left when the vault was walled up, more than twenty centuries ago. This sight generally disappears in a few minutes. The air, on penetrating these funeral chambers which had been so long closed, rapidly decomposed the bodies, reducing them to dust before the eyes of the visitors. " 'Twas an evocation of the past that had not even the duration of a dream." Besides the arms, the beds, and the sarcophagi, the tombs contained articles of toilet, mirrors, weapons, and, above all, vases. Almost all these movables have disappeared; they were too tempting to robbers. Even in ancient times, despite the respect professed for the dead, the temptation to pillage old tombs was irresistible. Theodoric, judging it better to authorise what he could not prevent, allowed anybody to appropriate the gold found in them, when they no longer had a lawful owner (*aurum sepulchris´ juste detrahetur, ubi dominus non habetur*).[1] The moderns have continued to profit by the permission, and so well that nothing now remains which could be carried off—that is to say, the mural paintings.

I cannot think of taking the reader successively through all the tombs of Corneto, and describing them one after the other. It would be a tiresome enumeration, for which a good guide may be substituted with advantage.[2] I prefer to suppose the visit paid. We have gone through the most important tombs by the wan light of the *cerini;* the *custode* has shown the paintings that decorate them; and we have looked with interest upon all these scenes, some half destroyed by damp, others preserving after so many centuries an extraordinary brilliancy and freshness. Having finished our round, let us try to sum up the impressions left and the reflections suggested by it. Let us ask ourselves what it can teach us of the people who built these tombs, and whether it be possible to draw from it as to their manner of living, their character, and their beliefs.

---

[1] Cassiodorus, *Variar.*, IV. 14.

[2] M. L. Dasti, the Mayor of Corneto of whom I have just spoken, has published two pamphlets, entitled *Tombe Etruche di pinte*, and *Museo etrusco Tarqueniese*, which will be of great use to visitors of these tombs. I may add that this essay has been translated into Italian, and is sold at Corneto as a kind of guide for strangers. I recall this fact merely as a testimony to the exactness of the descriptions.

II.

IMPORTANCE OF SEPULTURE AMONG THE ETRUSCANS—THE PAINTINGS IN THE TOMBS—FEW SCENES OF SADNESS ARE FOUND AMONG THEM—HOW IT IS THEY SO OFTEN REPRESENT BANQUETS AND GAMES—THE EXACTNESS OF THESE PAINTINGS—THE COSTUME OF THE PERSONAGES IS THAT OF ANCIENT ROMANS—THE SMALL NUMBER REPRESENTING MYTHOLOGICAL SUBJECTS, AND THE CONCLUSION TO BE DRAWN FROM THIS CIRCUMSTANCE—THE ETRUSCANS ACCEPT THE FABLES OF GREECE—*TOMBA DEL' ORCO*—WHAT HAPPENS TO THESE FABLES AMONG THE ETRUSCANS.—CHARÙN.

What first strikes us is the importance attached to sepulture. All ancient nations doubtless gave the matter great weight, but still they have left us palaces, temples, and theatres as well as funeral monuments; of the Etruscans we have nothing but tombs. They evidently, then, built them with more care than all the rest, and their minds must therefore have been much taken up with death. But what idea had they of it? One would think that this must be an easy thing to find out, and that in order to do so we need only look at the pictures which decorate the tombs. Unfortunately, these paintings are not all of the same epoch, and many represent very different states of mind. Under the influence of their neighbours, the Etruscans have more than once changed their opinions. These variations must be taken into account, in order that we may not draw too general opinions from a single

picture, or attribute to one period what belonged to
another.   Nor let us forget that ancient religions had
no precise dogmas, since it is truth we shall always
have before our eyes when studying Antiquity.   The
Etruscans doubtless possessed a great number of sacred
books ; but although we have lost them, we can be sure
that none of them contained a religious teaching, in the
sense we attach to the word.   There, as elsewhere, the
priests only busied themselves with regulating the
practices of religion, all the rest being left to the free
interpretation of the faithful.   Even on the question
which to us seems the most important of all—about
death and what follows it, about hell and about Elysium—
everybody thought merely what he chose.   Hence the
artists of the tombs of Corneto were not, like those of
the Catacombs, fettered by fixed beliefs, and rigorously
bound to conform to them.   They could abandon themselves more to their caprices.   To press too far the
meaning of the scenes they portray ; to attribute
formal intention to the least details of their pictures, as
has been sometimes done, and infer a certain and
general doctrine from what was sometimes only an
individual fancy, would be to risk self-deception.

With these reserves, there are a certain number of
observations which may be risked without fear, being
based upon too many proofs to be contradicted.   We
shall, for example, remark that, at least in the earlier
times, death does not seem to inspire the Etruscan
artists with very sad thoughts.   Mournful subjects
which seem in place on the walls of a tomb are very
rare at Corneto.   In the Tomba del Morto we are shown
an old man stretched on a magnificent bed.   He has

just died. Before him a young woman with dishevelled hair, probably his daughter, seems to be fastening or pulling down over her face the cap which covers her head. At the ends of the bed two men raise their hands in an attitude of the most poignant sorrow. This scene is like the one painted in the Tomba del Morente, where a whole family is seen plunged in grief near a dying man. But these, I repeat, are exceptions. The artist, in general, has been lavish in cheerful pictures. One would think his desire had been only to paint, in this abode of death, that which gives life a value. Above all, banquets are frequently represented, and there is scarcely a tomb which does not contain one. The guests recline on sumptuous couches, and hold large goblets in their hands; their women are placed beside them; everything breathes joy; wreathes of flowers hang from the roof, the tables are served, and we can distinguish the forms of the dishes which cover it, and count their number. By the tables stand slaves bearing amphoræ, and ready to pour out wine for the guests, while by their side musicians play the double flute or the cithern. We must not be surprised to see musicians figure so often in the paintings of Corneto, for music held a great place in the life of the Etruscans. Not only did they never celebrate a religious ceremony or a public festival without it, but it may be said to have accompanied all their actions. An historian cited by Athenæus declares that they kneaded their bread and flogged their slaves to the sound of the flute. A love of music naturally brings with it that of dancing, so at Corneto there are dancers in abundance. They are usually represented in violent attitudes, their hair dishevelled and their heads thrown back, as the Greeks love to paint the Bacchantes. We also very frequently see hunting scenes. In these gorges of the Appenines the chase must always have been a favourite amusement. The hunter is on foot or mounted. He pursues birds with the sling, and attacks the boar with the spear, while his servants carry upon their shoulders the beasts he has slain. Another subject the artists of the country delight to represent are the games, and especially horse and chariot racing. In the Tomba delle Bighe, the charioteers, clad in scarlet tunics, with reins in hand and bodies inclined, are about to dispute the prize. The riders are seated on one horse and hold another by the bridle, doubtless ready to spring from one to the other. Athletes and pugilists keep the crowd amused during the intervals of the races. Meanwhile the spectators throng into a kind of stand very like our own. We see them, men and women, dressed in their holiday clothes, and intent upon the show. Some persons who could not find any other place—slaves, perhaps—have crept beneath the tribunes, and look on from there, in company with some domestic animals. The scene has an incredible character of reality. Sometimes it is actors, pantomimists, or acrobats who are charged to amuse the public, and who do it with a will, making all kinds of contortions, climbing one upon the other, and walking upon their heads. Their costumes are at times rather strange. One of them wears a pointed cap with coloured stripes, and a little tuft of red wool at the end, just like that put by the Italians on their Punchinellos. So the tomb where it was found is called "la Tomba del Pulcinella."

What was the real meaning of these paintings? Why does the artist usually prefer them to others? And what can there be in them particularly suitable to a tomb? It is often said in explanation that they represent feasts given in honour of the dead, and at first sight this solution looks very probable. We know, indeed, what a great place festivities hold in the funeral rites of Rome. The ninth day after the funeral the family meets to dine round about the tomb. This repast is called the *cena novemdialis*; it is, strictly speaking, the octave of the dead. A year afterwards, and on the succeeding anniversaries, the repast is renewed, and reunites the relatives and all who still remember the friend who has passed away. So far-sighted people who wish their memory to be commemorated as long as possible are careful to leave by will funds to cover the expense of the feast. Christianity found these customs so enrooted that at first it did not dare to destroy them, and it was usual to come and eat and drink at the tombs of the martyrs on their anniversaries down to the time of St Ambrose. As for the gains, they were not, as one might be tempted to think, a simple gratification of vanity—a manner, like any other, of glorifying a man of importance who had died. They had a religious meaning of the deepest gravity. A Christian who assists at a sacrifice for the dead thinks that he is working by his prayers to ensure them eternal bliss, which is certainly to render them a great service; but a pagan who celebrated games in honour of one of his relations, actually helped him to become a god, which is a very great deal more. Such was the importance of worship in those old religions that not only could there be no gods without worshippers, but the worshipper is even suspected of contributing to the divinity of him he prays to.[1] Young races readily believe that the man who dies throws off the conditions of humanity and becomes a superior being. So then he is nearly a god (*dii manes*), and his divinity is completed, and the same honours are rendered to him that are assigned to the immortals. It is easy to understand that the games having this importance, it has been sought to preserve their memory, and that their image has been painted in the tomb of him who was honoured by them. It was a way of affirming his apotheosis.

In our days a new explanation has been imagined. These feasts, these games, we are told, are not, as it has been thought, a representation of honours rendered to the deceased, but an image of the felicity he enjoys in the other world. The scene had been laid on earth; in order to understand it, it must be removed to the sky. Among us, M. Ravaisson has maintained this opinion with great force. Apropos of a bas-relief recently discovered at Athens, where a young woman is seen holding out her hand to some old men, he bids us remark that we possess many such representations, and that hitherto antiquarians, believing they discerned an air of sadness on the faces of the personages, have supposed here scenes of adieu or separation. M. Ravaisson remarks that in the monument he is studying, the old men and the young woman, far from parting, are walking towards each other; and since Hermes, the god con-

---

[1] This is what Statius seems to me very precisely to express in his *Thebaid.* He represents a nymph who, by dint of adoring an oak, has rendered it a sort of divine power (*numenque colendo fecerat*).

ductor of souls, figures beside the woman, as if taking her to her relations. he thinks that the place where they are is the abode of happy spirits. Then extending to all monuments of this kind the explanation he has given of the one at Athens, he proposes to call them in future, not "scenes of adieu," but "scenes of re-union."[1] He believes them to be a fresh affirmation of the belief of the ancients in the persistence of life, a satisfaction given to that energetic hope which refuses to believe in eternal separation. He seizes the occasion to combat the doctrine of Lobeck, who holds that the Greeks, satisfied with the present life, long remain strangers to all serious concern respecting a life to come, and that they only began to grow anxious about it when political agitation came to trouble the serenity of their consciences and open them to religious terrors. To archæologists of this school, who decline to see in any monument allusions to what follows death, M. Ravaisson opposes the interpretation which he has just given of the so-called "scenes of adieu." To it he adds a new way of understanding the supposed funeral repasts. They are for him and many others[2] an expression of the divine condition of the soul when it has left

---

[1] M. Ravaisson's note was published in the *Gazette archéologique* of 1875. His conclusions can evidently not apply to all bas-reliefs without exception, and there are some where it is very difficult to see "scenes of reunion." Those spoken of by M. Brunn in the *Annales de correspondance archéologique* (1859, p. 325, *et seq.*), in which, beside the two spouses who press each other's hands, demons await death in order to proceed towards an open door, are indeed veritable "scenes of adieu."

[2] This opinion has been especially championed in Germany by MM. Ambrosch and Stephani.

the body, and a manner of showing the happiness it
will enjoy after death. So he would have them called
"Elysian banquets." To the reasons collected by M.
Ravaisson in support of his opinion, Dr Helbig adds
another, which is not without importance. He has
remarked that in the Tomba del Orco, to be noticed
further on, the artist has traced round the scenes where
the gods appear a line of dark blue, quite resembling
the nimbus by painters of the Middle Ages to distinguish the heads of the saints for the veneration of
the faithful. Well, this tomb, like almost all others
contains a banqueting scene, and this banquet is surrounded by the same nimbus, from which it may be concluded that the guests are also inhabitants of heaven.

Whatever be the force of these arguments, I fear
that those who visit the frescoes at Corneto will
retain some doubts. They have a character so frankly
terrestrial ; they reproduce with so much truth the
actions of ordinary life, that one has great difficulty to
conceive that the artist has thought of painting gods
and transporting into Elysium. In the Tomba del Vecchio
an old man, whose white beard contrasts strongly with
his swarthy hue, reclines near a young woman,
familiarly holding her by the chin. An air of sensual
satisfaction is spread over his features, and the woman
herself acquiesces willingly enough in his caresses.
While looking at them it costs us a violent effort to
persuade ourselves that we are no longer upon earth.
For the hunts, the games, and the dances, the difficulty
is still greater. It would doubtless be very natural to
see in them an image of the pleasures in which the
blessed indulge in the world beyond the tomb. "Some

of them," says Virgil, "exercise their limbs in the games
of the palestra, and wrestle with each other on the
yellow sand; others beat the ground in cadence. The
taste they had in life for chariots and horses does not
quit them after they have ceased to live."[1] But however inclined one may be to regard these frescoes as
the picture of a kind of pagan paradise, one lights at
every instant upon details that bring one back to earth
again. In the Tomba del Cacciatore, one of the personages who pursues birds with a sling is so carried
away by his ardour that he falls from a high rock
into the sea. That is an accident to which one
would think immortals could not be exposed. It is all
very well to say that in those remote times the future
life was thought to be exactly like the present one; it
is difficult to admit that the dead could have run a risk
of killing themselves.

Perhaps it is more simple and probable to suppose
that it is not merely a question either of Tartarus or of
Elysium here, but of future life as all primitive races
picture it to themselves. It is known that this second
existence appeared to them to be a dark sequel to the
first, a twilight after the day. Man continues to live in
the tomb, but with lessened wants, and passions grown
more feeble. In order that he may not perceive too
great a change, they build his sepulchre on the model of
his house. There are tombs at Corneto arranged quite
like ordinary habitations. The one called the Tomba
degli Scudi is composed of four rooms; one being placed

---

[1] *Æn.*, VI. 642. I may add that those personages who dance or
ride seem indeed to be quite alive, and that the artist has sometimes
written their names above their portraits.

in the middle, like the *atrium* of the Romans, and all
the others opening out of it. In this house great care
is taken to place all the objects which the deceased
liked for his use or his adornment—his arms, his gems,
the carpets and the vases which he paid so dearly for,
in order that he may find them if he needs them. It is
with the same idea that his " eternal abode " is decorated
with the scenes he loved in life. It is hoped that
all these pictures of feasts, games, and dances of which
he is supposed to be still cognisant, will console him for
his long, sad solitude. The reality charmed him when
he was alive ; it is thought the picture will suffice him
now that he is nothing more than a shade. Only these
paintings, in order to produce their effect, must be faithful and carefully executed. They are done for him
alone, since the tomb, once closed, is not opened again to
the living : but what of that ? They shall be made as
beautiful, as exact as possible for him. When they
meet that eye which we believe to be not entirely
sightless, it must be able to draw illusion and life from
them. Unless I am mistaken, this is how it became
customary to paint such animated and joyous scenes in
the tombs.[1]

These scenes, precisely because they are so faithful,
have the advantage of taking us into the midst of
Etruscan life. We see them as they were five or six

---

[1] In Greece too, in spite of the progress of ideas, this primitive conception of the other life was never effaced. When at Tanagra and
elsewhere those charming statuettes were placed in the tombs, which
have come out of them again after so many centuries, and which
amateurs contend for with such fury, it was doubtless that they might
keep the dead company.

centuries before our era, at the beginning of the Roman Republic. We divine their tastes, their habits, their everyday life, and their favourite occupations. War was evidently not among the latter; for we have re-marked that it never figures among the tombs at Tar-quinii. We find a few warriors, it is true; but equipped with such brilliant arms, and covered with such coquettish ornaments, that they are evidently more ready for show than for battle. But if war is absent from these pictures where the artists painted what the Etruscans liked to see, it proves that the Etruscans had no taste for war. All antiquity reproached them for their love of peace, and even gentle Virgil himself could not help falling foul of them. He supposes one of their chiefs, whom they have deserted in battle, to address them in these cruel words: " Of what use to you are your glaives, and what do you do with those darts which you hold in your hands ? You have only heart for pleasure; you are only brave in the combats of the night. Listen ! The crooked flute announces the feasts of Bacchus. To sit at a well-furnished board, and stretch your hands towards full cups—these are your delights. These are your wonted exploits.". [1] It must be owned that the paintings of Corneto show these re-proaches not to have been unfounded. They give us the idea of a rich society anxious to enjoy its fortune. Good living and the arts are its passion ; it passes life joyously ; its manners are not austere. The women sit at the feast with the men, which was not allowed at Rome until very late. The highest personages do

---

[1] *Æn.*, XI. 734.

not scruple to take part in the dance ; they even wish it to be known, as if it were a distinction, and in the frescoes in which they figure they have their names written above their heads. These are portraits, then, that we are looking at, and although the originals no longer exist, we see very well what they must have been. Men and women appear to us in their wonted attitudes, with the very dresses they used to wear, and which the artist has copied minutely. These details of costume, to which we are at first tempted to pay but slight attention, must not be neglected, and Dr Helbig's labours show the profit to be drawn from their close study. What adds to their importance is that the Romans and Etruscans of this period must have dressed much in the same style. We know that the Romans borrowed from the Etruscans the ornaments of their magistrates and the insignia of their priests. It is very probable that private people also imitated their attire. They had then too much to do themselves to trouble about such grave trifles ; besides, they lacked the species of ingenuity and inventiveness of mind needed for the contriving of a costume, and found it very simple to take their fashions from their neighbours. We have no monument remaining such as would bring the Romans of the first century before our eyes. " If," says Professor Helbig, " we would animate the streets of the great city, and see them as they were on holidays, we must in thought fill them with the men and women portrayed in the old tombs of Tarquinii. The women walk about in that high, conical, parti-coloured cap called *tutulus.* A broad riband fastens it towards the middle of the head, while another fixes it on the forehead. A sort of veil, red or brown in colour, hangs from the top of the *tutulus* or is draped upon the shoulder. The men wear the *pileus*, a high stiff cap, something like that of the women."[1] This is how we must imagine the contemporaries of Camillus to have dressed, and not in the fancy costumes given to them by our painters and sculptors. These fashions, derived by the Romans from the Etruscans, lasted until the time when Greece made them adopt hers, and it may be said that the women never quite gave them up. When they left off the ungraceful cap they had worn for so many centuries, they kept the ribands which surrounded it, and turned it into an ornament to twine in their hair. These fillets and the long robe descending to the feet, were the adornment and distinction of honest women, courtesans being forbidden to wear them. Thus Ovid, who desires it to be well known that he is only addressing light women, takes care to say: " Hence, O ye elegant bandlets, badges of modesty! with ye have I nought to do " (*Nil mihi cum vitta !*)[2]

Herr Brunn, the learned professor of Munich, rightly observes that, among the Etruscan monuments remain-

---

[1] The *pileus* was the head-dress of freemen, and was placed on the heads of slaves when they are enfranchised. It thus became for the people a symbol of liberty. On the coin struck by Brutus after the death of Cæsar is found a *pileus* between two daggers with these words, " *Eidus Martiœ,*" which recalls the date of the Dictator's assassination. During the French Revolution, the cap of liberty and the Phrygian cap, which are not quite the same thing, were confounded. The latter, on Phrygian coins, is worn by Midas. The French are said to have adopted it because it was worn by the Marseillais when they entered Paris singing the hymn of "*Rouget de l'Isle,*" (See Professor Helbig's note on the *pileus* published in the *Sitzungsberichte* of the Bavarian Academy of Sciences, 1880, I. 4.)

[2] Ovid, *Remed. am.*,386.

ing to us, those which seem the oldest do not contain
any representation of a mythological subject.   Not only
are there no scenes borrowed from the Greek legends,
but even the Etruscan gods themselves are absent from
them.   Only the dead is thought of: his pleasures, his
honours, the feasts and dances of which it is desired
to give him the spectacle, and the games celebrated at
his funeral.   The legitimate conclusion seems to be
that the Etruscans were then less superstitious than
they became later on.   With nations, as with individuals,
age often enfeebles belief; but it rendered the Etruscans,
on the contrary, more devout.   Greece soon offered
them all her fables, and they were accepted with remarkable eagerness.   There is at Corneto an important
tomb which enables us to be present, as it were, at this
invasion of Greek mythology.   As it contains a painting of Tartarus, it has been called the Tomba del Orco
It is easy to see that it was not all decorated by the
same artist, and one feels different epochs and different
hands.   We find first, near the entry, one of those
feasts of which I have already spoken, and which
are so common in the sepulchres of Etruria.   It
is treated in the usual manner of the painters of the
country.   The personages are portraits; the scene is
stamped with a grand character of simple truth.
Suddenly the system changes, and we enter upon a
cycle of new subjects.   The artists take to representing Grecian legends, and interpret them by processes
familiar to Greek art.   We have Pluto seated on his
throne, and Proserpine standing at his side.   The attitude of the king of Hades is full of majesty.   He
stretches his hand towards a three-headed warrior in

front of him, as if to give him orders. This warrior,
covered with the armour of a knight, is Geryon, son of
the Earth, the giant who revolted against Jupiter, and
who became, as a punishment for his insolence, one of
Pluto's servants. A little further on, a venerable old
man, his head covered with a mantle, leans upon a stick.
His eyes are closed, he leans forward as if to listen
to someone who is questioning him, his features have
an air of melancholy. We do not need to read the inscription by which he is designated in order to recognise
in him Tiresias, the divine blind man. Opposite to the
old man, and as if to form a contrast to him, Memnon—
handsome Memnon, as Homer calls him—in an elegant
effeminate attitude and clad in a sumptuous costume,
personifies the heroes of Asia. Between Memnon and
Tiresias rises a large tree, upon whose branches climb
a crowd of strange little beings resembling men. These
are probably the souls of the vulgar dead, of whom
Virgil tells us that they crowd on the shores of the
Styx more numerous than the flocks of birds that
assemble to flee the first winter colds, or than the
leaves when the winds of autumn sow them on the
roads.[1] Behind these figures were doubtless many others
representing the chief inhabitants of hell; but now
only that of Theseus is clearly distinguishable. He
gazes sadly upon a personage whose features are very
much obliterated, and who must be his friend Pirithous.
They had planned together to carry off Proserpine, and
are cruelly expiating their crime in hell. A horrible-
looking demon called Tuchulcha (the artist has taken

---

[1] *Æn.*, VI. 309.

care to tell us his name), shakes over their heads a furious serpent. His mouth, or rather beak, is wide open, as if uttering a frightful yell. Perhaps he is emitting the vengeful cry which Virgil makes re-echo in hell around Theseus :

" Discite justiciam moniti et non temnere divos." [1]

In the midst of all these pictures of Tartarus is found, one knows not why, an almost comic scene borrowed from the *Odyssey.* It represents Ulysses blinding the Cyclops. It is a much less careful picture than the rest, the treatment being perfunctory. The Cyclops, in particular, with his great ears sticking up and his gigantic face, quite resembles a caricature. It is difficult to understand what the adventures of Ulysses and Polyphemus have to do here, or what reason there could have been to represent them in a tomb.

The decoration of the Tomba del Orco is, then, nearly all Greek.   The artist who painted on these walls Pluto and Proserpine, Tiresias and Theseus, doubtless imitated some work known and admired among the Greeks, as that of Polygnotus adorned the famous portico of Delphi.   Yet there is a personage in the fresco of Corneto who seems to belong especially to Etruria. It is the one called Charun. He appears again and again, and is always represented with a sort of complacency. Charun is a fiend upon whom popular imagination seems to have accumulated all that could render an inhabitant of hell at once repulsive and formidable. His flesh is green, his mouth immense and furnished with menacing teeth, and his nose is bent like a vul-

---

[1] *Æn.*, VI. 620.

ture's beak; he has large wings on his back, and in his hands he grasps a double hammer. Although this figure is quite foreign to Greek art, Dr Helbig bids us remark that the Etruscans borrowed it from Greece. The name Charun shows the origin of the personage. He is old Charon, the ferryman of hell, whom Virgil represents with a disordered beard, flaming eyes, a dirty garment cast over his shoulder, and an oar in his hand, which served him to keep off the crowd of the dead.[1] In the alteration to which the Etruscans subject him in order to transform him into the tormentor of souls,' they have still imitated Greece, whom, it would seem, they were unable to do without. When Polygnotus wished to represent Erynomos, the demon of putrefaction, it occurred to him to give him a dark blue colour like that of the flies which infest meat. But with Greek artists these are but the fancies of a moment. Their caprice satisfied, they soon abandoned them in order to return to simplicity and nature. In painting hell, they have as much as possible replaced the monsters by allegories—Terror, Grief, Sleep, etc.—which gives them an opportunity to depict noble attitudes and beautiful forms. The Etruscans, on the contrary, have plunged into the horrible, and their imagination has taken pleasure in the most repulsive spectacles. It is evident that this community, in growing old, gave itself up to the terrors of the other life. It takes pleasure in peopling that other world with monsters, and makes it a place of dread. It invents all kinds of tortures for the dead, and supposes that in becoming unhappy they

---

[1] *Æn.*, VI. 299.

become maleficent and cruel. Formerly they pleased them with joyous festivals, now they require executions; they wish their tombs to be sprinkled with blood, and Etruria, to satisfy them, becomes more prodigal in gladiatorial combats. Hunting scenes or dances are no longer represented on the walls of their tombs, but are replaced by scenes of murder. A tomb discovered at Vulei by Alexandre François is adorned with excellent paintings, comparable in execution with the finest remaining to us from antiquity. The subject was drawn from the *Iliad*, but by a strange and lugubrious caprice the artist has seen fit to choose from the Homeric poem that scene which shocks us the most—that where Achilles, having taken twelve noble and brave Trojans in the River Xanthe, brings them "like young fawns trembling with fear," and with his own hand immolates them at the tomb of his friend Petroclus. Homer seems only to speak with repugnance of this action of his hero, and condemns him in relating it. "Achilles," he tells us, "was shaken by sombre and cruel thoughts." How happens it that several centuries after, in the full bloom of civilization, a painter has chosen to reproduce precisely what the simple poet of a barbarous age would have palliated? He even seems to have found the subject not repulsive enough for him, for he has felt it necessary to add to it the hideous and bestial figure of Charun. The demon stands beside Achilles, and seems to incite him to accomplish the bloody immolation. This sinister personage evidently troubled the imagination of the Etruscans. They were indeed so terrified at it themselves that they believed other people would be afraid of it likewise. Titus Livius relates that in their fights with the Romans in defence of their independence, their priests flung themselves upon the enemy "with blazing torches, with serpents in their hands, and aspects of fury,"[1]—that is to say, imitating as far as possible their Charun. Is it not curious that this country, which four or five centuries before Christ concerned itself so much with the other life and made such horrible pictures of hell and its inhabitants, should be the one where, in the Middle Ages, the poem of Dante and the frescoes of Orcagna were produced? In every epoch the Devil filled it with the same terrors.

III.

THE PAINTINGS IN THE TOMBS THE ONLY MEANS WE HAVE OF BECOMING ACQUAINTED WITH ETRUSCAN CIVILIZATION—ANCIENT TOMBS—THEY DO NOT DIFFER FROM THOSE OF OTHER ITALIAN RACES—THE DATE AT WHICH WE FIND AMBER, AND WHY WE CEASE TO FIND IT A LITTLE LATER— *VASI DI BUCCHERO NERO* — INFLUENCE OF THE CARTHAGINIANS—AT WHAT MOMENT IT MUST HAVE BEGUN—HAVE WE A RIGHT TO INFER FROM THE PRESENCE OF PHŒNICIAN OBJECTS IN THE TOMBS OF ETRURIA THE EASTERN ORIGIN OF THE ETRUSCANS?—THE INFLUENCE OF GREECE—AT WHAT EPOCH WAS IT EXERCISED?—CAN IT BE SAID THAT ETRUSCAN ART NEVER POSSESSED ORIGINALITY?— PAINTINGS AT CŒRE — DECADENCE AND END OF ETRUSCAN ART.

What gives a peculiar value to these tombs and their paintings, and explains the interest taken in their study, is the circumstance that they alone at the present day can

---

[1] VII. 17.

afford us some light respecting ancient Etruria. We
could do without them more easily, and should have a
more direct and certain means of acquainting ourselves
with the Etruscans, if we knew their language; but this
has hitherto remained a riddle. Science has in our
days tackled problems apparently more difficult, and
solved them. She reads the inscriptions graven on the
monuments of Egypt and Assyria, and she has found
again the language of the Persians, and restored their
sacred books. The Etruscan tongue did not seem to
be more unyielding. It was spoken or understood down
to the time of the Roman Empire. Many of their
inscriptions remain to us, whose characters are easy to
read; and as they are all epitaphs, their meaning may be
approximatively guessed. So it cannot be said that no
one understands them. On the contrary, everybody
flatters himself that he can explain them; but each
explains them in a different manner, which is worse
than not understanding. In reality, when we would
analyse scientifically, distinguish the verb from the
noun, and seek the exact sense of the words, everything
escapes us. After a century of efforts we are no further
advanced than Lanzi, when in 1789 he published his
work entitled *Saggio di lingua Etrusca*. It was impossible not to nourish some hopes when fifteen years
ago it was known that a distinguished *savant*, W.
Corssen, known for his fine works on the old Latin
tongue, was about to apply the sagacity of his mind
and the certainty of his method to the interpretation of
Etruscan. But Corssen was not more fortunate than
others. He died, one may say, in harness, and his book,
which was published after his death, has only added a

few hypotheses more to those already ventured. However mortifying the avowal, it must be owned that Science has this time been beaten. We must therefore resign ourselves to ignorance, and wait until some new discovery allows our philologists to try their fortune under better conditions.

Since the inscriptions remain undecipherable, we have no other means of entering this unknown world than by the study of the only monuments it has left us —that is to say, the tombs, with the articles that furnish and the frescoes which decorate them. But the tombs can only be of any use to us if we manage to fix their age. Until we have established a kind of chronology between them, and distinguished the ancient from the more recent ones, we can deduce no conclusions as to the history of development and progress of the race who built them. Unfortunately this work is not only indispensable, but also very delicate. The monuments of Etruria having been almost always imitated from foreign models, it is by comparing them with those of Egypt, Assyria, and Greece that we may hope to find out to what epoch and to what school they belong. Those who undertake to make these comparisons must therefore bear in mind and before their eyes all the works of antiquity. Add that the relation between the original and the copy is usually very difficult to seize. It is often a detail insignificant in appearance—the arrangement of a dress, the ornamentation of a piece of furniture, a feature, a line in the face or the costume, which causes the imitation to be guessed and the original to be found again. The undertaking was very difficult; it required very sagacious critical power and an infinity of knowledge.   I think, however, that it may be said to have succeeded admirably.

It is true that among these tombs the most ancient are easy to distinguish.   Here antiquity betrays itself by certain signs, and error is not possible.   Of late years the excavations at Corneto have brought to light a great number which go back to a very distant epoch.   They are all composed of a round hole a mètre and a half broad and from two to three mètres deep.   At the bottom of this kind of well was placed the urn containing the ashes of the deceased.   In ordinary sepulchres it rests directly on the earth, but it has sometimes been enclosed in a kind of round or square recipient, for its better protection.[1]   Around the funeral urn, the piety of the survivors has placed divers objects which must have then been precious.   There are necklaces, bracelets, bronze fibulæ; and there are also vases of a grey or blackish colour, made of a somewhat impure clay, and formed by hand.   Some of these vases are without any ornament whatever, while others have lines in the form of circles or squares, traced upon the fresh clay with a pointed instrument.   This is what is called, in the language of archæologists, the geometrical decoration.   Almost all important museums contain these primitive vases; and although they are not very beautiful, I must own that I cannot look upon them without a certain emotion.   This, then, is how the taste for art first manifested itself in man.   These clumsily traced

---

[1] In the Museo Civico just established at Bologna, under the intelligent direction of M. Gozzadini, the happy plan has been followed of placing some of these tombs with all the objects they contained. It is a very curious and most instructive exhibition.

lines prove that to provide for his nourishment and his safety no longer sufficed him; that he was sensible of a want to beautify the utensils which served his needs; that beyond the necessary he caught a glimpse of something else, and began to feel the value of the useless. It is a new instinct revealing itself in him, and which will not cease to grow and become more perfect. In these rough designs lay ingermed all the progress of the future. If, after having glanced at these humble beginnings, we can connect them with the marvellous paintings of the white lecythes of Athens, we shall embrace at a glance the way which human industry travelled in a few centuries.

The study of these ancient sepulchres suggests some important reflections. First of all, it must be remarked that neither iron nor gold is found. This is a proof that they belong to a time when these metals were unknown, or at least very rare, and they probably go back to the epoch when the Age of Bronze finishes and the Age of Iron begins. In what are called the *terremare* of Northern Italy, some remains of villages built on piles in the first times of the Age of Bronze have been discovered. Among all sorts of detritus, fragments of pottery remained, which were carefully collected. It has been found that the vases discovered at Corneto are only an improvement on those met with in the *terremare* of Emilia. Here, then, thanks to them, is a gap filled up. We now possess the whole series of the generations who have inhabited Italy, and we see the march of progress uninterruptedly, from the most utter barbarism down to the most complete civilization. Let us add that the use of these vases was not peculiar to Corneto; they have been found at Bologna (the ancient *Felsina*), at Cervetri (*Cære*), at Palo (*Alsium*), at Orvieto (*Vulsinii*)—in short, all over Etruria. There is nothing in this to excite our surprise, for it is natural enough that cities of the same race should possess the same industry. What is really astonishing is that similar vases exist among Italian races of a different origin from that of the Etruscans. Of late years the taste for archæological studies has greatly spread in Italy, and every city having been seized with an ardent desire to know its past, excavations have been carried on methodically from one end of the peninsula to the other. We may say that nearly everywhere, when the deep stratum containing the most ancient tombs has been penetrated, the soil has rendered the same kind of remains. What has been discovered at Corneto has also been found in the old cemeteries of Campania, of Picenum, of the Sabina, of Latium,[1] and of Rome, in the sepulchres of the Esquiline and the Viminal. What must we conclude from this? That the races who then shared Italy were less separated from each other, and less unlike than we are tempted to believe. Their frontiers were not rigorously closed, and merchants passed through bearing the utensils necessary to life, and the ornaments which adorn it. There were then, even in this primitive and savage epoch, some elements of commerce—that is to say, some elements of civilization. The chief difference between these peoples is the

---

[1] The custom of giving funeral urns the form of little cabins was thought to be peculiar to Latium ; and until lately urns of this kind had only been found in the territory of Alba. Some have, however, just been found at Corneto exactly similar to those of Latium.

greater or less rapidity with which these germs developed among them. There are some for whom this first period lasted longer, while others passed through all the stages more rapidly. One is tempted to believe that directly Italy was conquered by the Romans it became quite Roman, and that being reduced by the same domination, all its peoples took to living the same life. This is a delusion that must be got rid of. There are some whose position and whose character long defended them against the influence of the Imperial city. We must picture to ourselves that in this large country, which now seems to us so enlightened and so prosperous, there still remained islets of barbarity, as it were, in the midst of the general culture. History cannot teach us this, for it does not descend to such details, but Archæology reveals it. It puts this persistence of ancient customs, this struggle of the local mind, obstinately resisting the language and usages of Rome, vividly before our eyes. In some recent excavations at Este (the ancient *Ateste*), tombs were discovered containing vases of rather rough make, and inscriptions in the old dialect of the country. One would think they dated two or three centuries before our era, had not a medal of Augustus been found in one of them. It is clear that these countries had not quite submitted to Roman influence at the end of the Republic. It was the Empire which united in the same civilization first Italy, and then all the world.

Etruria had progressed much more rapidly. Above all, Tarquinii, near the ocean, and seeming from her mountain height to call the stranger to her, was early visited by bold merchants who brought her the products of their industry. So her progress was very rapid. A curious tomb, discovered not long since, enables this to be verified. In one of those cylindrical holes of which I have just spoken, above the cinerary urn at the bottom, was found a stone sarcophagus, containing the remains of a little girl whose body was not burnt; and with the poor child they buried all her jewellery. This chiefly consists of rings and necklaces of bronze, only differing from those of the preceding epoch by their more skilful workmanship. But there are also some gold ornaments, and some pieces of amber. This tomb, placed so close to the other, and doubtless belonging to nearly the same epoch, marks a first step in that career of luxury and elegance in which Etruria was to stop no more.

I would it were possible, *a propos* of the amber ornaments in this tomb and in many others of the same period, to analyse in detail a memoir of Dr Helbig touching the employment of this precious substance in ancient times. It is an interesting chapter of this history of ancient commerce, which also has a bearing on that of Greek art. The few words I may say on this work will show its importance. Dr Helbig begins by confirming the particulars which the ancients give us touching the origin of this amber. It travelled by land, passing through the whole of Germany, tribe by tribe. The Rhône took it to the great *entrepôt* at Marseilles, whence it was distributed among the Hellenic nations, and it entered Italy by Pannonia and Venetia. The banks of the Po seem to have always been the centre of this commerce whence it penetrated among the peoples of Italy.

Amber is not found in the tombs reaching back to the Age of Bronze, but a little later it abounds. Coquetry and superstition united to augment its value. Ornaments were made of it to set off the beauty of women, and amulets to preserve them from throat diseases and the effects of the evil eye. What is most curious is that it did not long hold its own. In many parts, and especially among the richer and more civilised people, amber suddenly passed out of fashion. After having been found in abundance among tombs of a certain antiquity, it is no longer seen in more recent ones—that is to say, at the very moment when, international relations becoming more frequent, it was easier and less costly to preserve. It is a strange fact, of which Dr Helbig has been the first to give us the reason. According to him, all is explained by the ascendency acquired by Greece over the Italians. Greece never cared to execute her masterpieces in amber, and it is easy to understand why. "It is a fundamental principle of Art," Dr Helbig tells us, "to subordinate the material to the adequate expression of the idea." In order that it may entirely obey the will of the artist, it must have no exigencies of its own. Well, amber only produces its full effect under certain conditions, and if certain properties are respected which are peculiar to it. It does not then lend itself with docility to all that one would fain do with it. It has this disadvantage: its transparency and the brilliancy of its surface mar the clear perception of forms. This is what made the Greeks averse to amber. It is from a similar motive that, although they use opaque glass, they never employ the transparent material. They know that the latter does not admit of perfectly clear and defined forms being given to objects, and that when they are looked at, the lines of the reverse mingling with those of the front produce a confused whole. It must, however, be remarked that they were not always of this way of thinking. In the Homeric age, when they did not know these refinements, they esteemed it much, and used it in their jewellery. One of the suitors of the steadfast Penelope can think of no better means of seduction than to offer her " a gold necklace with beads of amber, which is like the sun." They ceased to prize it directly a more elevated sentiment of art awoke among them. They communicated their repugnance for this rebellious material to all the peoples subject to their influence, which proves to what a degree their tastes dominated those who learned from them, and what faithful disciples they made of their imitators. In Etruria, in Latium, in Campania, so long as Greek art flourishes, amber is absent from the tombs. It only becomes fashionable again at the beginning of the Roman Empire. Professor Helbig infers that at this moment classic traditions are about to be lost; and his conclusion is legitimate. Doubtless people prided themselves then on a passionate love of Art, and the number of amateurs who paid dearly for statues and pictures was never greater; but their taste is no longer so pure. The extraordinary and the costly are more sought after than the beautiful. Precious materials are loved for themselves, because of the price they cost, and they are employed in works for which they are unsuited. In architecture, for example, peperino and travertine, the fine stones which served for the construction of the majestic monuments of Rome, are disdained; white marble itself seems too bare and cold; and from far-distant countries rare stones and marbles are sent for, porphyry and obsidian, to surprise the eye and strike the imagination by the richness of the materials. That amber should profit by this change in public taste is easy to understand. The infatuation inspired by it reached its climax under Nero. It being found that it did not arrive in sufficiently large quantities, a Roman knight was sent expressly across Germany, as far as the North Sea, to stimulate the commerce in it. It was made into necklaces, rings, and bracelets for the toilet, into statuettes to adorn the house, and in the heats of summer amber balls were held in the hand, to refresh and perfume at the same time. In the rough, or worked, it was used everywhere, and the Emperor Heliogabalus grieved that he had not enough to pave the streets through which he must pass.

Let us return to the tombs of Etruria, and to the attempt which has been made to classify these according to their age. We stopped at the point when amber and gold made their first appearance, and when the brown vases with geometrical designs begin to assume less crude forms. The following epoch presents a more sensible progress. It is then we meet for the first time those beautiful black vases called by the Italians "*vasi di bucchero nero*," first quite smooth and then ornamented with reliefs. They must have been regarded as marvels of elegance among people who had but just become acquainted with the precious metals, and who were wont to content themselves with their primitive pottery. Later, when the painted vases of Greece were known, they passed out of fashion and fell into discredit. We see that it was "the thing" among the fops of Rome to laugh at "this old black crockery," and that Martial was obliged to remind these scorners that a powerful king, Porsenna, had formerly been satisfied with it.[1]

The tombs in which these vases are found contain much more curious objects, which must for a moment arrest our attention. These are *scarebei* of hard stone, jewels of very delicate workmanship, and perfume vases ornamented with strange figures. Winged sphinxes are seen; fantastic beasts; stiff personages in little tunics, like those covering the obelisks; thick-set, bearded giants holding lions by the paw, as in the bas-reliefs of the palaces of Nineveh. The origin of these objects is not doubtful. We have before our eyes the products of an Oriental art, and we recognise at once in their jewels and these vases importations from Assyria, Egypt, or some neighbouring nation. How is it that they come so far, to be buried in Italian sepulchres? Can we find out who undertook to bring them, by what road they travelled, and to what date this first invasion of the East goes back? Grave problems these, which were long discussed, and whose solution is now foreseen.

First of all, it is certain that the Etruscans did not receive them direct from Egypt or Assyria. The Egyptians, whom Professor Helbig styles "the most hydrophobic nation of the ancient world," did not willingly venture on these long voyages. As for Assyria, its natural frontiers were at some distance

---

[1] XIV. 98. The Louvre Museum contains a great number of these "*vasi di bucchero nero.*"

from the Mediterranean, which it only touched at moments and as the result of ephemeral conquests. But between Assyria and Egypt there was a nation who undertook to trade for its neighbours, viz. the Phœnicians. Uninventive themselves, they excelled in making use of the inventions of others. Like the genuine traffickers they are, they have not, so far as they themselves are concerned, any care for originality; they simply manufacture at home and send abroad goods that are sure to find a market. As those from Egypt and Assyria seem to please foreigners, they imitate, sometimes also spoiling them, and spread them through the entire world. So thus they came into all the countries where we find them through this intermediary. Greece herself, in spite of the superiority of her genius, of which she was always conscious, and although she had already produced great poets, was first tributary to Oriental art, and it is in imitating that she learned to surpass it. Much more then did the Italians, less happily gifted by nature and less intrinsically rich, undergo its charm. It must be remarked that the Latins welcomed it not less warmly than the Etruscans. In 1876, near Palestrina, the ancient Præneste, a veritable treasure was found, composed of objects formed of gold, silver, ivory, amber, bronze, glass, or iron, and containing vases, tripods, jewellery, arms, and utensils of all kinds; above all, cups, of which one is decorated inside with different subjects chiselled in relief. This is assuredly one of the most curious pieces of Oriental goldsmiths' work we possess.[1]

---

[1] This cup has been studied by M. Clermont, Gannau, in his work entitled *l'Imagerie phénicienne.*

That these cups, these vases, and this jewellery was brought into Italy by the Phœnicians can be the less doubted from the fact that one of the' objects found at Palestrina bears a Phœnician inscription. But what Phœnicians do we mean? Under that name two peoples may be understood, whose destinies were very different, although their origin was the same. One of them inhabited the borders of Asia; the other, an off-spring of the first, had established itself in Africa. Did the merchandise we find again in Italy come from Tyre or from Carthage? Dr Helbig answers without hesitation that they came from Carthage. The chief reason he has for his belief is that we know of no relations entertained by the people of Tyre with the Italic races, whereas it is certain that the Carthaginians frequented the ports of the peninsula, and brought thither the products of their industry. Supposing the hypothesis to be sure, we at the same time succeeded in fixing with great probability the epoch when this commerce was carried on. Dr Helbig thinks him-self justified in affirming that it does not go back further than the seventh or eighth century before our era. In the sixth century the relations between the Carthaginians and the Italians became closer. They united to oppose the progress of the Greeks, who were masters of Southern Italy, and wished to push their dominion further. It cannot be doubted that clever traders like the Carthaginians profited by this circum-stance to place their wares favourably. They did not like war for its own sake, cared but little for glory, and only sought conquests or alliances with a view to creating outlets for commerce. So we find that at the

end of the sixth century they signed with the young
Roman Republic a treaty of commerce, a translation
of which Polybius has preserved for us. Rome was
then of very small importance; but when one is astute,
one must foresee all, and Carthage meant to prepare
the future for herself. It is in consequence of this
treaty, and of the alliance with the Etruscans, that the
Carthaginian ships, certain of not being molested, brought
into Italy all those precious objects with which the contemporaries of Brutus and Porsenna adorned themselves
during their lives, and which, after death, were buried
with them. The sixth century before our era, and the
beginning of the fifth, are then the epoch when this
commerce was the most active ; and it is, above all, to
this moment that it is natural to attribute those great
importations of Oriental objects found in the tombs of
Italy.[1] And this settles a question. Everybody knows
how many discussions have been raised, and how many
hypotheses started, with regard to the origin of the
Etruscans. The presence among them of objects of
Oriental make has often been invoked in these discussions as a decisive argument. It was for many *savants*

---

[1] François Lenormant, while generally accepting Dr Helbig's
opinions, subjects them, however, to a restriction. He thinks that
some of these apparently Oriental objects were brought into Italy, not
by the Carthaginians, but by the Greeks. The Greeks also imitated
the East, and at this moment the products of Ionian industry did
not much differ from those of the Asiatics. Lenormant brought
home from Vulci and Cervetri vases whose style seemed at first sight
absolutely Egyptian or Phœnician. But on observing the paintings
on them more closely, it is perceived that they depict purely Greek
fables. According to him, then, even in this primitive commerce we
must give some place to the Greeks.

a manifest proof that Herodotus was right in saying they came from Lydia. " See," they used to say, " how faithful they have remained to the art of their country. In leaving Asia, they evidently brought the taste with them, and kept it in their new fatherland." This seemingly victorious argument has now no longer any force. We know at what moment the Etruscans received among them the products of the East, and who taught them to know and love them. They had then already been several centuries in Italy, and had had plenty of time to forget their origin. So the favour with which they received the merchandise brought them by the Carthaginians is not accounted for, as is asserted, by the charm of memory, but by the attraction of novelty. It is a mistake to think they had piously preserved Oriental custom from the day when they quitted their native land. I have just shown that we possess monuments more ancient, and nearer the period when they entered Italy; and these monuments contain nothing recalling the East. It is certain, then, that the influence of Asia upon the art and industry of the Etruscans has nothing to do with the problem of their origin. This, I repeat, is a settled question. We still remain in ignorance as to their race and the country they came from,[1] but the ground is cleared of an hypothesis, which will make the solution of the problem more easy.

We are coming to a revolution which took place in Etruscan art. The vessels of Carthage must have met

---

[1] In our days one is inclined to think there is no truth in the pretty story of Herodotus, and that the Etruscans probably came by way of the Alps. But of the race to which they belonged we are in absolute ignorance.

in the ports of Etruria those of the Greeks, and the
merchants of the two countries probably entered into a
sharp competition with each other. The relations of
the Etruscans with Greece began very early, and of this
we have a certain proof. Dr Helbig has shown by
ingenious deductions that they must have become
acquainted with writing about the eighth century B.C.,
and we know that they had it from the Greeks. The
alphabet they used is that of the Phœnicians, but increased by the letters which the Greeks had added. So
that before the seventh century B.C. they knew Greece,
entertained relations with her, and had already been to
her school. If her influence over them was not at first
sovereign, it is because she herself had not yet found
her way, and was still content to imitate Egypt and
Assyria. But she was not made to remain long sub-
servient to the foreigner. Her natural originality
ended by re-awaking, and she brought to every market
the products of a freer, younger, more living art, in
which the West recognised her genius. Etruria was
seduced before the other Italian nations, and from that
moment she ceased to copy the East, and imitated
Greece.

Greek art is chiefly represented in Etruria by sepul-
chral frescoes ; and they were all painted under her
influence. Those of Corneta being more numerous, and
having all been executed in the same place and under
the same local influences, it is easier to compare them
with each other, and in comparing them to arrive at a
classification. This work, begun by Prof. Brunn, has been
pursued with still greater rigour and success by Dr
Helbig. His judgment is determined by reasons of

many kinds, some of them rather belonging to the
domain of taste, while others are derived from his
erudition.   A painting bears its date in the manner of
its execution, and a practised critic, on looking at it,
can tell the period of art it belongs to and the school
that produced it.   But this sort of intuition is not
enough.   In order that the critic's decision may be
accepted without contest, it is well for it to be based
upon more precise proofs.   The processes used by the
artist in the details of his work may furnish them to
him.   We see, for example, that Pliny says of
Polygnotus : *Primus mulieres tralucida veste pinxit;*[1]
so that as often as we see a picture with this transparent
clothing which allows the forms to be guessed, we have
a right to suppose it posterior to Polygnotus.   Precious
indications may sometimes be drawn from a circumstance which at first seems trivial.   Thus in the Tomba
del Vasi Depinti the artist has represented the interior of
an Etruscan house.   Vases are arranged on a table or on
the floor.   Their form is elegant, and they bear black
figures on a reddish ground.   This detail, to which we
do not at first pay great attention, is not without interest.
We know pretty nearly about what century this kind
of decoration came into fashion for painted vases, and
when it was replaced by red figures on a black ground ;
so we are here in possession of an approximate date.
With the help of these indications, and of many
others which I am obliged to omit, Dr Helbig has
established that the oldest tombs of Corneto are not
anterior to the middle of the fifth century B.C.   This is

---

[1] *Hist. Nat.*, XXXV. 9 (35).

a very important result for the history of the art and civilization of Etruria.

He has also shown, by the progress remarked among the frescoes, that Greek art was not introduced among the Etruscans suddenly; that it penetrated little by little, insinuating itself more and more every day, and becoming more and more dominant, until the moment when it triumphed, without dispute and without a rival. The history of these various phases would be an interesting study. It would perhaps show that after having exalted the Etruscans too highly, we now give them a worse reputation than they deserve. Prof. Mommsen, their great enemy, compares them to the Chinese, who are incapable of finding anything for themselves, and will only allow them "the secondary genius of imitation," while even as imitators he puts them below all the other Italian peoples who were inspired by Greek art. But we are going to show that there was an epoch when they were not quite the slaves of their teachers, and when they knew how to put a certain originality into their imitation. We possess at Paris paintings which show us what the Etruscans could do when they dared to trust to their own genius. One of the most interesting rooms in the old Musée Napoleon III., at the Louvre, is that in which some of the most beautiful antiquities have been placed that come to us from ancient Coere. The public lingers willingly there, to look at a large sarcophagus occupying the middle of the room, and on which two personages, a husband and his wife, lie half reclined. Their strange costumes, their animated faces, their little bright eyes, attract the attention of all who pass. This itself is a very curious specimen of Etruscan art; but still more curious ones are to be seen in the glass cases. Some terra-cotta slabs have been placed there, which formed the lining of ancient tombs. These are covered with paintings executed after the manner of the archaic school, and on the model of the old masters of Greece. The gestures of the personages are stiff, the forms clumsy, the extremities of the hands incredibly elongated, the drapery regular and heavy. When sitting, they look like wooden figures that have been bent in order to put them on the chairs; when they stand, their attitude is contrary to all static laws, and one can see that they will fall if they begin to walk. All these defects do not prevent them from being perfectly lifelike, and such is the attraction of life, that we look at them with pleasure, in spite of the imperfections of this primitive painting. One of these scenes struck me above all. It represents two aged men seated opposite to each other on those seats handed down by the Etruscans to the Romans, and which became the annuli chairs. One of them, who seems to be the gravest and most important, holds a kind of sceptre in his hand. He is speaking, and the other listens. The latter, listening figure leans his chin upon his hand in a natural attitude of meditation; a profound melancholy is impressed upon his features. It is someone in affliction, whom a friend is consoling for a cruel loss he has suffered. Towards the top of the picture a little winged figure, a woman covered with a long red robe which hides her feet, flies in space towards the two old men. She represents the soul of the dead coming to assist at the conversation of which she is the subject—a touching idea certain to come to this people so occupied with the future life. People so convinced that existence continues beyond the tomb were naturally brought to believe that our cherished dead listen every time we speak of them.

Certainly everything in this picture is not original, the painter-imitates the processes of a foreign art; but one feels that he is their master, and that he appropriates them freely to his thoughts. The sentiment is his, and he renders it as he feels it. When looking on these beautiful frescoes of Coere, and others scattered among the Italian museums, it is impossible not to own that the nation which in those remote times possessed artists capable of thus reproducing life, and giving to the figures they drew this air of simple reality, were capable of going further, and creating a national art. It seems to me even that we can guess from these beginnings what would have been the dominant character of Etruscan art, could it have developed itself in liberty. It would, doubtless, have cared but little for the ideal; it would not too eagerly have sought after dignity and grandeur. We have seen that in the frescoes of the tombs the artists love to paint scenes of real life—games, hunts, and feasts—which they depict as they see them, without any attempt to ennoble them in execution; that their personages are portraits, and that not only do they try to make them as like as possible, but they endeavour to reproduce the least details of costume. This anxiety to copy the reality exactly is so natural to the Etruscan artists that it is found among the sculptors as well as among the painters. On visiting the room where the sarcophagi are collected in the museum at Corneto, one experiences a strange impression. The dead are sometimes represented stretched full length upon their tombs as they are on the pavements of our cathedrals, and sometimes raised upon their elbows. The artists have been careful to give them a religious attitude: men and women hold a *patera* in their hands, as if death had surprised them while they were engaged in making a sacrifice. But in spite of the gravity of the act they were accomplishing, their faces are frequently vulgar. The attire and the lower part of the body are often treated with elegance. The sculptor must have had books of models, and have prepared in advance and at leisure those parts of his work which did not change. The face is that of the dead. The artist added it at the last moment, and reproduced it with perfect fidelity. When he has old men or women to represent, he does not spare us any of the deformities inflicted by age upon the human face. He shows us with complacency the furrows of the brow, the projection of the features, the hanging flesh, the flabby breasts, and the skinny necks. This realism, sometimes coarse, at times powerful, was the tendency of Etruscan artists; and this is the way they would have continued, had they followed their natural instincts, to the end.

But they turned aside from it in order to draw nearer to Greek art. So long as Greece had only sent them the works of her first masters, full of inexperience and gropings, their admiration had not been sufficiently strong to paralyse all originality. But when the masterpieces came, the seduction was so strong that they quite forgot themselves. In the presence of these marvels they were completely subdued and vanquished, and only thought of reproducing them. Dr Helbig makes us follow the ever more and more powerful influence of Greece in the frescoes of Corneto. There are tombs—the more ancient ones—where national art timidly tries to resist, and where the characteristics of the two schools are sometimes found clumsily mingled. But in the following, Greece rules with undivided sway. Her victory is revealed by the presence of scenes and personages borrowed from the Homeric poems, by the employment of the nude, and by the idealistic character of the paintings. In the school of the Greeks, the taste of the Etruscan artist becomes more refined and his hand more skilful. His defects disappear or diminish, he produces more elegant works, but his inspiration is no longer so sincere. He temporises his natural qualities, and does not succeed in equalling those of his masters. Soon decadence is visible. It is already seen at Corneto, in the Polyphemus of the Tomba del Orco. The defeat of Tarquinii and its submission to the Romans made it irreparable. There happened then in Italy what we again see going on before our eyes. All those little cities which had preserved a distinct physiognomy so long as they remained free and sovereign, those small capitals of small states, where a certain activity of mind reigned, which cultivated art and formed independent schools, were absorbed in the great Roman unit. Life, as usual, was borne towards the centre. The municipalities, carried away in the general movement, with their eyes fixed upon Rome, no longer had any character of their own, and the little originality that Etruscan art had left finally disappeared.

H

This is the most important thing we learn from the latest works upon the Etruscans. These works, as we have just seen, embrace all their history. Without leaving the hill of Corneto, we may have the spectacle of all the revolutions that this mysterious race passed through from its advent into Central Italy down to its defeat by the Romans. Doubtless all is not completed. There remain in this history conjectures to verify, gaps to fill up, and we may be sure that the excavations, which continue, will add much to our knowledge. Yet the great lines are traced, and we hold the sequence of the chief facts. We have even succeeded in fixing some rather probable facts in the midst of this dark night. We know pretty nearly at what date Etruria began to undergo Phœnician influence, and when Greek art was revealed to her. These results are not, perhaps, so striking and unforeseen as certain discoveries. They were attained slowly by dint of minute observations, by the efforts of assiduous labour, by collecting the shreds of vases, by scrutinising old texts, and by amassing small facts. This road seems long to the impatient, and pleases not the makers of brilliant generalisations. Of the erudite sciences it is the usual mode of progression: they walk by small steps, but they advance always, and one cannot measure the road they have made in these few years and despise them. We have suffered many disappointments in our day, and we have more than once been forced to abandon hopes whose realisation seemed certain. Science alone has kept all her promises. It is needless to recall here all the light she has thrown upon the past since the beginning of this century ; the study I have just made shows that at

the moment of its conclusion she was not yet exhausted.
We owe her great gratitude, not only for the honour we
shall derive from her discoveries in the future, but for
the good she now does us. She has afforded curious
minds, captivated by the quest of the unknown, the
liveliest joys they can experience ; she makes them forget bitter deceptions ; she raises, she sustains them, and
despite the sadness of the eve and the cares of the
morrow, she allows them now and then to say, like the
Romans of the Empire when the advent of a good
prince made a break in the stormy sky, *vivere lubet.*"

CHAPTER III.

I HAVE just read the *Æneid* in the country which inspired it, in the very place where the events related in it passed; and in doing so I experienced the most lively pleasure. Of course I do not mean to say that it cannot be understood without taking this long journey, and that the sight of Lavinium and Laurentum is fraught with revelations as to the merits of the great poem; for this would be a ridiculous exaggeration. Virgil, like Homer, belongs to the school of poets who put the man first, and only consider Nature in its connection with him. They rarely describe her for her own sake, as we so willingly do nowadays. When they offer us the picture of a conflagration devouring the harvest, or of a torrent inundating the land, they are careful to place, somewhere on a neighbouring height, a husbandman or a shepherd, whose heart is wrung at the sight of the disaster:

> "*Stupet inscius alto*
> *Accipiens sonitum saxi de vertice pastor.*"

Virgil, then, is not one of those who indulge in needless descriptions; he describes places as little as possible. Only, we may be sure that what he says is always scrupulously true. The ancient poets love precision and fidelity; they do not draw imaginary landscapes, and usually only show us those they actually have before their eyes. They paint them with one stroke, but that stroke is always true, and one feels great pleasure, when this is possible, in verifying its exactness.

Be assured that it is not merely an inquisitive, profitless pleasure: the study of the great writers always gains by these researches. They rejuvenate and refresh our admiration for them, which is at times not unnecessary. The greatest peril that can menace them is only to inspire in their worshippers an enthusiasm conventional and made to order; and that they may escape it, it is as well now and then to change the point of view from which we regard them. All that stimulates us to draw nearer to them, all that puts us into direct communication with them, re-animates in us the feeling of their true beauties.

And such is the profit I have just derived from this manner of studying the *Æneid* in its home. It seemed to me that in reading it again by Mount Eryx or the Tiber, in the forest of Laurentum, and on the heights of Lavinium, the tales of Virgil became more living to me, that I understood them better, and that they struck me more forcibly. Although this kind of impressions are of a strictly personal character, and it is not easy to communicate them to the public, I will nevertheless try to do so, although scarcely hoping that these studies will have for others quite the same interest I felt in them myself.[1]

---

[1] In beginning this work, I must not forget that it was anticipated more than eighty years ago, in a book which still enjoys a merited

I.

THE LEGEND OF ÆNEAS.

I.

THE LEGENDS—WHY THEY DESERVE TO BE STUDIED—THE LEGEND OF ÆNEAS—HOW IT AROSE—ÆNEAS IN THE *ILIAD*—HOMER SUPPOSES THE RACE OF THE ÆNEIDES ESTABLISHED ON MOUNT IDA — THE JOURNEYS OF ÆNEAS—HOW IT CAME TO BE SUPPOSED THAT HE LEFT ASIA—THE WORSHIP OF APHRODITE, MOTHER OF ÆNEAS—GENESIS OF THE LEGEND.

IT seems to me that before starting to accompany Æneas on his adventures, it will not be unprofitable to make ourselves acquainted with the personage, to know whence he came, what was related of him, and how the history of his fabulous journeys obtained credence. If we would appreciate Virgil's masterpiece, and form an exact estimate of the author's originality, we must first ask ourselves what was furnished him by tradition, and what he himself invented. It is generally affirmed that the *Æneid* is a national poem, and that this is one

interest. M. de Bonstetten, an enlightened Swiss, who had taken part in the affairs of his country during the Revolution, had travelled in the north of Europe, and made a long stay in Italy, published in 1804 a work entitled *Voyage sur la scène des six derniers livres de l'Eneide.* This book contains ingenious and correct ideas, and I have used them. But politics hold a greater place in it than literature. M. Bonstetten is a man of the world, who did not pursue the study of Virgil very deeply, and who went over the coast of Latium, thinking more of the economical conditions of the country than of Æneas and his companions, so I thought there was still something to be done after him.

of its chief merits.   In order to decide how much foundation this statement has, we must find out whence came the fables that tell of the establishment of the Trojans in Latium, whether they sank deeply into the memory of the people, and what memories the poet, in relating them, awakened in those who listened; for this is the only means of knowing whether his poem was ever popular.   It is clear, then, that any thorough study of the *Æneid* must begin with the examination of the legend of Æneas.

The science of former times had no liking for legends. When the rules of rigorous criticism are applied to them, they certainly, for the most part, do not stand the examination.   Daunon, who in his *Cours d'Études historiques*, had occasion to relate the one with which we are about to busy ourselves, does so with great repugnance, and feels a sort of irritation in the presence of so much nonsense.   It seems to him " a tissue of ridiculous fictions, of romantic and incoherent fables ; " and he declares that he only takes the trouble to relate them in order to show their extravagance, the only conclusion he draws from them being that " the histories of all nations begin with puerilities."   We have become less severe, and these " puerilities " do not seem to us deserving of so much contempt.   Even supposing, which is rare, that they are no aid to the knowledge of the past, we remember that the legend has everywhere been the first form of poetry, and this is enough to entitle it to some consideration in our eyes.   It is rightly said that the child foreshows the man ; and so a nation is already revealed in the fables that cradled its youth.   In order to gather exactly the original qualities of its mind and natural bent of its imagination, we must go back to those old, old tales that were its first creation, or at least the first food of its fancy.

The learned have of late years been much busied with the Ænean legend. There are few since Niebuhr who, in studying the past or the institutions of Rome, have not found it in their path and endeavoured in their own manner to explain it.[1] I am about to use all these works in order to explain in my turn how the legend seems to me to have been formed, how it was introduced and spread among the Latins—in short, what reasons Virgil had for making it the subject of his poem. These are small problems, yet difficult to solve, and despite the efforts of learned criticism, everything has not yet been made clear. We cannot always hope to arrive at certainty in researches of this kind, and must sometimes be content with probability. Having lost the ancient chroniclers who related this series of fabulous events, and being obliged to reconstruct the narrative from incomplete accounts, gaps remain which it is impossible to fill up. The study of legends resembles railway journeys in mountainous countries, where one passes so quickly from tunnel to tunnel; light and darkness follow each other at every moment. However annoying these inevitable alternations, it seems to me much that some intermittent

---

[1] M. Hild, a French professor, has taken up the question again in a very careful and complete memoir entitled *La Legende d'Énée avant Virgile*, in which he summarises the ideas of German *savants*, adding his own.

light should have been cast upon fables so many centuries old.

Æneas first appears to us in Homer's *Iliad*, and the place he holds there has long since struck the critic. The poet clearly tries to give him a great part. He loads him with praises and puts him beside the bravest. In council and battlefield he and Hector are the first of the Trojans. The people honour him as a god; and it is he who is fetched to face the enemy in perilous crises, when the body of some hero just slain is to be defended, or when Achilles is to be prevented from entering the walls of Troy. Æneas is in no wise backward; and, whoever the rival pitted against him, throws himself resolutely into the fray. His first appearance on the battle-field is terrible: " He walks like a lion, confident of his strength; he holds before him his spear and his shield, which everywhere covers him, ready to kill whoever shall come to meet him, and sending forth cries which strike dismay."[1] What does him much honour and helps to give a great idea of him is, that the gods who protect the Greeks get frightened when they see him, and tremble for the days of the enemy he is about to challenge, even when that enemy is Achilles. But the exploits of Æneas never last long, and he nowhere fulfils the great expectation he has raised. Hardly does he enter the field when he is stopped by some vexatious incident. It is true, this very incident redounds to his honour, for it shows how dear he is to all the gods. At the first danger he runs, all Olympus

---

[1] *Iliad*, V. 299.

is astir. Venus, Apollo, Mars, Neptune, hasten to his assistance; they defend him turn by turn, they tend him when he is wounded, and they enclose him with a protecting cloud to screen him from the hazards of the fight.

Sainte-Beuve, who has very delicately analysed the manner in which Æneas is treated in the *Iliad*, and makes some very ingenuous remarks on the subject, points out especially the advantage which Virgil afterwards drew from it in the composition of his poem. "If Homer," he tells us, "had made Æneas one of his heroes of the first rank, if he had caused him to perform exploits equal to those of Hector and Achilles, he would have left his successor nothing further to do, and would have exposed him to dangerous comparisons. If, on the contrary, he had made an insignificant figure of him, and represented him as quite a secondary and obscure personage, it would have prejudiced him, and unfavourably disposed the readers of another epic; for that Virgil should have chosen one of the lesser heroes of Troy to give him the first part in a new adventure would have appeared unseemly. He would have been blamed for wanting to make an immense oak and the great founder of Roman fortunes issue from a feeble stem! But having highly extolled him without making him do much, having aroused attention to him without satisfying it, having everywhere announced his exploits and nowhere narrated them; it really looks as if he had foreseen that this personage would be the hero of a second epic poem, had held him in reserve, and prepared him with his own hands for the use another poet was to make of him." [1] In reality Homer could not of course foresee Virgil, and it is impossible to suppose in him as much benevolence towards an unknown successor; so we must seek elsewhere for the reason he may have had in giving Æneas this attitude. This reason is not difficult to find, for he has been at the pains to tell us it himself. In the twentieth chapter of the *Iliad*, when gods and men are grappling in a terrible affray, Æneas, having been persuaded by Apollo to attack Achilles, is about to perish. Fortunately Neptune perceives the danger he is in. He addresses Juno, the great enemy of the Trojans, and reminds her that it is not in the fate of Æneas to fall before Troy, and that the gods preserve him in order that some relics may remain of the race of Dardanus. Then he adds these significant words: " The family of Priam have become hateful to Jupiter, and now it is the turn of valiant Æneas to reign over the Trojans, as well as the children of his children who shall be born in the future." [2] Here is a formal prediction. Well, we know that although poets are naturally bold, they do not, for the most part, venture to predict an event with this assurance until after its accomplishment. We are bound to believe, then, that at the time when the *Iliad* was composed there was somewhere a little nation who claimed to be a relic of the inhabitants of Troy, and that its kings called themselves sons of Æneas. It is in order to flatter the pretensions of these princes and glorify them in the

---

[1] Sainte-Beuve, *Étude sur Virgile*, p. 127.
[2] *Iliad*, XX. 20, 306.

person of their great ancestor, that the poet treats him with such consideration, that he presents him as a kind of rival of Hector, a pretender to the throne of Ilium, and heir-designate of Priam, and that, not being able to celebrate his exploits, he has at least announced the greatness of his race. Supposing these kings to be generous, that they received epic singers well, and that they granted them the same honours which Demodochus receives at the table of the king of the Phæcians, it will be easily understood that the rhapsodist acknowledged this hospitality by loading the ancestor of his benefactor with praises.

In these remote times, the authority of Homer was admitted without dispute, and there was no other history than that which he related. So, that Æneas had survived the ruin of his country, was a tradition accepted by all the world. Touching the manner of his deliverance, very different tales were in circulation. Some said that he came to an understanding with the Greeks, and others that he escaped them, either on the day or on the eve of the taking of Troy; but all agreed in affirming that after the disaster he gathered the survivors together and settled with them somewhere in the neighbourhood of Mount Ida. Such is the basis of the legend. Homer shows it to us at its starting-point, and although it afterwards has to suffer many changes, it always keeps something of its origin. The character of Æneas does not change, and it is remarkable that it should, from the first moment, have taken the features it was to keep to the end. With Homer, Æneas is a hero, but still more a sage. He speaks wise words and gives good counsels. Above all, he respects the gods.

Neptune, when he wishes to save him, recalls "that he offers without ceasing gracious gifts to the immortal gods who inhabit the vast heaven." [1]   So he is their favourite, and we have just seen that they are always on the alert to protect him.   Such are the distinctive qualities of the personage; he will not lose them either in the popular tradition or in the narratives of the poets, and Virgil, who has been so much abused in this matter, was not free to represent him otherwise than he had been made.

But the first form of the legend is about to undergo a notable change.   At an uncertain point of time,[2] while continuing to believe that Æneas fled at the last moment from Troy, people begin no longer to admit that he settled in some town of Mount Ida, to leave it no more, and he is made to undertake wonderful journeys in search of a new country.   He leaves Ilion guided by a star which his mother causes to shine in the sky for his direction.   Some are content to send him towards neighbouring countries, and suppose him to stop at the borders of Thrace at the mouth of the Hebrus, where

---

[1] *Iliad*, XX. 298.

[2] It has hitherto been generally thought that this new form of the legend first appeared in the works of Stesichorus,—that is to say, about the sixth century before our era.   In confirmation, the *Iliac Table* was relied upon, a monument dating from the Roman Empire, in which all the adventures of Troy, down to the settlement of Æneas in Italy, are roughly portrayed in a series of bas-reliefs.   It is said that the last pictures, namely those dealing with the journeys of Æneas, were composed in accordance with the narrations of Stesichorus.   But M. Hild thinks there are reasons for not giving too much importance to this testimony.   It seems to him that in these pictures the influence of Sesichorus may have been modified by recollections of Virgil.

he founds the town of Æneos; others take him a little further, to Pelos, to the Adriatic, along the Gulf of Ambracia. Once started, he cannot stop. He advances further and further towards the "Hesperides"; he doubles the coast of Bruttium; makes a promontory in Sicily, which tradition represents as full of souvenirs of the Trojans; touches at Cumæ, where he buries his pilot, Misenus, on the cape which still bears his name; skirts the coast of Italy, and definitively settles in Latium. This time the journeys of Æneas are over; the legend has taken its last form, and we are on the road which will take us directly to the *Æneid*.

Whence comes the change which it has undergone since Homer wrote? What reason could there have been to tear Æneas from the Trojan land where the *Iliad* shows him, to take him to so many different spots? It is difficult to say with certainty, and this is just one of those gaps which I just now anticipated. But if it be surprising that the Homeric narrative should have been thus modified, it is much more so that the Greeks should have spread the legend under its new form, and it is difficult to understand that they should have been at pains to attribute such glorious adventures to a Trojan hero. Why did they undertake to celebrate the glory of an enemy, and whence the goodwill that prompted them to make so fine a history of him? It may be confidently answered that none of the personages who figure in the *Iliad* was a stranger to them. Such was the prestige of this poem, that Greece, unwilling to lose any of it, had adopted the vanquished as well as the victors, and acknowledged them all more or less as her children. It may also be added that among the Trojans none was less an enemy of the Greeks than Æneas. Homer depicts him as greatly irritated against the divine Priam, who does not honour him as he deserves. So wise a man as he could not much approve the conduct of Paris; and according to some, he always advised that Helen should be restored to her husband. It is also said that, foreseeing the coming ruin, he came to an agreement with the enemy, and made his peace independently. Of all the Trojans he was therefore the one against whom the Greeks must feel the least resentment, and whose origin they could most easily forgive. Yet however plausible these reasons may appear, they do not prevent one from feeling surprised that the Greeks should have paid such honour to a companion of Hector, who had fought so vigorously against Diomedes and Achilles. Had they been quite free to choose the personages to whom they should grant the honour of these great adventures, they would doubtless have given the preference to one of their own chiefs. They had one—the most glorious and most beloved of all; he, who best represented their character and country, and of whom so many surprising stories were already told that it would have cost little to attribute a few more exploits to him. This was Ulysses. He was then, if tradition may be trusted, in some isle near Italy, where the enchantress Circe kept him. Nothing was easier than to suppose that he had passed thence into Latium, and to make him the ancestor of the great Roman family. We have proof that some tried to give this turn to the legend, and to substitute Ulysses for Æneas. If, in spite of national vanity and the attraction of a popular name, this version did not survive; if the Greeks accepted the other, although it glorified a Trojan to the detriment of a hero of their blood, we must believe that they were not free to act differently, and that it was somehow or other forced upon them.

There is yet another observation which one cannot fail to make when reading the different accounts of the journeys of Æneas. Each of these narratives descriptive of his arrival in a different country supposes that he stops there and leaves it no more; and that his permanent settlement may be the more certain, it tells us that he died in the country, and that his remains are preserved there. This multiplicity of tombs, all consecrated to the same person, occasioned some embarrassment to good Denys of Halicarnassus, who took the whole fable seriously. It simply proves that the legend was not made all at once; that it was not born entirely in the imagination of one man; that each of the excursions of Æneas formed a particular and isolated narrative; and that they were only joined together to form an entire history later on. Whence I conclude that if, as I have just said, the legend of Æneas is not a pure fancy, a capricious invention of the Greeks, but involves some circumstance independent of their will, which forced it on them, as it were, we must believe that this circumstance was presented to them several times in succession, and in different places.

Can we take another step in the midst of this darkness? Dare we guess what this circumstance was which gave rise to the legend? Conjectures, it may well be thought, have not been wanting; but I only see one that can quite satisfy us and account for all; this is the suggestion of Preller in his *Mythologie Romaine*.[1] According to him, the legend arose from the worship rendered by sailors to Venus, or rather to the goddess Aphrodite, as the Greeks called her. Aphrodite is not only the personification of beauty and love; she was born of the foam of the waves and sways the sea. Lucretius, in the hymn which he sings in her honour at the beginning of his poem, addresses her thus: "Before thee, a goddess, the winds fly away. When thou appearest the clouds disperse; the waves of the sea seem to smile, and the heavens for thee are all gleaming with tenderest light."[2] The Greek sailor who has put himself under her protection when landing on some strange shore does not fail to build a shrine to her, or at least to raise her an altar. It is a witness to his gratitude for the safe voyage he has made. Aphrodite and Æneas are intimately bound together; and the homage rendered to the mother at once recalls the son— the more so that this divine mother bears a name which quite reminds one of the Trojan hero being called the "Ænean Aphrodite."[3] We know from Denys

---

[1] Preller, *Römische Mythol.*, 667, *et seq.*

[2] Lucretius, I. 6.

[3] This name of Ἀφροδίτη Αἰνειάς has been explained in various ways. Some see in it, indeed, a souvenir of Æneas, and think it was intended to connect the name of the son with that of the mother, while others believe it an epithet, meaning "the noble, glorious Aphrodite." Herr Wärner, who studied the legend of Æneas, says in an interesting memoir (*Die Sage von den Wanderungen des Æneas*, Leipzig, 1882) that the worship of Astarte may possibly have preceded that of Aphrodite in the various countries where Æneas is

of Halicarnassus that sanctuaries of this kind were very frequent on the coasts of the Mediterranean. They existed at Cythera, at Zacynthus, at Lemas, and at Actium, in every place where maritime commerce was a little brisk, and in all of them the name of Æneas was joined to that of Aphrodite. When a Greek vessel touched at these shores, and the mariner worshipped at the rough shrine raised by his predecessors, could he hear names which the *Iliad* had made familiar to him from his youth without a world of mythological memories awaking in him? As it is in his nature to create fables, and his vivid imagination unceasingly revives the past, he thinks he perceives the exile of Troy seeking a home for his banished gods. "It is doubtless here that he settled, and as if to take possession of the country, he built a temple to his mother." It is true that in another voyage he may find elsewhere a tomb of Aphrodite like the one he has just seen, and which calls up the same memories in him. He will simply apply to the new country what he said of the other, and affirm that this time he has found the real dwelling of Æneas. Thus, little by little, the legend was formed, lengthening at each voyage, ever finishing and ever beginning again, until it occurred to a compiler more clever than the

---

supposed to have landed. The vessels of Tyre, coming before those of Greece, may have left shrines there which afterwards, when the Greek navigators got the upper hand, were consecrated to the Greek goddess. In this case Æneas may possibly have taken the place of some Phœnician hero, who was worshipped together with Astarte. This hypothesis is ingenious, but in the prevailing darkness I nevertheless prefer not to go further back than the Greek navigators.

rest to weld together all these separate narratives in one whole. He took Æneas on his departure from Troy, on the day when he carried off his father and his gods from his flaming home; he made him touch in turn at all the ports of the Archipelago where some local tradition indicated his presence; he then led him to the shores of Sicily and Italy; and as the town of Ardea in Latium was the last spot where he raised a temple to Aphrodite, he supposed this to be the end of his long journey, and that the great traveller had at last found that new country " which fled unceasingly before him."

The legend thus related became quite different from what it was in Homer. Homer shows us Æneas quietly installed with his people in the neighbourhood of Troy; the new narrative presents him incurring all kinds of adventures, to found at last a city as far off as Latium. Nothing more contrary could therefore be imagined. But scrupulous scholars were found who endeavoured to arrange everything. They supposed that after sailing to the Italian shores and building Lavinium, Æneas left his new kingdom to his son, and returned with part of his people to his residence on Mount Ida. This was an ingenious way of contenting everybody; yet the compromise was not favourably received, and at the risk of running counter to the *Iliad*, Æneas was left to live and die on the banks of the Tiber, where such great destinies awaited his descendants.

II.

HOW THE LEGEND OF ÆNEAS PENETRATED INTO ITALY—
OPINION OF NIEBUHR—IT DOES NOT REPLACE THE
ITALIAN LEGENDS, BUT RATHER OVERLAPS THEM—
IT IS CONNECTED WITH THE ORIGIN OF LAVINIUM—
HYPOTHESIS OF SCHWEGLER—THE PROCESS OF ASSIMI-
LATION BY WHICH ÆNEAS CAME TO ASSUME AN
ITALIAN PHYSIOGNOMY—HOW THE GREEKS COMMUNI-
CATED THE LEGEND TO THE ITALIANS—IN WHAT
MANNER IT WAS RECEIVED—THE ROMANS NOT HOSTILE
TO FOREIGN IDEAS AND USAGES—THE INFLUENCE OF
GREECE ON ROME IN EARLY TIMES.

The legend is completed; it has taken its place among
the multitude of marvellous stories which feed the Greek
imagination.   But thus far it is known to the Greeks
alone, and it remains for us to see how they transmitted
it to the Latins.   We must above all get to understand
why the Latins received it so submissively; how it was
that they yielded to the imposition of unknown ancestors; and how they consented to accept a vanquished
and proscribed foreigner, of whom they had heard
nothing, as the first author of their race.

This appears to Niebuhr to be quite inexplicable.

It does not seem to him possible " that so proud a
State as Rome, which despised every foreign element,"
should have been so condescending on this occasion,
when it was a question of the history of its origin—
that is to say, of traditions which ancient peoples
regarded as sacred, and on which they usually based
their national religion.   So he takes the pains to

imagine an hypothesis which will accommodate everything. According to him, the inhabitants of Latium
were Pelasgians, like the Teucrians, the Arcadians, the
Epirotes, the Œnotrians, etc. Early separated, established in distant countries, these peoples, notwithstand-
ing, never lost sight of each other. Religion formed a
bond of union between them; they visited together the
Isle of Samothrace, where great mysteries were celebrated. It is here, in these friendly meetings, that the
legend must have arisen. It was only a more lively
and striking manner of expressing the relationship of
these different peoples, and preserving its memory.
To state that a chief from Troy had gone through
the world, leaving in certain countries a part of the
people who accompanied him—what is this but
affirming that all those who inhabit these different
countries sprang from the same stock, and remem-
bering that they are brothers? The legend is therefore
natural and indigenous among them. It does not come
from abroad; they created it themselves, and this alone
can explain its having become popular. Such is
Niebuhr's opinion, which he sets forth with profound
conviction, and which appears to him to be truth itself.[1]
Unfortunately it is only a conjecture, and I think it
entirely lacking in probability. The little nation of
husbandmen and bandits who inhabited the plains of
Latium had neither ports nor vessels. If they had been
obliged to go and seek the legend in the sacred Isle of
Samothrace, I think they would never have known it;

---

[1] " The hypothesis I have just advanced is not for me a desperate
attempt to find some outlet or other; it is the result of my conviction."

it was the legend which came and sought them out. It is believed now that they held it from the Greek navigators, and that it came to them along with many others, which ended by modifying their religious beliefs. From the moment we do not accept the hypothesis of Niebuhr, we have to solve the problem which he avoids. We have, then, to look for the reasons which permitted the Latins so readily to accept the ancestors presented to them by the Greeks.

I imagine, to start with, that if they did not feel much enthusiasm for the legend the first time that it was related to them, it did not, on the other hand, inspire them with one of those repugnances which habit does not overcome. This was the essential point: before being accepted, it had to be listened to. It is probable that it would not have been listened to, but would have been rejected at once, had it pretended to substitute itself for any of the ancient traditions of the country. But it was not so audacious or so clumsy. The Romans related the foundation and the first years of their city in a certain way. They recounted the miraculous history of the twins, that of the king-pontiff, that of the conqueror of Alba, etc. Æneas took care not to meddle with Romulus, Numa, the kings of Rome, or to appropriate their exploits. He was merely made the ancestor of the first of them, and placed in those remote times to which the most ancient Latin traditions did not reach back. The popular traditions were therefore not interfered with, and the history of Rome was only made to begin a little earlier, which could not wound its pride. Thus, the new legend having taken care to fix itself in a void, had sheltered itself from all objection.   But it was not enough for it to be listened to without ill-will; it had to gain foothold in a land where it had no roots.   A legend is by its nature light and volatile.   If it remains in the air, it is liable to be blown about by all the winds, and, after a few years, to be dispersed and lost.   In order to live, it must lean on something lasting.   Either it must be incorporated in certain religious rites, and become a sort of explanation of them, when the persistence of the rites preserves the memory of the legendary narrative; or it must become connected with a town, and insinuate itself among the fables related concerning its origin, which assures it the longest duration.   But with regard to Rome, there was nothing to be done, the ground having been taken up long since; so they contented themselves with Lavinium, and Æneas passed for its founder.   It remains to be seen why this town was chosen in preference to others, and what special facility it offered for the establishment of the legend.   An ingenious hypothesis of Schwegler[1] renders the task easy.   Lavinium was the holy city of the Latins.   Each town, each state, like each family, had its protecting gods, which were placed in a consecrated spot, and to which great homage was rendered.   Those of the Latins dwelt at Lavinium.   This town was therefore for the entire confederation what the shrine of the Lares was for the house of a citizen, and the Temple of Vesta and of the Penates were for Rome— that is to say, the religious centre and spiritual capital of the league.   Schwegler concludes, from some particu-

---

[1] In his excellent *History of Rome*, which death prevented him from finishing.

lars furnished by the ancient scholiasts, that it was built
especially for the part it was destined to play, and that
round about the abode of the common Penates the entire
confederation sent a certain number of colonists, charged
to honour the gods of the country. It resembled one
of those improvised centres which formed themselves
in Asia Minor near the theatres and the temples where
the festivals of the federated cities were celebrated.[1]
We may say, then, that it had no particular founder,
since it was founded by a federation of cities; and as
such artificial creations do not favour the growth of
legends, probably none were related concerning its
origin, and so that of Æneas met with no competition.
It had the advantage of furnishing a fabulous past to a
city devoid of one; why should it find a bad reception?
Besides, was not so wise, so pious a hero, the son of
Venus, the favourite of the Olympian gods, completely
fitted to figure as the founder of a holy city?

Here then is Æneas established at Lavinium as its
acknowledged founder. But the Latins still had among
them an alien by birth, and as such it was difficult for
him ever to become popular in his new country. We
are about to see how this disadvantage, without quite
disappearing, which was impossible, was at least
mitigated in the sequel. It has been remarked that in
young races the memory of facts is generally more

---

[1] Does not the sight of these cities, founded expressly to be the
religious centres of confederated peoples, remind one of Washington,
which owes its birth to analogous reasons? Politics have done
in the United States what religion did among the confederations of
antiquity.

tenacious than the memory of names; that they do not forget the marvellous incidents they heard related in their youths, but that they seldom remember to whom they were attributed; so that these tales, gradually becoming detached from the personages to whom they were at first attributed, end by floating in the air, ready to fall again on all who successively occupy public attention. Several generations of legendary heroes are thus often seen to inherit the same adventures in turn. There was a certain number of these roving legends among the Latins, as elsewhere. These settled upon Æneas, and a whole history was composed for him, of which Greece, most certainly, had no idea. It was doubtless still said that he came from Troy; he was still the same wise, religious hero of whom Homer had sung; and he was still represented, according to usage, bearing off his father and his gods upon his shoulders, to save them from the conflagration. Then comes the first serious change. In the Latin legend, the gods he carries off are no longer the same. The Greeks supposed him to have saved the Palladium, the miraculous statue involving the destinies of Troy; the Latins substituted the Penates for the Palladium. These were especially Italian gods, quite peculiar to the race, and bearing its mark. All the nations of antiquity imagined protecting gods of the family, and made them according to their idea. Those of the Romans were gods of " alimentation and nourishment," and they received their name from the very place where the household food was kept (*penus*). Such are the gods which the brilliant son of Aphrodite, the protected of Apollo, carries away with him, and for which he desires to build a city. He only builds this city in accordance with the formal behoof of Fate ; but whereas among the Greeks destiny is expressed by the voices of the priests of Delphi and Dodona, the Latins substituted for these predictions the oracles of the country, which are far from being so poetic. Thus, in the new legend, Æneas is told that he will not succeed in his enterprise until he has immolated the white sow with her thirty little ones, and when his companions, in their voracity, have devoured even their tables. These are fables which, by their great simplicity, betray a Latin origin, and have nothing at all in common with Greece. The death of Æneas, like his life, conformed to the legends of Latium ; and what is told of the old kings of the country when they die is repeated of him : one day he disappears and suddenly ceases to be seen (*non comparuit*), and it is supposed that he plunged into the waters of the Numicius, a sacred river. Thenceforth he is honoured as a god, by the name of the very divinity in which he was lost, and is no longer called Æneas, but *Jupiter indiges*. This is not how the Greeks deified their heroes. They openly placed them in Olympus, preserving their human features, and honouring them by their names. But Æneas was to become quite Latin ; and from the moment he touches Italian soil, his new country takes possession of him. She gives him adventures, she gives him a legend, she ends by even taking from him the name by which Greek poets sang of him. This was the only way the legend could become acclimatized in the country where it was to be definitely fixed. It had to assume its spirit and its character, and to lose, little by little, all, whether in the personage or his history, that might be repugnant to the Romans.   It would, of course, be a great mistake to believe that all these changes were meditated and thought out; that they were the fruit of deep combinations.   Such processes are not at all suited to primitive epochs.   But while admitting that, on the whole, the work was done by chance and unconsciously, it is none the less true that the legend must have profited by the facilities it found, and that it followed the natural paths which lay before it in order to penetrate into the heart of the country.   Doubtless we cannot hope, at this distance of time, to distinguish very exactly how things happened; yet the knowledge we possess of the manners and customs of different peoples allows us to form some very probable conjectures.   For example, it will not cost a very great effort of the imagination to picture to ourselves what usually took place when Greek navigators touched at these coasts six or seven centuries before our era.   They almost always found the place taken.   The Phœnicians had preceded them, and had long since been masters of the commerce.   But the Greeks possessed advantages over them which they well knew how to use.   The Phœnician was before everything a greedy merchant, who only thought of selling his carpets, his stuffs, and his cups of chiselled metal, as dearly as possible.   Of course the Greek did not disdain good profits; there never was a more heedful and adroit merchant; but he took with him into the countries he visited something more than the products of his industry.   Roving the world for his pleasure, almost as much as for his profit, when business was over he was not always in a hurry to lock up his money and be off.   He was already that " little Greek " whom the Romans so often laughed at—supple, curious, chatty, insinuating; soon at ease in the homes of others, and knowing how to make himself necessary there. Like his great ancestor Ulysses, he loved, when visiting cities, "to know the customs of the peoples." While selling his goods, he looked and observed. Being sharp and perspicacious, he was not long in remarking that these peoples, whom he treated as barbarians, had beliefs and usages much resembling his own. When he heard them talk, he seized words and phrases that recalled his own tongue. In these days such resemblances no longer surprise us; for everybody knows that all these peoples belonged to the same race of men, that after living long together they separated with a common stock of words and ideas, and that it is not astonishing that this stock should be recognised in their civilizations and their idioms. But this was unknown to the Greeks and unsuspected by all around them. There was only one means of explaining everything, and they made great use of it. They supposed that their ancestors, or, if not a Greek, at least one of the Trojans celebrated by Homer, had been to these shores and perhaps founded a colony. Henceforth there was no longer room for surprise that the inhabitants of the country should have retained ways of speaking and acting which recalled Greece; it was a heritage that had come to them, without their knowledge, from these old travellers. But the Greeks were not people to stop at a vague hypothesis: in such fertile brains suppositions soon became realities. As generally happens to the self-confident, everything served to convince them of the truth of their conjectures; and the adventures of the hero of Troy, of which their memory was full, recurred to their thoughts *à propos* of everything. The names of persons and places met with on their road suggested unexpected connections to them at every moment. They made their hosts talk, scarcely listened to them, and always found in their narratives some detail that set them thinking of their own legends. Having received from heaven over and above everything the charming gift of invention, they added much to what was told them, and from all these different elements, to which they gave a uniform colouring, they excelled in manufacturing amusing fables, which they were never tired of relating.

Let us go further. Can we, after imagining how these fables must have come into being, picture to ourselves the manner of their reception ? No one has told us ; but there is something which brings it to our knowledge more surely than if anybody had been at the pains to instruct us. They were *remembered*, and those who heard them told gave them a place beside their national traditions, which they sometimes supplanted. This is the victorious proof of the success obtained by them. This success should not surprise us. We know a little better now in what state of civilization were the nations of antiquity when the Greeks began to visit them. In various parts of Italy deep excavations have been made, which brought to light some very ancient tombs. The objects found in them are exceedingly rough. They are usually vases fashioned by hand, of impure clay, imperfectly polished, and with their grey or blackish surface ornamented merely with lines and circles—that is to say, the first decoration men ever thought of. Evidently those who used those vases and possessed no others were still almost barbarians. But those barbarians were not people to acquiesce in their barbarism, and they asked nothing better than to leave it. The proof of this is, that near this primitive pottery were found pieces of amber from the North Sea, scarabei and cups brought by the Phœnicians, and, in more recent tombs, cups with archaic figures of Greek origin. Those people then, so rough and savage in appearance, were nevertheless endowed with the taste for a more exalted art. They did not disdain its products, but welcomed the merchants who introduced it to them, and probably paid them highly.

This characteristic is striking among the most ancient Romans. As we have just seen, Niebuhr states that Rome in her pride "despised all foreign elements." The truth is just the contrary. She doubtless had a great opinion of herself, and early foresaw the part she was to play in the world; but this legitimate pride never degenerated into ridiculous vanity. She did not despise her enemies even after they were vanquished, knew how to acknowledge what was good in them, and when necessary she appropriated it. "Our ancestors," said Sallust, "were people as wise as bold. Pride did not prevent them from borrowing the institutions of their neighbours when they saw any profit in them. Their arms are those of the Samnites, and to the Etruscans they owe the insignia of their magistrates. Whenever they found among their allies or their enemies anything worth taking, they sought to introduce it among themselves. They preferred rather to imitate others than to envy them."[1]   This is the true character of the people.   If they sometimes appear vainly self-complacent, and impertinently disdainful of the foreigner, it is mere comedy.   The attitude a Roman thinks himself obliged to assume in public, the way he talks when others are listening, his manner of acting when looked at, are not always in conformity with his true sentiments.   This is remarked in his dealings with the Greeks.   He doubtless affects to laugh at them in public, but he cannot do without them ; and we may be certain that the very first day he saw them he submitted, without being able to help himself, to the ascendency of that witty and insinuating race who brought him such beautiful works and told him such good stories.

When speaking of the introduction of Greek civilization into Rome, the mind is generally carried back to a precise date, and thinks of the day in the year 514 B.C., when a captive of Tarentum caused a regular drama imitated from the masterpieces of Greece to be played in a theatre which had hitherto only been used for Etruscan dancers and Italian buffoons.   It is, in truth, a decisive moment in the history of Rome.   That day the door was for the first time flung wide open to Greek literature, and by the way which had been thus prepared for her, she soon passed bodily through.   But when this species of *coup d'état* took place, Greece had long since gradually and noiselessly penetrated Rome, and what she had done in those few centuries was more important than what remained to be accomplished.   To

---

[1] Catiline, 51.

give Rome a literature was doubtless a great undertaking; but was it not a much graver one yet to modify
the manners of the city, and by a secret and continuous
process to introduce a new spirit into it? She gained
this result in that first intercourse of which history has
not preserved the memory. Above all, the national
religion came out quite changed. We know what was
the essential character of the old Roman religion. The
gods it honoured had scarcely taken human form; they
still lacked individuality and life, and behind them
were seen the forces and phenomena of the nature they
faintly personified. It is from Greece that the Romans
learned to make entirely animate beings of them, to
give them passions, and to attribute adventures to
them. They doubtless went about it in earnest. Prof.
Hild bids us remark that those vague divinities, which
a father of the Church calls " incorporeal and intangible
shadows," offered but meagre food to the imagination of
the crowd. Having once beheld the living figures of
the Hellenic Pantheon, it would have no others. Thus
was introduced into Rome the Greek mythology, which,
in creating a history for all these stiff and inanimate
gods, gave them life; and thus was established the
worship of the heroes, sons of the gods, a sort of intermediate being between divinity and manhood, from
which the poetry of the Greeks had drawn such great
advantages. Æneas entered with the others, and, like
them, met with a good reception.

III.

AT WHAT MOMENT DID THE LEGEND FIRST BECOME KNOWN TO THE ROMANS ?—IT IS FIRST MENTIONED AT THE TIME OF THE WAR WTIH PYRRHUS—THE IMPORTANCE IT TAKES AFTER THE PUNIC WARS—THE LEGEND AMONG THE POETS, NÆVIUS—THE LEGEND AMONG THE HISTORIANS AND SCHOLIASTS, CATO, VARRO—THE LEGEND AMONG THE ARTISTS—WHY WAS IT MORE SPREAD AMONG THE ROMANS THAN AMONG THE GREEKS ?

Only one point remains to be cleared up; but it is perhaps the most obscure. Can we ascertain at what moment the legend of Æneas became known among the Romans ? We do not hope to attain to a precise date, as may well be imagined. We must not be exacting, but content ourselves with little, when so distant an age is in question.

First of all, it is indisputable that the first intercourse of the Romans with the Greeks goes back very far. It is no longer a matter of doubt that they received the art of writing from them ; for in the most ancient Latin inscriptions the form of the letters is that of the Æolo-Dorian alphabet. This alphabet was doubtless communicated to them by one of the Greek colonies established in Southern Italy or in Sicily. It probably came to them from Cumeà, whose vessels did a great trade along the Italian coasts. But when did they begin to use it ? When the ideas of Niebuhr upon the beginnings of Roman history were dominant, it was customary to make this epoch as late as possible, in order to leave the field the longer free for the formation of primitive epics, and it was even asserted that the Romans did not learn to write until the time of the Decemvirs. These are ideas which have now been exploded. It is certain that writing was known to the Romans at a very early date, and in a recent publication M. Louis Havet has tried to show that their alphabet was fixed before the time of the Tarquins.[1] We must admit, then, that the Greeks frequented the markets of Rome from the day of its foundation. This opinion, a prediction of philology, has been confirmed by the archæologist. In the excavations made on the Viminal, tombs were reached under what is called the Wall of Servius, and which must consequently be more ancient. These tombs contained, among other objects, Chalcidian vases, which doubtless came by way of Cumea. From the moment the Greeks knew the road to Rome, they

---

[1] See M. L. Havet's opening lecture at the College de France, 7th December 1882. The consequences of the fact pointed out by them do not lack importance, and he does not shrink from them. After establishing the fact that writing was known in the time of the Roman kings, he adds : " But," it will be asked, " did those old kings really exist ? " And why not ? If the Romans could write at that time, why should they not have transmitted a few authentic names to posterity ? It is very remarkable that with regard to these facts, formerly so much contested, French, Italian, and even German criticism seems to have become conservative again. At the same time that M. L. Havet's pamphlet appeared, M. Gaston Paris published in the *Romania* a very important article on the legend of Roncevaux. This article ends with the following words: " While following up these studies of critical analysis, now only in their beginning, we shall become more and more convinced that in being distant and anonymous the epic is not differently circumstanced than other births of human poetic activity ;

brought the products of their industry thither, and with them their ideas, their civilization, and their legends. But must we believe that the legend of Æneas was already among them ?   Upon this point the learned are divided, and the most opposite opinions are offered. While some believe it to be as ancient as Rome herself, others will not admit it to be anterior to the Punic Wars.   On which side does the truth seem to be ?

To those who would take it back to the very beginning of Rome, it has been rightly replied that, had it existed at the time when the Roman religion was formed, it would hold some place in it.[1]   Denys of Halicarnassus, in expounding it, says "that it is confirmed by what takes place in the sacrifices and ceremonies"; but he must have been mistaken.   The most ancient festivals of Rome are known to us, and Prof. Mommsen thinks we can reconstruct the calendar of Numa.   There is no mention of Æneas in it.   He is first heard of in history in connection with Pyrrhus.

---

that it is only developed by a series of individual innovations, doubtless marked in the corners of their respective epochs ; and which have nothing unconscious or *popular* in the almost mystic sense sometimes attached to the word.   Everything here, as elsewhere, has its explanation, its cause, its reason to be and to cease."   Here we are, then, very far from the assertions which made the glory of Wolff, Lachmann, and Niebuhr.   It is curious to realise, just at the end of this century, that after having run through a whole cycle of seductive hypotheses, and of audacious destructions and reconstructions, the evolution is finished, and brings us back very nearly to the point of departure.   But we return to it with more exact ideas, and with a clearer view of the past ; and if all those great systems which reigned for a few years were only errors, they were at least fertile errors, which have renewed criticism and history.

[1] *Antiq. rom.*, I. 49.

We are told that the king of Epirus was induced to declare war against the Romans by the memory of his ancestor Achilles, there being a family quarrel between him and the Trojans of Rome, which he desired to settle.[1] So the legend existed at that time, and a contemporary historian, Timæus of Tauromenium, tells it nearly in the same way that it is known to us. Is it probable that it was quite recent at this moment, or that the war with Pyrrhus gave rise to it? I find it difficult to believe. Prof. Hild is right in saying "that a belief or a worship is never implanted all at once by hasty adoption or violent annexation." It must then have been working its way, and insinuating itself into Rome for some time past; but it only began to assume a certain authority there shortly before the war with Pyrrhus. What also leads me to the same conclusion is, that about this time I see it accepted in an official manner by the Roman authorities. When a State is wise, it does not give in too soon to contested novelties; and in order that a sort of public consecration should have been accorded to the legend of Æneas at Rome, it must have been pretty widely spread at the time and accepted by many people. In 472, according to Prof. Mommsen, and, according to Nissen,[2] fifty years later, the Acarnanians being engaged in a struggle with the Ætolians, asked Rome to help them. Their ground of appeal was that of all the Greeks their

---

[1] This is at least what Pausanias says, although his sources are not known.

[2] Nissen, *Zur Kritik des Æneassage* (*Jahrb. für class. Phil.*), 1865, p. 375, *et seq.*

ancestors alone had taken no part in the Trojan War. They doubtless thought that this motive would suffice to soften the Senate, and that the heirs of the Trojans would not decline to pay their ancestors' debt. From that time texts abound to prove that belief in a Trojan origin had become among the Romans a maxim of State, alleged without hesitation, even in diplomatic documents. When, after the disasters of the Second Punic War, Rome asked the inhabitants of Pessinonte to let them have the statue of the Mother of the Gods which was to restore their fortunes, she did not forget to remind them that her ancestors were Phrygians by birth, and, consequently, their countrymen. A little later, in treating with Antiochus, king of Syria, whom she had vanquished, she takes care to stipulate that he shall set free the inhabitants of Ilion, who are related to the Roman people. During the wars in Asia, the generals who passed by the ancient town, are careful to stop there and make sacrifices. Æneas, thenceforth, has taken his place among the ancestors of the Romans; he figures at the head of the list, and public honours are rendered to him. In the Forum of Pompeii, along a monument which ornaments one side of the square, four niches are distinguished, which used to contain statues, now destroyed. Æneas and Romulus occupied the two first; while Signor Fiorelli supposes the two others to have contained Cæsar and Augustus. These were the four founders of the Roman State. Some fragments of the inscription graven below the image of Æneas still remain. They recall all the legend in a few words: the flight of the hero carrying with him his gods and his father; his arrival in Italy; the foundation of

Lavinium; his miraculous death; and his apotheosis as Jupiter Indigos.[1]

Latin poetry also takes early possession of Æneas. We know that he figured in the first orational epic Rome possessed. When the rough plebeian Nævius, so ardent for the glory of his country, undertook to sing the First Punic War, in which he had been a soldier, he began by going back to the Trojans. At this moment the history of Æneas is enriched by a new incident on which Virgil was afterwards to shed an immortal brightness. Nævius imagines Æneas to have been driven by the wind from Troy to Carthage, where he was received by Dido. He was not, I think, the first to bring together these representatives of two races, and this is how they come to be connected. On the western coast of Sicily, on the summit of Mount Eryx, there rose one of these temples of Aphrodite to which allusion has already been made. The position of Eryx between Africa, Gaul, Spain, and Italy, made it one of the spots where merchants of all countries came together. The Phœnician was constantly meeting the Greek there. Each of the two peoples brought with it its national traditions, and in their reciprocal communications, when one told the story of Æneas, the other replied with that of Dido. And so by dint of talking about them, they came to join them in the same legend. Allied together so long as their nations were united, they became

---

[1] It is true that among the paintings at Pompeii there exists one which is a kind of parody of the official legend. It represents a monkey, clad in a coat of mail, carrying an old monkey on his shoulders and dragging a young monkey by the hand. Æneas, Anchises, and Ascanius are meant.

mortal enemies as soon as the war broke out between Carthage and Rome. Then the hatred of the children is made to go back to that of the ancestors, and the meeting of the queen of Carthage with the Trojan hero takes tragic colours. It is doubtless Nævius who gave this new character to the ancient legend. To account for the animosity of the two races, he supposes that they had ancient grudges to avenge, and that their enmity began with their very existence. Ennius also thinks he must take up Roman history at the fall of Troy, as is seen in the short fragments of the First Book of his poem which remain to us. We have especially the verse in which he begins to relate the adventures of Æneas :

"*Cum veter occubuit Priamus sub marte Pelasgo.*"

The remainder took up very little place, and half a Book sufficed Ennius for the narration of what occupies twelve in Virgil. The malicious said that while laughing at his predecessor Nævius, whom he accused of writing in a barbarous rhythm and having no care for elegance, he avoided repeating what the rough poet had done, in order not to clash with him, and that he was like certain heroes of Homer, who shout all kinds of nonsense to their enemy, and let fly an arrow or two from afar, but withdraw as soon as he advances. However this may be, it is curious to remark that the first time the Latin Muse tackles the epic, she goes straight to the subject which Virgil was to handle. Is it not to the point here to recall Sainte Beuve's remark with reference to Homer? He says there was a sort of unconscious conspiracy among all these ancient writers to prepare the matter on which their illustrious successor was afterwards to work.

From the hands of the poets the legend fell into that of the chroniclers and scholiasts. It had no reason to rejoice thereat. The moment that the learned seize upon these old legends, and undertake to make them clearer and wiser, is a crisis for them. The learned are not light-handed. They want everything to be rational and sensible, which is surely a most legitimate desire; yet, somehow or other, from the moment you try to put reason into popular fables, and take too much trouble to make them probable, they become ridiculous. Virgil had afterwards much ado to restore to his hero the poetic tinge of which his prolonged sojourn among scholiasts and chroniclers had deprived him. Yet they rendered him a signal service, since their minute researches and learned labours contributed to establish the authority of the legend more solidly. So long as it was only found in the verses of the poets, it might be suspected of having no other foundation than those thousand Greek fables which no one took in earnest. But from the moment serious people, who did not make it their trade to amuse the public, took the tronble to busy themselves with it, in books where they studied the laws and religion of their country, it seemed to deserve more confidence. Cato, a consul, a censor, an enemy of the Greeks, related it without hesitation in all its details, and did not hesitate to give, respecting the exact extent of the territory ceded by Turnus to the Trojans, and the different struggles which Æneas and Ascanius sustained against Turnus, details as precise as if contemporary events had been in question. Varro, "the most learned of the Romans," who was a man of war as well as a scholar, and commanded the fleet of the Adriatic while Pompey was tracking the pirates, profited by a little leisure to follow up Æneas, do his journeys over again, and visit with his galleys the different ports at which he had touched. He was so convinced of the reality of his adventures that he thought he found indisputable traces of his sojourn everywhere. We see in the fragments of his works still extant that he speaks of these distant events in a tone of extraordinary assurance. "Is it not certain," he says, "that the Arcadians, under the leadership of Evander, came into Italy, and settled on the Palatine?"[1] It seems really a crime to doubt it.

I know that to these reasons, which induced us to believe that the legend was then very widely spread and generally believed in, it has been objected that it was utterly unknown to Roman Art. How is it possible to admit that, being so popular as is asserted, it so rarely tempted sculptors and painters? It is certain that no fresco or bas-relief of any importance is known anterior to the Empire, having the history of Æneas for its subject. M. Brunn thought he had found one on one of those metal coffers called *cists*, which come to us from the tombs of Præneste. He fancied that he recognised on one of the sides the battles of the Rutuli and the Trojans, while on the plaque in the cover he saw Æneas presenting the old Latin king with the spoils of Turnus whom he has just killed. Beside him is Lavinia, who is about to be delivered to her husband,

---

[1] Severus, in *Æn.*, VIII. 51.

while Amata, her mother, retires, furious, in order not to witness this marriage.[1] This is quite the subject of the *Æneid*, and, as M. Brunn supposes this work of art to be anterior to the First Punic War, he admits that the legend was then fixed in its most minute details, and that Virgil only translated faithfully the popular fables which existed more than two centuries before his time. Unfortunately, M. Brunn's explanation is now strongly contested, and it is questioned whether the coffer does not belong to a more recent epoch, or whether the subject represented is really what M. Brunn imagines it to be. But on the other hand, since the time when M. Brunn, erroneously or not, placed the adventures of Æneas on the *cista prænestina*, they have been found, and this time indubitably, in a Roman tomb. In 1875 excavations were undertaken by an Italian Society at the extremity of the Esquiline, in the space extending between Santa Maria Maggiore and the little monument known as the Temple of Minerva Medica. Here lay one of the important roads of Rome—that leading to Præneste. Along the Roman roads one is always sure to find tombs. One of those excavated contained frescoes which had unfortunately suffered much when, in the third century, the custom of burying the dead having replaced that of burning them, alterations were made to the tomb in order to adapt it to this new practice. However, enough remains of the paintings to enable one to grasp their subject quite clearly. It is the early history of Rome from the arrival of Æneas in Italy. We first see him founding Lavinium and

---

[1] *Ann. de l'Inst. de corresp. arch.*, 1864, p. 356, *et seq.*

fighting Turnus. In the pictures, which follow each other without being separated, like those on the column of Trajan, all the phases of the great battle fought on the banks of the Numicius can be followed. Then comes the foundation of Alba by Ascanius, and lastly, the story of Rhea Silvia and the twins.[1] What adds value to these paintings is that they must be contemporary with Virgil's works, and as they do not reproduce exactly the tradition followed by him, and were probably not executed under his influence, they show how the events sung by the poet were understood by people round about him. But whatever importance may be attached to them, it must not be forgotten that they are the only work of art of any value anterior to the *Æneid* treating of Æneas and Lavinium; and it must therefore be owned that down to the time of Virgil, the journeys of the Trojan hero, which had inspired so many poets, had busied sculptors and painters but little.

Does this justify us in stating that the legend was but little known at that time? I do not think so. Let us remember that the arts were in the hands of the Greeks, and that the Greeks only liked to busy themselves with themselves. It has been remarked that they hardly ever reproduced events of Roman history in bas-reliefs or frescoes. It is true that having created the Ænean legend, as we have seen, they might have been expected to feel more taste for the work; but

---

[1] This monument was first described by M. Brizio in his work entitled *Pitture e sepolcri scoperti sull' Esquilino.* The subject was treated afresh by M. Robert in the *Annales de l'Institut achéologique de Rome* (1878, p. 234, *et seq.*). I have followed M. Robert's explanations.

unfortunately this legend had come into existence but recently, when their imagination was beginning to tire of reproducing fables. Besides, it is obviously less rich in poetic details, more sombre and dry than others. Nor had it enjoyed the good fortune to please a great poet, and be transfigured in his song. These were depreciating circumstances which little recommended it to the choice of artists. In conclusion, they had a special reason for forsaking it, on which I must for a moment dwell; because in teaching us why it was neglected by the Greeks, it at the same time shows us one of the reasons, and perhaps the strongest, which attracted the Romans to it.

When the legend of Æneas began to spread among the Greeks, Rome, too feeble as yet to cause them uneasiness, was yet powerful enough to inspire them with a desire to attach her in some way or other to their country, and thus take part in her glory. A century later all was changed. She had subdued Greece, she had just invaded the East, and she openly coveted the empire of the world. The Greeks, vanquished and humiliated, no longer felt the same alacrity to adorn with poetic fables the origin of a people who oppressed them. This legend—although their own work—seemed to give their rivals a too advantageous past. They began by speaking less and less of it, and ended by forgetting it. Denys of Halicarnassus states that in his time there was hardly anybody left in Greece to whom it was known. Its place had been taken by quite contrary fables. There existed then, at the courts of the little Asiatic princes and of the barbarian kings, quite a school of historians who made it their business to say as much ill as possible of the Romans, and as much good as possible of their enemies. They naturally shared the fate of those whose cause they championed, and it is conceivable that the conqueror whom they insulted should not have been solicitous to preserve their works. We possess Polybius, who wrote the history of the Punic Wars in the Roman interest; but we scarcely know the name of that Philinus of Agrigentum who extolled the Carthaginians, and turned everything to their glory. The usual tactics of all these enemies of Rome consisted in ridiculing the baseness of her origin. They said that she had been an asylum for bandits; that she owed her birth to wretches, vagabonds, and slaves. These calumnies made Halicarnassus indignant, and he undertook to reply to them by writing his *Roman Antiquities*. In order to show their falseness and victoriously refute them, he related the legend of Æneas in all its details. Addressing his countrymen at the commencement of his book, he says: "Trust not at all those lies (with regard to the foundation of Rome); they only spread fables. I will show you that those who founded her were not vagabonds snatched by chance from among the most contemptible nations. They were Trojans, following a famous chief, whose deeds were sung by Homer. Or rather, since the Trojans are of the same origin as we, they were Greeks." [1]

Denys well knew that this conclusion was quite to the taste of the Romans, and that it flattered the secret

---

[1] All these ideas are developed in the Preface to the *Roman Antiquities* of Denys of Halicarnassus.

instincts of their vanity. They had long borne without loss of temper the stigma of "barbarians," which the Greeks gave to all who were not of their race. When they better understood the worth of letters and of arts, they disliked to be put thus summarily and with a word beyond the pale of civilization. They wished to re-enter humanity, and in some way connect themselves with Greece, if only by their distant origin. The legend of Æneas gave them the means, and they grasped it with alacrity. The great lords delighted to imagine themselves descended from the most illustrious companions of Æneas; and there was even a certain number of families for whom this origin was not contested. These were called " Trojan families "; and Varro, desirous to please everybody, wrote a book in support of their chimerical genealogies. Simple citizens could not have such exalted pretensions; yet though they did not dare to claim the honour of having Trojan chiefs among their ancestors, they were still proud to be descended from common soldiers. In the famous prediction announcing the disaster of Cannæ, the soothsayer Marcius, addressing the Romans, called them "children of Troy" (*Trojugena Romanœ*).[1] In giving them this name he evidently meant to please them. A little later the poet Attius, having composed a national piece on the devotion of Decius, of which the Romans were so proud, entitled it *The Sons of Æneas or Decius* (*Æneadœ sive Decius*). Writers of tragedy or comedy generally seek to give to their works titles attractive to the public. Attius, then, supposed that

---

[1] *Titus Livius*, XXV. 12.

the Romans would like to hear themselves called sons of Æneas. And thus the general vanity became a factor in the success of the old legend.

IV.

WHAT REASON HAD VIRGIL TO CHOOSE THE LEGEND OF ÆNEAS FOR THE SUBJECT OF HIS POEM?—THE HISTORICAL EPIC AND THE MYTHOLOGICAL EPIC—THE *ÆNEID* IS BOTH A MYTHOLOGICAL AND AN HISTORICAL EPIC—WHY DID VIRGIL PREFER ÆNEAS TO ROMULUS?—IN WHAT SENSE MAY THE *ÆNEID* BE SAID TO HAVE BEEN POPULAR?

We at length bid adieu to darkness and uncertainties, and emerge into full light: we have reached Virgil. After having sought to discover whence the legend of Æneas came, what were the elements that formed it, and why the Romans received it so favourably, it remains for us to ascertain the reasons that may have induced Virgil to make it the subject of his poem.

We run no risk of committing an error when we assert that he did not do so without reason, and that, in the conception of his works, he left nothing to chance. Voltaire relates that when, at the age of twenty, he took it into his head to compose an epic, he scarcely knew what an epic was. Virgil would not have displayed such levity. He was not one of those poets of impulse of whom Plato tells us that they do not know what they are about. He meditated and reflected long before writing. He was a sad and timid man, and had not a sufficiently good opinion of himself to think he was capable of improvising masterpieces. All his works bear traces of patient labour and obstinate effort. The wonder is that in his case toil never hampered inspiration.

We may be certain that after deciding to write an epic poem, he first of all asked himself what the subject of this poem was to be. The reply to this question would be different, according to the school the poet belonged to. There were two at the time disputing and dividing public suffrage. The one clung to the past, and wished simply to continue it. It was composed of admirers of the old Latin poets, and counted especially among its ranks those wise and ripened minds to whom innovations are unpleasing. The other had chosen new models, and professed to rejuvenate poetry by imitating the younger poets. As always happens, these had the young people and the women on their side. Each of the two schools looked upon the epic differently. The old school was especially partial to the historical poem—that is to say, the poem which relates the deeds of our ancestors; and it must be owned that its taste was in conformity with the peculiar genius and natural aptitudes of the Roman race. This race was, above all, military and practical, and only loved literature on condition of its containing lessons for the conduct of life. The ideal and fanciful, by which the Greeks were moved, left it somewhat indifferent. It had little inclination for legends in which imagination has so great a place, and the poetry of its preference was that dealing with real facts and personages. So the Latin poets, as soon as their wings had strength to bear them, turned

in that direction. Nævius sings the First Punic
War; while Ennius, giving his work the very Roman
title of the *Annales*, relates all the history of Rome,
emphasizing the events he has himself seen, and can
speak of as a witness. The success of his work was
very marked. Rome recognises herself, and for a
century epic-makers followed in his tracks. Even in
Virgil's time, and round about him, poems were composed on the defeat of Vercingetorix and the death of
Cæsar. Lucretius, the greatest poet of the age, also
holds to the author of the *Annales*, and although he
did not write an epic tale, he proclaims himself the
disciple of Ennius, and congratulates him on having
brought from Helicon "a crown whose laurel leaves
shall never fade." The other school sought its inspirations among the Alexandrian poets. In spite of the
reputation they enjoyed in the Greek world, Rome had
remained long without knowing and applying them.
She liked to keep to the classic epoch; but when her
conquests had brought her into more frequent contact
with Asia, her generals, her proconsuls, her merchants,
who frequently visited the large towns, read these
poets with whom everybody around them busied themselves, and were charmed. They did not find it
difficult to communicate their feelings to their friends;
for there was then at Rome a polite and refined society
which was beginning to tire a little of the old writers
and to seek new objects for admiration. These graceful and delicate works, where care for form is pushed
so far; where so many learned allusions, so many
surprises of expression and imagery are found; where
the mode of speech is so ingenious that it stimulates

the mind and makes it pleased with itself when it has grasped its refinements, were well made to captivate. Naturally, after admiring, Rome imitated. The first to write verses in the Alexandrian style were at the same time young men of talent and heroes of fashion — Licinius Calvus, Cornelius Gallus, and above all, Catullus, the greatest among them. They obtained much success. One of their usual methods was the frequent employment of mythology. Some were content to make use of it in short allusions in their elegies, while others spread it out in epic poems. The histories of the gods and the heroes, the adventures of Hercules and Theseus, the war of Thebes or that of Troy, the conquest of the Golden Fleece, furnished them in abundance epic subjects, which they preferred to all others.

Between these two schools Virgil had to choose. Each had its merits and its advantages. The historical poem, preferred by the old school, most pleased the greater number, and had the better chance of becoming popular. Rome was always proud of her past, and she lent a willing ear to those who celebrated her glory. But this style also presents great difficulties of execution. It is always awkward for Poetry to have to compete with History. If she reproduces facts exactly as they have happened, she is accused of sinking into dryness, and being nothing but a chronicle; if she attempts to mingle a little fiction with it, serious people find that the truth prejudices the fable, while the fable discredits the truth; that one does not know on what ground one is walking, and that this uncertainty spoils all the pleasure of the work. The mythological epic is not exposed to this danger. All in it is of the same nature, and from the first verse it introduces the reader into a world of fancy and invention which he leaves no more. The *genre* once accepted, the mind is at rest, and does not experience the unpleasantness of being hauled backwards and forwards between fiction and reality. It is a kind of dream, to which it can confidently abandon itself; and it is at least sure of following it to the end without any rough incident coming to dissipate it. But, on the other hand, the public to which this kind of poetry appeals is limited, since it does not possess what attracts the crowd. In order to understand it one must have the delicacy of an artist and the learning of a scholar. Above all, at Rome, where artists and learned men were rare, it would have to resign itself to the indifference of " the profane vulgar," and be the charm of a few refined natures. Virgil did not servilely adhere to any school, and in this he shows his originality; his taste, broad and free, sought its inspirations everywhere. He began by a liking for Theocritus, an Alexandrian, while in his last work he so closely imitated the ancients that Seneca calls him an Ennianist down-right, which in his mouth is a grave reproach. In order to create the language, at once so firm and supple, which he used with such admirable effect, he did not scruple to join together the two great repre-sentatives of the opposed schools, Lucretius and Catullus. From the one he borrowed more especially the vivacity of his turns, and the energy and brilliancy of his expressions, while from the other he took his neater phrasing, and his easier, more flowing rhythm. From this combination arose that marvellous poetic language which Rome spoke without much change until the end of the Empire.

The same mind is found again in Virgil's choice of a subject. It is of a kind to satisfy everbody, and holds a middle place between the historical and the mythological epic. It has been supposed, with sufficient probability, that he hesitated some time before deciding. We know that when he finished his *Georgics*, he read them to the Emperor in the retreat at Atella, whither Augustus had gone to take a little rest and nurse his throat complaint. Was it on this occasion that he composed the brilliant prologue with which the Third Book opens? It is natural to believe so. In this prologue he announces the *Æneid*; but it has obviously not yet taken in his mind its definitive form. At this moment he seems quite disgusted with mythology. The young Roman poets had made such an abuse of it that in a few years it had lost all its freshness. "Who does not know," says Virgil, "pitiless Eurystheus and execrable Busiris? Who has not celebrated young Hylas, and Delos, dear to Latona, and Hippodamia, and Pelops, the fiery rider with his ivory shoulder?" All these subjects, fitted to please idle minds, seem to him exhausted (*omnia jam vulgata*). He desires to walk far from the crowd, and try new roads that will lead to glory. There are moments when, fashion having run for some time in a different direction, the old becomes new again. It would seem then, that Virgil intended to return to the tradition of the old Latin poets, and compose an entirely historical epic. In fact, he announces to Augustus that he is about to sing his combats:

" Mox tamen ardentes accingar dicere pugnas
Cæsaris."

He fortunately changed his mind. In taking for his subject the wars against Brutus and Antony, he would have found himself contending with the difficulties which Lucian, in spite of his genius, failed to overcome. He did well to go back further, to the very beginnings of Rome. His poem has not the less remained thoroughly historical, not only because of the constant allusions made to historical events and personages, but from the very nature of the subject, which is the glorification of Rome, and from the grave and sustained tone of the narrative. And yet it is mythological too, since gods and goddesses are the principal actors in the drama, and Olympus and the earth are spoken of in the same breath. By placing his fable in an epoch when legend and history are confounded together, he has suppressed their antagonism, and has thus been able to combine the advantages of both schools without incurring their disadvantages.

But may it not be objected that he went back too far? It may appear that, since he wished to glorify Rome in her foundation, it was not Æneas he should have chosen. Æneas only founded Lavinium, and is for the Romans but a very distant ancestor. The ancient chroniclers made him the father or the grandfather of Romulus, which brought him near enough to the birth of Rome; but later on, in order somehow or other to bring the legend into harmony with chronology, it was found necessary to intercalate between them the interminable series of Alban kings. It is indeed strange that a poet who desired to celebrate Rome should have chosen an epoch when it did not yet exist, and a hero who lived more than four hundred years ere its foundation. Virgil would have apparently done better to stop at Romulus, for he would have found himself in the very heart of his subject. Romulus was then much more popular than Æneas. Everybody knew his name; on the Palatine, the cabin where he lived was shown; and the little grotto, shaded by a fig-tree, where it is said the wolf had nursed him, was an object of devotion. Poetry had seized on these relics at a very early date, and in singing them had lent them splendour and force. The passages of the First Book of the *Annales* of Ennius, where he relates the dream of the vestal, the birth of the son of Mars, and his struggle with Remus, were in the memories of every educated Roman; and all repeated with emotion those beautiful lines, at once so strong and tender, expressing the gratitude of all the Romans to him who gave their city its life :—

> *"O Romule, Romule die*
> *Qualem te patriæ custodem di genuerunt !*
> *O pater, O genitor, O sanguen dis oriundum !"*

Nevertheless Virgil preferred Æneas to Romulus, and he had many reasons for doing so. One of the chief was certainly a desire to please the Emperor. Among all the families who boasted of a Trojan origin, the Cæsars held the first place. While the Memmii, the Sergii, and the Cluentii were content to have for ancestors lieutenants of Æneas, the Cæsars boldly connected themselves with Æneas himself, and claimed descent from his son Iulus. In singing the father of the Romans, Virgil celebrated the ancestor of the Julii. This was a means of giving the Emperor's power an appearance of legitimacy, and of making him, across the centuries, the natural heir of the kings of Rome. He thought then to serve his country, while paying to the prince his debt of personal gratitude. At the same time he fulfilled the promise he had made him in the *Georgics*, to raise him an immortal monument. It was, of course, no longer an historical poem devoted to a recital of the Emperor's exploits; but he was easily recognised under the features of the chief of his race. The glory of the ancestor illumined the descendant, and although the name of Æneas was inscribed on the pediment of the building, it might be said that Augustus was its centre, and that, in reality, he occupied it all:

> "*In medio mihi Cæsar erit, templumque tenebit !*"

Virgil had yet another reason for preferring Æneas to Romulus and the others, which must have seemed to him important. Æneas already figures in the *Iliad*, and his name recalls both the battle in which he took part and the warriors whom he knew. To speak of him, then, was a natural occasion to multiply allusions to the Homeric poems and re-animate the heroes of the Trojan War. This is a pleasure which Virgil indulges in as much as he can. Although he knows the danger there is of provoking disadvantageous comparisons, he exposes himself to it at every moment. He seeks every means to connect his poem with that of Homer;

he imitates the chief incidents, and causes the personages to live again. Hector is re-born in the words of
Andromache; Diomedes is found again in Southern
Italy, and does not want much pressing in order to
talk of his old deeds; Ulysses is traced in the
enchanted palace of Circe, and in the isle of the
Cyclops, while Hecuba, Helen, and Priam are seen
once more during the last night of Ilium. For Virgil,
as for us, Homer was not only a great epic poet; he
was the Epos personified. So he must have deemed
himself happy to draw as near to him as possible, both
by the subject and the personages of his poem. And
this completes our understanding of his reasons for
choosing the legend of Æneas.

Was he right or wrong in doing so? May it be said,
with certain critics, that in the *Æneid* the choice of
the subject has prejudiced the success of the work—
that a poem whose hero was a foreigner and a stranger
was doomed in advance never to become popular and
national? After the long study just read, the reply to
this seems easy. Doubtless the legend of Æneas is of
Greek origin; but we have seen that it soon became
acclimatised in Rome, that it took a Roman colouring
by its mixture with the legends of the country, and,
finally, that the State, far from combating, at an early
date officially adopted it. When Virgil took possession
of it, it had been related by the historians and sung by
the poets for more than two centuries. We cannot
then regard it as one of those frivolous fables which the
poet invents at his fancy, and pretend that Æneas, son
of Venus, was as indifferent to Romans of the Augustan
epoch as was Francus, son of Hector, to Frenchmen of
the sixteenth century.

Does this mean that it was as popular in Rome as the stories of Achilles and Ulysses were in Greece? To suppose this were to forget the radical differences between the two countries. In the Greek cities the disdain for foreigners, the dominating passion of the Hellenes, maintains the race in its purity. There may be diversities of rank and fortune between the citizens; but they have all the same origin. The national traditions are a treasure belonging to all, and which none allow to be lost. The poet who undertakes to celebrate them is understood by every one; he sings for the poor and for the rich, for the lettered and for the ignorant; and when he succeeds, his success is truly popular, since there is no one in the whole nation who does not take pleasure in listening to him. It could not be thus in a city like Rome, formed of a mixture of different races. A population constantly renewing itself, and composed of heterogeneous elements, has few common traditions, and quickly forgets them. I suppose that the plebeians, whose recollections did not go back very far, knew indeed but little about all these ancient fables collected by the learned, and that they left them very indifferent. Nor was it for them that Virgil wrote. He knew that he would have lost his time, and that it was not possible to interest the entire people from base to summit in his work, as could be done in the case of the Greeks. He only addressed the enlightened classes—the noble by birth or fortune, the upper citizen circles, and persons of education. All these people — some from aristocratic vanity and others in order to imitate those above them—willingly recurred to the past. They preserved its memory and liked to hear it spoken of. It is in this class of society that Virgil was popular; and as it was educated, so it had read the Homeric poems, and knew the *Annales* of Ennius and the works of the Latin chroniclers, therefore the legend of Æneas was quite familiar to it. In choosing it for the subject of his poem, Virgil was certain neither to surprise nor displease the public for whom he wrote.

II.

ÆNEAS IN SICILY.

IT would be a very charming journey to accompany Æneas from Troy to Laurentum, *viâ* Thrace, the Cyclades, Crete, and Epirus, stopping at Carthage to receive the hospitality of Dido. But, unfortunately, everybody has neither the time nor the means to undertake so long a jaunt, and one must know how to limit oneself. Furthermore, these ports and isles are for Æneas merely stages where he touches, and Virgil does not take the trouble to describe them. He scarcely tells us anything even of Africa itself, where his hero remains longer than he ought to do. This is not the true country of the *Æneid;* we must reserve this title for Sicily and Italy. Those are the lands known and loved by the poet, whither he likes to lead Æneas, and which he is happy in describing. We are about to try and go over them with him.

I.

HOW VIRGIL CAME TO KNOW SICILY—POLLION COUNSELS
HIM TO IMITATE THEOCRITUS—BY WHAT QUALITIES
THEOCRITUS MUST HAVE PLEASED VIRGIL — THE
MORETUM—WHY VIRGIL DID NOT CONTINUE TO
WRITE REALISTIC POEMS—SICILY IN THE *BUCOLICS.*

We learn from Virgil's biography that he was very
fond of Campania and Sicily, and that he often lived
there.   Born at the foot of the Alps, where the winters
are often rainy and rough, he doubtless felt the kind of
instinct which impels people of the north towards
southern countries.   Perhaps he found, too, that warm
climates better suited his health, which was always bad.
He did not like Rome, although he possessed a house
on the Esquiline, near the palace of Mæcenas.   It was
too noisy and busy a town for him, and he could only
write amid calm and silence.   In order to give the last
touch to his *Georgics*, he ran away to Naples; and when
the *Æneid* was in question, he felt it necessary to go
further still.   We are told that he composed a part of it
in Sicily.

He probably owed his first revelations with regard to
Sicily to the idylls of Theocritus, and learned from them
to know and love it.   Well, we know at what moment
and in what manner his attention was first drawn to
the Sicilian poet.   He was twenty-five years old,
and lived on the farm of his father, a well-to-do
peasant, who had given him the education of a great

lord. He had returned thither after the conclusion of his studies, and probably did not think of leaving it again. While he was leading an indolent, dreamy existence in that beautiful country "where the Mincius rolls its lazy course," poetry fermented in him, and sought an outlet. His imagination, still imperfectly regulated, drew him in every direction. He seemed not to know himself, and could not settle. Sometimes he composed little occasional pieces on the trivial events spoken of round about him; at others he raised his voice, and, passing from one extreme to the other, sketched the beginning of an epic. The verses he wrote thus at haphazard were read to his friends, and made him a certain reputation in the neighbourhood. Pollion then governed Cisalpine Gaul. He was a clever man, who devoted his leisure to history and poetry, and always delighted to patronise literature. He doubtless divined the young man's talent, and regretting the indecision in which so fine a genius was tarrying, he resolved to put him in a regular way, and pointed out a model for him to follow.

That model was Theocritus, whom the Romans seem hitherto to have neglected. The study of Theocritus charmed Virgil so much that for at least three years he did nothing but imitate him. Although no ancient critic has told us by what qualities this author must have chiefly pleased him, it does not seem to me difficult to guess. I imagine that in this confusion of his first years, when the component elements of his genius were not yet united and welded together, he must have felt two different tendencies drawing him in contrary directions. He had, in fact, received two different educations, whose impress he kept to the end. Nature had first been the master whose lessons had charmed him, and whom he ever passionately loved. His childhood was passed in the fields, and for him who understands them, the fields are a school of nature and simplicity. They give a taste for the true, the artless, the sincere, and a hatred for the affected and the mannered. Such must have been the lesson learnt from this first contemplation of Nature, and which remained at the very root of his talent. But he also began early the study of books. At Cremona, at Milan, at Rome, he frequented the scholiasts, the rhetoricians, and the philosophers, and he also became acquainted with Greek literature, reading Homer, Socrates, and Plato. It was another intoxication, and his soul, which felt nothing by halves, gave itself up entirely to this admirable poetry. The masters charged with the explanations of its beauties were generally ingenious, refined minds, who above all sought to imbue their pupils with a feeling for its delicacy and grace—that is to say, for its literary merits. Virgil, like a docile pupil, prized these charming qualities highly, yet without losing sight of the others; and it was doubtless from the two educations which he had successively received that he imbibed both the sentiment of the simple grandeur which rural life teaches us to love, and the more artificial beauties learnt in the schools; that, in short, he became an artist and remained a countryman.

If, as I think, he was in this frame of mind when he read Theocritus, I am not surprised that he should have been so impressed by him; for it is just this quality of uniting Art and Nature which the Sicilian poet possesses in a wonderful degree.[1]

At heart he is an exquisite, a friend of the poets of Alexandria; mused, like them, "in the aviary of the Muses;" but this does not prevent him from choosing as the usual heroes of his verses goat-herds and drovers. To descend to them while remaining himself does not cost him an effort. He makes them sing under the great trees, "while harmonious bees hum around the hives, the birds warble under the leaves, and the heifers dance on the thick turf,"[2] and their songs have at one and the same time a rustic accent and all the refinements of laborious art. They sometimes coarsely attack each other; like villagers, they revile their masters, they insult their rivals; and all this abuse is composed of the most exquisite sounds, which sing to the ear like music. It is a succession of complicated rhythms, that, calling and answering each other, contrast and combine according to learned laws, of which a herdsman certainly never had an idea. The shepherds of Theocritus are generally simple, superstitious, credulous folk, who spit three times in their bosoms to escape witchcraft,[3] and who think their mistress is about to return when they feel a twitching in their right eye.[4] But they are also artists who understand and who enumerate all the beauties of a vase whose sides are covered with delicate carving, and skilful singers, who draw harmonious sounds from the syrinx, and who find "that summer and springtime

---

[1] On Theocritus, see M. Girard's two studies in the *Revue des Deux Mondes* of March 15th and May 1st, 1882. M. Couat also treats of the Sicilian poet in his *Poesie Alexandrine.*

[2] VI. 45. [3] VI. 39 [4] III. 31.

are not so sweet as the Muse."[1] All are amorous, yet their manner of loving is not the same. While some impress their passion in a few words of deep and simple truth, others describe it with ingenious refinement, like clever people on their guard, as one had to be in the court of Ptolemy or Hieron. When deserted by their mistresses, some moan and complain gently, as becomes well-bred people, while others are less enduring and less proper. There are even some who unceremoniously give the faithless one a blow on the nape of the neck, soon followed by a second.[2] There is the same variety in their pleasures. One thinks it the greatest bliss of all to watch in winter the beech log burning on the hearth, and "the smoking tripe cooking on the fire." Others are not so easily satisfied ; they are only pleased when couched on thick beds of odorous mastic or new-cut vine, while the poplars and young elm-trees wave above their heads, and a sacred stream flowing from a nymph-haunted grot harmoniously murmurs at their feet. To bring together and unite these contrary elements required all the suppleness of the Greek genius; but no poet ever so perfectly blended them as Theocritus. With him all contrasts are merged in the charm of light and shade enveloping the whole. From his entire work, composed of such different parts, results a singular impression, which gives to the refined the illusion of Nature, and enables the simple to define the seduction of Art. Virgil, as we have just seen, was both. He loved Art and Nature equally, and found in Theocritus the wherewithal to gratify both his passions

---

[1] IX. 28. [2] XIV. 34.

at once. This is why he was so happy to read and so eager to imitate him.

Among the works attributed to him is a piece one would fain think his, since it is very charming, and seems to have been composed in his youth. It is a picture of country life, very different in character from those he drew in the *Bucolics*. Here his only aim is to paint exactly a vulgar truth. It is what in our days we should call a realistic piece. Although very ancient, it seems composed according to all the rules of the new school. The author has not been prodigal of invention or style; he merely contents himself with reproducing what he has before his eyes, without pretending to change anything. He describes the morning of a peasant, from the moment he rises to the hour he goes to work. Let us first remark that the man is not called Tityrus or Menalcus, as in an idyll, but " the flat-nosed " (*Simulus*), which is quite a Roman name.[1] We see him slowly rise from his couch. The night is black, and, half asleep, he gropes with his hands before him towards the hearth. When he gets to it he says, " Here I am." Then he lights his lamp with all kinds of precautions, " stretching his hand towards the east wind to prevent the light going out." He soon wakes an only servant, an old negress, of whom he draws us a striking portrait. " She has frizzled hair, a thick lip, a large bosom, hanging breasts, a flat stomach, thin legs, and a foot which spreads at ease : "—

> " *Pectore lata, jacens mammis, compressior alvo,*
> *Cruribus exilis, spatiosa prodiga planta.*"

---

[1] When speaking of a flat-nosed girl, Lucretius calls her " *Simula.*"

'Helped by his servant, Simulus bakes his bread, and prepares the dish which he is to carry away for his dinner. It is a national dish called *moretum*, from which our poem takes its name. The author is careful to give us the recipe, which does not much tempt us to imitate it. It consists of garlic, onion, celery, rue, and cheese. All these ingredients are put into a mortar, and while Simulus pounds them, an acid odour seizes his nostrils, his brows wrinkle, and anon with his hands he wipes his weeping eyes. When the pestle no longer jumps, he passes his two fingers round the mortar, in order to bring to the centre what covers the sides. The operation finished, he puts on his strong boots, claps his *galerus* upon his head, goes out to his work—and here our little poem ends.

The work is piquant and curious in its rusticity; nor would it surprise me if, with our present bent and the taste prevalent among the public, it were at the present time preferred to the *Bucolics*. It will certainly be asked why Virgil, supposing him to be its author, did not continue to describe country life in this manner? Why did he change his method, and having begun to walk in a new path, abruptly leave it to follow in the steps of Theocritus? We must believe him less satisfied than ourselves with his work, and that these servilely exact pictures did not appear to him the perfection of art. Perhaps he thought that our every-day existence being usually so mediocre and flat, it is really not worth while to live it twice—in reality and in dreamland! Being sad by nature and inclined to look at things from their worst side, to escape for a moment from real life seemed to him sweet; and he must have clung more than any one to that imaginary existence in which we can at least correct the miseries of the other, and find help to bear them. The perusal of Theocritus revealed to him a kind of literature in which reality is spiced with a flavouring of the ideal. This was what suited his tastes, and thenceforth he knew no other.

Here, then, he is plunged into imitation of the Greek poet. At the same time his Muse must become in some sort expatriated and wander from the spots it first frequented. Tityrus and Menalcus cannot, like Simulus, be dwellers on the banks of the Po ; for never did such shepherds lead their flocks in the plains of Cisalpina. In order to admit their being, it is needful to imagine them to have come from far. Theocritus places them in Sicily, an admirable country in which to house fancies partaking at once of reality and the ideal. Virgil had nought better to do than to leave them there. Sicily therefore became for him the land above all others of the eclogue, and at times even Arcadia scarcely disputes with it this privilege. When he wants to draw shepherds playing on the syrinx and making rustic songs, he dreams of Sicily. The land enthralls his fancy ; it is everywhere recurring in his verses, and when about to sing new songs, the Muse he invokes is a Sicilian one :

" *Sicelides Musæ, paulo majora canamus.*" [1]

Rural poetry calls up in him the memory of Syracuse, and he begins his last eclogue by saluting the

---

[1] *Æn.*, IV. 1.

charming fountain of Ortygia, of which poets relate so many legends :

> "*Extremum hunc, Arethusa, mihi concede laborem.*" [1]

When Corydon wishes to dazzle his friend by a picture of his wealth, he renders him an account of his sheep which feed on the pastures of Sicily :

> "*Mille meœ siculis erant in montibus agnœ.*" [2]

Although suspected of being a Cisalpian, and of scarcely ever having quitted Mantua, he tells us, like Polyphemus, that he has seen his form in the placid sea, and did not find himself ugly :

> "*Nec sum adeo informis ; nuper me in littore vidi.*
> *Quum placidum ventis staret mare.*" [3]

That sea, let us doubt not, is the one in which the heights of Taorminus or the slopes of Ætna are seen to sparkle in the sun—the sea spoken of in those divine verses of the shepherd of Theocritus : " I crave not to possess the fields of Pelops, or pile up heaps of gold ; nor would I fly more swiftly than the winds ; but may 'neath this rock but hold thee in mine arms, and, looking on my feeding sheep, launch forth my songs towards Sicilia's sea." [4]

---

[1] *Æn.*, X. 1.   [2] *Ibid.*, II. 21.
[3] *Ibid.*, II. 25.   [4] *Ibid.*, VIII. 53.

II.

SICILY IN VIRGIL'S TIME—CHARACTER OF THE GREEKS OF SICILY—WHY THEY WERE ATTACHED TO ROMAN RULE—SICILY RUINED AND PILLAGED BY ROMAN GOVERNORS—WHAT TRAVELLERS WENT TO SEEK IN SICILY—MARVELS OF NATURE—MARVELS OF ART—THE MONUMENTS OF THAT TIME—PUBLIC TEMPLES PRIVATE GALLERIES—SHRINE OF HEIUS—TASTE OF THE ROMANS OF THAT TIME FOR WORKS OF ART—THE PORTRAIT OF VERRES DRAWN BY CICERO—ATTRACTIONS OF SICILY FOR VIRGIL.

It was thus Virgil became acquainted with Sicily, and as he at first only knew it from the idylls of Theocritus, it was difficult for him not to become enraptured with it. We must believe that when later on he visited it himself, his pleasure was as intense, and that the reality confirmed all his dream illusions. Sicily is one of these beautiful countries where deceptions are not to be feared, and which fulfil everything that is expected of them.

We have the somewhat rare good fortune to know approximately in what condition Virgil must have found it. As a rule, the condition of Roman provinces is but little known. Nobody tells us of them, all eyes being turned towards the capital, from which they are not wont to be diverted towards the surrounding country. But in consequence of a certain event some years previous to the Augustan epoch, general attention was for a moment fixed on Sicily. A great lord who ruled it in the name of the Roman people, having as usual treated it very harshly, the Sicilians attacked him before the tribunals of Rome. They were supported by the democratic party, who wished, in the person of the extortionate prætor, to discredit all his caste, and Cicero was charged to prosecute him. Causes of this kind were very common at the time, and once decided, they were soon forgotten. Thanks to the orator's talent, that of Verres became immortal. The orations of Cicero have fortunately been preserved, and they abound in curious details on the condition of Sicily. Let us draw from this inexhaustible source, and ascertain what it was at that moment, and the effect it must have produced on Romans who went to visit it.

We are told, to start with, that although the population of Sicily was very mixed, one of the elements composing it had nearly absorbed all the others, and that a single tongue—the Greek—ruled in the entire island. The Romans were surprised to see that the Greeks of this country did not quite resemble those they met elsewhere. They had, like their countrymen, much delicacy and charm of mind as well as their taste for argument, and, above all, their liking for raillery. "In their greatest trials," says Cicero, "they always find some occasion to jest."[1] But they were also sober and laborious, two qualities not met with in a like degree among the inhabitants of Greece proper or the Greeks of Asia.[2] Cicero adds that the Roman domination had been well received by them. They willingly associated with the merchants of Rome who brought

---

[1] II., *Verr.*, IV. 43.   [2] *Ibid.*, II. 3.

them their capital and their industry, and they worked
their lands conjointly with them, as they afterwards
did their vines and their sulphur with Germans and
Englishmen. This does not mean that they had a
particular liking for the Romans, but that they felt
it impossible to do without them. They reckoned on
their help to escape a danger from which they could
not defend themselves alone. The cultivation of cereals
was the great industry of Sicily, and the peasantry
having become scarce there as elsewhere, it was
necessary to replace them by slaves. We know that
rich persons possessed several thousand. These slaves
were not settled in the villages or scattered over the
farms, as field labourers are with us, since Sicily could
not then possess more villages and isolated farms than
she does in our days. They were assembled in great
troops, like those labourers we see perform the sowing
or the harvest in the plains of Southern Italy. Ill-fed,
ill-clad, hardly treated, they were led to work by
villici, who must have borne a strong likeness to the
caporali of to-day. They worked with shackled feet, and
during the daytime the superintendence of the *villicus*
prevented them from communicating with each other.
But at night, in their temporary camps, it was easy
for them to concert together. It is thus that, within
a few years, two revolts broke out which terrified the
world. A Syrian and a Cilician, at the head of more
than sixty thousand herdsmen and labourers, were seen
holding Roman generals in check, devastating the
provinces, and spilling the blood of freemen in torrents.
From that moment the Sicilians lived in a sort of
perpetual terror. Laws were made forbidding slaves

ever to carry arms about them, on pain of death, and
these laws were observed with the utmost rigour.
"One day," says Cicero, "an enormous boar was
brought to Domitius the prætor. Surprised at the
animal's size, he wanted to know who had killed it.
They told him the shepherd of a Sicilian, and he
ordered him to be sent for. The shepherd came in
haste, expecting praise and rewards. Domitius asked
how he had slain this formidable beast. 'With a boar-
spear,' he replied. And instantly the prætor had him
put on the cross."[1] To this ever-menacing scourge,
another had of late years been added. Fleets of pirates
from Cilicia covered the Mediterranean. Their light
vessels passed through the squadrons sent to watch
them, and laughed at the heavy Roman galleys. One
day they were seen to enter in bravado the port of
Syracuse itself, and after going the round of the quays,
quietly leave it, without anybody daring to follow
them.[2] Against all these dangers the Sicilians needed
the support of Rome, and thus, since the Punic Wars,
they had always shown themselves submissive subjects.
They were continually paying court to their conquerors,
and Cicero remarks, with some surprise, that many
among them took Roman names, which appeared to
show a desire to renounce their ancient nationality and
accept that of their new masters.[3] The two races were

---

[1] II., *Verr.*, V. 3.

[2] *Ibid.*, V. 37.

[3] *Ibid.*, V. 43. It was Antony who, after the death of Cæsar, gave
the right of Roman citizenship to all Sicily. He pretended to have
found the decree, which he published in the Dictator's papers; but
Cicero thinks the Sicilians had paid him to fabricate it.

therefore beginning to mix together, and that assimilation of Sicily with Italy which in our time has become so complete was already in preparation.

Not that Rome always afforded the Sicilians very efficacious protection. She sometimes chose to govern it people who performed their functions very badly, and who pillaged those they should have defended. Verres, by keeping for himself the money destined for the support of the fleet, and by placing it under the command of his mistress's husband, whose incapacity as an admiral equalled his marital complacency, had delivered it to the pirates. He himself, during the two years of his prætorship, had only been solicitous to fill his coffers and his galleries. He had put up all the municipal offices of the province for sale, had made the peasantry pay twice as much as they ought, and, under pretence of imaginary crimes, had confiscated the fortunes of the richest and most distinguished persons. "Sicily," said Cicero, "is to-day so enfeebled and forlorn, that she will never more regain her ancient prosperity."[1] This was a prediction, and it was accomplished to the letter. The Empire doubtless gave to Sicily, as to the rest of the world, peace without and security within. For nearly three centuries the pirates were no longer heard of. There were a few more revolts of slaves—for example, that of Selurus, who was called "the son of Ætna," because he for a long time overran and devastated the environs of that mountain. Strabo saw him devoured alive by the beasts in the great circus of Rome, after a combat of

---

[1] *Verr.*, I.

gladiators. "They put him," he says, "on a very high scaffolding representing Ætna. Suddenly the scaffolding came to pieces and fell in, and he was hurled into the midst of cages filled with wild beasts that had been placed beneath."[1] As we see, these attempts were vigorously repressed, and they never assumed the terrible character of those of Eunus and Athenion. Yet, in spite of the calm enjoyed by the province under the Empire, it never recovered.[2] Is it not strange that the peace, which it had so longed for and so little known, could not give it back for a moment that prosperity, that brilliancy, that intensity of life, that glory of letters and of arts, which had favoured it so wonderfully while struggling amidst fearful disorders?

There happily remained to it what it held from nature, and nothing could take away: the riches of an inexhaustible soil, in a small space an astonishing variety of sites, picturesque mountains, wastes well outlined, and a climate of admirable serenity which struck even Italians with surprise. " It is affirmed," said Cicero, "that at Syracuse there is no day so dull but the sun shines some few moments."[3] Add to this all those volcanic phenomena so complacently mentioned by Strabo, and which excited wonder in proportion to the impossibility of explaining them : those burning fountains gushing from the earth; those

---

[1] Strabo, VI. 2-5.

[2] The Emperors seem to have become discouraged from busying themselves about Sicily. It is one of the few provinces where no milestones, so frequent elsewhere, have been found, which seems to show that there were no great highways, or that they were not kept in repair by the public authorities. See Mommsen's reflections on the subject (*Corp. insc. lat.*, X. p. 714).

[3] II., *Verr.*, V. 10.

mountains flinging torrents of fire or mud; those
flames running capriciously over the waters; those
islands rising suddenly from the sea and sinking into
it again; in short, all those extraordinary sights which,
their reasons being unknown, were accounted for by
legends, and gave Sicily the reputation of being a land
of wonders.

But it was not this which chiefly attracted travellers.
The author of a poem on Ætna complains that people
trouble themselves but little to admire the great
sights of Nature, whilst they traverse countries, cross
seas, and give themselves a thousand pains for the
sake of contemplating celebrated pictures or old
monuments.[1] So the curious went to Agrigentum or
Syracuse, as they went to Athens or Corinth, to visit
the masterpieces of Greek art. It is certain that their
expectation was not deceived, and that they did not
regret their journey. Let us remember that all those
buildings whose ruins astonish us, although we have only
their skeletons left, were then intact and complete.
The temples still had their pediments and sculptured
friezes; the wind and the rain had not worn the fluting
of the columns. These were covered with a coating of
stucco strong enough to protect them, yet sufficiently
thin not to appear heavy, like those transparent
draperies which so perfectly show the forms of ancient
statues. The Metopes produced their full effect, placed
above columns in the very spot for which they had
been made, instead of being ranged along the walls of
a museum, as we see them to-day. It must be added

---

[1] *Ætna,* 563, *et seq.*

that all this Doric architecture, which seems to us so majestic and so grave, was then set off and brightened, as it were, by colours long since effaced by time. · It is now known that the Greeks used to apply to marble and stucco paintings which at first served to correct the crudeness of the natural tones, and later, as the monuments grew old, prevented them from assuming those varieties of tint so destructive to the unity of the whole. Let us make an effort of the imagination, and strive to picture to ourselves the aspect those fine edifices must have presented. The great exterior parts are usually painted light yellow, a colour less dazzling in the sun and less crude than white, which comes out better against the clouds, and contrasts more pleasantly with the verdure. On this uniform ground the decorative details are picked out in livelier tints. The triglyphs are painted blue, the background of the Metopes and the pediments red, while the columns spring lightly from a darker basement. Sometimes delicately traced lines indicate the jointing of the stones. Pliny, speaking of a temple of Cyzicus, says that " the gold seemed only a pencil-mark as fine as a hair," and that " nevertheless it produced marvellous reflections." Towards the top, along the friezes and above them, the ornaments are more numerous, and the colours more varied and lively, as if to form a sort of crown to the edifice.[1] So much for the outside. We

---

[1] I here use M. Hittorff's ideas, and often his very expressions. As is well known, it was he who, not without raising violent disputes, first maintained that Greek monuments were covered with colours, and it was his studies on the temples of Segestes and Selinonte which revealed this truth to him. His great work, *The Ancient Archi-*

see how greatly it differed then from what it is to-day.
As for the interior, we have nothing left of it. The
walls of the *cella*—that is to say, of the very dwelling of
the god—have disappeared almost everywhere, and this
is a great pity, for they were often covered with fine
paintings. At Syracuse, in the temple of Minerva,
there were a series of pictures representing the
incidents of a cavalry battle fought by Agathocles.
" There is not," says Cicero, " a picture more famous, or
which attracts a larger number of strangers."[1] In the
same temple they also went to see sculptured doors, as
we visit those of Ghiberti, at Florence. They were considered an admirable work, and critics of Greek art had
composed many treatises to set forth their beauties.
What appeared more curious yet was to see ranged
along the walls the gifts that had been offered to the
gods. Pliny the Younger relates that, having received
an inheritance, he had ventured to purchase a statuette
of Corinthian bronze, representing an old man, standing,
which seemed to him a fine work. " I do not mean to
keep it for myself," he tells us. " I wish to offer it to
Como, my birthplace, and place it there in some frequented place, preferably in the Temple of Jupiter. It
is a gift which seems to me worthy of a temple, worthy
of a god." In truth, fine statues are not out of place

---

lecture of Sicily, which he left incomplete, was finished by his son,
M. Chas. Hittorff, and published in 1870. M. Chas. Hittorff sought to
efface himself before his father, of whom he was a most devoted fellow-
worker, and would not put his name to the first page ; but this filial
piety must not deprive him of the share of credit justly due to him for
his part in a common work.

[1] II., *Verr.*, IV. 55.

there, even when they do not represent the divinity one
comes to pray to; but there was much besides. Only
to speak of the temples of Sicily, Cicero reports that
tables of marble were seen there, bronze vases, ingots of
gold, with ivory tusks of extraordinary size; and hanging from the walls were helmets and cuirasses tastefully
wrought, as well as wooden pikes, which had doubtless
served the ancient kings of the country as sceptres.[1]
The temples, then, were not merely museums, as has
been often said, but genuine storehouses of curiosities.

It must have sometimes been difficult for the inex-
perienced traveller to find his way in the midst of all
these heaped-up riches. Happily he could apply to
zealous and obliging persons, whose race is not extinct
in Italy, and who made it their profession to guide
strangers and make them admire the ancient monuments. They were called " mystagogues " or *periegetes*.
There were many of them in Sicily, as well as in all
Greek countries visited by the curious, and Cicero
describes them as very much perplexed after Verres had
cleared out all the temples. He says: " Being no longer
able to show the precious objects, they were reduced to
pointing out the places they used to occupy,"[2] which is
not quite the same thing.

Independent of the public monuments, gymnasiums,
theatres, or temples, which contained so many remarkable works, there were in Sicily many galleries belonging to private persons, which strangers were permitted to visit, as is still the case in Rome and

---

[1] II., *Verr.*, IV. 56.   [2] *Ibid.*, IV. 59.

other important towns in Italy. Cicero speaks of many of these rich collections, which, to their misfortune, excited the covetousness of the Verres. But there are two which he especially praises: that of Stenius, at *Thermæ Himerenses* (now Termini), and that of Heius, at Messina. It had occurred to Heius to bring together the masterpieces of his gallery in a room expressly arranged for the purpose, a thing that was done long afterwards in the Tribuna of Florence, and is being imitated in nearly all the museums of Europe. He possessed a little chapel, very quiet, very retired, with altars before which to pray to the gods, and had adorned it only with four statues, four marvels: the Cupid of Praxiteles, the bronze Hercules of Myron, and two canephoræ of Polycletes. The Cupid had made the journey to Rome. The ædile, C. Claudius, had borrowed it of his friend Heius to embellish a festival which he gave to the Roman people. This was told without fail to visitors, just as, in our days, the value of a picture is thought to be increased by relating that it was among those taken away by the French, and placed in the Louvre. The chapel of Heius was open every day, and strangers who visited Messina did not fail to go and see it. "This house," says Cicero, "did no less honour to the town than to its master."

So people went to visit Sicily then for the same reasons that they go now. Above all, she attracted artists, connoisseurs, or those who deemed themselves such, and admirers of Greek art, who knew her to be at the least as rich in ancient monuments as Greece or Asia. The journey was doubtless not so convenient and rapid as to-day, although perhaps easier to perform than it was a few years since. Cicero states that when he had to draw up the indictment against Verres, he went over the whole island in fifty days, " so as to collect all the complaintsof the towns and private persons,"[1] which supposes somewhat easy means of getting from place to place. And indeed many Romans visited Sicily. In the *Verrines*, every time the orator speaks of some important city, or of some famous monument, he seems to suppose that there are persons among his audience who know them.

This is precisely what excites in us a certain surprise. We are astonished that there should be so many people at Rome who took the trouble to go so far to see fine buildings and rich museums. The Romans had long ostentatiously pretended to have a sovereign contempt for the arts, and officiating magistrates and orators who desired to appear serious affected never to have heard of the great artists of Greece. But this was a comedy. In reality the very men who took pleasure in mangling the names of Praxiteles or Polycletes in the tribune were beginning to pay very high prices for their works, and at Rome a middle-sized bronze had just been sold for 120,000 sesterces (or about £960), the price of a farm.[2] Verres happened to be one of those Romans whom Greek art had captivated; but as he put himself above prejudices, and prided himself on not practising the ancient virtues, he had the courage to own his tastes, and was not squeamish as to gratifying them. His being sent to Sicily was a great misfortune for him. The sight of the masterpieces of which that country

---

[1] *Verr., prima act.*, 2.

[2] II., *Verr.* IV. 7.

was full inflamed his passion and goaded it to every
excess. I imagine that, before our tribunals, the kind of
fury that had seized him for objects of art would have
earned him some indulgence,—at Rome, on the contrary, it contributed greatly to his ruin. Had he contented himself with taking the money of the provincials,
he would have created less scandal, since it was then a
very common crime, and people were used to it; but to
see a Roman compromise himself so for the sake of
stealing statues and pictures was not at all a usual
thing, and indignation was increased by surprise. So
extraordinary a crime seemed unworthy of pardon.

The portrait drawn by Cicero of Verres must be a faithful one, and I have remarked that certain details of the
figure have not ceased to be true. It is an original of
which we have copies. It is not enough to say that he
had a taste for works of art—he had a mania for them.
Cicero reports that a few days before his suit was tried,
he assisted at a feast given by Sisenna, a rich Roman,
and in order to do honour to the guests, all the curiosities possessed by the master were brought out. Verres
had a great object in appearing indifferent to this sight,
since it was important for him to hide his folly in order
not to prove his accusers in the right. But it was
impossible for him not to approach these paraded
riches, to see them nearer, to touch them, to handle
them—to the great fright of the slaves, who knew his
reputation, and did not lose sight of him.[1] When an
object pleased him, he could no longer do without it—
desire of possession became mania. He asked to take it

---

[1] II., *Verr.*, IV. 15.

away for a few days and did not return it. Often he proposed to buy it, and at first the owner refused. "The Greeks," says Cicero, "never willingly sell the precious objects they possess."[1]   But Verres was absolute master of the province, and had a thousand means of ruining those who did not show themselves willing to oblige him. After begging, he threatened, and the poor wretches ended by resigning themselves, groaning all the while. This is how he came to give only 6500 sesterces (about £52) for four fine statues, and to pay 1600 sesterces (about £12, 16s.) for the Cupid of Praxiteles.[2]   It was a manifest theft; but Verres only called it a bargain. This is a good word to disguise a doubtful business, and collectors like to use it. Nothing pleases them so much as not to pay its proper price for a thing. They thus at one and the same time gratify their love of economy and their vanity. When it was a question of despoiling the public monuments, Verres met with still less resistance. They were more directly under his hand, besides which each of us is usually less eager to defend what belongs to all. Once, however, he was obliged to give way. His agents arrived by night in Agrigentum to take away a statue of Hercules, honoured by the inhabitants with a particular worship. "The chin and lips," says Cicero, "were quite worn away with its adorers' kisses."[3] Unfortunately for Verres, the slaves who guarded the temple gave the alarm, and the Agrigentines assembled from all quarters of the town, and put the robbers to flight with stones.

---

[1] II., *Verr.*, IV. 59.   [2] *Ibid.*, 6.   [3] *Ibid.*, 43.

But he was not accustomed to find himself face to
face with such determined adversaries, so he had no
need to restrain his passion, which had indeed nothing
to hamper it. He not only sought after statues of
bronze or marble, Corinthian vases, famous pictures—
all those objects, in short, which the curious contended
for at immense prices—his mania included everything.
He also collected jewels, carpets, furniture, and plate.
All the rich families of Sicily possessed *patera*, incense
pans, and precious vases used in the worship of their
domestic divinities. When Verres had the discretion
not to take them, he at least removed the metal
ornaments in which they were enclosed, and which were
generally remarkable works of art. Then he fixed these
ornaments on gold cups, and thus manufactured sham
antiques. At Syracuse there were studios where skilful
artificers worked for him, and there he passed entire
days, dressed in a brown tunic and a Greek mantle.[1]
This is again a very common fancy among collectors.
They imagine that by these repairs and restorations—
by allowing themselves to finish and modify the works
of the masters, they become their collaborators, and
their love increases for works into which they have put
something of themselves.

Cicero adds, as a last touch to the picture, that
Verres was at bottom very ignorant, and little capable
of appreciating all these works of art which he
amassed. He had at his orders very experienced Greek
artists, whose duty it was to inform him. " He sees with
their eyes," says Cicero, "and takes by their hands." [2]

---

[1] II., *Verr.*, IV. 23.   [2] *Ibid.*, IV. 15.

Amateurs are not always connoisseurs, which, however, does not prevent them from passionately loving objects whose full value they do not understand; for it is well known that the least enlightened passions are sometimes the strongest. That of Verres was increased by the spice of violence and coarseness usually existent in the Roman soul. They were still soldiers and peasants. Greece had not succeeded in destroying the foundation of barbarism and brutality derived from nature, and they still occasionally united outbursts of savagery with the delicate tastes of civilized beings. Let us suppose an amateur of this character to possess unlimited authority, that he is in a conquered country with submissive subjects at his feet, and assiduous flatterers around him; he will soon lose his head and think everything allowed him. It was this intoxication of absolute power in an odious nature, joined to an unwholesome admixture of the Roman and the Greek, which, under the Empire, produced Nero. Verres was a sketch for Nero under the Republic.

Happily for Sicily, the Romans who came to settle there were not all like Verres. To return at last to Virgil, whom we have left too long, there is no doubt that he also was sensible of the beauties of Greek art. Let us be assured that he did not pass through such towns as Selinus, Agrigentum, or Syracuse without lively emotion. He certainly visited their theatres and their temples, and admired the statues and pictures remaining in them after the thefts of the terrible prætor: but he, at least, was content to admire. We may believe that the memory of the monuments he has seen in Sicily recurred to his thoughts when he had to describe similar edifices. Has he not Agrigentum or Segesta in mind when he talks to us of those temples "that rise upon an ancient rock, with pinnacles upborne by a hundred columns"?[1] Does not his mind go back to the rich colouring to which I alluded just now when he describes those magnificent roofs sparkling with gold (*aurea tecta*)?[2] Yet I am tempted to think that having come to Sicily chiefly to seek repose, he was still more touched by the charms of the climate and the beauties of nature. I imagine that he must have chosen somewhere in a pleasant place, on these mountains sloping to the sea, a solitary dwelling where he could work without distraction at his great epic. Sicily had for him the merit of recalling Greece. While still young, he had expressed in celebrated verses the happiness he should feel in traversing the beautiful valleys of Thessaly or of Thrace, and in seeing the young Spartan maidens bound on the heights of Taygeta :

> *"O ubi campi*
> *Sperchiusque, et virginibus baccata Lacænis*
> *Taygeta !"*[3]

It is most astonishing that he should not have undertaken this longed-for journey till the last year of his life. Probably Sicily inspired him with patience —Sicily was Greece too, but a Greece nearer to him, more within his reach, and, above all, almost Italian. This was for Virgil a great reason for loving it. Indeed he makes great efforts to join it to Italy entirely. He

---

[1] *Æn.*, III. 84 : " *Saxo structa vetusto* " ; VII. 170 : " *Contum sublime columnis.*"

[2] *Ibid.*, VI. 13.   [3] *Georg.*, II. 487.

affirms that it originally formed part of Italy, and that in reality it belongs to the country, although Greek in appearance and in language. "These parts," he tells us, "were formerly shaken and overwhelmed by deep convulsions. The two lands formed but one, when the furious sea forced itself a passage between them and divided them with its waves. It was thus they became violently separated one from the other, and that a narrow channel ran between these towns and fields, formerly united."[1] Hence Virgil found himself authorised to confound them in his affection, and treat Sicily like the rest of Italy. The origin of the two countries being the same, he could well give it a place in the national poem, which was to contain all the traditions and all the glories of the Italian fatherland. This place, as we are about to see from his poem, was very large, and only Latium has a greater one. Sicily fills one entire Book of the *Æneid*, and nearly half of a second.

III.

THE THIRD BOOK OF THE *ÆNEID*—ÆNEAS IN EPIRUS—HE TOUCHES AT ITALY—TARENTUM—HE PASSES INTO SICILY—ÆTNA—THE ISLE OF ORTIGIA—THE FOUNTAIN OF ARETHUSA—AGRIGENTUM—WHAT VIRGIL'S FEELINGS MUST HAVE BEEN WHEN HE WENT OVER THE RUINS OF GREEK CITIES IN SICILY—DREPANUM—DEATH OF ANCHISES.

The Third Book of the *Æneid* shows us Æneas seeking a new abode. The poet tells us that after escaping

---

[1] *Æn.*, III. 414.

from Troy, he took refuge in the high valleys of Ida, where he passed a season in resting from his fatigues and preparing for his voyage. He then starts, without well knowing whither he is going. He has resolved to be guided by the oracles, but oracles, as we know, are not always very clear, and it is not easy to understand them. They advise Æneas to withdraw to Hesperia, that is to say, the regions of the west. This is a very vague expression, which shows him approximatively the direction he is to follow, but does not tell him the precise spot he must stop at. Even when the prophetess Cassandra talks to him about Latium and the Tiber, their names, quite unknown to an inhabitant of Asia Minor, do not teach him much. As for the other direction, that he must return to the land whence came his forefathers, it would have been necessary, in order that it should suffice him, for him to thoroughly know the history of his most remote ancestors, and we see that the memory of them was lost. It is not surprising that having so imperfect a knowledge of the country whither the gods ordered him to go, he should have so often lost his way. Thus it happens that, after many mistakes, a wind sent by Providence blows him into the Adriatic, opposite Italy, and then impels him into the Gulf of Leucate; that is to say, to the very spot where the battle of Actium was fought. One might be tempted to think that Virgil had invented this incident, which allowed him to connect the fortunes of Æneas with those of Augustus. But this is not so, for the legend was much older than those of Augustus or Virgil, since Varro had related it. But of course the poet turns it to great account. He is happy to take the Trojan hero to the shores where his great descendant is to gain the victory that will make him master of the world, to show him to us stopping there with satisfaction, foreseeing confusedly, and by a kind of divination, the great destinies for which these places are reserved, and already celebrating with his followers games that seem to foreshadow and prepare those which the great Emperor will establish after the defeat of Antony.

From Actium Æneas repairs to Epirus, where he finds Andromache again, with Helenus, her new husband. Helenus is a very skilful seer, and as Æneas never misses an occasion to inquire the will of the gods, he takes great care to consult him. It is from him he learns with some clearness the road he must follow. The Fates order him to bear his gods into Italy, but the part of Italy in which he must settle is not that seen opposite Epirus. He must skirt the coasts of Calabria, "his oars must beat the waves of the Sicilian sea," he must visit Campania, and he must see closely the rock of Circe, before he can reach that peaceful shore where he is to fix his dwelling. This time Æneas is very clearly directed, and "when he spreads the wings of his sails to the breath of the winds," he knows where he is going and the road that will take him to the goal of his enterprise.

It is on this journey that we are about to follow him.

But, it may be asked, are these poetic fictions to be taken seriously? Must we accompany the hero of a legend step by step, try to find places to which he never went, and take the trouble to draw up a regular plan of his wanderings, as if real travels were in question? Why not? Ancient poets love to put reason into fancy, and give to fable the colouring of truth. When we read them, good sense has only a single concession to make. It must accept the fictitious personage presented to it, and the marvellous premises of the tale it is about to hear; that done, we enter the domain of reality, and do not leave it again. This imaginary hero will now, on the whole, only do reasonable things, and his existence will usually unfold itself under the ordinary conditions of human life. This manner of introducing truth into the legend, and satisfying imagination and good sense at the same time, is one of the greatest charms of ancient poetry. Let us then follow Æneas without repugnance, and be convinced that Virgil is about to describe perfectly real landscapes to us, and that the greater part of the time he will only depict what he has himself seen.

Æneas must first pass from the shores of Epirus to those of Italy. There is a narrow arm of the sea to cross, a few hours' passage, which would be mere child's play for a vessel of our days. But then pilots did not dare to leave the shore. We must see the precautions taken by the pilot of Æneas before risking himself amid the floods, and daring to lose sight of the land. " Night, led by the hours, had not yet reached the middle of the sky, when watchful Palinurus rises, inquires of all the winds, and lends his ear to the least breath. He observes the stars which glide through silent space: Arcturus, Hyades, the two Bears, Orion, with his sword of gold. Then, when he sees that all is calm in the tranquil sky, from the height of the poop he gives the signal of departure." [1] The voyage is accomplished

---

[1] *Æn.*, III. 512.

without accident.   At the first rays of morn, the Trojans see before them a promontory crowned by a temple, and at the foot of the hill a natural port open towards the east, where they shelter their ships.[1] Here it is that Æneas for the first time touches Italian soil. He piously salutes it, but, true to the orders received from Helenus, he only remains there a few hours, and then continues his way, skirting the coast.

"Then," he adds in his rapid recital, "we arrive at the entrance of the Gulf of Tarentum. From the other side rises the temple of Juno Sacinia; further on Gaulon and Squalan are seen, fruitful in wrecks."[2] That is all, and three lines suffice him to depict all the coast of Apulia and Calabria—that is to say, one of the most beautiful landscapes of Italy. I think it must have cost him something to be so moderate. Had he not resolved to sacrifice everything to the unity of his work, he would have found it difficult not to dwell with pleasure upon this beautiful land, and his Muse would willingly have lingered there awhile; but he belonged to a severe school, who made it a law to abridge needless descriptions. So he resigned himself to saying nothing of the famous cities that decked this coast; nothing of Sybaris, whose luxury was so renowned in antiquity; nothing of Crotona, where lived Pythagoras; nothing of Metapontum, where he died. He has only made an exception for Tarentum, and even here he only mentions its name, which is strange, if one remembers the im-

---

[1] The description is so exact that the place meant by Virgil was recognised without difficulty. It is the little village of Castro, a few leagues from Otranto, not far from the promontory of Japagia, now called Santa Maria di Leuca.

[2] Æn., III. 550.

portance it then had, and the place it held in the life
of some rich Romans. Tarentum had become one of
the summer haunts they preferred, although it had the
inconvenience of being at a great distance from Rome.
But when a generation of the bored is attacked by a
mania for travelling, and feels a need to leave home
and business during a part of the year, it does not
usually long remain faithful to the spots wherein it
goes to seek repose. Like all remedies, they soon
cease to be efficacious, and no longer cure it of tedium.
Others must then be sought, possessing the charm of
novelty; and it generally chooses them farther off, and
less accessible than the others, in order that they may
render the pleasure of changing place more keen.
For a long time the great lords of Rome were content
to reside at Tusculum or Veii, when they desired to
refresh themselves from the fatigues of political
life. Then they went a little further—to Præneste, to
Tibur, and afterwards, when all Italy was conquered,
to Naples, to Baia, to Cumæ, to Pompeii, which was
indeed a journey. At the point of time we have arrived
at, Baia seemed to many of these disgusted ones a spot
too hackneyed, and almost vulgar; and in order to get
further off, they fled as far as Tarentum. It must
be owned that "soft Tarentum" deserved the pains
people took to get to it. Horace was right when he
said that nothing in the world seemed to him prefer-
able to this corner of earth :—

> " *Ille terrarum mihi præter omnes*
> *Angulus ridet.*" [1]

---

[1] *Carm.*, II. 6, 19.

It was a town of delights, made as if expressly to be the favourite sojourn of an Epicurean,[1] and which, rocked by the waves and perfumed by the odour of its gardens, had for the last century been finally and gently dying out in idleness and pleasure. It is placed between two seas. On the one side is the gulf bearing its name which Æneas crossed when sailing towards Sicily; on the other, a vast interior lake, 50 kilomètres round, only communicating with the gulf by a narrow cutting, and which the tongue of land the city is built on shelters from tempests. In bad weather nothing is more interesting than the contrast between the troubled and the tranquil waves. While in the direction of the high sea one beholds storm-beaten ships, in the interior sea little fishing-boats go quietly about, casting or raising their nets.[2] A little further on a vast plain lies spread out, devoid of great landscape features, but rich and smiling, such as the ancients loved. It rises little by little towards the mountains that shut it in to the north, and whence descend the little streams which throw themselves into the sea, after scattering a little freshness on their way. One of these is the Galesus, sung by Virgil in his *Georgics*— for Virgil, like Horace, was a frequenter of Tarentum. It is impossible to forget the picture he draws us of that good old man who, in happy spots " where black Galesus winds through meadows gold with grain,"[3]

---

[1] Cicero, *Ad fam.*, VII. 12.

[2] Even in antiquity the *Mare piccolo* had the character of an incomparable fishing-ground. Horace tells us that gourmets held the shellfish of Tarentum in high esteem : *Pectinibus patulis jactat sc molle Tarentum.—Sat.* II. 4, 34.

[3] *Georg.*, IV. 126.

clears a few acres of abandoned land. After sowing there amid the brambles squares of vegetables, surrounded by a border of lilies, vervain, and poppies, and planted a few elms and plane trees to shelter his rustic table, he thinks himself equal to a king, because he culls first of all men the rose in spring, and fruits in autumn. It is in this charming passage of the *Georgics* that we must seek the impression made on Virgil by Tarentum. In the *Æneid*, as his hero does not stop there, he has not thought fit to stop there either, and contents himself with mentioning the name. But he was quite sure that the name would suggest to his readers memories which I would fain recall by the way.

In the meantime Æneas continues to skirt the coasts of Calabria. Having reached the extremity of the peninsula, and passed the last promontory, "Capo Spartivento," he suddenly perceives a magnificent spectacle. It is Sicily, whose coasts he beholds receding in the distance, and, above all, Ætna rising before him. Ætna holds a great place in the admiration and curiosity of the ancients. It is known, however, that they were not very sensible to the beauties of wild sites. The glaciers dismayed them, and they seem never to have brought themselves to examine the Alps closely, so loath are they to speak of them. But Ætna, placed in the very heart of a country they loved to visit, forced itself on their attention. It too often met their sight, and was the theatre of phenomena too terror-striking for them possibly to be silent about it. And this is why, in spite of their preference for calm and reposeful landscapes, they busied themselves a great deal about the terrible mountain. There were then, as in our days, very many tourists who risked the ascent; Strabo, who tells us so, invoked their testimony several times.[1] They started from the little town of Ætna, as we do now from Nicolosi. They rose painfully through a desolate region, across cinders and snow, to the approaches of the summit. Along the way they sometimes witnessed singular spectacles. Priests bending over the mouths of the volcano made sacrifices, or, by the aid of various practices, sought to divine the future. Nearly arrived at the end of the journey, some superstitious persons stopped, seized by a kind of sudden terror. They feared, by finishing the journey, to surprise secrets whose knowledge the gods reserved to themselves. Others, more daring, went forward as far as it was possible to go. The more truthful relate that it was almost impossible to reach the brink of the crater, to which access was barred by smoke and flame. However, their accounts seldom agree. Strabo infers from that that the top of the volcano must not always wear the same aspect, and that, doubtless, each eruption changes its form. The testimony of modern travellers quite confirms this opinion.

Another kind of curiosity very conceivable in people who were so often the witnesses or the victims of the fury of Ætna was to inquire, and, if possible, discover, its cause. How can it be that at certain moments showers of cinders cover the mountains, and rivers of lava flow down to the sea? As was natural, the reasons first given were borrowed from mythology. It was the vanquished of the great battles of Olympus, whom the

---

¹ Strabo, VI. 2, 8, and the poem of *Ætna*.

triumphant gods had hurled into the abyss. It was
Typhon, it was Enceladus, it was the fabled giants
pressed down by the heavy mountains, and whose
breasts, crushed by the weight, vomited flames. " Every
time," says Virgil, "they turn their weary sides, the
whole of Sicily trembles and roars, and the sky is
veiled in smoke." [1] These poetic and childish explanations, with which Æneas contents himself, did not
always suffice. A century after Virgil, a writer, apparently belonging to the bold school of Seneca, an enemy
of the ancient traditions, sought to give another reason
more serious and more learned.[2] He supposes that the
waters of the sea engulf themselves in the depths of
Ætna by underground cavities, while the wind pene-
trates it by other openings. Once in, they naturally
meet in these narrow passages, and, clashing together,
have terrible struggles which make the earth tremble,
and when at last they find some issue they escape in
a tempest of flames. Such is the system somewhat
heavily expounded by the poet in a poem of more than
600 lines. He does not quite guarantee its certainty,
and more often gives it as an hypothesis. However, he
is very pleased to develop it, since it exonerates him
from believing in the mythological fictions. He is a
freethinker, very proud of being so, who abuses his
unfortunate brethren much, when they venture to talk
of Enceladus or of Vulcan, and who for his part pro-

---

[1] III. 581.

[2] It is thought, although it is not certain, to have been Lucilius, to
whom Seneca addressed his famous letters. He was intendant of
Sicily, and while sojourning there had an opportunity of studying
Ætna.

fesses only to care for the truth, in *vero mihi cura*.[1] But in spite of this bragging, he is at heart only a timid freethinker, ill weaned from those fabulous stories he laughs at, and who commits the very weaknesses with which he sternly reproaches others. Before beginning his poem he invokes Apollo, under the pretext that " this god helps us to walk with more assurance in unknown ways;"[2] and in order to make us understand the terrible beauty of the eruptions of Ætna, he seriously tells us that "Jupiter himself admires from afar the jets of flame, and fears that the giants are thinking of taking the field again, or that Pluto, discontented with his share, desires to exchange hell for heaven."[3]   This poet, so well pleased with himself, seems to me the faithful image of the society in the midst of which he lived, and which was wrought by contrary instincts. Sceptical and believing, at the same time mocking and devout, it laughed at the old gods and looked around everywhere for new ones.

However rapid the voyage of Æneas, it was impossible for Ætna not to arrest his attention for a moment. Virgil was therefore obliged to describe it. He does so in a few lines, in which he represents it at times launching into the air clouds of smoke mixed with burning cinders, and flames that touch the stars, and at others vomiting calcined stones and melted rocks, while the mountain boils down to the deepest of its abyss :

> " *Horrificis juxta tonat Ætna ruinis,*
> *Interdumque atram prorumpit ad æthera nubem.*
> *Turbine fumantem piceo et candente favilla,*

---

[1] *Ætna*, 90.　　　[2] *Ibid.*, 8.　　　[3] *Ibid.*, 200.

Attollitque globos flammarum et sidera lambit :
Interdum scopulos avulsaque viscera montis
Erigit eructans, liquefactaque saxa sub auras
Cum gemitu glomerat, fundoque exæstuat imo." [1]

These sonorous and brilliant lines were from the very first appreciated by connoisseurs, and cited in the schools as a finished model of description, so much so that Seneca, not a partial judge, declared that he had nothing to find fault with in it or to add to it.[2] Yet a critic of the second century, usually very respectful of established reputations and received opinions, took it into his head to protest against this general admiration. He pointed out many weaknesses in this so - called masterpiece, and concluded that it was one of those passages which the author would have recomposed if he had had time, and whose imperfection tormented him on his death-bed. This is doubtless a great exaggeration, and Scalager had no trouble in proving that the famous passage contains many fine lines. For my own part, I might be tempted to think them perhaps too fine. One perceives that the poet seeks effective expressions and piles up hyperboles. If I must say all I think, I, like Aulu-Gelle, find a little verbosity and effort in it.[3] It is not Virgil's fault, but Ætna was here in question. The poet felt himself grappling with an important, difficult subject that absorbed people's imaginations, and overdid himself a little, in order to fulfil public expectation.

Æneas is too prudent to remain long at the foot of Ætna. Besides, he has to avoid the anger of the

---

[1] III. 571.   [2] Sen., *Epist.*, 79, 5.
[3] Aulu-Gelle, XVII. 10 : *In strepitu sonituque verborum laborat.*

Cyclops, who are the inhabitants of the country, and
of Polyphemus, their chief, who would like to avenge
upon him the harm done him by Ulysses. So he starts
again as soon as possible. The Trojan ships pass quite
close to these immense blocks of lava near Aci Castello,
which were flung into the sea by the volcano. The
people call them "*scogli de' Ciclopi*," and suppose them to
be fragments of rock hurled by Polyphemus after the
escaping Ulysses. For my part, when I viewed their
dark mass covered by white foam from afar, and dominating the waves by more than 60 mètres, I thought
I had the Cyclops themselves before my eyes, advancing into the sea in pursuit of Æneas. "We see them
erect," says Virgil, "threatening us with their fierce
eyes, and raising their proud heads to the heavens.
Fearful assemblage! (*concilium horrendum!*)"[1] Æneas
escapes, thanks to his oars. Ætna recedes little by
little on the horizon; Pantagia is passed; the Gulf of
Mægara and of Thassus "prostrated to the sun;"[2] and
they only stop a little further on, " at the spot where
an island advances into the sea of Sicily, opposite Plem-
myrium, watered on all sides by the waves. This isle
bears a name illustrious in history ; the first inhabitants
called it Ortygia." It is here that Syracuse began.
Later on, the immense town overflowed upon the con-
tinent. It advanced, without stopping, into the plain as
far as the heights of the Epipolæ, and to the fort of Euryalus ; but the island always remained the heart and
centre of the great city. Hieron had built his palace
there ; Denys crowded it with magnificent monuments ;

---

[1] *Æn.*, III. 688.   [2] *Ibid.*, 689 : *Thapsumque jacentem.*

and it was the residence of the Roman prætors. Now the entire city, like Tarentum, is included within its ancient acropolis. There, imprisoned on all sides by the waves, defended by the bastions of Charles the Fifth, with its narrow streets, its old houses, its monumental windows, it carries the traveller some centuries backward, and gives him the pleasure of forgetting for a moment the trivialities of modern towns. Of all these curiosities, Virgil only mentions one—that which Syracuse owes to Nature, and which must have been with her from all time. This is the fountain of Arethusa, about which the Greeks told so many wonderful tales. We may well think that pious Æneas, hurried though he be, stops on this shore to offer his prayers at the sacred spring. Modern travellers do as he did, nor fail in passing to go and see Arethusa. A few years since they underwent a great disillusion in visiting it. It was then very much neglected, and the women of the town, who did not at all resemble Nausicaa, used to come without ceremony and wash their clothes there. It has since been repaired and we see it in about the same condition as it was in the time of Virgil. It is a semicircular basin, in which papyrus grows, and which a narrow jetty separates from the sea. It is filled with limpid water, and contains fish of all kinds and aquatic birds of every colour in abundance. The day I visited it the sirocco blew violently, and the waves broke foaming against the shore. I had truly a legendary scene before my eyes: Neptune, furious against a poor nymph who resisted him, trying to force the quiet refuge whither she had retired. I must say that Arethusa

did not appear at all troubled by this uproar. While
the sea raged, the fishes continued to swim after the
bits of bread which children threw them, and the
swans sailed gravely among the tufts of papyrus. Yet
when I heard the dull noise of the billows, and saw the
plumes of foam rising above the jetty, I could not help
fearing that the sea would prove the stronger. Looking
at the narrow tongue of land by which the sacred spring
is protected, I trembled for it, and was tempted to
repeat the cry of Virgil:

" Doris amara suam non intermisceat undam ! " [1]

On leaving Ortygia, Virgil passes the promontory of
Pachinum, one of the three which give Sicily its form.
He then skirts all the coast parallel to the shores
of Africa, on which the Greeks had planted their
colonies. It was a country illustrious among all, and
had held a great place in the history of humanity. But
Æneas passes quickly by it. He tells us he is impelled
by a favourable wind, and he must profit by it to go
whither the gods send him. He has only time to point
out a few of the towns he sees in passing. There is
Camarina, Gela, Agrigentum, " which rises on the
height, and shows the traveller its vast ramparts ";
there is Selinus, with its belt of palms; there,
finally, is Lilybæum, " which hides beneath its waves
perfidious rocks." In these rapidly composed lines, I
see nothing to retain but the picture of Agrigentum:

" Arduus inde Acragas ostentat maxima longe
Mœnia." [2]

Ruins still remain of those immense walls that sur-

---

[1] *Egl.*, X. 5.   [2] *Æn.*, III. 703.

prised Virgil ; and beside large blocks of stone overthrown
by time we may see a series of temples, half destroyed,
which, when they were intact, formed a sort of crown
to the ramparts. The effect must have been striking
when there were seen from below : first a line of temples
and walls, and then the town, with its admirable edifices
mounting stepwise to the rock of Minerva (*Rupe*_
Athenæ) and to the acropolis. Virgil's verse gives
us a sufficiently good idea of this spectacle, and the
precision of his description shows us that he had
Agrigentum before his eyes when he wrote. He seems
to have cared little to know whether at the time of
the Trojan War it was as he described it. This was
a point to trouble an historian or an archæologist, and
touched him little. Some rigorous critics have blamed
him for this, while others have sought to defend him, by
saying that, in fact, Agrigentum was not founded until
several centuries after the voyage of Æneas ; but that
there was already, upon the spot where the Greek city
was to rise, a little town of Sicilians, and that the poet ·
means to speak of the latter, though he gives them the
name of the former. This dispute is of little importance ;
but here we are at any rate certain that Virgil visited
what in his day remained of the Greek cities along the
African sea. They could not have been in quite the same
state as that in which we see them to-day. Camarina
and Gela had not entirely disappeared, and the columns
of the Temple of Selinus did not strew the ground.
Yet Strabo plainly states " that the coast extending
from Cape Pachinum to Lilybæum is deserted, and
that one finds but few remains of the settlements
which the Greeks established there." We should like

to know the effect they produced upon Virgil, and the thoughts that arose in his mind as he passed through the streets of these abandoned cities, and wandered in those large empty spaces whence life had withdrawn. He has nowhere told us so, yet I do not think it would be rash to imagine them. He called up before his eyes the history of these unhappy cities, torn by factions, passing from extreme liberty to the hardest servitude, always ready in their domestic quarrels to invoke the aid of the foreigner, and destroying each other without pity. He doubtless said to himself that a nation is not made solely to build admirable monuments, to have musicians, sculptors, painters, poets; that, above all, it must be capable of wisdom, moderation, and discipline, and that it must know how to conduct itself, to keep peace within, and live on terms of amity with its neighbours. Then his mind reverted to his own country, so poor in art and literature; and I suppose that he must have felt reconciled to this inferiority when he saw it possess in such a high degree the political qualities whose absence had ruined the Greeks: respect for authority, the acquiescence in leadership, forgetfulness of private quarrels in face of a public enemy, and strict union of the citizens for a common purpose. It seemed to him then that, however great the glory of Greece, Rome in other respects could bear comparison with her, and that it was surely a great nation which, by knowing how to govern itself, had become worthy to govern the world. This is the sentiment expressed by him with admirable brilliancy in those lines of the Sixth Book, which some critics, I know not why, have reproached him with. " Others will

know better how to animate bronze and make it supple,
to cut living figures in marble; and they will speak
more eloquently. Thou, Roman, remember that it is
thy glory to command the universe, to force the nations
to keep peace, to spare the vanquished, to humble the
proud—these are the arts which thou must cultivate."

"Excudent alii spirantia mollius æra . . . .
Tu regere imperio populos, Romane, memento !" [1]

I cannot but think that, in visiting the ruins of
the Greek cities of Sicily, the contrast between
the two countries, between their contrary qualities
and their different destinies, must have struck Virgil
more forcibly, and that it inspired these beautiful
lines.

We have now come to the end of Æneas' first voyage
in Sicily. From Lilybæum he directs his course
"towards the sad shore of Drepanum," [2] and there, at
the moment when he thinks the end of his labours is
approaching, he loses his father. The legend fixed the
burial-place of Anchises in different spots, and his tomb
was shown in almost all the countries where the Trojans

---

[1] *Æn.*, V. 848.

[2] III. 707: *Drepani illætabilis ora.* Does he only call it so
because he lost his father there ? Commentators bid us remark that
this coast is marshy and sterile. For the ancients it had been a
desolate country ever since the combat between Eryx and Hercules,
and it long kept this appearance. Now everything is in a state of
transformation. In the lower part, salt-pits have been established
which seem very flourishing, and the surrounding plain is becoming
covered with new houses. Near the port of Trapani an attempt has
even been made to plant a garden, whose trees courageously resist the
north-west wind which bends their heads.

had stopped. Virgil was therefore free to make him die as he liked. It was to his purpose to let him accompany his son as long as possible, since it suited him to place at the side of the pious Æneas a kind of interpreter of the gods, to explain their oracles and communicate their will. But he could not keep him any longer without serious inconvenience. We have just got to the moment when a tempest is about to throw Æneas on the coast of Africa, where he will meet with the hospitality of Dido, and pass the whole of a long winter in pleasure.[1] What kind of a figure would the virtuous Anchises have made in the midst of this amorous adventure? He could not have prevented it, since the gods consented, nor permitted it without compromising the dignity of his character: so it was better for him to be absent. Virgil therefore lets him opportunely vanish.

After his father's death, Æneas leaves Sicily, though not for ever. He is to return a few months later, on his flight from Carthage, and sojourn there during the whole of the Fifth Book.

IV.

RETURN OF ÆNEAS TO SICILY—FIFTH BOOK OF THE *ÆNEID* — MOUNT ERYX — TEMPLE OF VENUS ERYCINA — FUNERAL GAMES IN HONOUR OF ANCHISES—COURSE OF THE SHIPS—BURNING OF THE FLEET—SEGESTA— DEPARTURE OF ÆNEAS FOR ITALY.

It has often been remarked that the Fifth Book of the *Æneid* is not very closely connected with the rest of

---

[1] *Æn.*, IV. 193: *Hiemen luxu quamlonga fovere.*

the poem. It might be suppressed without loss, if not to the charm of the work, at least to the development of the action. We have nothing but ceremonies and spectacles, and the desperate struggle of a man to accomplish a divine mission against adverse divinities, which is the subject of the *Æneid*, seems to rest for a while. Æneas, obeying the orders of Jupiter, has just abandoned Dido, and is steering towards Italy. Suddenly the breeze freshens, and the pilot, who soon gets frightened, declares that he dares not continue his course with so threatening a sky. The prudent Æneas easily allows himself to be moved by these misgivings, and consents to stop on his way. Sicily is near. It is a beloved country, ruled over by a Trojan, old Acestus, and contains the tomb of Anchises. It is nearly a year since Anchises died; and as the opportunity is offered of celebrating this anniversary, it must be taken advantage of.

Here then is the Trojan fleet returned to the port of Drepanum. The part of Sicily where Æneas stops has not had quite the same lot as the rest of the isle. It early escaped the Greek domination, and was occupied by the Carthaginians, who were its masters for more than two centuries. It is clear that this long sojourn of the Semites must have exercised some influence over the ancient inhabitants, although it is now difficult to distinguish it. After the first resistance, the Greeks of this part of the country had to come to an understanding with the conquerors, in spite of the differences of manner and of race, and it was arranged to live together, as the Sicilians and Arabs agreed to do in the Middle Ages. A *tepera* preserved in the museum of Palermo represents on one side two hands clasped together, and on the other bears an inscription which informs us that Imilcon Hannibal, son of Imilcon, has made a pact of hospitality with Lison, son of Diogenetes, and his descendants.[1] Contracts of this kind could not have been uncommon between the two peoples. It is also probable that the conquerors, although their minds were not turned that way, did not entirely resist the seduction of Greek art. When they took Segesta, they carried off a bronze statue of Diana which passed for a masterpiece. "Transported into Africa," says Cicero, "the goddess only exchanged altars and adorers. Her honours followed her into this new abode, and thanks to her incomparable beauty, she found again among the enemy the worship she had received at Segesta."[2] Carthage dominated in all the western part of Sicily; but in order not to weaken herself by scattering her forces, she had fixed herself strongly in three important cities: at Lilybæum (Marsala), at Drepanum (Trapani), and at Panormos (Palermo). Above Drepanum, in the centre of the coast occupied by the Carthaginians, rises Eryx (now Monte San-Juliano), which they had made one of their chief citadels. We must first go over it and describe it, for all the action of the Fifth Book takes place around this mountain.

The reputation of Mount Eryx was very great in ancient times. Although it barely rises 800 mètres above the sea, and although there is in Sicily many a peak,

---

[1] Salinas, *Guida del museo di Palermo*, p. 40.

[2] II., *Verr.*, IV. 83.

without counting Ætna, greatly exceeding it in height, it is of so fine a form, so regularly cut, so well posed, and is seen from all sides to so much advantage, that its name occurs of itself to Virgil when he wants to give us the idea of a high mountain: *Quantus Athos aut quantus Eryx!*[1] Access to it is now easy. A fine winding road leads to Trapani, and the summit is reached in three or four hours. One is surprised to find there certainly one of the most curious little towns that can be seen. Shut in by solid walls which go back to the most remote times, defended by towers and bastions, San Juliano contains nearly four thousand inhabitants within its gates. The town has an antique and severe look, and very little has been done to improve it. As we pass through these narrow steep streets, bordered by little houses with low doors and few windows, we feel the bitter north-east wind that blows even on the finest days, and reflect that in winter the weather here must often be very rigorous, and we ask ourselves how men could have been tempted to place their dwelling so high. Yet this spot must have been peopled very early in the world's history, for remains of flint weapons have been found here, proving that it had inhabitants before the use of metals was known. An isolated mountain, easy to defend, whose foundations are planted in the sea, and which is provided at its summit with inexhaustible springs of water, offered a sure asylum to those who wished to place their lives and fortunes beyond danger of sudden attack. Later on

---

[1] *Æn.*, XII. 701.

it served as a fortress to all the conquerors of Sicily, and the Greeks, the Carthaginians, and the Romans disputed its possession with fury. Its inhabitants were more numerous than ever amidst the violence of the Middle Ages, and it is then that, in order to make room for them, the houses had to be crowded together one upon the other, as we see them. Now, when men can live without danger in the plain, the mountain is gradually becoming depopulated, and the time is not far distant when the almost deserted little town will only be frequented by the curious who visit the country in search of memorials of antiquity.

What chiefly draws them hither is the renown of the famous Temple of Venus which formerly crowned the mountain. They will no longer find it. The temple has perished entirely, and it is scarcely possible to do more than recognise its site. A little above San Juliano extends a broad plateau, reached by a small walk planted with trees and bordered with flowers. This plateau must originally have been very narrow. It was increased in extent by enormous substructions, which sometimes sink very low, and rest on projections of the rock. Works of this kind were frequent among the ancients, who did not recoil from any labour in order to fix the bases of their edifices solidly. But this one struck even the ancients themselves by its vast proportions, and, not knowing its architect, they attributed it to Dædalus, the legendary artist, just as we sometimes talk about monuments being Cyclopean. These kinds of expressions teach nothing, but they are convenient to disguise ignorance. We are now farther advanced than the ancients, and we can say what people built at least the lower layers of these immense walls. M. Salinas, a distinguished Palermitan archæologist, has discovered that the large blocks of stone on which the walls rest bear letters, and that these letters are Phœnician.[1] We have thus a proof that the first works to fix the foundation of the temple and of the town were carried out by the Carthaginians. But we have just seen that Mount Eryx was peopled long before their arrival in Sicily, and there is nothing to prevent us from believing that on the site on which they raised their sumptuous buildings, there already existed a modest sanctuary built by the old inhabitants. And this confirms Virgil's account in every respect. He shows, on the approach of Æneas, the people of the country, who from the top of the mountain have their eyes fixed upon the sea, observing from afar the unknown guests whom the waves are bringing them. He depicts them as rough and half savage, as they must have been, "holding javelins in their hands, and covered with the skin of a Libyan bear."[2] As for the old sanctuary which preceded the Phœnician temple, he attributes its foundation to Æneas himself. At the moment of leaving, "the hero," he tells us, "on the crown of Eryx raises to Venus, his mother, a sacred habitation near the stars."

The divinity of Eryx had the advantage of being recognised and honoured by all the peoples who navigated the shores of the Mediterranean. Under different names, the Phœnican, Greek, Etruscan, and Roman sailors paid homage to a goddess of the sea, whom they

---

[1] Salinas, *Le mura fenicie di Erice*, an extract from *Notizie degli scavi* April 1883.

[2] *Æn.*, V. 35, *et seq.*

called on in times of danger, and to whom they believed they owed their safety. Whether they named her Astarte, Aphrodite, or Venus, she was in fact the same for all. They gave her the same attributes; they acknowledged in her the same power. In her sanctuary on Eryx there were found, side by side with Greek and Latin inscriptions, *ex-votos* in which Phœnicians or Carthaginians put themselves under the protection of Astarte, " who gives long life." As all equally honoured the goddess, it came to pass that, in spite of their furious rivalries, her temple was never laid waste, and went unharmed through these terrible wars in which the combatants allowed themselves every license. This happy fortune augmented the credit enjoyed by it among the devout. It was the more extraordinary from the circumstance that the Temple of Eryx was considered one of the richest in the world. Thucydides relates that the inhabitants of Segesta took the Athenian envoys thither when they wished to deceive them as to the resources at their disposal, and that they made them believe they were the masters of all the treasures deposited there.[1] Among the gifts presented to the goddess, Elienus particularly mentions rings and earrings,[2] which reminds us of the *Madonna di Trapani*, whose church is just at the foot of Mount Eryx. She is a miraculous Virgin, in whose favour many women of fashion have despoiled themselves of a portion of their ornaments. She is a overladen with diadems, necklaces, bracelets, jewels, which sparkle in the light of the tapers, and even wears, hooked to the bottom of her dress, a number of

---

[1] Thucydides, VI. 46   [2] *De Anima*, X. 50.

watches of every age and style, that would fill a collec-
tor's heart with joy.   According to the report of Elienus,
I suppose that something similar must have been found
in the Temple of Venus Erycina, so it was thought that
the goddess was well pleased with so rich a dwelling-
place, and loved to abide there.   It was one of her
favourite residences.   Theocritus says, in invoking her:
"O thou who dwellest in Golgos, Idalia, or on high
Eryx."[1]   The people of the country asserted that she
only left it once a year, in order to make a tour
in Africa.   Her absence was known by the sign
that not a single dove was seen around Eryx.   She
took them all with her on her journey.   Nine days
afterwards she came back, and the doves with her.
Her departure and her return were the occasions of
brilliant ceremonies.

The worship of Venus Erycina had the sensual and
voluptuous character usual in the religions of the East.
The goddess was served by young and beautiful slaves,
called in Greek *hierodules*.   In the Temple of Aphrodite,
at Corinth, there were a thousand of these, who, when
ships' captains tarried there a few days, made them
forget the weariness of their long voyages.   It must
have been the same at Eryx.   Passing sailors came
there to celebrate Venus with those transports and
excesses which heighten the joys of life in people
always in danger of death.   On one of the slopes of
the mountain a great heap of broken *amphoræ* has
been found, whose handles bear Greek, Latin, and
Carthaginian inscriptions.   It is likely that the mariners

---

[1] XV. 100.

of all countries who climbed Eryx brought their wine
with them, and drank it up there in merry company.
The *heirodules* helped them to spend the money they
had laboriously amassed in the course of their dangerous
voyages. Thus some of these women soon managed
to make a fortune. Cicero speaks of one of them,
named Agonis, first a slave, and then a freedwoman
of Venus, who became very rich, and who possessed,
in particular, slave musicians who were a source of
envy, and were at last taken away from her.[1] These
pleasures of all kinds which were found on Eryx make
it easy to understand the renown it must have enjoyed
among seafaring people all over the Mediterranean.
The temple, poised on the top of the mountain, was
seen from afar, like a beacon. I suppose that the
pilot or the captain who had just made a long voyage
full of fatigues and perils felt his heart beat with joy
when, coming from Africa or Italy, he saw this place
of delights appear on the horizon, where he was about
to forget his hardships for a moment, and that when he
left Drepanum, he must have kept his eyes long fixed
upon the mountain which called up in him such
pleasant memories. However, it was not only people
of this sort who came to honour Venus Erycina in her
sanctuary; for sometimes visitors of more importance
were seen there. Diodorus tells us that the most
important magistrates of the Roman people, consuls,
and prætors, when their functions called them this way,
mounted to the Temple of Eryx. He adds that their
forgetting their gravity for a moment, and rendering

---

[1] *Divin. in Cæcil.*, 17.

homage to the goddess by lending themselves to the pleasantries and games of the women who served her, was appreciated. They found it an easy manner of performing their devotions.[1]

Now the plateau of Eryx is deserted. The temple of Venus, the residence of the *hierodules*, all those edifices consecrated to pleasure, have disappeared. These spots, where for so long festive songs resounded, have become silent. What remains to them is the admirable view enjoyed from the top of the mountain, the series of smiling plains and hills following each other to beyond Cape San Vito, that immense extent of sea rolling out before us as far as the coasts of Africa.

Yet do not let us look so far, but content ourselves with a more restricted horizon. For we must keep our eyes fixed upon this narrow strip of land stretching at our feet between the mountain and the sea. It was chosen by Virgil for the scene of his Fifth Book, and from the heights on which we are standing we are about to follow its different incidents without trouble.

We have seen, higher up, that what determined Æneas to stop a second time in Italy was the opportunity offered to visit the tomb of Anchises, and render him fresh honours. As soon as he has disembarked, he assembles his soldiers, and from the top of a mound,

---

[1] The women of Eryx are considered the most beautiful in all Sicily, and this is all that the country retains of the protection of Venus. They already had this reputation in the Middle Ages. The Arab traveller, Ben Djobair, who makes this statement, adds : "May God make them captives of the Mussulmans !"

like an emperor, makes them one of those solemn harangues so pleasing to Roman gravity :

"*Dardanidæ magni, genus alto a sanguine divum,*"[1] etc.

In this speech he announces to them the series of festivals he is preparing in honour of his father's memory, and everything is carried out in acccordance with his word. First they visit the tomb of Anchises, to scatter flowers there, and pour out libations of milk, wine, and blood. The ashes of him who was honoured with the love of Venus, and who is the father of Æneas, are not those of an ordinary being. He is a god, and makes the fact well known to his son by calling up the serpent which issues from his tomb, and comes to taste the meats consecrated to him. Æneas does not at first grasp the meaning of this marvellous apparition, and asks himself whether he has just seen the familiar genius of the place, or whether it is a kind of domestic demon who serves his father in the other life. At last he understands, and sacrifices sheep, swine, and bulls to him, whom he regards as a new divinity. This is a timid and somewhat confused sketch of apotheosis. A few years later, when Augustus died and was proclaimed a god by the Senate, the ceremonies of his funeral were minutely regulated, and the ritual of imperial apotheosis was fixed. "Soldiers with their arms, and knights with their insignia, running round the funeral pyre, threw into it the rewards they had received for their valour. Then centurions approached and set fire to it. While it burned, an eagle rose, as if to carry with

---

[1] *Æn.*, V. 45.

it the soul of the prince. These ceremonies, it must
be owned, seem grander than the libations of milk and
wine poured by Æneas on the tomb of his father, and
the mysterious serpent gliding from the mausoleum;
but Virgil did not foresee what would be done after
him, and contented himself, as was his wont, with
appropriating the ancient practices of the national
religion to new circumstances. The funeral games,
announced in advance to the soldiers by Æneas, take
place nine days after the sacrifice. Such was the
usage, as Servius tells us.[1] The trumpet gives the
signal; the Trojans and the people of the country
hasten to assemble in order to assist at them, and the
poet employs more than five hundred lines, nearly the
whole of the Fifth Book, in their description. In order
to understand why he gives them so great a place in his
work, we must recall that which they held in the
lives of the Romans of his time. Since politics
had become indifferent to them, they had grown
to be their chief interest, and the amphitheatre or the
circus occupied the time left free by the forum. In
order to please them, it had been necessary to multiply
their games without measure, and in the first century
of the Empire, when those which seemed useless had
been suppressed, they still took up one hundred and
thirty-five days of the year. So Virgil was certain of
charming his readers by entertaining them with that
which was their most ardent passion. He also found
in them the advantage of being able to imitate Homer,

---

[1] Servius, in *Æn.*, V. 64: *Unde etiam ludi qui in honorem mortu-
orum celebrantur novemdiales dicuntur.*

who had also taken pleasure in describing at length the games instituted by Achilles at the funeral of Patroclus. This part of Virgil's work is chiefly copied from the *Iliad;* but here, as elsewhere, he knows how to maintain an air of independence, even in the midst of the most exact translations. He assimilates what he reproduces, and, in spite of the empire exercised over him by his great predecessor, he preserves the character of his own genius. There are, however, two of these pictures which belong to him entirely. Firstly, he has replaced the chariot race by that of the ships. It is easy to see how the idea of this change was suggested to him. The Trojans, who had been sailing about for seven years, could not have had many horses [1] at their disposal, and, in any case, they had not had opportunities of practising their management. As they have only applied themselves to the handling of their ships, it is in this species of exercise that it was natural to make them contend with each other. The chariot races were common ground, which Greek poetry had hackneyed; ship races had been described less often, and they might furnish some new descriptions. The other spectacle which Virgil did not borrow from Homer is what is called the "Trojan game" (*ludus Trojanus*), a kind of *carrousel* in which the youth took part in games of skill and strength, and to which a very venerable antiquity was attributed. These evolutions of the young folk before the eyes of their fathers had in themselves something graceful and

---

[1] Virgil is very careful to say that the horses ridden by the youths in the *ludus Trojanus* were furnished by Acestes.

touching which must have pleased Virgil. He knew, moreover, that in describing them he was seconding the designs of Augustus, who brought them into repute again, doubtless in order to make his grandchildren shine in them, and show the people, in the midst of ancient pomps, the future masters of the Empire. The poet is here faithful to his usual system, which consists in connecting the present with the past, and restoring life to these old tales by animating them with the passions of his own time.

I will not analyse these accounts, which could not have the same interest for us that they possessed for the contemporaries of Virgil. Let it suffice to say that here, as everywhere, the poet has exactly described the scene of his drama. From the height of Eryx, one can fancy one sees the various games by which Æneas honoured the memory of his father, and enjoy the spectacle of them. There is first the ship race, by which the festival begins. The starting-point is not given, but is doubtless some mooring stage near the port of Drepanum, where they had taken refuge during the bad weather. But, on the other hand, the place towards which they are to steer is indicated very clearly. "Amidst the waves, facing the surf-beaten shore, stands forth a rock, by raging billows scourged and hid, when winter storms obscure the sky. Silent in calm it sways the placid flood, and sea-birds love to rest there in the sun." [1] I perceive it a few kilomètres from the beach, and Virgil's description has helped me to recognise it. It is now called

---

[1] *Æn.*, V. 124.

the Isola d'Asinello. The vessels must round this little island, decorated for the occasion with oak branches. This is certainly the rock where Sergestus broke his oars and his prow. I think I see him trying painfully to advance with his remaining sails, " like a snake o'er which a waggon wheel has passed in the middle of the road, which exhausts itself in useless efforts, and bends upon itself, without being able to progress a single step," while the vessel of Mnestheus, with its panting rowers bent to the oar, passes before it like lightning. This first contest over, Æneas, who has witnessed its varying fortunes from the neighbourhood of the port of Drepanum, proceeds, skirting the shore, " to a meadow surrounded by a belt of hills shaded by forests." It would be easy to find, along the slopes of Eryx, more than one spot answering to Virgil's description. Eryx does not descend towards the sea with a uniform slope ; but undulates to right and left in advancing ridges that enclose little verdant valleys nestled to the mountain side. To use the poet's expression, these little valleys closely resemble the circular part of an ancient theatre, and appear made expressly for crowds desirous to assist conveniently at some spectacle. Let us picture to ourselves Æneas sitting at the end of this species of circus, upon a more elevated seat. Round about him, the Trojans and Sicilians place themselves as they can upon the slopes of the hills, and thence all watch the foot race, the palestra, and the archery.[1] But while all are engrossed

---

[1] The spot where these different games take place is the same where Anchises was buried. Virgil says so, positively, in lines 550 and 602. Probably there was some old monument there, which the people of the country called the Tomb of Anchises.

in the pleasure they derive from the complicated evolutions of the Trojan game, the spectacle is cut short by an unforeseen incident. A messenger hastens up to announce that the women, who had been left at Drepanum, desperate at the prospect of having to start again, and yielding to the bad advice of Juno, have set fire to the ships. From the spot where he is, the port is hidden from Æneas, and it is not possible to see the burning fleet; but above the heights the smoke is seen rising into the air like a cloud. Iulus first, and then all the Trojans after him, rush to quench the conflagration.

Despite the promptness of the aid and the help of Jupiter, all the ships cannot be saved. Some are quite destroyed, or too much damaged to be repaired, so it is no longer possible for Æneas to take away the whole of his people with him, and he must make a selection. The bravest, the most resolute, will alone accompany him; as for those " who feel not the want of glory,"[1] they will stay in Sicily. He leaves the women there, too, who are worn out by seven years of exhausting adventures. But, before departing, he sets to work to build them a town, whose boundary he traces in the Italian manner, with a plough, and which he places under the authority of good Acestus. This town is Segesta, important in its time, and which, in order to conquer its rival Selinus, called the Athenians and the Carthaginians to its aid. It had already much declined when the Romans became masters of Sicily. It then remembered at the right time that it was said to have been founded by Æneas, and tried to make

---

[1] *Æn.*, V. 751 : *Animos nil magnæ laudis egentes.*

capital out of its Trojan origin. In support of the tradition, it showed an ancient chapel which it had raised to its founder, and recalled that two little brooks which flow at the end of the valley had received the names of Simois and Scamander. The Romans received its advances favourably, and looked on it as an allied and kindred town. They affected to treat it honourably, and exempted it from taxation, while Virgil celebrated its birth in his poem. But these honours did not stay its decadence ; under the Empire it became more and more impoverished and forlorn, and in the Middle Ages it had entirely disappeared.

Yet people still go to view the site it occupied ; for if the town exists no more, two monuments of it remain—a temple and a theatre—which preserve its memory and attract the curious. The temple is not, perhaps, the most beautiful of those still possessed by Sicily, but there are none which more deeply impress travellers. In order to enjoy and appreciate it at its full merits, it is well to view it from a little distance, it being a characteristic of Greek monuments that they are made for the place they occupy, and that their position is one of the elements of their beauty. Here the temple rises upon a height, and the very hill on which it is built serves it as a pedestal. It is one with it, it is its crown, and to isolate were to dismember and mutilate it. Its aspect changes entirely according to the point of view. Coming from Calatafimi, it is caught sight of suddenly at a turn of the road, through a break in the rocks, and the view is marvellous. It appears in profile, and its columns stand out against the sky with wonderful clearness.

From the foot of Monte Barbaro, we have a front view.
Its pediment is outlined against a fine mountain, rising
behind and serving it as a background. It thus
appears more substantial, more powerful, more severe.
This is the quality which prevails as one approaches.
When we are quite close, the whole may even appear
heavy and ungraceful. The columns, as in all Sicilian
temples, are very near each other, less slender and more
massive than in the buildings of Greece proper. But
let us reflect that here the architects had a difficult
problem to solve. They built with inferior materials
upon an agitated and moving soil, and they had to
sacrifice lightness to solidity. They succeeded, since
their monuments still exist. It is, moreover, a defect
to which one soon becomes accustomed. The first
surprise over, we admire without reserve this noble
Doric architecture—so sober, so vigorous, so clear, so
rational; where there is no ornament without its
explanation, not a detail but conduces to the effect of
the whole, and which is a satisfaction to the mind as
well as a feast for the eye.[1] The Temple of Segesta was
not finished. The fluting of the columns is scarcely
begun, and the friezes were never ornamented with
sculpture. Very likely the building was in progress
when Agathocles took Segesta by assault. It is known
that he ruthlessly massacred ten thousand of its inhabi-

---

[1] In connection with these qualities of the Gothic order, the first
pages of Burckhardt's *Cicerone* may be read. This excellent book,
found so useful to serious travellers desirous of forming a true judgment of the masterpieces of art, is now entirely at our disposal, having
been translated into very elegant French by M. Auguste Gerard
(Paris, Firmin Didot).

tants and sold the rest.   Since that terrible event, the city did nothing more than vegetate, and never found resources to complete the temple begun by her on so large a scale in the time of her prosperity.   It had to be adapted to worship as best it might, and was used in this condition for centuries.   This is what has since happened to many Gothic cathedrals overtaken by the Renaissance or the Reform before their completion.

As for the town itself, it was situated on a neighbouring hill, Monte Barbaro.   We climb up to it with difficulty, amid fallen rocks; and in the ascent we come across a few fragments of wall, a few thresholds of the Roman epoch, and this is all we have left of Segesta. One of the things that most astonish us, while roving the world in search of relics of the past, is to see important towns, like this which resisted Syracuse, perish so completely that scarcely a trace of them is left.   Only the theatre, cut into the rock, has survived the common ruin.   The orchestra and the stage may be distinguished, while the rows of benches, with the steps by which the spectators reached their places, are nearly intact.   If we except that of Taormina, which is a marvel, I do not believe there is another in Sicily whence a more extensive or more varied view is enjoyed.   It is bosomed in the midst of a circle of picturesque mountains, whose tops sometimes form great majestic lines, and at others fantastic, intricate zigzags. Before it, the plain extends as far as the sea, seen on the horizon in a frame of hills, with the little town of Castellamare, which without doubt formerly served as a port to Segesta.   Looking down below us, we are struck by the variety of different aspects the country presents at its various heights. At a glance we may pass in review all the different cultivations forming its wealth. Below, near the streams, are orange and lemon trees, whose yellow fruit stands out upon the dark-green leaves. A little higher, half-way up, we have corn, the vine, the olive—all those products which made Sicily, as Cato said, the granary of Italy. Higher yet, along the abrupt slopes, are seen dwarf palms, aloes, a vigorous vegetation reaching nearly to the top of the hills, and cropped by sheep and goats. But in spite of the admiration this sight produces, it is impossible not to feel intense surprise. As far as sight can penetrate, neither village, farm, nor cottage is to be seen ; and with the exception of a few wild-looking herdsmen, not a human form. The workmen only come here when they have to sow or reap. Their labour done, they return home, and this fertile country, for a while so full of life, once more becomes a desert. The solitude is then so profound, that one finds it very difficult to picture to oneself that these spots, where no human sound reaches the ear, were once so well peopled and so animated; and did one not see at one's feet the seats of a theatre, and on a neighbouring hill the temple with its empty *cella* and sunken roof, one would never imagine one was standing on the site of a great town.

After Æneas has founded Segesta, and settled the Trojans there whom he is not to take with him, nothing more remains for him to do in Sicily. So he takes leave of Acestus, sacrifices sheep and bulls to the gods, and orders the cables which hold the ships to the shore to be cut. "Himself erect upon the prow, his head encircled with an olive wreath, and raising the cup he holds in his hand, he flings into the salt sea the entrails of the victims, and pours libations of wine upon the waves."[1] The wind blows from the poop, and bears him to Italy, where he must fulfil his destiny.

III.

OSTIA AND LAVINIUM.

I.

THE TWO PARTS OF THE *ÆNEID*—CHARACTER OF THE LAST SIX BOOKS—VIRGIL IS HERE IN THE HEART OF HIS SUBJECT—PERFECTION OF THE STYLE—THE POET'S AIM COMES OUT BETTER—VIRGIL'S PATRIOTISM—HOW HE HAS GROUPED ALL ITALY AROUND HIS WORK.

THE *Æneid*, as we know, is very exactly divided into two equal parts, of six Books each. The first portion contains the adventures of Æneas up to the moment when he disembarks at the mouth of the Tiber. The other relates how he manages to establish himself in the country assigned him by the Fates. These two parts have not quite the same character. It was long since remarked that the one more resembles the *Odyssey*, the other the *Iliad*. The first is most generally preferred by amateurs and critics, who find it more interesting, more agreeable, and more varied. They find the second

---

Æn., V. 774.

greatly inferior, some even suspecting that Virgil felt this inferiority, and that this is why, when dying, he wished to destroy his work. " It is not vouchsafed to men to be perfect," says Voltaire, alluding to this. " Virgil exhausts all that the imagination has of greatest in the descent of Æneas to hell ; in the loves of Dido he has said all that can be said to the heart ; terror and compassion cannot go further than in the description of the ruin of Troy. From this high elevation which he had reached in the midst of his flight, he could only descend." Chateaubriand was, I think, the first among us to protest against the opinion of Voltaire. In that part of the *Genius of Christianity*, where he treats of literary criticism, and where, in spite of his defective knowledge, he has cast so many new ideas, he makes the curious remark that the most touching lines of Virgil, those whose memory has lingered in all hearts, are found in just the last six Books of the *Æneid*. He infers from this that in drawing near to the tomb the poet put something more celestial into his accents, " like the swans of Eurotas, consecrated to the Muses, who, according to Pythagoras, before expiring had a vision of Olympus, and expressed their ravishment by harmonious songs."

What is true above all, and impossible to contest, is that in these six Books we are really in the heart of the subject. Virgil has taken care to tell us this himself. At the moment when his hero disembarks upon the coast of Italy, he interrupts himself, in order to invoke the Muse, and ask her aid, for he needs it more than ever on account of the importance of the events he is about to sing:

" Major rerem mili nascitur ordo,
Majus opus moveo " [1]

We see that, far from believing, as Voltaire would have it, that at this moment "his subject declines," he proclaims that he has reached the culminating point of his work. There are even some critics who, taking advantage of his avowal, reproach him with having got there too late. They find that it is much to spend six Books out of twelve in the narration of preliminary adventures, and that it is surprising that in a poem whose fine ordering everybody extols, half of the work should be beside the real action. But it seems to me that people who so reason do not take Virgil's aim into account. He wants to relate how Æneas brought his gods into Latium and built them an asylum there, so that the action begins at the moment when Hector confides them to him. All the dangers he dares by land or sea are equally part of the subject; and if Virgil seems to have chosen to multiply them at pleasure,[2] it is because they foreshadow the great destinies of the city that is about to come into being. The hostile gods would not rage against her with such cruel obstinacy did they not know that she is to be queen of the world. This is why, after having recalled all the obstacles that oppose its birth, and which appear to him the gauge of its glorious future, the poet concludes his enumeration with this triumphant line:

----

[1] *Æn.*, VII. 44.

[2] Heyne (*Æn.* III., *excursus* II.) has shown that while the ordinary traditions suppose the voyage to have lasted three years, Virgil makes it last seven.

" Tantæ molis erat Romanam condere gentem." [1]

Thus the trials of all kinds inflicted by the anger of Juno on pious Æneas are included in the subject of the *Æneid*, and Virgil was within his right in relating them to us; but as the adverse duties must redouble their efforts in proportion as the hero nears the goal, it is natural that his last struggle should also be the most perilous. Before gaining a decisive victory, he must brave his most inveterate enemies and fight the most hazardous battles. Virgil was therefore right in saying, at the moment when he was about to begin the narration of these last combats, "that a vaster career was opening before him, and that he had arrived at the most important part of his work."

It was also the most difficult part. In the remainder he is supported and sustained by Homer and the other poets, epic or lyric, who sang the adventures of the Greek heroes returning home after the fall of Troy. Thanks to these poets, all the isles of the Archipelago, all the shores of the Ionian Sea, were peopled with charming fancies which they had sown in the path of their heroes. Virgil had only to choose; to whatever spot he led Æneas, he was sure to awaken poetic memories in every mind. Homer, Sophocles, Pindarus, and the others thus became his fellow-workers, and he gave his poem the advantage of the admiration inspired by their works. But once alighted in Italy, all these resources fail him. On this ungrateful soil, which Poesy has not touched with her wing; which, instead of the treasure of Greek fables, only offers him a few

---

[1] *Æn.*, I. 33.

meagre and prosaic legends, he must draw upon him-self for almost everything. I will not pity him too much on this account; since if from this moment his work becomes less easy and pleasant, it gains in originality, and belongs to him more. It is this indeed which gives us his true measure. Whatever admiration one feels for the marvels he has crowded into his first six Books, there is in the others more invention and veritable genius, and it is by them he should be judged.

In the first place, their style is perfect. The efforts the poet must have made to impart beauty to matter in itself sufficiently arid, and to put something of variety into a rather monotonous theme, are not perceived. The incidents are so skilfully introduced, and seem to arise so naturally from the subject, that it is difficult to realise how much imagination and artifice were needed to weld them together. This merit does not strike one in reading a good poem. Order and connection are such natural qualities that one does not think of remarking them. In order to appreciate their value, we must read those devoid of them. From this point of view, it may be said that the perusal of the epic poets of the decadence, who took so much trouble to be interesting, and succeeded so poorly, redounds much to Virgil's credit. Valerius Flaccus, Silius Italicus, and, above all, Statius, that man of so much refinement and talent, whose poem is only a mass of brilliant episodes, laboriously brought together without being united, makes us duly appreciate in the *Æneid* the simplicity of the action, the dexterous joining of the

parts, and the harmony of the whole. But we shall be
more sensible of these merits if we compare different
parts of Virgil's work. In the first Books of his poem,
the narrative sometimes wanders; and there is even
one, the Fifth, which, strictly speaking, might be
omitted. Nothing of the kind is found in the second
part of the work. There everything is connected and
linked, and the author walks straight on without ever
straying from his road. The action, urgent and swift,
lingers not for a moment. It is so simple that it
may be taken in at a glance, and nothing is easier than
to sum it up in a few words. Throughout three Books
Fate is adverse to the Trojans. Juno succeeds in
frustrating the alliance they were about to make with
Latinus; all the Italian peoples take arms against
them; and while Æneas is gone to obtain the support
of Evander and the Etruscans, Turnus besieges his
camp and almost succeeds in taking it. In the Tenth
Book Æneas returns with fresh troops, and on his
arrival fortune changes. He begins by beating back
the Latins, who attack his soldiers; then he in his
turn pursues them as far as Laurentum, and ends the
war with the death of Turnus. This arrangement
is nearly the same as that of the *Iliad*, where
we see Hector advance nearer and nearer towards
the vessels of the Greeks, and then retire before
Achilles as far as the walls of Troy, where he is
slain. But in Homer events are so crowded that
the wealth of detail does not always allow of a just
conception of the whole. In Virgil, who is more
sober and terse, the general plan is better seen, the
double movement constituting the progress of the

Q

action is better understood, and the unity of the work being more apparent, the interest seems to be more lively.

I also find that in these last Books one is more struck by the poet's aim, and that the idea which animates the work is more visible here than elsewhere. This thought, it may be said, is found everywhere; for there is not a verse of the *Æneid* in which Rome is not glorified, and just at the end of the Sixth Book there is an admirable summary of its history. Virgil's patriotism is so ardent that he everywhere seeks and finds occasion to display it. One feels some surprise at this, when one reflects that this poet who sings of Rome with such passion was not quite Roman by birth. For a long time the aristocratic party had obstinately refused to grant the right of complete citizenship to the inhabitants of Cisalpina. These vain great lords took pleasure in making them feel, by every kind of outrage, that they were still subjects and a conquered people. Virgil, in his youth, must have heard the story of the decurion of Como, whom Marcellus one day caused to be beaten with rods, in order to prove to him that he was not a citizen. It was not until 712, after the battle of Philippi, that the inhabitants of Cisalpina, who had received from Cæsar the right of citizenship, were placed upon quite the same rank as other Italians. Virgil was then twenty-eight years old, and a Roman at heart. Rome must truly have exerted an extraordinary attraction over people, for her former enemies so soon to have become her faithful allies and devoted citizens. She is usually represented as an object of execration to the vanquished; this is a great mistake, at least so far as the West is concerned. She knew how, in a few years, to make her conquest forgotten. It is remarkable that those who loved her most, who served her with the greatest zeal, and celebrated her with most affection, did not belong to her by birth, and were descended from peoples she had roughly subdued. Virgil, then, was a patriot, almost before he was a citizen, only his patriotism is not quite like that of the old Romans of the Republic. The latter only saw Rome, and the great town was all in all to them. Virgil also admires it much; but he does not separate it from Italy. The country, for him, is not entirely included within the wall of Servius; it includes the lands contained by the Alps and the sea. And he is tenderly attached to this great country, which had been so unhappy during the civil wars, and which he saw so rich and flourishing under Augustus.[1] He had already sung it in admirable lines in his *Georgics* :—

> " *Salve, magna parens frugum, Saturnia tellus,*
> *Magna virum !* "[2]

When, later on, in response to the wish of the Emperor and the desire of all the Romans, he resolved to write his epic, he quite intended to associate all

---

[1] The scholiast Servius tells us: "It is well seen that Virgil was very much interested in all that concerned Italy" (*Æn.*, I. 44). Although his history is not well known, it may be affirmed that he had often visited it, admiring its beautiful spots and its fine views, and inquiring into the ancient history of all the towns he passed through.

[2] *Georg.*, II. 173.

Italy in the glory with which he meant to crown Rome.
He started with this thought, but could only quite
realise it in his last six Books. The action, which
hitherto had travelled all over the world, then centres
in the plains of Latium. The theatre in which this
great drama is played is really very limited, and does not
extend beyond four or five square leagues; but in this
little plain reaching from Ostia to Laurentum, and
from the hills to the sea, Virgil has had the skill to
group all Italy. There are in the army of Turnus,
Latins, Sabines, Volsci, Marsci, Umbrians, and even
Campanians—that is to say, representatives of all those
noble races of Central Italy that furnished so many
soldiers to the Roman armies. Æneas joins to his
Trojans the Greeks of Evander, and the Etruscans of
Tarchon; and as at this time Etruria extended her
dominion as far as the Alps, the poet takes occasion to
put Ligurians and Cisalpians among the troops of
Æneas, and to say something by the way of his beloved Mantua. Only the point of Southern Italy, then
in the hands of the Greeks, remained outside his
subject; but he finds means of some sort to connect it.
He imagines that Turnus sends an embassy to Diomedes,
who reigns over those parts, in order to ask his alliance.
Thus, although Diomedes refuses to take up arms, his
name and those of the towns he governs are not quite
absent from the *Æneid*. And so the poet caused all
the races of Italy to figure in it, creating for them
common memories in the past, at the moment when
they had just been united under the hegemony of
Rome, and interesting them all in the success of his
work.

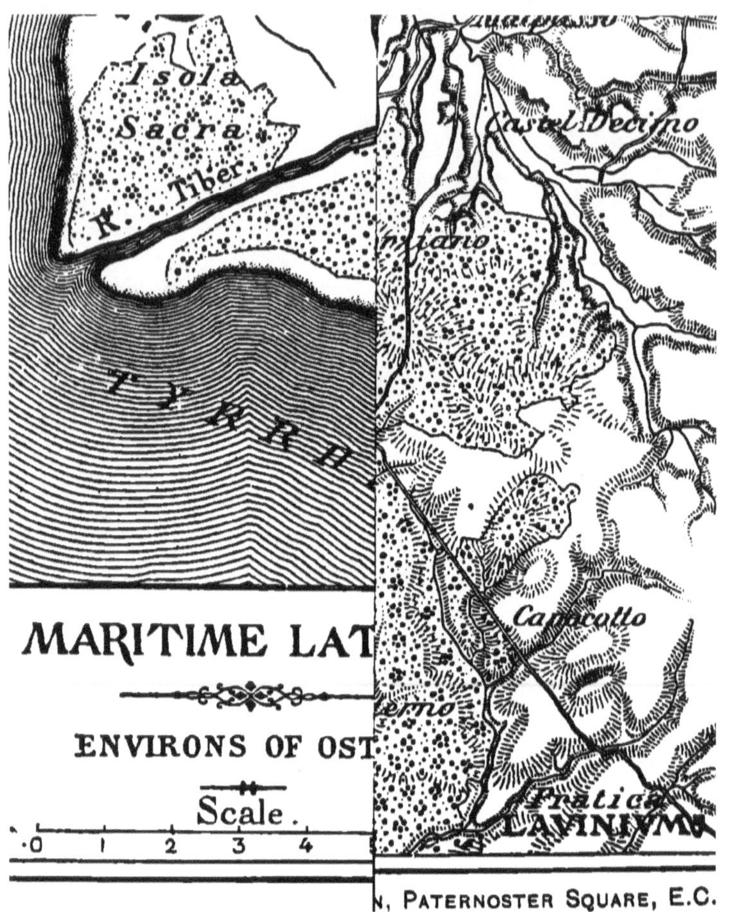

MARITIME LAT

ENVIRONS OF OST

Scale.

·0   1   2   3   4

N, PATERNOSTER SQUARE, E.C.

These general reflections ended, let us enter at length upon the study of the chief events narrated in Virgil's last six Books, and follow them, as far as possible, over the country which was their theatre.

II.

ÆNEAS LANDS ON THE COAST OF OSTIA — VIRGIL'S DESCRIPTION OF IT—ITS ASPECT IN OUR DAYS—HOW ÆNEAS KNOWS THAT HE HAS REACHED THE END OF HIS VOYAGE—MIRACLE OF THE EATEN TABLES—THE WHITE SOW AND HER THIRTY LITTLE ONES—ORIGINAL MEANING OF THIS LEGEND, AND THE CHANGES IT UNDERWENT.

In the course of his long voyage Æneas has more than once approached Italy. On quitting Epirus, where Helenus and Andromache had just given him such a good reception, he perceived in the distance before him low lands and misty hills. It is Italy. "Italy!" exclaims first Achates. "Italy!" join in all his companions, saluting it with a joyous cry. The heart of Æneas beats with pleasure on first nearing the country promised him by the Fates, and which his race is to make so glorious. But he is not to enter on this side. The soil before his eyes is all Greek, and peopled with enemies. He contents himself with secretly passing a night there, and continues his way along the Gulf of Tarentum. Later on, after his sojourn in Carthage and in Sicily, where Acestus, another fugitive from Troy, affords him hospitality, he stops at Cumæ to consult the sibyl and descend into Hell. But this is not yet the spot where he is to settle; he must re-embark and turn towards those Latian lands "which seem ever to flee before him." Finally, after touching at Misenum, at Palinurus, and at Caieta, to bury there the companions he has lost, he doubles the promontory where the enchantress Circe holds her court, and arrives at the mouth of the Tiber.

"The sea was already becoming tinged with the rays of dawn, and Aurora clomb to the horizon on her rosy car. Suddenly the winds fall, the breeze ceases to blow, and we must wrestle with the oar against the passive wave. Then Æneas sees upon the shore a tufted wood, and in the midst the Tiber winds his smiling course, bearing his yellow sands, and flinging himself with rapid whirlings into the sea. Along and above his waters birds of varied hues, the wonted dwellers of the wood and stream, enchant the air with their accents, and flutter amid the trees. Æneas orders his sailors to direct their course on that side, and turn the prows towards the shore, and then he enters joyously the shady bed of Tiber."[1]

I have more than once gone over this coast where, one spring morning, the pious Æneas landed; and I own that the spectacle I had before my eyes is not quite what Virgil drew. The Tiber continues to flow noiselessly, fretting its banks, and rolling its yellow waters towards the sea; but trees are rare on this desolate shore, and I never heard birds sing there. In lieu of this idyllic picture, one has before one a monotonous and silent landscape that awakens in the

---

[1] *Æn.*, VII. 24.

soul an impression of sadness and of grandeur. It was
otherwise in Virgil's time; and if he adorned his picture
with such cheerful colours, it is because he drew these
spots as he saw them. Near the Tiber's mouth rose Ostia,
the old port of Rome, growing each day in importance,
as the relations of Italy with foreign countries became
more frequent. The moment was approaching when
the great city, unable any longer to feed herself, would
be forced to ask neighbouring lands for her food—oil
from Spain, corn from Africa and Egypt. All the
merchandise of the world was beginning to pass
through Ostia, which grew more and more populous
every day. It is at this time that Virgil visited it,
and he saw the Tiber as those enriched merchants, who
came thither to enjoy a little freshness and repose upon
its banks after the fatigues of the day, had made it.
All this part of the country had then a very different
aspect from that which ten centuries of desertion and
solitude have given it. The sacred isle between Porto
and Ostia has become a desert where a few wild oxen
graze, and which the traveller hardly dares to cross.
was then a much-frequented place, whither the Præfect
of Rome came with a part of the Roman people to celebrate brilliant festivals. We are told that throughout the
year the ground formed a veritable carpet of verdure,
and that in spring so many roses and flowers of all
kinds grew there that the air was perfumed, and it was
called "the abode of Venus."[1] The banks of the Tiber,

---

[1] See what Wernsdorff says in the Preface of *Pervigilium Veneris*
about these festivals which used to be celebrated at Ostia (*Poetæ Lat.
minores*, Lemaire's edition, II. p. 485).

as far as Rome, were covered uninterruptedly with fine villas. "He alone," says Pliny, "has more than all other rivers together."[1]   Near the immense city it was bordered by delicious gardens, where the great lords loved to assemble their friends of both sexes for joyous feasts, during which they amused themselves by watching the boats pass up and down the stream.[2] One cannot doubt but that Virgil assisted more than once at these amusements of the Roman aristocracy, and he must have had them in mind when describing in the Eighth Book the journey undertaken by Æneas to the town of Evander.   It would be impossible to imagine a more pleasant voyage: "The vessels glide upon the waters, the river is astonished, the forest looks with surprise at this new spectacle of gleaming bucklers and brightly-coloured ships that swim upon the waves. The rowers work without ceasing, and advance through the long windings of the Tiber; they pass beneath a thick vault of trees; and their prow seems to cleave the forest whose image is reflected on the placid water."[3]   Except the sinuosities of the sluggish river, nothing is now left us resembling this seductive picture.   An old writer, a century earlier than Virgil, and who doubtless lived at a time when the work of man had not yet transformed this thankless nature, speaks very differently from him.   He describes Æneas as seized with sadness at the sight of this country which Latinus makes over to him, and where he must henceforth live.   "He was very ill pleased," he tells us, "to have fallen upon so arid and sandy a soil: *ægre*

---

[1] *Hist. Nat.*, III. 5 (9).   [2] Propertius, I. 14.   [3] *Æn.*, VIII. 91.

patiebatur in eum devenisse agrum macerrimum litorosissimumque." [1]   This energetic sentence represents admirably the aspect of the country as we see it to-day. When from the height of one of these mounds, formed by the accumulation of ruins, we cast our eyes around us, it is impossible not to pity the poor Trojan chief who has just left the rich fields of Asia, and whom the gods have made pay with so many toils and perils for the possession of a few leagues of sand.

Virgil attributes other feelings to him. He represents him as enchanted at the spectacle before him, and overjoyed at touching this unknown shore. For he hopes that he has at last reached the end of his journey, and that the soil he is about to tread is the land whither the Fates have led him. But when we know pious Æneas, we shall be certain that he will not lightly trust to his hopes. Before beginning to found a stable settlement, he will wait until the gods have shown him by manifest signs that he is not mistaken; and in order that he may have full confidence, they must prove to him twice, by successive prodigies, that he is in the land where he is to remain. These wonders, related by Virgil circumstantially, have in his work a particular character. They already astonished the critics of antiquity; they still more surprise modern readers,[2] and have given rise to great dis-

---

[1] Servius, in *Æn.*, I. 7. These are the words of the historian Fabius Maximus.

[2] Voltaire is so afraid they may be found ridiculous that he finds it necessary to excuse Virgil for having related them. "Is it not true," he says, "that we should allow a French author who took Clovis for his hero to talk about the holy *ampulla* brought by a dove from heaven into the city of Rheims to anoint the king, and which

cussions. Since we are just upon the spot where they took place, let us occupy ourselves with them for a moment.

We know what a great part religion plays in the *Æneid*, and that this religion in its essence is the religion of Homer. I cannot here relate how it happens that the gods of Greece and Rome, which originally did not resemble each other, finished by being confounded. The friends of Greek literature doubtless helped much in this confusion; in any case, it was very advantageous to them. When they composed some poetical work, they allowed themselves to make Jupiter and Minerva talk like Zeus or Athene, and to freely imitate those masterpieces with which their imaginations were charmed. There can be no doubt but that Virgil also accepted it very willingly. He loved Homer too much not to seize with alacrity all opportunities of drawing near to him. It is, however, clear that he endeavoured somehow to preserve for his mythology a national character, and this stamps his originality among his country's poets. In the first place, we see that when he borrows a fable from the Greeks, he takes care to place the scene of it in some corner of Italian ground. Instead of calling up the dead on a field of asphodels, on some unknown isle of the ocean, like Ulysses, Æneas descends into Hell near Lake Avernus, at the spot where the people

---

is still preserved with faith in that town? It is the fate of all those ancient fables to which the origin of every nation goes back, that their antiquity is respected while their absurdity is laughed at. After all, however excusable it may be to use such tales, I think it would be better to reject them entirely. One sensible reader whom these things offend deserves more to be considered than the ignorant vulgar who believe in them."

of the country place an entrance to Tartarus. The abode where Vulcan forges the arms of the gods is no longer at Lemnos, but near Sicily, in one of those volcanic isles " whence fires are seen to gush like those of Ætna." [1] When Tisiphone has finished her work of discord and wishes to leave the earth, she plunges into the . Lake of Amsactus, which exhales pestiferous vapours. [2] Finally, Juno, desiring closely to watch the last combats of Turnus and Æneas, quits Olympus and stations herself on the heights of Mount Albanus, where, later on, the famous and national Temple of Jupiter · Latialis rose. [3] It was a way of connecting this foreign mythology with Italy, and of interesting all Romans in attaching it more closely to them. But he had still more in view. The introduction of the Hellenic religion had not suppressed all the ancient fables of the Italian races. Some survived in connection with towns or temples, whose birth they explained. They were rude, like the people who had created them ; and men of the world, who found that they recalled the rusticity of their forefathers, took pleasure in laughing at them. Virgil treated them with more respect. Their antiquity endeared them to him, and he thought that, having cradled the infancy

---

[1] *Æn.*, VIII. 416. [2] *Ibid.*, VII. 563.

[3] *Ibid.*, XII. 134. It is curious, in this connection, to note in what degree Horace and Virgil have contrary tendencies. While the patriot Virgil, who would fain impart a Latin colouring to the Greek fables, seems to wish to confound Olympus with Mount Albanus, Horace, very indifferent to such a care, laughs at those who would identify Mount Albanus with Parnassus, and who pretend to make it the abode of the Muses : *Dictitet Albano Musas in monte locutas* (*Epist.*, II. 1. 27).

of the Roman people, they had a right to figure in a poem telling of its foundation. It was doubtless not an easy task to place them beside the Homeric fables, usually so elegant and so graceful, and they ran a great risk of making but a sorry figure there; but this danger did not stay the poet, whose aim it was that Æneas, on setting foot in Latium, should be welcomed and greeted, as it were, by an old Latin legend.

The Trojans, he tells us, had just fastened their ships to the green banks of the Tiber. Æneas, with the principal chiefs and handsome Iulus, are resting beneath the branches of a high tree. They prepare their repast. First, among the food they are to eat they place cakes of pure wheat (it was Jupiter himself who suggested this idea to them), and then they load this table, formed of the products of Ceres, with wild fruits. It happened that when all their food was exhausted, their hunger, still unsated, obliged them to attack those light cakes. "Ah!" exclaimed Iulus, jesting, "here we are eating our tables as well." He said no more; but this saying was enough to announce to the Trojans the end of their ills. Æneas at once receives it from the mouth of his son, and struck by the accomplishment of the oracle, he meditates upon it in silence. Then, suddenly, "Hail!" he cried, "land which the Fates did promise me! And you also hail, faithful Penates of Troy. Here is your dwelling, here is your country. My father Anchises (I remember him to-day) revealed to me in times gone by the secrets of the future. 'My son,' he said, ' when arrived on unknown shores hunger shall force thee, after eating all, to devour also thy tables, hope then for a fixed abode, and remember to trace on that spot the boundary of a new town.' Here, then, is that terrible hunger that was foretold to us. Yes, we have just borne the last trial which was to put an end to our uncertain wanderings." [1]

Heyne, who passed his life in commenting on Virgil, and usually professed a great admiration for him, cannot help being scandalised here. This legend of the eaten tables seems to him quite ridiculous, and unworthy of the majesty of an epic poem. It must be owned that it bears the character of a peasant's fable. They are very fond of telling these tales, which at first seem terrible, but end almost amusingly. The one in question was doubtless ancient, and had been repeated for a great length of time in the cabins of Latian husbandmen.[2] Virgil sought it there, and, far from blaming him for it, like Heyne, I think he must be congratulated on having had the courage to introduce it into his poem, and the more so that he was not unaware that it would shock many of his readers. He also knew those railers and sceptics whom Ovid addressed when, being about to talk of old Janus and his ridiculous surnames, he says to them, "You are going to laugh." He has

---

[1] _Æn._, VII, 107.

[2] Probably certain rites in the worship of the Penates had given rise to it. It was customary to offer those little gods the first fruits of the repast, and these were presented to them on slices of bread called _mensæ paniceæ_. Naturally they were sacred, and only in case of a terrible famine would anyone dare to touch them. To eat the _paniceæ_ would therefore simply mean to suffer from one of those scarcities which force one to respect nothing. Such must be the origin of the prediction made to the Trojans, and which frightened them so much. The good-humoured ingenuity of the Latian peasantry found the means related by Virgil to fulfil the oracle at small cost.

even made visible attempts to disarm them, and has obviously tried to prepare these malicious wits for this rustic story, and familiarise them with it. In order that they may be less surprised on hearing it told, he has it announced several times in advance. With this task he charges the Harpies, old Greek divinities— coarse, a little grotesque, and quite suited for the office. As for the narrative itself, I have just quoted it in full, and the skill with which it is managed is obvious. There are none of those little jokes, as in Ovid, designed to show that the poet is not taken in by the tale he is telling; all is simple and serious. Yet we must remark the part given to Iulus in this matter. It is he who perceives that they have eaten their tables, and who says it. In another mouth the thing might surprise; it is becoming in a child, to whom such little remarks are natural. Without apparent design, therefore, Virgil has set about making us accept this simple legend with great cleverness.[1]

The other was more important, and enjoyed a much greater popularity in the country. The first adventure, just related, assured Æneas that he had at length set foot upon the ground that had been promised to him, and ordered him to make a first settlement at the very spot where he had disembarked. But this was not the

---

[1] We have just seen in Virgil's narrative that Æneas only speaks of Anchises. It is he alone who predicted that he would be reduced to eat his tables. It is therefore likely that the prediction of the Harpies was added by the poet later on. I do not think it rash to suppose, as I have just said, that Virgil only did so because he feared the bad effect his narrative might produce on some readers, and wished to justify it, and prepare them for it in advance.

end of his fortune. The Trojans will not remain in this kind of intrenched camp which they are about to construct at the mouth of the Tiber. They must leave it, in order to advance to greater conquests, plunging deeper and deeper into the interior of the country, and building a new town each time they stop. This march, with Rome for its goal, must be known to Æneas. He deserves to be admitted to the secrets of the future, since he has had so much trouble in preparing it. Were he only working for himself, he would long since have been fixed on some quiet spot of earth, there to end his troubled existence in peace. But he belongs to his descendants, and must not deprive them of the country over which they are called to reign, or of the glory that awaits them. Is it not just that, to console him for the toils and perils he suffers, he may at least know what is to happen after him, and foresee the great destinies in the preparation of which he is working so hard? This is how the gods reveal the future to him.

When Æneas can no longer doubt the hostility of the Latins, he is anxious about the war that threatens him, and a prey to a thousand cares. As evening falls he stretches himself upon the river bank, "beneath the fresh vault of the skies,"[1] and only goes to sleep after the others, late in the night. During his slumbers, a god appears to him, "clad in a light purple tunic with azure folds, his head covered with a crown of reeds." He introduces himself. It is the river-god himself, by whose brink the hero is resting, the Tiber, beloved of heaven, who flows with full banks through fertile plains.

---

[1] *Æn.*, VIII. 26.

"Ego sum, pleno quem flumine cernis
Stringentem ripas et pinguia culta secantem,
Cœruleus Tibris, cœlo gratissimus amnis."

He begins by repeating to Æneas, who cannot know it too well, that this land is indeed the one where he must settle : " Thy promised home is here ; and here must thy Penates dwell." And that he may not think himself the dupe of a dream, a manifest sign of the divine will is announced to him : " Under the oaks that cover this shore, thou shalt find an enormous sow outstretched, which has just brought forth thirty little ones. She is white, and her little ones, white like their mother, hang from her teats. This is the spot where thou must raise the city thou art to build (Lavinium) ; it is the end of all thy toils. Thence, later on, after thirty years have come round, shalt start thy son, Ascanius, to go and found Alba, the noble city, whose name shall recall its origin (*Alba*, the white). Be sure that my predictions do not deceive thee." And indeed, on awakening, Æneas finds the white sow lying on the bank with her thirty little ones, and sacrifices them to Juno.

This legend, like the preceding, is a peasant's tale. The word-play forming its essence, and which explains the name of the town of Alba, sufficiently shows its origin. Those peasants, moreover, are inhabitants of Latium, a country whose swine form its chief wealth. Varro the Elder speaks with vanity of those which he raises in his domains, and calls his countrymen " pig-raisers " by way of compliment (*porculatores italici*). Strictly speaking, it may be said that these animals figure more advantageously on a farm than in an epic poem. Homer doubtless spoke of them without repugnance; yet when, in the *Iliad*, Jupiter wishes to restore courage to the combatants by a favourable omen, he usually sends them an eagle rending a serpent, or holding a fawn in his talons. An eagle, it must be owned, looks better than a pig or a sow. It has been remarked that Virgil himself, in his *Georgics*—that is to say, in a work in which he sang of Italian agriculture—did not give these animals quite the place they deserved to fill. He only speaks of the pig two or three times; and again in one of these passages he has thought fit to lend him an almost heroic attitude entirely out of keeping with its nature:

> " *Ipse ruit dentesque sabellicus exacuit sus,*
> *Et pede prosubigit terram.*" [1]

We no longer find the same timid precautions in the *Æneid*. He did not hesitate to introduce the white sow and her little ones into it, nor did he ask himself what the fastidious would think about it. Here again we must in some degree approve his courage.

All agree that when Virgil reproduced the legend it had been greatly modified by time; but even his own narrative of it admits of its being brought back to its primitive form. Whatever he may pretend, it was not created to explain the rise of Lavinium. Those who first imagined this artless fable had Alba, then the metropolis of the Latin League, in mind. They related that they were one day assembled at the foot of Mount Albanus, their sacred mountain, consulting the gods as

---

[1] *Georg.*, III. 255.

to the spot where they should build their capital. Suddenly, during the sacrifice, the pregnant sow they were about to immolate escaped towards the mountain. They followed her at a distance, and at the place where she stopped to give birth to her young ones, they founded their city. Legends of this kind were not uncommon in the ancient mythology of the Aryan races. At Bovillæ it is a bull, at Ephesus a boar, which, escaping from the hands of the sacrificers, indicated the spot where the town was to be raised. Here the sow was preferred, because it is the animal which it was customary to immolate on the occasion of treaties of alliance, and the thirty little ones represented the thirty cities composing the Confederation. As we see, everything is simple and natural in the primitive story, and we do not need an augur or an aruspice to enable us to grasp its meaning.

Later, when the legend of Æneas was implanted in Rome, and the Trojan hero was made the founder of Lavinium, the sacred city of the Penates, it was desired to transplant the marvellous tale, which had been invented for the ancient capital of the Latin League, to the new one. But it could not be adapted to its new purpose without undergoing some changes. It was supposed that the white sow stopped where Æneas built Lavinium; but at the same time it was still admitted that it had given its name to Alba, so the prodigy found itself relating to two cities at once, which is difficult to understand. Moreover, it was imagined that the thirty little ones meant the thirty years separating the foundation of the two cities. Virgil was forced, by the very subject he had chosen, to adopt this last form of the legend, which was not, as we have seen, the most simple and most natural. But what mattered those little obscurities of detail in the narration of a miracle? The substance of the adventure remained; it was still a question of the sow and her little ones, and people whose youth had been charmed by these wonderful tales were happy to find them again in Virgil's poem.[1]

III.

LAVINIUM—ITS DECADENCE UNDER THE EMPIRE—WORSHIP OF THE PENATES—VESTIGES OF THE ANCIENT CITY — PRATICA — OUTLOOK FROM THE BORGHESE TOWER—THE PLAIN OF THE LATIUM—LATIN AND SABINE ELEMENTS IN THE ROMAN CITY.

By the prediction of the Tiber, we are now led to speak of Lavinium. This town is often mentioned in the *Æneid*, although it does not yet exist. This is because in reality it forms the only link connecting the legend of Æneas with the history of Rome. In itself a small

---

[1] Virgil has even introduced a new obscurity and inaccuracy into the legend. Admitting the white sow to have been found, as he says, on the banks of the Tiber, it should have been supposed that she fled to the spot where Lavinium was to rise. But he thought it would be a ridiculous sight to show Æneas and his soldiers running for nearly eight kilomètres after a sow, so he once more bravely made up his mind, and had her immolated on the spot where she was found. But then one no longer understands the expression "*Is locus urbis erit,*" for Lavinium is six miles from the banks of the Tiber. Servius says we must translate as if there were "*in ea regione*"—that is to say, in the country, in the environs—which is very vague and arbitrary.

hamlet in the midst of a solitary plain, it must be very indifferent to the masters of the world. Virgil several times made a point of reminding them of the right it had to their respect and their affection. At the very beginning of his work, Jupiter, consoling Venus for her son's misadventures, unveils to her the future reserved for his descendants. He first shows her Æneas founding Lavinium, in order to establish his homeless gods there. It is the starting-point of those glorious destinies. Later, from Lavinium will issue Alba, and Alba in its turn will give birth to Rome, so that all the greatness of Rome is referable to the founding of the city of Æneas. The Penates, for whom he must build a dwelling on a hill of Latium, are the pledge of the eternal empire promised by the gods to the nation who wear the toga:

> *" His ego nec metas rerum nec tempora pono ;*
> *Imperium sine fine dedi."* [1]

In Virgil's day the little town must already have been half deserted. Such, indeed, was the common lot of most of those he speaks of, and which make so great a figure in his poem. He himself tells us, with regard to Ardea, the capital of the Rutuli, " it has still a great name, but its fortune is past." [2] I picture to myself that Ardea was then, as now, a village of a few houses surrounded by old walls, upon a steep hill. Strabo, who went over the whole of this country in the time of Augustus, tells us that, after the ravages of the Samnites, it could not raise itself from its. disasters,

---

[1] *Æn.*, I. 278.
[2] *Ibid.*, VII. 412.

and that, of the ancient and illustrious cities dating from Æneas, only vestiges remained. A hundred years later Lucan bears witness to the same abandonment. He says: "The sites of Veii, Gabii, and Cora are marked by ruins. Where Alba rose, or the Penates of Lavinium had their temple, nothing but uninhabited fields are any longer seen."[1] He adds that everywhere the walls of cities are too vast for their inhabitants; that the fields lack husbandmen, and that a single city suffices to contain all the Romans. He doubtless means that this town has ended by absorbing Italy.[2] Rome was already making a vacuum around her, and from the Augustan age it might be foreseen that she would end by encircling herself with a desert. It is therefore likely that most of the Latin towns, when Virgil knew them, had already begun to assume the desolate look they wear in our days. It was a reason for him to love them more. They must have even pleased him by their very sadness and their solitude; and rich, flourishing, populous, they would have inspired him with less affection. His biographers relate that he felt ill at

---

[1] Lucan, *Phars.*, VII. 391.

[2] Bonstetten, describing the state of this part of the country in 1804, speaks very much like Lucan: "Some of the fifty-three nations that formerly existed in Latium are represented by a single house. The great city of Gabii is now merely the abode of a herd of cows. Fidenæ, where so many thousand men perished by the fall of an amphitheatre, is a broken-down sheep-stall; and Cures, the illustrious country of Numa, an inn. Antemnæ, with its superb towers, Collatia, Cenina, Veii, Crustumerium, and so many other towns which proved the flourishing state of Latium, were swallowed up in a few years by infant Rome, already taught to devastate the earth, and we are still searching for the spot where they existed."

ease in large, populous towns, and shunned them as much as he could. On the other hand, he must have visited these poor abandoned cities willingly. The striking contrast between their ancient fortune and their present wretchedness the more endeared them to him, and one feels that he never speaks of them without emotion.

Among all these half-ruined and deserted ancient cities Lavinium had a particular importance. " Here," said Varro solemnly, " here are the Penates of the Roman people " (*ibi dii Penates nostri*).[1] They had shown in an important circumstance that they would not dwell elsewhere. It was related that Ascanius having tried to take them with him to the town which he had built, they twice left their temple at Alba, although the doors had been carefully shut, and returned by night to Lavinium. They had to be left there, since they would not leave their old home ; and as they would have been angry had they lost all their worshippers, six hundred inhabitants were sent, who were forced to dwell there and offer them sacrifices.[2] Thenceforth Lavinium was entirely consecrated to their worship. It was a kind of holy town, like a few that are still left in Italy, containing nothing but churches and convents, and where only monks are met with. There was no dearth of priests in Lavinium either, if we are to believe the inscriptions, which mention a great number, and even bid us observe the very characteristic circumstance, that they kept the ancient costume in all its

---

[1] *De Ling. Lat.*, V. 144.

[2] Denys of Halicarnassus, *Ant. Rom.*, I. 67.

rigour, whereas at Rome it had been modified, in order
to make it more convenient.[1] The Temple of the Penates
was doubtless the most important in the country. It
was much visited, but it not being allowed to penetrate
into the sanctuary, considerable uncertainty existed
as to what these gods might be. Some stated that
they were represented under the form of small seated
statues with spears in their hands, and others that they
were merely pieces of iron or bronze, not even formed in
the human shape. The devout Denys of Halicarnassus,
very much perplexed between these contrary assertions,
gets out of the difficulty by saying one must not speak
of that which the gods do not allow one to know.[2]
However, it was not neccesary to know in order to
respect them, since they had worked miracles that
proved their power. It is said that two young maidens,
doubtless two vestals, having come to sleep in their
temple in order to be relieved of certain reproaches of
which they had been the object, one of them, who was
not quite stainless, was in the course of the night struck
by a thunderbolt, while the other slept at her side without awaking.[3] There were also at Lavinium other
religious edifices, which naturally claimed to go back
to the time of Æneas, and in their neighbourhood his
tomb was shown. "It is," says Denys, "a little mound,
about which have been disposed trees in admirable
order, and worthy to be seen."[4] In the Forum of the
city statues of bronze recalled some of the legends that

---

[1] Servius, in Æn., VIII. 661.   [2] Antiq. Rom., I. 67.
[3] Servius, in Æn., III. 12.   [4] Antiq. Rom., I. 64.

had announced his prowess. As may be imagined, the famous sow with its thirty little ones was not forgotten. It was often in question in Lavinium. It was thought they possessed the cabin where Æneas had immolated it; and what is still more surprising, the priests showed the sow herself to visitors, preserved in brine.[1] We thus see that the worship of relics is of ancient date in Italy.

Holy towns are usually dull ones. People are so busied there with sacred interests that worldly pleasures are neglected, and so there is generally a lack of animation and gaiety. Lavinium could not have been an exception to the common rule. Yet the old town had its days of festivity. Every year, at fixed dates, priests came there from Rome to celebrate ancient ceremonies, and the first magistrates of the Republic, dictators, consuls, prætors, came there to sacrifice to the Penates, when they took office.[2] A general would not have undertaken a great military expedition without having first gone there to consult the gods. It is related that when the consul Hostilius Mancinus went thither to consult the augurs before leaving for Spain, the sacred chickens fled into the woods. The consul paid no heed to the warning, but went and got beaten by the Lusitanians.[3] But beyond these solemn occasions which from time to time enlivened the town, it is probable that life then was very monotonous, and that it declined day by day. It is not known at what date and in consequence of what events it was joined to its neighbour

---

[1] Varro, *De re rust.*, II. 4, 18.   [2] Servius, in *Æn.*, III. 12.
[3] Valerino Maximus, I. 6, 7.

Laurentium, the ancient city of Latinus, which was
drawing its last breath beside it. Thenceforth its
citizens took the name of *Laurentes Lavinates*, and the
town itself was sometimes called *Laurolavinium*. Inscriptions show us that the Emperors made a few efforts
to arrest its decadence. It was naturally those most
zealous for the worship of the gods, or most friendly to
the ancient traditions, who chiefly cared to busy themselves about it; for example, good Antoninus, who all
his life showed so much respect for the old memories of
Rome, or Galerius, the ardent persecutor of the Chris-
tians. We still find in the correspondence of Symmachus,
the last of the pagans, a mark of affection towards this
town, which he calls " *religiosa civitas.*" At this moment
Christianity was victorious, invasion was approaching,
and Lavinium was about to vanish entirely, with the
worship of the Penates.

Nothing now remains of the ancient town, and its
name is no longer found upon the map. Its situation,
however, may be given with accuracy. The learned
agree in believing that it was replaced by Pratica, and
everything proves that they are right. Like Lavinium,
Pratica is 16 miles (24 kilomètres) from Rome, at 24
stadia (4 kilomètres) from the sea, and about half-way
between Ostia and Antium. In turning up the soil at
haphazard many ancient remains have been found,
proving that on this spot must formerly have risen a
town of some importance; and as these remains are sometimes fragments of vases belonging to ancient buildings,
and sometimes pieces of marble and porphyry which
recall the most sumptuous periods, Nibby concludes
that this city must go back to the most ancient times,

and that it still existed under the Empire. Finally, numerous inscriptions have been found at Pratica or in the vicinity, some of them bearing the name of Lavinium, which definitively settles all doubts.

Pratica occupies a plateau of slight extent, rising on nearly every side precipitously from the plain. When we have been round it, and seen how difficult of access are the houses of the village, firmly supported as they are by the rock, we easily understand the reasons Æneas may have had for building his town in this place. He found himself safe there against the unforeseen attacks of the Rutuli or the Volsci, of all those peoples whose habit and pleasure, according to Virgil, was to live by rapine :

> *" Semperque recentes*
> *Convectare juvat prædas et vivere rapto."* [1]

On the other hand, the narrowness of the plateau explains that it could not long suffice a population which, in the beginning, was continually on the increase.[2] We have only to glance at Pratica in order to understand the account of Livy, who tells us that Ascanius, seeing that his father's town could not spread, resolved to quit it and found a new one on Mount Albanus, between the mountains and the lake.

Pratica can only be entered by one road, which is

---

[1] *Æn.*, VII. 759.

[2] Pratica only occupies the site of the citadel of Lavinium. The town itself probably extended into the plain, towards Ardea. Many remains of walls have been found in this direction, which may have been the city's boundary. In any case it was small, and hampered in its development by accidents of the ground.

probably the one followed by the procession of consuls and prætors when they came to perform some sacred ceremony at the Temple of the Penates. The roadway, after circling the village for a short distance, rises to it abruptly by a somewhat rude causeway, and enters it beneath a gate which might be easily defended. All here is evidently well prepared to offer a safe asylum to a few husbandmen desirous to protect themselves from pillage. The same cause explains the founding of Lavinium and Pratica. The people who, after the ruin of the ancient town, assembled anew on this narrow table-land, wished to find safety from the incursions of the Barbary pirates who, until the taking of Algiers, never ceased to infest these shores. When night fell, the husbandmen hastened to quit the plain, climbed into their little fortified enclosures, and the door once well secured, they could at least sleep in peace. It is thought that the village of Pratica,[1] whose name is first heard in the ninth century, was in the course of the Middle Ages several times abandoned and rebuilt. As it stands, it is not more than two or three centuries old. It contains but one piazza and a few streets somewhat less dirty than those of other Italian villages. The piazza, regular and sufficiently large, has been decorated with a few fragments of antiquity. These are the little village's titles of nobility.[2] There are capitals of

---

[1] The primitive form of this word seems to have been "Patrica." Nibby thinks this name must be derived from that of *Pater Indiges*—that is, of Æneas—who was chiefly honoured at Lavinium. By its modern name it would be the City, *Æneas civitas Patris*.

[2] The statues and inscriptions have been lately placed in the court-yard of the Borghese Château.

columns, fragments of statues, inscriptions in honour of Antoninus and Galerius, and lastly, a sort of pedestal bearing the words "Silvius Æneas, son of Æneas and of Lavinia." If this monument was not the work of an amateur of the sixteenth century, as it very possibly may be, it is perhaps the base of some statue which ornamented the Forum of Lavinium. One side of the Piazza is formed by the front of a large house, devoid of any architectural pretensions. This is the Palazzo of the Borghese family. Pratica has belonged to them for nearly three hundred years, and constitutes one of their most important baronies.

This does not imply that the village is very populous. It numbers but the seven or eight families who dare to remain there all the year round. The rest of the population is nomadic, and consists of peasants who in the winter descend from the mountains, and return home as soon as the heat approaches and the malaria begins to be dangerous. It is much the same from one end of Italy to the other, wherever marsh fever rages. François Lenormant, when travelling in Grecia Magna, found the custom again there.[1] The colours in which he painted the miseries of those poor Calabrian peasants, who come every year to work in this unwholesome soil, have not been forgotten; and I bear witness that the pictures he drew of them produced the liveliest emotion in the country itself: so true is it that one becomes indifferent to spectacles which one has daily before one's eyes, and that it is good for a stranger now and then to tell us what happens in our own home. Not long since,

---

[1] *La Grande Grèce*, by François Lenormant.

M. de la Blanchère, who made a stay at Terracina and courageously explored the Pontine marshes, had an opportunity of observing and describing the same customs. There, too, the fields are deserted during half the year—the emigrants arriving in the month of October. Generally the same persons settle in the same spots. They descend the Apennines and the Abruzzi together, and come to resume their work. "Each," says M. de la Blanchère, "goes to find his *lestra*—that is to say, a clearing made by himself or a predecessor—often by an ancestor—for families are perpetuated during centuries upon the same soil. A *staccionata*, or rough fence of brambles, contains the beasts; hive - shaped cabins shelter the people. On his own account, or that of another, the occupant carries on one or many of the thousand vocations of the *macchia*—shepherd, cowherd, swineherd, for the most part; sometimes a woodcutter, and always a poacher and a prowler, using the *macchia* without scruple, like a savage of the virgin forest, he lives, and by his work makes a revenue for his own and the soil's master, who has confided his beasts to him—that is to say, when they are not his personal property. Thus six or seven months pass. June comes, the marshes dry up, the pools of the forest are exhausted, the children tremble with fever, the news from the country is satisfactory, and in a fortnight the roads are covered with people going back to the mountains again. Family by family, *lestra* by *lestra*, the *macchia* empties. Only men exhorting their horses, asses, or their women, laden with what is to be brought away, are met with; and those whom July surprises in these regions are few indeed. The forest is abandoned to twenty species of gad-flies and insects, which make life there impossible."[1]

This is what happens on almost all the coast of Latium. I own, however, that at Ostia the picture seemed to me sadder than M. Blanchère represents it. There the immigrants are all husbandmen who come to sow the ground and get in the crops. At night they crowd together in cabins made of old planks covered with straw. I visited one, narrow and long, which resembled a passage. It had no windows, and was only lighted by the doors placed at each extremity. The arrangements were of the simplest; in the middle the saucepans in which the soup is made; on either side, in dark recesses, men, women, and children lie pell-mell on heaps of straw that are never renewed. Directly you enter the cabin a fœtid odour seizes you by the throat. As you pass on, eyes unaccustomed to this darkness can make out nothing. You only hear the moans of the sick whom the fever holds to their straw, and who lean forward to ask the passer-by for alms. I should never have believed that a human being could live in such a hole. At Pratica there are at least houses decent enough in appearance. They are empty half the year, and much too full the rest of the time; but the immigrants who crowd them have not to suffer like those who wallow in the barracks at Ostia. The little village, moreover, does not look very miserable. It even possesses a great luxury in the shape of an *osteria con cucina*, which remains open during all the winter season, and does not seem to lack customers. In spring the land-

---

[1] De la Blauchère, *Terracine*, p. 11.

lord takes flight like everybody else, only leaving a
wretched servant, a victim to the malaria, to take care
of the house. I found myself there with some people
of the country one day when it poured with rain; for
want of anything better to do, they played at cards.
They were *caporali*, or labour-masters, and their
dignity was seen in their costume. They wore under
their large green-lined brown mantles a gallooned
waistcoat. These insignia, together with their short
breeches and pointed hats ornamented with feathers,
gave them a melodramatic air, of which they seemed
very proud. Looking at them, I thought that certainly
no village inn in France could offer a collection
of such types. The French peasant does not care to
assume theatrical poses, or to attract the attention
of strangers. On the contrary, he is so timid and
cunning that he will rather give himself an air of simplicity and innocence in order that he may not be
mistrusted. One has to be careful not to judge him
quite by his appearance, or think him as foolish as he
looks. The peasantry of these parts have not the same
character. Nature has given them a ferocious look, and
to nature they willingly add. One would think they
desired to inspire fear, and to appear more brigand-like
than they really are. But, however this may be, vulgar
faces are rarely found among them, and a glance at
them suffices to convince one that they belong to an
energetic and intelligent race. Since they all come
from the Appenines and the neighbouring heights, I
have no difficulty in believing that I have before my
eyes descendants of the Marsi, the Equi, and the Samnites, of all those rough mountaineers whom Rome had

so much difficulty in subduing, and who afterwards helped her to subdue the world.

One of the curiosities of Pratica is the tower rising from the middle of the Borghese Palace. It is seen from every direction, and serves to direct shepherds and travellers in a country where beaten roads are not always found. It was doubtless built to overlook the vicinity at a period when unforeseen piratical attacks were to be feared, and it enables one to penetrate all the windings of the valleys, and observe all the shore from Ostia to Porto d'Anzio. From the uppermost storey the view is marvellous, but I will not proceed to describe its beauties. However great the desire in these high spots to cast one's eyes afar, and although the spectacle of these beautiful lines of mountains that close the horizon is incomparably grand, I own that I feel rather tempted to look down at my feet. I am absorbed by an entirely historical interest. I think of Rome, whose belfries and houses I can distinguish, and I endeavour to follow hence the phases of her budding fortune. This ground which surrounds me on every side is Latium—"Old Latium" as it was called (*Latium vetus Prisci Latini*). It is here, according to a celebrated expression, "that Rome struck her first roots" (*ex hac tenui radice crevit imperium*); it is in this little corner of the land that the Romans must have become imbued with their fundamental qualities. I take it in entirely, and while carefully examining it, I ask myself whether there is anything in the configuration of the soil and the nature of the country to account for the character of the inhabitants.

From this height at which the inequalities of the

ground disappear, Latium seems to be a vast uniform plain. On looking at it, a reflection of Schwegler's, from which he drew important conclusions, occurs to my mind.[1] He bids us remark how easy to traverse and how accessible to the stranger this plain appears to be at first sight. Towards the south I see neither mountains nor river separating it from the Volsci; to the north it is bathed by a navigable stream, the sea bounds it to the west, and it possesses a long line of coast. The ancients had already observed that the countries bordering the sea are those which most quickly attain to a brilliant civilization; but that, in general, they pay for this rapid progress by an early decay. "They are prompt to change," says Cicero, "and greedy of novelty. They like to listen to all those travellers, who bring them their ideas and their customs with their wares. They end by resembling those isles of Greece, more troubled and unstable in their institutions than the wave that beats their shores."[2] Happily, Latium is not quite what it seems when viewed from aloft and from afar. This plain, at first sight apparently quite unbroken, hides undulations of ground, heights and valleys, which sometimes render circulation sufficiently inconvenient. This navigable river is not easy of access, on account of its shifting sands; this long coast has no natural ports. It follows that the visits of the foreigner did not produce all their usual effects. External influence doubtless made itself felt, but it was tempered by a groundwork of natural

---

[1] *Röm. Geshichte*, I. 4.
[2] Cicero, *De Rep.*, II. 4.

S

qualities which nothing would quite destroy. I do not know how; but the taste for novelties and the love of tradition blended. Commerce and industry did not replace agriculture. Nature and the soil had made the Latins husbandmen, and field-work was always the most honoured of all vocations among them. But these husbandmen do not remain isolated in their farms; they possess a certain intelligence of political life, and feel the want of a national existence. Families group together to form cities, and cities unite in a common alliance to form a nation. It is not quite the same among the people who were their nearest neighbours, almost their brothers—the Sabines. I see before me their mountains, forming a sombre line on the horizon. In that country, scarcely accessible to people from without, there dwelt an almost savage population of husbandmen and shepherds, resolutely attached to their old customs and their ancient beliefs, and resolved not to change them. With regard to political organisation, they remained faithful to patriarchal rule. Their ideal form of government was family government, and they did not, like the Latins, get so far as to establish veritable cities. "Their towns," says Strabo, "are scarcely hamlets."[1] So Schwegler thinks that in the union of the two peoples which formed the Roman nation, each had its share and played its part. The Latins represent that love of progress, those broad views, those humanitarian instincts, which are the characteristic and the honour of the Plebeians, while the Sabines, a race energetic but narrow, severe to hardness, devout even to superstition,

---

[1] Strabo, V. 3.

brought into the mixture that love of ancient usages, that respect for old maxims, that spirit of resistance and conservatism which animated the Patricians. The struggle between these two opposite tendencies lasted, under different forms, for six centuries, and explains the whole of Roman history down to the time of the Empire. Many sages and patriots who were witnesses of it or its victims deplored it bitterly. They believed and have said that Rome would have been much happier and greater could one of these two elements of discord have disappeared. I think this a mistake, and that, in combating, they restrained and tempered each other. Their opposition prevented stability from becoming routine and reform revolution. It may have rendered progress slower, but it made it more sure; and, thanks to it, everything was done with order and in its due time. The very struggle of the two hostile principles, far from being a cause of weakness to Rome, is perhaps what gave it most spring and motion. In these daily assaults of which the Forum was the scene, characters took that energetic temper, that ardour of generous rivalry, that mettle, and that vigour, which, turned against the stranger, conquered the world.

But we have wandered very far from our subject. Roman history is full of attraction, and if we give way to the reflections suggested by the sight of the plains of Latium and the mountains of the Sabina, we shall not be able to stop. It is high time to descend from the Borghese tower and return to the camp of Æneas.

IV.

ÆNEAS GOES TO SEE EVANDER AT PALLANTEUM—THE TRO-
JAN CAMP AT OSTIA—IT IS BESIEGED AND ALMOST
TAKEN IN THE ABSENCE OF THE CHIEF—BURNING OF
THE SHIPS—EPISODE OF NISUS AND EURYALUS.

The god of the Tiber, in his prediction which kept
us so long just now, is not content to announce to
Æneas the destinies of his race, and give him explanations regarding the foundation of Lavinium and Alba.
After busying himself with the future, he thinks of the
present, and teaches him how to escape from the
dangers that threaten him. All the Italian people
unite against him, and he cannot oppose them without
soldiers, so Tiber tells him how to find them. He
must implore help from the enemies of the Latins, and
he will be enabled to resist Turnus by the help of
Evander and the Etruscans. In order to procure these
precious alliances, and obey the orders of the gods,
Æneas leaves his camp, embarks on the Tiber, and
proceeds to visit King Evander in his little town of
Pallanteum. This is an ingenious means found by
Virgil to get out of one of the greatest difficulties of his
subject. His aim is to sing the glory of Rome; and
Rome, at the time in which he places his epic, does not
yet exist; she only figures there by means of the
predictions unceasingly made of her greatness and her
glory. To render her more present in this epic of
which she is the soul, the poet has had the happy idea
to send his hero to the very spot where she is one day
to rise. If he cannot see, he must at least divine and

foreshadow her. On this predestined soil there is something of her already. At the foot of the Aventine, the worship of victorious Hercules is celebrated, Salian priests sing around the *ara maxima;* on the slope of the Palatine the sacred grotto of the Lupercal is shown, and when the Arcadian shepherds pass before the bushes which cover the rocks of the Palatine they think they hear Jove shake his thunder, and take to flight, terrified. Virgil's Eighth Book is one of those written by him with most ardour and passion. This first view of Rome before her birth entranced him, and the picture he drew of it was of a nature to enrapture his contemporaries, who loved to contrast this town of marble which Augustus flattered himself with having built, not only with the brick Rome of the Republican period, but with the straw houses of the age of the kings. I wish I had time to follow Æneas in this excursion, in which he salutes in advance the city destined to be the world's marvel (*rerum pulcherrima Roma*); and I should like also to accompany him to Cœre, where the enemies of Mezentius await him with their alliance. It would be interesting to see how he speaks of the Etruscans, and the impression which this strange race makes upon him, but I must limit myself, for the journey would take us too far. Let us be resigned, then, to allow him to start alone, and not leave the camp where he has placed his soldiers.

All who wrote the history of these ancient events have spoken of the camp of Æneas, and agree in calling it Troy (*Troja, castra Trojana*); but they place it at different spots. Many supposed that Æneas stopped between Lavinium and Ardea, near the temple raised to Venus, where a statue of the goddess was shown, said to have been brought thither by himself.[1]

Virgil decided for another part of the shore. Faithful to his custom of connecting the present with the past, he chose to consecrate his beginnings of an important town by a great memory, and placed the camp of Æneas at the very place where King Ancus Marcius was afterwards to found Ostia. We have seen the Trojans arrive at the mouth of the Tiber, and penetrate into the " shady bed of the river." After advancing a little way along its banks, they stop and disembark. It is there that recent excavations have brought to light the foundations of vast magazines that encroached upon the Tiber, and still contain large corn jars in which the food of the Roman people was placed in reserve. Ostia is now about four kilomètres from the sea; but we know that at the time of its prosperity it was quite close to it. In the *Octavius* of Minucius Felix, the first work written by a Christian in Latin, the author and his friends leave Ostia one morning for a walk on the shore, and it seems from the

---

[1] Another reason they had for making Æneas come to this spot was that the sacred river *Numicus* or *Numicius* was generally placed here. Denys of Halicarnassus and Pliny seem indeed to say that it flows near Lavinium, and it is usually identified with the *Rio Torto*, or some other of these rivulets found between Pratica and Ardea. But Virgil puts it quite close to Ostia. When on their arrival the Trojans seek to find out where it is they have landed, they send people to explore the neighbourhood, and these report that they have just seen the marshes where the Numicius rises (*Fontis stagna Numici*), which would seem to point to a rivulet issuing from the *Stagno di Levante* and flowing towards the sea. However, it was said that this rivulet had dried up, which explains the discussion as to its position.

narrative of Minucius that they only have to go a few
steps. They soon arrive at their goal, and find themselves on a kind of carpet of sand, which the tide seems
to have spread at their feet to make an agreeable walk.
A century and a half before, when Virgil went over this
shore, it must have been in nearly the same state; and
in accordance with his custom, he supposes that it had not
changed since the time of Æneas. Wishing to do for Ostia
what he had done for Rome, he has reverted to the time
when cabins of straw held the place of marble palaces.
His fancy, in love with simplicity and fond of contrasts,
has delighted to place the poor shelters of an improvised camp where he saw wide streets bordered by
porticoes and full of the most sumptuous merchandise,
and to assemble a few frightened soldiers in the very
places animated in his time by the movement and
noise of business. This camp of Æneas is a kind of
little town, imagined by the poet on the model of the
castra stativa in which the Roman legions were wont to
retrench themselves when they had a rather long stay
to make. The boundary, according to an ancient usage,
is traced with the plough, a deep ditch is dug all
around, and the earth drawn from it serves to form an
entrenchment furnished with battlements and loopholes.
In front, like advanced sentinels, rise wooden towers,
joined to the fort by drawbridges, to be lowered or
raised according to the needs of the defence. The
town (as Virgil calls it) is only provided with a
rampart on the left side; the right being built upon
the river, the poet supposes that it does not want protecting. This circumstance affords him the *dénouément*
of one of his most brilliant episodes. He relates that

Turnus, pursuing the fugitive Trojans, enters their camp with them, unperceived. The fugitives' first care is hurriedly to close their gates, and they thus shut within their walls the very man they would have avoided. On recognising the tuft of red feathers that waves upon his head, and the lightnings flashed by his shield, they are seized with unspeakable terror. Turnus chases and slays them "like a tiger surrounded by timid cattle." They end, however, by seeing that he is alone; and having united, they gradually force him to retire from the combat. Before this crowd, every moment increased by the timid who are taking heart again, he withdraws little by little and step by step, holding them all at bay, but exhausted by the unequal contest. "The sweat rolls in black waves over his body. He can no longer breathe, and his pantings shake his breast." Borne back at length against the Tiber, as there is neither retrenchment nor wall on this side, he flings himself into the river, "which raises him softly on its waters, and gives him back to his companions cleansed from the soils of the fight."

This combat, which takes place while Æneas is absent, fills the whole of the Ninth Book of the *Æneid*. In the course of it, the Trojans, bereft of their chief, are very badly used by Turnus, and besieged in their camp, which is on the point of being taken. Of all this struggle, which it would be of slight interest to study in detail, I only give two episodes, not because they are finer than the rest, but because they seem to me to become somewhat clearer when read upon the spot, and because they fit themselves better into the landscape, as it were.

The first is that in which the poet tells us of the metamorphosis of the Trojan vessels into sea-nymphs. When Æneas landed on Italian soil, his first care was to place his ships in safety. He could not think of leaving them in the river. The famous port of Ostia, before the works of Claudius and Trajan, was not a port. Strabo tells us that the shoals caused by the sand carried by the Tiber did not allow vessels of heavy tonnage to approach the coast. "They cast their anchors and remained at large, exposed to all the roughness of the open sea. Meanwhile, light craft came to take their merchandise and bring them other, so that they left without having entered the river."[1] Æneas, in order to avoid these dangers and place his vessels in safety from the sands and the waves, has them drawn up upon the shore. This custom, already existent in the time of Homer, was not abandoned in the second century of the Empire.

Minucius Felix tells us that while walking about Ostia (at the very place where the Trojan fleet must have been) he met with "ships taken out of the water, and resting on wooden stays, in order to prevent them from being soiled by the mud."[2] The vessels of Æneas were placed on the left bank of the Tiber, in the space of four stadia (720 mètres) which separated the Trojan camp from the sea. They had been hidden as well as possible, and, like the camp itself, they were defended by a sort of entrenchment on the side where the river did not protect them. But they did not escape Turnus. Going before the main body of his

---

[1] Strabo, V. 3, 5.　　　　[2] *Octavius*, 3.

soldiers, who did not march fast enough, the chief of
the Rutuli, with a few chosen horsemen, turns on the
Trojan camp "like a famished wolf around a well-
filled, well-shut sheep-fold, when, through the night,
mid wind and storm, he hears the lambs bleat peace-
fully beneath their dams."[1]   While looking on all
sides for some opening through which to strike his foes,
who will not come out, he espies the vessels, and
prepares to hurl blazing torches against them. But at
this moment Cybele, mother of the gods, steps in and
saves them. Since they were built with trees of the
sacred forest of Ida, she will not have them perish like
ordinary craft, and obtains from Jupiter leave to change
them into goddesses of the sea. She has only to say a
word. "At once the vessels break the bonds that held
them, and like plunging dolphins sink in the abyss.
Soon after, on the surface of the waves, as many youthful nymphs were seen to rise as prows of bronze had
been along the shore."[2]

Naturally this miracle does not please Voltaire, and
we must believe that it caused some surprise even in
ancient times, since the poet feels it necessary to defend
it. Like the authors of the *chansons de geste*, who, after
relating anything incredible, never fail to state that
they read it in the Latin work of some well-informed
monk, Virgil invokes tradition. "It is a very old
story," he tells us, "but its fame has been preserved
throughout the ages."[3] This precaution shows us that
he foresaw some objection. He well felt that in his
work the tale he was about to tell bore quite a new

---

[1] *Æn.*, IX. 59.   [2] *Ibid.*, 117.   [3] *Ibid.*, 79.

character. In Homer's poems and in his own the gods very frequently intervene; but for the most part it is not to disarrange the regular order of the world, and produce effects contrary to good sense. The supernatural, as they understood it, is usually a very natural thing. In those primitive times which we are depicting, men were accustomed to attribute all that happened to them to a divine influence.

When they watched some violence of the elements, or when they felt some furious ardour arise in their hearts, they were tempted to think that the divinity could not be a stranger to it. "Is it true," says one of Virgil's heroes, "that the gods inspire in me a great design; or does not each of us make a god of the passions of his soul?"[1] It is in consonance with this idea that the ancient poets so often represent Mars, Minerva, and Apollo going about the field of battle, and at the critical moment appearing to a combatant to stir up his ardour or suggest some enterprise to him, and it almost always happens that they only advise him what should have occurred spontaneously to his own mind. When Virgil shows us Alecto inspiring the Italians with anger on the coming of Æneas, we cannot help thinking that the Italians must of themselves have felt very irritated at seeing a stranger land among them, and without more ado come to settle on their lands, under pretext that the gods have given them to him. Elsewhere he shows us Juno, Venus, and Cupid plotting together to make Dido fall in love with Æneas. Do we need the intervention of so many divinities to

---

[1] *Æn.*, IX. 184.

explain to us that a woman, young, beautiful, and who has loved much, one day takes a fancy to a hero who relates his misfortunes and his adventures to her in so touching a manner ? We are not surprised that Æneas, when he begins to love Dido, forgets for her that Italy which the Fates promise him ; and we also understand that when he has nothing more to desire, in the first weariness of sated love, he begins to think of it again. Was it absolutely necessary to trouble Mercury in order to remind him of it ? It were possible, then, in the examples I have just given, to suppress the marvellous without grave damage to the action ; for it is only a means of better explaining natural incidents which, strictly speaking, could explain themselves. But the legend we are studying has not quite the same character. It is a downright miracle altering the laws of nature.

It was imagined to amuse the mind for a moment by the unexpectedness and strangeness of the invention, and is indeed a wonder of fairyland, foreshadowing Ovid's *Metamorphoses.*

Of the other story I will say scarcely anything, for fear of not saying enough ; it is the episode of Nisus and Euryalus. Virgil has put all his soul into it, which does not prevent everything in it from being exact and precise, so that on the spot the least details can be followed and understood. In a purely imaginative narration the poet gives us the complete illusion of truth. Here is the camp of Æneas as we have just described it, between the Tiber, the plain of Laurentum, and the sea. We first assist at the military vigil of the Trojans, in face of a threatening enemy. They are uneasy

about the absence of their chief, and fear to succumb
on the morrow beneath the attacks of Turnus. Nisus,
who guards a gate with Euryalus, reveals to him that
he has formed a plan to cross the encampment of the
Rutuli, and go and inform Æneas of the danger which
his soldiers are exposed to. In lines impossible to
forget Virgil relates the conversation of the two friends
and their noble struggle, a dispute between tenderness
and heroism, in which heroism finally triumphs. He
then takes them to the assembly of the chiefs. While
the soldiers sleep, the chiefs standing in their midst,
leaning upon their long lances, seek some means to warn
Æneas, when the two friends come to announce that
they have undertaken the enterprise. Nisus knows
the way that must be followed in order to reach him.
Beneath that hill which he points out to the right, he is
sure to find a road that in a few hours will bring him
to Pallanteum, the nearest houses of which he has seen
from afar in his adventurous hunting excursions.[1]
Accompanied by the good wishes of Iulus and the Trojan
chiefs, they start. Here our topographical knowledge
enables us to follow them step by step. Virgil tells us
" they left by the gate nearest to the sea," and we are
at first rather surprised at this. It is just the contrary
road to the one they might have been expected to take,
since by following this direction they turn their backs
on Pallanteum. Are we to believe, with Bonstetten,
that the course of the Tiber then approached the large
marsh known as the *Stagno di Levante;* that, towards

---

[1] *Æn.,* IX. 244. Bonstetten calls attention to the fact that from
Castel Decimo the houses of the Roman outskirts are plainly seen.

Rome the morass and the river joining, formed, as it were, a boundary to the camp of Æneas, and that there was no issue on this side ? Or is it not more simple to suppose that Nisus and Euryalus chose the way skirting the sea, because it was least defended ? Nisus, in fact, has remarked that the Rutuli, who have passed the night in playing and drinking, do not keep guard. Hardly any fires shine in their camp. Plunged in sleep and drunkenness, some are stretched on the grass, while others are more softly couched on heaped-up carpets ; all are sleeping with a will. So the two friends easily effect a great slaughter. They even tarry longer than they should over this easy victory, and, tempted by the rich booty they have won, lose time in carrying it off. Poor Euryalus, quite a youth, with the vanity of his age, cannot refrain from covering himself with brilliant arms, which, struck by a moonbeam, will presently betray him and cause his death. They at last perceive that day approaches, that they have got to the extremity of the Rutuli camp, and that they must hasten to leave it.

They now change the direction of their way. The poet has told us that at starting they found two roads before them : one doubtless leading straight to the sea, the other turning to the left, skirting the shore, and holding the place of the Via Severiana, constructed by Severus, from Ostia to Terracina. As long as they were traversing the camp of Turnus, Nisus and Euryalus followed the latter road. On leaving it, they turn to the left, their intention doubtless being to take the end of the *Stagno di Levante*, and thence proceed in a straight line to the city of Evander. In order now to

go from that spot to Rome, we should have to make
Malafede or Castel Decimo by some cross-road, and
take the Via Ostiensis or the Via Laurentina, which
would quickly bring us there. So we can very clearly
picture to ourselves where the unfortunate youths were
when the Volscians, coming from Laurentum to bring
Turnus part of his troops, perceived them. They must
have been close to that fine park of Castel Fusano one
never fails to go and see when visiting Ostia, at the spot
where the Selva Laurentina begins. Virgil thus describes the forest they tried to cross:

> *" Silva fuit late dumis atque illice nigra.*
> *Horrida, quam densi complebant undique sentes ;*
> *Rara per occultos lucebat semita calles."* [1]

Bonstetten bids us remark that this description has
not ceased to be true. Now, as in the time of Æneas,
the whole of this region abounds in impenetrable
thickets where bushes and brambles interlace, and it
is impossible not to lose one's way. I remember a little
wood between Castel Fusano and Tor Paterno which I
was so imprudent as to enter, and from which I only
escaped with much difficulty and many scratches, very
far from the place whither I desired to go. Evidently,
had Volscians pursued me with 300 horsemen, I should
not have saved myself. Yet Nisus manages to get off.
The poet, bent on being precise above all things, tells
us he had got to that spot called later " the Alban field," [2]

---

[1] *Æn.*, IX. 381.

[2] I have some difficulty in understanding how this passage of the
Æneid could have given interpreters so much trouble. It is clear
that neither the town founded by Ascanius, nor, as Heyne supposes,
the lake situated at the foot of Mount Albano, is here in question.

when he saw that he was alone. Euryalus, less skilful and resolute, and encumbered by the spoil with which he had loaded himself, had lingered on the road Nisus does not waver; he plunges into the forest, and returns to die with his friend.

I will not be so imprudent as to relate their death when Virgil has so ably done so. I prefer to leave the reader the pleasure of going over the entire episode again in the *Æneid*. This pleasure will be complete if he have the good fortune to read this admirable narrative at Castel Fusano itself—that is to say, in the place that inspired it. I can imagine none in the world where the soul could better yield itself up to this grand poetry. In our bustling towns it is very difficult to abstract oneself from the present; it seizes on us, and holds us fast on every side. At Castel Fusano nothing draws us away from the memories of antiquity. In order to belong quite entirely to Virgil, I would rather not have before my eyes even the stern palace of the Chigi, as much like a fortress as a country house. I would place myself opposite the avenue paved with the slabs of the Via Severiana, and leading to the sea, beneath the shade of those great parasol pines, the most beautiful found in the Roman Campagna. "This shade," says Bonstetten very happily, "is like no other. You

---

These are much too far from the shore, and it would have taken Nisus a long day's journey to go and return, whereas he must have been much less than an hour on his way. Virgil means some spot on the territory of Laurentum to which, for reasons unknown to us, had been named *loci Albani*, and was so called in his day. The care he takes to point it out well shows the desire he had to be precise, and connect the scene with a definite spot.

walk between the gigantic trunks of these trees as between columns, and although in a wood you see the sky and the horizon all round. The eye reposes gently, as if under a gauze veil, in a light having neither the darkness of shadow nor the brightness of the sun. In order to be aware of the light parasol spread out in the air between the sky and earth, you must raise your head." Certainly, as I have already said, Virgil's verses may be understood and enjoyed everywhere; but it seems to me that in this solitude and this great silence, in the midst of this fine park surrounded by a desert, and among all these relics of the hoary past one finds in them one charm more. Perhaps, too, seeing how exactly places have been described and scenes narrated, we better understand how it is that a work of imagination, a creation of the poet, should have become for us more living and more true than many a real story, and how the prediction of Virgil was accomplished, who announced to his personages that nothing could efface their names from the memories of men:

> " *Fortunati ambo, si quid mea carmina possunt !*
> *Nulla dies unquam memori vos eximet ævo.*" [1]

----

[1] *Æn.*, IX. 466.

T

IV.

LAURENTUM.

I.

TENTH BOOK OF THE *ÆNEID*—ASSEMBLY OF THE GODS—
RETURN OF ÆNEAS—WAR IN VIRGIL'S POEM—HIS
PORTRAYAL OF THE DIFFERENT ITALIC RACES—WHY
HE DID NOT PAINT THEM MORE DISTINCTLY.

AT the end of the Ninth Book of the *Æneid*, the
Trojans are besieged in their camp during the absence
of their chief. The attempts made by them to warn
him have failed; they have lost their bravest soldiers,
and their affairs seem desperate; but fortune is about
to come back to them with the return of Æneas, and
thenceforth their success will continue to grow until
the end of the poem. We have arrived, then, at one of
those decisive moments when events are about to take
a new turn. So Virgil abruptly breaks off his narrative,
and transports us from the earth to the sky, in order to
assist at an assembly of the gods.

It is a very brilliant episode, and very carefully worked
out, which is the more remarkable from its being the
only one of the kind in the *Æneid*. If Virgil did not
imitate Homer, who so often represents the gods
assembled and debating together, it is doubtless because
he felt some embarrassment as to doing so. It is in
such scenes that the Homeric gods most willingly give
way to all the violence of their humours; and this
violence is little in keeping with the idea formed by a
more enlightened age of divine majesty. Virgil, while

on the whole retaining the old divinities, aimed at
making them more grave and decent, and this attempt
was attended with some dangers. We can only accept
the Homeric gods by allowing our imagination to go
back to the age of Homer. In order that the simplicity
of certain details may not wound, it must abandon
itself entirely to the past, and believe itself to live
therein; but when we imprudently ask their acceptance
in connection with the present time, the imagination at
once becomes more fastidious, and, the illusion once
dissipated, contrasts irritate, and the corrections we
try to apply to the original figure, with the new
features we add, only serve to cast the strangeness
of the rest into higher relief. In the assembly of the
gods in the Tenth Book, although Jupiter has become
more majestic and dignified, we are less inclined to
congratulate him on the progress he has perhaps made
than struck by the extent to which he falls short of
the divine idea. Brought into a less unsophisticated
medium, we find that the speeches of Venus and Juno
contain outbursts of language, subtleties of reasoning,
and a whole rhetorical mechanism which seems to us
very much out of place in Olympus. We are above all
displeased to see that all this discussion leads to nothing.
Jupiter, who begins by appearing very angry, and who
seems to say that he is about to form the most serious
resolves, ends by declaring, amid thunder and lightning
and invoking the Styx to witness his words, that he
will do nothing at all, and that he lets events take their
course (*Fata viam invenient*).[1] It was not worth while

---

[1] *Æn.*, X. 113.

to call together the whole of the celestial body for so little.   This celebrated scene, then, which opens the Tenth Book in so brilliant a manner, seems to me to have only one result; it indicates with great solemnity that we have got to one of the chief crises of the action.[1]

It is, in fact, directly after the assembly of the gods that fortune changes.   Very early in the morning, Turnus, hoping to carry the Trojan camp before succour arrives, resumes the attack.   The unfortunate soldiers, who were so hardly treated the day before, and who had little hope of escape, " look sadly down from the towers, and their thinned ranks can scarcely man the ramparts." [2]   Turnus redoubles his efforts, attacks all the gates at once, throws flaming torches on the towers, and thinks himself sure of success, when suddenly a cry rings out upon the walls, a cry of joy and deliverance.   It is Æneas who is coming with the thirty vessels of the Etruscans.   The sun, rising at this moment above the Alban mountains, strikes his shield, and the flashes are easily seen from the Trojan camp, situated, as we know, four stadia from the sea.

Read in the poem, the events that follow appear

---

[1] The only positive result of this assembly of Olympus is that Jupiter, in his opening speech, prohibits all the gods from meddling in the quarrel of the Trojans and the Latins, and undertakes in his last not to meddle in it himself.   In the upshot, neither the gods nor Jupiter abstain from taking part in the fight.   I am therefore greatly tempted to believe that Virgil composed this brilliant digression separately, and added it, so that he had no time to harmonise it well with the rest.

[2] *Æn.*, X. 121.

somewhat confused, but they develop themselves, on the contrary, with great clearness when studied upon the spot. Æneas had caused the cavalry given him by Evander, and reinforced by that of Tarchon, to take the land route, while he himself brought the Etruscan fleet to the mouth of the Tiber. The road to be followed by the cavalry and the spot where it was to await him were settled in advance. All has been carried out exactly, and the cavalry has passed the Tiber somewhere between the Trojan camp and the Pallanteum. In order to escape Turnus, who keeps upon his guard, and wishes, above all, to prevent help from being brought to the besieged, it has ·been obliged to go a rather long way round, and has perhaps even skirted the *Stagno di Levante*. The poet tells us nothing of all these movements; but lets each imagine them according to his fancy. But it is certain that the cavalry has also arrived quite close to the sea, since Pallas, Evander's son, who has come in the ship of Æneas, manages to join it and put himself at its head. This, then, is the situation of the combatants when Turnus, still besieging the Trojans, without seeming to suspect what threatens him, hears their cry of joy and the distant salutation they address to their chief. Then he, too, turns to the ocean, and sees the Etruscan fleet nearing the shore. Hereupon, leaving a few soldiers around the walls, he rushes to make a furious attack on the newcomers. The combat goes on in two places at once—towards the mouth of the Tiber, where Æneas has just disembarked with the Etruscans, and a little farther on, towards Castel Fusano, where Evander's cavalry, commanded by Pallas, find themselves for a moment very much embarrassed among trunks of trees, and large stones rolled down by the waters of a torrent.[1] After a bloody struggle, the Latins give way, Turnus being withdrawn from the combat by a stratagem of his sister. The Trojan youth leave the camp where they were shut up, and all the troops of Æneas unite under his hand.

This Book and the two following, like the one preceding them, are almost entirely taken up with descriptions of battle. A certain monotony results, which explains the severe judgment sometimes passed against the end of the *Æneid.* It was unfortunately a necessity of the subject chosen by Virgil, and he could not escape it. Since Æneas must conquer by arms the country where he is to settle, of course the poet had to sing of war. He did not love it, however, and always remembered that it had troubled his youth. At twenty-six years of age, when he was given up to the pleasures of country life and the love of the Muses, he had seen with terror the undisciplined legions of Antony and Octavius pass, ravaging all upon their way. They returned soon afterwards, made more insolent by victory, and claiming from their chiefs the rewards they had been promised, and he had nearly lost his life in defending his little field from them. We must

---

[1] This seems to Bonstetten very improbable. "The Tiber," he says, "never rolled rocks." I add that the Arcadian horsemen do not fight on the banks of the Tiber, but a little farther on. The mountains are very far from the spot where they are placed, and the water flowing from them would fall into the *Stagno di Levante,* which bars the way. So it is very difficult to understand what Virgil means in this passage.

not be astonished that he should have retained a sort
of horror of war. Peace was his ideal and his dream.
He loved to foresee it in the future, and hailed in advance
a happy time when differences would no longer be
settled by arms, when all old quarrels would be forgotten, and when concord and justice would at length
reign over the world.

> "*Aspera tum positis mitescent sæcula bellis.*
> *Cana Fides et Vesta, Remo cum frate Quirinus*
> *Jura dabunt,*" [1]

and among the reasons he had to love Augustus—the
strongest, certainly—was his having closed the Temple
of Janus and bidden the Empire be at peace. At the very
moment when forced by the necessity of his subject to
tell of battles, he never ceases to load war with the
hardest epithets (*horrida, insana bella; lacrimabile
bellum*). He puts himself on the side of the mothers
who curse it, and, in a deathless line, shows them at
the first noise of battle pressing their children to their
breasts :

> "*Et pavidæ matres pressere ad pectore natos.*" [2]

Nor could he help communicating this feeling of his
to his hero. Æneas makes war as Virgil sings it—very
much in spite of himself.

It may indeed be said that Homer sometimes talks
like Virgil. It also happens to him to be deeply
touched by the ills inflicted on men by war. When a
young man dies, he pities him "for sleeping a brazen
sleep far from his wife, of whom he has received but

---

[1] *Æn.*, I. 291.   [2] *Æn.*, VII. 518.

few caresses."[1] He has words full of melancholy on
the fate of poor mortals carried off, like the leaves of
trees,[2] but it is only a flash. Once plunged into the
scrimmage, he is seized with the intoxication of combat.
He triumphs with the victor, he strikes the vanquished
without ruth, he is full of violent insults and cruel
ironies, and it seems natural to him for a warrior to
threaten his enemies "to eat their quivering flesh, to
spill their brains like wine, and to reach the infant
even in its mother's womb."[3] He finds no greater
happiness for Jupiter than "to sit apart from the
other gods and rejoice in his glory, while he watches
the glint of the bronze and the warriors who slay and
are slain."[4] How strange is the nature of the poet! He
understands everything, and everything enchants him!
He describes contrary sights with a like pleasure, feels
opposed sentiments with the same force, and puts
himself equally into all that he does without showing a
marked preference for anything. This is doubtless one
of the reasons which have caused his existence to be
doubted, although it is of course impossible to imagine a
work without an author. A man's personality is shown
by the qualities which dominate him, and it is usually
the absence of some among them that throws the others
into relief. So Homer, who seems to have all in the
same degree, appears to us less living and less real
than Virgil, whose character is drawn and defined as
much by what is lacking in him as by what he possesses.
It must be owned that the incomparable gentleness of

---

1 *Iliad*, XI. 240.   2 *Ibid.*, VI. 147.
3 *Ibid.*, XX. 346 ; VI. 9.   4 *Ibid.*, XI. 75.

soul, which is its chief feature, little predisposed him to be the bard of battles. He has done his best to imitate his great predecessor; he, too, represents insolent, implacable warriors, cutting off arms and legs, insulting the enemy before fighting him, jeering at him when vanquished, and treading upon him when he is dead. But do what he will, his heart is not in all these horrors, and we always feel that the gentle poet has to do himself a violence when he must be cruel. Whatever talent he exhibits in these descriptions, he is no longer quite himself in them, and they give us little pleasure.

Yet it seems there was a means of introducing a little variety into the accounts of these combats. This was to profit by the diversities existing among the Italic races before Rome united them under her dominion, and describe each of them with its peculiar manners and distinguishing features. He has exactly tried to do so, and this effort deserves the more to be remarked, because it was an innovation. In Homer, the Greeks nowise differ from the Trojans, and exactly resemble each other. The famous catalogue of the Second Book of the *Iliad* contains scarcely anything but proper names and a few general epithets. This long enumeration of nations that took part in the Trojan War is, in itself, of but small interest.[1] What gives it its importance is that later on Greek cities considered it a title of nobility to figure there. But no difference appears between them. Virgil, too,

---

[1] See the enumeration of the Italian warriors in the Seventh Book, ine 647 to the end.

when he placed at the end of the Seventh Book of the *Æneid* a list of the Italic peoples allied to Turnus, chiefly desired to glorify their past, and give them an antiquity that would do them honour; but he does not content himself with drily enumerating them, he adds to their names some mention of their histories, curious particulars concerning their usages, with descriptions of their costumes and arms. He shows us, for example, the Volsci, the Hernici, and the people of Præneste and Anagnia, who wear a wolf-skin upon their heads, and who march to battle with one foot bare and the other with a leather covering; the Falisci and the mountaineers of Soracte, who advance singing the praises of King Messapus, the horse-tamer; the Marsi, whose chief is a priest skilled in the art of charming serpents; the Osci, the Aurunci, and the Sidicii, armed with a short javelin which they launch by means of a strap, and with a curved sword; the inhabitants of Capræ, of Abella, and of the banks of Sarnus, wearing cork helmets and carrying long lances which they use in the Teutonic manner. All these details of picturesque history, not yet hackneyed, must have occasioned the contemporaries of Virgil the liveliest pleasure, and, indeed, he was considered as a great archæologist and antiquary; but, in our days, we have become more exacting. We have been spoilt by pictures of this kind being heaped upon us, and never have enough of them. Many, instead of being thankful to him for what he has done, are tempted to find that he stopped too soon. It appears to them that he has not painted the various Italic nations in strokes sufficiently marked and distinct, and they especially resent his not having made more of the Etruscans, of whom he speaks still less than of the Latins. If we except a word he says in passing about their taste for gaudy costumes and glittering arms, he indeed only emphasizes one side of their character—their passion for good cheer and women. In the midst of a battle, their chief Tarchon, who sees them fleeing before Camillus, reproaches them "with loving only to sit at a well-furnished table beside a full cup, and with only having courage for Venus and her nocturnal combats."[1] These are vivid strokes, it is true, but they would not have sufficed a modern poet. He would have given greater relief and a more original attitude to this strange people, of whom an ancient author already said that in its language and mode of life it resembled no other nation in the world.[2] Virgil did not choose to do so, and for this he doubtless had some reason. The writers of antiquity, historians as well as poets, were above all artists, and their first care was the unity of their works. They did not treat the various parts irrelatively, but held that each of them should add to the general effect. Our authors have not exactly the same cares. In the romance of *Salammbô*, where Flaubert seems to have undertaken to remake with realistic treatment the prose epic of Chateaubriand, he is brought, like Virgil, to enumerate the different peoples who form the army of Carthaginian mercenaries. This method is very simple. He merely gathers from everywhere, without choosing, all the archæological curiosities he can find, to dress up his characters in.

---

[1] *Æn.*, XI. 735.　　　　[2] Denys of Halicarnassus, I. 30.

He describes successively "the Greek with his slim waist, the Egyptian with his high shoulders, the big-calved Cantabrian, the Libyans daubed with vermilion and looking like coral statues, the Cappadocian bowmen, who with the juice of plants paint great flowers on thin bodies," etc. Each of these traits may be striking in itself, but the whole forms the most incongruous and bizarre picture possible to imagine. It is not an army, or even a crowd; it is a masquerade. It is hard to understand how men, whom we know to have differed so utterly from each other, could have been brought to combine in common action, to become the instrument of a single will, and, under Hannibal's leadership, to bring about the destruction of the Roman legions. In his striving after absolute accuracy of detail, Flaubert seems to have failed to impress us with an idea of the truth of the whole; he gives us a series of *genre* pictures instead of composing a great historical masterpiece, as was his original intention. It is a serious fault; and when we come to see the bad effects produced in his work by over-colouring, I think we shall be less tempted to reproach Virgil with the sobriety of his descriptions.

The battles in the *Æneid* are treated in the same manner as the battles in the *Iliad*: they are given their proper value. Virgil, like Homer, alternates general *melées* with hand-to-hand fights; and it is not to be denied that after a time this proceeding becomes somewhat monotonous. His description of the single encounters is sometimes very fine. We take great pleasure, for example, in carefully studying the struggle between Turnus and Pallas, between Æneas and Lausus and Mazentius; but we take less interest in the accounts of the general skirmishes; that is to say, in descriptions of warriors who slay and are slain, without always being able to make out to which side they belong:

> "*Cædicus Alcathoum obtruncat, Sacrator Hydaspem.*
> *Partheniumque Rapo.*"

On this account I spare the reader all the details of the battles which were fought around the Trojan camp. It will be enough for him to know that, at the end of the Tenth Book, the Rutuli are completely vanquished and pursued by Æneas as far as Laurentum, whither we are about to follow him.

II.

LAURENTUM—HOW THE OLD TOWN DISAPPEARED—WHERE COULD IT HAVE BEEN SITUATED?—CANAL OF THE *STAGNO DI LEVANTE*—THE *SELVA LAURENTINA*—THE BOARS OF LAURENTUM—ASPECT OF THE SHORE—PLINY'S VILLA.

This is not too easy an undertaking, for nothing remains of Laurentum. It was said that the ancient town built by Faunus, where King Latinus dwelt with Amata his wife and his daughter Lavinia at the time when Æneas set foot in Italy, was later on abandoned for Lavinium, as Lavinium was for Alba, and Alba for Rome. It continued, however, to live on obscurely, while Rome was accomplishing her great destiny, although so well forgotten, that in 565, during the *feriæ Latinæ*, they forgot to apportion it part of the victims, as was customary for all the members of the confederation. Happily the gods remembered the town, showing their displeasure by numerous prodigies, and the sacrifice was recommenced.[1] It certainly deserved greater consideration on the part of the Romans, for it had remained faithful to them at a serious crisis, when the Latin League took up arms against them, and they were deserted even by Lavinium.[2] The war over, it had been decided that, in recognition of this fidelity, the treaty between Rome and Laurentum should be renewed year by year, on a fixed day. We may well believe that in this country, where nothing was lost, some vestige of the ancient ceremony would still remain in the time of the Emperor Claudius. At Pompeii an inscription of that period has been found, in which a certain Turranius a vain and pedantic personage, who seems to have been very solicitous of religious dignities, tells us that he has been appointed by the inhabitants of Laurentum to renew the old alliance with the Roman people.[3]

---

[1] Titus Livius, XXXVII. 3.

[2] The conduct of the people of Lavinium on this occasion is very racily told by Titus Livius. After long wavering between the two parties, they had at last sent forces to help the Latins, but scarcely had the first troops passed the gate when they learnt that the Latins had been beaten. The general, while getting his men in again as fast as possible, could not help saying: "This is a little journey which will cost us dear" (*Pro paulula via magnam mercedem esse Romanis solvendam*). And, in fact, the Romans sternly punished Lavinium for the intention the town had had to harm them.—Titus Livius, VIII. 2.

[3] Prof. Mommsen has lately found another inscription of this same Turranius at Patrica, the ancient Lavinium.

But these memories of a glorious past did not prevent the town from becoming depopulated, and we have seen that it was at last united to Lavinium, which proves that it had then no longer much importance. The precise moment of its final disappearance is unknown.

Since the Renaissance, the learned have at different times turned their attention to it, and endeavoured to discover where it could be. It has most often been placed at two spots situated not far from each other, namely, the farm of Tor Paterno and at Capo Cotta. Let us take up the question in our turn, and go over the country with a view to discovering which spot best agrees with the descriptions of the *Æneid*. This little journey in itself is not without its charm; the country is curious, not much known, and full of great memories, and I think we need not regret having ventured into it, whatever the success of our researches.

Our best plan to avoid losing our way is strictly to follow Virgil. He supposes that the first care of Æneas, on landing on the banks of the Tiber, is to win the friendship of the people of the country. For this purpose he chooses a hundred of his companions, whom he sends under the leadership of prudent Ilioneus to greet King Latinus and ask his alliance. They leave for Laurentum on foot, accomplish their embassy, and return within the day. This proves that the town of Latinus is not very far off; and we are set at rest, at starting, as to the length of the journey we have before us. Here we are, then, starting from Ostia, like the embassy of Æneas, and following the shore. At about 4 kilomètres distance our way is barred by a tolerably broad canal, which carries the waters of the *Stagno di Levante* into the sea. In ancient times, as now, this canal was passed by means of a bridge, and near here an inscription has been discovered, stating that certain emperors (probably Diocletian and Maximian) have repaired this bridge, which was falling into ruin, and that they have done so in the interests of the inhabitants of Ostia and of Laurentum (*Pontem Laurentibus atque Ostiensibus vetustate conlapsum restituerunt*). The canal, then, formed the boundary between the territory of the two towns, and we are certain, when we pass the bridge, to set foot in the domains of Laurentum.

A little further on we discover another relic of the old city, which proves that we are, indeed, on the road that must take us to it. On leaving Castel Fusano, we enter a large forest which to the left extends as far as Decimo, and is called in modern maps Selva Laurentina, the name it bore in antiquity. The forest of Laurentum, with its dense thickets and quagmires covered with reeds, was much frequented by Roman hunters. They found there plenty of very wild boars, which showed good sport. Virgil, in order to describe the energetic resistance of Mezentius, surrounded by enemies who harass him, compares him to a boar of Laurentum, whom the hounds have driven into the toils. When he sees himself shut in them, he quivers with rage and sticks out the bristles of his flanks. None dare approach him. It is from far, and sheltered from danger, that the hunters press him with their darts and their cries. The fearless beast stands at bay on every side, grinding his tusks and shaking

the darts fixed in his back.[1] Horace tells us, however, that "he wasn't worth the pains he cost and the
dangers he made his captors run." "As he lives in the
marshes and among the reeds, his flesh is flabby and
insipid ; he is far from equalling that of Umbria, which
feeds only on acorns."[2] It must be remarked, however, that Horace does not here express his own opinion ;
the person he makes speak is a professor of gastronomy
whose niceties he desires to ridicule. As a rule, folk
were not so fastidious, and Martial, when he sends one
of his friends "a boar of Laurentum, weighing a good
weight,"[3] thinks that he makes him a handsome present.
The excellent Pliny the Younger, though by nature
neither a warrior nor a sportsman, nevertheless yielded
to the fashion, and when at his country house near the
sea went like the rest to await the boar in the woods
—but his was a peculiar mode of hunting. "You are
going to laugh," he writes to his friend Tacitus, "and I
allow you to do so willingly. I, that hero whom you
know, have taken three boars, and the fattest in the
forest. 'Eh, what! Pliny?' you will say. Yes; Pliny
himself. But I managed everything so as not to break
with my ordinary tastes and my love of repose. I sat
quietly near the nets, and had at hand not a pike or a
spear, but the wherewithal to write. I reflected and
took notes; for I wanted to be sure, in case I might
return empty-handed, at least to bring away full tablets.
Don't despise this way of working. It is wondrous to
see how bodily movement enlivens and stimulates the
mind. The forests that surround us—the solitude, the

---

[1] *Æn.*, X. 707.   [2] *Sat.*, II. 4, 42.   [3] Martial, IX. 49, 5.

U

silence, makes thoughts dawn within us. I advise you, then, when you go hunting, to take writing tablets with your stores, and you will find, from experience, that not only Diana walks the woods, but that Minerva, too, is sometimes met there."[1] Things have not much changed in the Selva Laurentina since Virgil and Pliny's time. Boars still abound there, and the king of Italy has no more favourite relaxation than to leave his austere Roman residence and go and hunt there from time to time.

Along the shore, between the forest and the sea, there stretches a sandy plain, fringed by a chain of dunes, called by the people of the country "Tumoletti." It is quite uninhabited, and from Castel Fusano to Tor Paterno, for more than 9 kilomètres, one finds not a house, and rarely meets a human being. Yet formerly this was one of the most populous and most agreeable places in the world; nowhere, perhaps, were so many rich country houses found so close together. Pliny tells us: "They followed each other, sometimes separate, often contiguous, and seemed to form so many little towns."[2] Does this mean that the nature of the soil and the conditions of the climate have changed, and that in former times one was not exposed there to the terrible fever scourge? We are bound to think so, since this country, once so densely peopled, has become a desert. But the change has not been so great as is usually asserted, and we may suspect that, even then, one could not live there quite free from peril. Pliny says in so many words:

---

[1] *Epist.*, I. 6. [2] *Ibid.*, II. 17, 27.

"The coast of Etruria in all its length is dangerous and pestilential;"[1] and we know from Strabo that the soil of Terracina, Setia, and Ardea, and all this coast in general, was marshy and insalubrious. Yet the evil was clearly much less grave than it is now, for Strabo immediately adds: "But it is nevertheless pleasant to live there, and the ground is not seen to be worse cultivated."[2] It was doubtless this cultivation that rendered the soil more wholesome, and, without quite subduing the malaria, made it less offensive. Probably there, as at Rome, "the first fig brought a few fevers, and opened a few successions";[3] but little heed was paid to this, and we shall see that the doctors themselves ended by recommending their patients to live at Laurentum. The Romans had managed to make it a place of rest and pleasure. For them it had the advantage of being far enough from Rome to enable them to escape the importunate, and yet sufficiently near to enable them to get there in a few hours. "I need only start," says Pliny, "when I have finished my business, and my day is ended."[4] So this neighbourhood had early begun to be fashionable. Scipio already used to come here with his friends and taste that pleasure, so fraught with charm, of making oneself young for a moment, when one feels oneself on the eve of ageing altogether. Tradition loved to show Lælius and him playing like children with shells on the sea-beach.[5] The orator Hortensius also possessed a celebrated villa at Laurentum, of which Varro speaks

---

[1] *Epist.*, V. 6, 2.   [2] Strabo, V. 3, 12.   [3] Horace, *Epist.*, I. 7, 5.
[4] *Epist.*, II. 17, 2.   [5] Valerius Maximus, VIII. 1.

with admiration. It comprised a wood of more than
50 jugera (12 hectares, or nearly 30 acres), in which
there were a great number of animals that had been
accustomed to come together at the sound of a trumpet.
This enabled the proprietor to offer his guests, while
dining, a very curious entertainment. The repast was
served on a hill; an artist, clad as Orpheus, with a
long robe and a cithern, was introduced; and on a
signal, to complete the illusion, the artist sounded a
trumpet, when stags, boars, and all the beasts of the
forest were seen running up. Varro says: "It was
a spectacle as fine as that one in the Great Circus
during the games given by the Ædiles, or the hunts
that are made with the beasts of Africa."[1] But of all
these country houses, where the great lords of Rome
passed a good half of their lives, none is so well known
to us as that of Pliny. Under pretext of inducing his
friend Gallus to come and see it, he gives him, in a
celebrated letter, a detailed description of it which
places it quite before our eyes. The perusal of this
letter is of the greatest interest to all who would
have some idea of the magnificent Roman villas. It
shows us to what degree everything was arranged in
them for the comfort of life. To our taste, nothing
is wanting but a park and grounds. Such a fine
house would have needed a better surrounding. But
perhaps the very reason Pliny prefers it to all his
other villas is because he is not harassed there with the
cares of property—is freer, more at his ease, and, being

---

[1] *De re rust.*, III. 13.

distracted by nothing, can work better than elsewhere.
" Here," he says, " I hear no one speak evil of others and
myself speak evil of none, if not of myself when ill
content with what I have done. Here I escape from
fear and hope, and laugh at all that may be said; I
only hold converse with myself and my books. O sweet
and good life! Pleasant repose, worth more than what
is honoured with the names of work and business!
O sea, O shores, my true study-rooms! What a source
of inspiration you are to me!"[1] We know, as surely
as possible, where Pliny's villa must have been. He
has taken the trouble to indicate its site with such
exactness that there is no possibility of mistake. He
tells us it is on the sea-shore, 17 millia (a little more than
15½ English miles) from Rome; that one can get there
by the Via Ostiensis and the Via Laurentina; but that
one must leave the former at the eleventh, and the
latter at the fourteenth mile. With a compass, then,
on a well-made map, we can mark the place exactly.
It is at a little distance from Castel Fusano, towards
the spot called " La Palombara," where it is usually
located. As for thinking that some ruins of it may be
found by excavating the soil here, this is an illusion
and a chimera. The dwellings of private persons are
not made to last for ages. That of Pliny, from Trojan
to Theodosius, must have often changed owners, and as
each of its new owners doubtless desired to accommodate
it to his taste and his fortune, it is probable that, even if
it still existed at the end of the Empire, it was no longer
the same house. Nibby was right, then, in saying that

---

[1] Pliny, *Epist.*, I. 9.

nothing now remains of it but the pleasant description left us by Pliny.

III.

TOR PATERNO—CHARACTER OF THE RUINS FOUND THERE—
   THE VILLA OF COMMODUS—MARCH OF ÆNEAS ON
   LAURENTUM—AMBUSH OF TURNUS—PROBABLE SITUA-
   . TION OF LAURENTUM.

After traversing this desert for several kilomètres, we at length descry before us a vast habitation, with strange and massive forms. It is Torre di Paterno, or, in common parlance, Tor Paterno, a very large farm belonging to the King of Italy. It is situated not far from the sea, to which we are brought by an avenue of trees, ending in a little pavilion built in the midst of the sands of the shore.

What gives this its importance in our eyes is that nearly all the learned consider it built on the site of Laurentum. The illustrious antiquarian Fabretti was, I believe, the first to pronounce this opinion.[1] In connection with an inscription he had found in this vicinity, and was studying, he related that he had seen considerable ruins at Tor Paterno, and did not doubt but that they were the last remains of the town of Latinus. He added that, being eighty years of age, he much feared that he had neither the strength nor the time to prove this. In fact, he has nowhere done so ;

---

[1] Fabretti, *Inscr.*, p. 752.

but he has been believed upon his word, and his opinion has gained ground.

On reaching Tor Paterno, a fine modern inscription first meets our eyes, informing us that we are indeed at Laurentum, the very place which was the cradle of Rome.

LAVRENTVM

ROMANÆ VRBIS INCVNABVLA.

The inscription then records that, on 14th October 1845, Pope Gregory XVI., an ardent lover of antiquity, visited this spot, and that the very fields trembled with joy at the honour done them by the Sovereign Pontiff. This noble visit seemed officially to consecrate the right of Tor Paterno to identify itself with Laurentum.

At Tor Paterno, and in its vicinity, considerable ruins have certainly been found; and one is at first inclined to think that a spot where antiquity has left so many relics must have held a certain place in history. This is the basis of Fabretti's opinion, and what gave it so much credit down to our days. But is it possible for a moment to admit that these are the ruins of a town? This is the whole question, and it seems to me that a rapid examination will suffice for its solution.

They are chiefly accumulated about the farm. The modern house has lodged itself in their midst anyhow, leaning its little rough-cast and whitened shell against huge walls of red brick, that dominate it on every side. In order to understand the extent and grandeur of the ancient monument, we must go over the habitation. For the present edifice, it has only been possible to

utilise a part of them. Behind, in a sort of enclosure
contiguous to the farm, rise great fragments of wall,
higher and more massive than those of the façade, and
sometimes supported by buttresses. Long study is not
needed in order to recognise the kind of edifice to
which these remains belonged. It is impossible to see
them without thinking of the great buildings on the
Palatine, and, above all, of the villa built by Hadrian
at Tivoli.   Although in a worse condition and of more
modest dimensions, they are of the same family and
nearly of the same period. We have before us a palace
of the Imperial epoch; and it is easy to recognise
the great halls with their arched doorways and the
vaults which decorated their interiors. Outside the
farm, in the fields extending towards the right, ruins
are met with everywhere. These are usually masses
of cement and brick from some fallen wall or vault,
with, from time to time, fragments of walls in better
preservation, and even halls of which we can distinguish
the ground-plan.   At every turn there are pieces of
marble or stucco; capitals and shafts of columns, and I
even found a headless bust, whose drapery was carefully
done, and which appeared to belong to the time of
the Antonines. On the other side, we can trace the
remains of a large aqueduct reaching out into the
country. Pliny remarks that this neighbourhood has
the disadvantage of possessing no springs. In his
time people were content to dig wells there, which,
although very near the sea, yielded limpid and pure
water.[1] It is therefore probable that the aqueduct

---

[1] *Epist.*, II. 17, 25.

which brought water at great expense from the mountains was only built after Trajan's time.

Our walk ended, it is easy for us to solve the problem we set ourselves just now. Surely these are not the ruins of a town that we have just visited. A town, especially when ancient, like Laurentum, contains monuments of various epochs, and, furthermore, the dwellings of both rich and poor are found there. Here everything seems to be of the same age; brick constructions of the Antonine period predominating almost throughout, and, mutilated though they be, retaining an air of power and grandeur which forbids us to think they were the hovels of poor people. We have then, before us, the dwelling of a rich man—probably the palace of a prince. Let us push our conjectures further, and seek to ascertain what emperor could have had his residence here. It is not a difficult task. In 189, Rome was ravaged by a plague which filled its inhabitants with the most terrible dismay. "One met nothing," says Herodian, "but people filling their nostrils and ears with the most powerful scents or unceasingly burning perfumes." The doctors pretended that these odours, by occupying the passages, prevented the bad air from entering, neutralised its powers by their own, and stopped its effect.[1] These remedies were of course useless, and, as they did not prevent people from dying, the Emperor Commodus, as cowardly as he was cruel, sought a more efficacious means of escape from the scourge—he left Rome. His physicians, among whom was perhaps Galen, coun-

---

[1] Herodian, I. 12.

selled him to take refuge at Laurentum. The reason they had for recommending this town was that it was built in a very bracing country, and was surrounded by laurel woods which had given it the name it bore. They doubtless attributed to the laurel some of those qualities we assign to the eucalyptus. It was certainly not in the town of Laurentum itself that the Emperor came to ask an asylum. He probably possessed some country house in the neighbourhood, which he had built or embellished, and went there to pass all the time that the malady lasted. Nothing then prevents us from supposing that the great walls of Tor Paterno are what remains to us of the villa of Commodus.[1]

But the problem is not yet quite solved. Supposing, as seems to me certain, that the ruins we have just visited are those of a palace and not of a town, it may be admitted that the town was near the palace, and Laurentum may still be placed, if not at Tor Paterno itself, at least in the vicinity. Bonstetten quite refuses to believe this, and it seems to him that the place in no wise fits in with Virgil's narrative. Tor Paterno, he says, is only 500 mètres from the shore: Laurentum must have been much further. In none of the battles that took place round the town of Latinus is the sea mentioned, whereas Virgil constantly spoke of it while they were fighting before the Trojan camp.

---

[1] Gell, in his *Topography of Rome*, calls attention to certain analogies of construction between the ruins of Tor Paterno and those found on the Appian Way, and to which the name of *Roma Vecchia* is given. These latter belong to a villa belonging to Commodus, and which he had repaired. The architecture of the two edifices seems to him to be of the same time.

This reasoning quite convinced Nibby, and is what decided him to withdraw Laurentum inland, as far as the *Casali di Capocotta*, where he had discovered some ancient remains. Let us take up the question again in our turn, and see whether they have both well interpreted what Virgil tells us.

First of all, is it true that he makes no allusion to the neighbourhood of the sea, in the two last Books of the *Æneid?* Bonstetten says so, and Nibby repeats it after him, but I think they both go too far. King Latinus, in the sacrifice preceding the combat of Turnus and Æneas, begins by calling the earth, sea, and sky to witness that he will be true to his promises: *Cœlum, mare, sidera juro.*[1] Well, we know that the Romans were very precise and circumstantial people, who liked, above all things, to be perfectly well understood by those with whom they had to do. So in addressing the gods, they were in the habit of touching or showing the things whose names they pronounced, in order that no confusion might be possible. I therefore think the sea must have been pretty close to the spot from which Latinus spoke—that it could at least be seen—and that his hand stretched towards it at the moment when he invoked it in witness of his sincerity must have added precision and solemnity to his oath. A little further on, when the combat has begun, he alludes to a wild olive, dedicated to Faunus, rising in the midst of the plain. " It was a tree venerated by sailors. When they were saved from the wreck, they came to bring it their offerings, and hung their

---

[1] *Æn.*, XII. 196.

clothes upon its branches."[1] I own my inability to suppose that "the tree venerated by sailors" grew inland. Catullus tells us that in their dangers they are accustomed to address "the gods of the shore;"[2] so it must have been to some tree near the shore that they came to hang their soaking garments when delivered from peril and safe on dry land. It is natural that they should be in haste to return thanks to the gods for their protection, and that they should do so in the very face of the floods by which they had nearly perished. Thus we see that in ancient pictures representing the sea-shore, the artists love to paint little chapels decked by the gratitude of sailors with garlands and festoons.

These are a few reasons for thinking that Laurentum could not be far from the sea, but it is true there are others which might prevent us from thinking it could have been very close. The Eleventh Book of the *Æneid* contains an account of a military incident deserving close study. I said just now that Virgil's battles quite resemble Homer's; but we must make a reservation. War in the *Æneid* appears less primitive, more intricate, and more learned than in the *Iliad*. In Homer, each fights for himself and follows no inspiration but his courage, whereas, among the soldiers of Æneas and Turnus, there is more discipline and concert. The *mêlée* still remains sufficiently confused; but, with the exception of these furious encounters, where every one presses forward and has no other fixed idea than to go as far and hit as hard as he can, one

---

[1] *Æn.*, 766.　　　　　[2] Catullus, 4, 22.

feels a little more art and tactics in their manner of fighting. Turnus, for example, conducts the siege of the Trojan camp with a certain skill. Messapus, whom he chooses to blockade the enemy, commands fourteen Rutuli chiefs, and each of them has a hundred soldiers under him. Guard is mounted, too, or relieved, and bivouac fires are lighted. Preparatory to giving the assault, the wall is beaten with a ram, and then the troops advance tortoise fashion—that is to say, raising their shields above their heads to protect themselves from the enemy's missiles. These are devices of which Homer's heroes never thought. But more remarkable than all the rest is the way in which Æneas sets to work to take Laurentum. The Latins, beaten on the banks of the Tiber, have just fled, and have sought refuge in the town of Latinus, which is about to become the centre of the final combats. Æneas decides to follow them. May I be permitted to say that, in order to insure success, he imagines a "turning movement"? The term is very modern; but there is no other so exactly expressing the process he is going to put in practice. Placed as he is at Ostia, and having before him the great pond called *Stagno di Levante*, he can get into the country facing him by both banks of it. He divides his army into two bodies, causing them to take two different ways. The horsemen under Tarchon advance along the sea-shore. The foot and the bulk of the army turn in the other direction; but, instead of following the edge of the pond, and not leaving the plain, they rise to the left and plunge among the hills. The poet does not tell us the reason that induces Æneas to undertake this delicate operation. Does he fear that the sandy roads of the plain will prove inconvenient for people heavily armed ? It may be thought so, but it is more probable that he hoped by debouching upon Laurentum by a road that was not the shortest and most natural, to be less expected, and have more chance of surprising the enemy. In that case he is mistaken, for Turnus, who possesses scouts, has discovered his designs, and is preparing to frustrate them. " There is," says Virgil, " in the recesses of the mountain, a deep valley, fit for surprises and the ruses of war, and surrounded on all sides by heights covered with thick woods. One gets there by a narrow path and by a close gorge, difficult of access. Above, towards the highest summit, is hid a plateau, which they do not know of ; a safe and convenient post, whether it be wished to rush upon the enemy, or whether it be preferred to remain upon the height and roll down huge rocks. It is thither the Rutuli chief proceeds by unknown roads. He seizes the position, and first finds himself in the perfidious forest." [1] But all his projects are crossed by unforeseen events. While he is awaiting his enemy, and hoping to crush him in his passage, they come in hot haste to tell him that Tarchon's horsemen have beaten his, and that, meeting no serious resistance, they are approaching Laurentum, in order to take it. He must, of course, hasten as fast as possible to defend his allies. " He leaves the hill which he occupied, and quits the impenetrable woods." [2] Scarcely is he lost from view and entering the plain, when Æneas, penetrating the

---

[1] *Æn.*, XI. 522.   [2] *Ibid.*, 896.

defile, henceforth free, crosses the heights and issues from the thick forest. Thus both march rapidly towards the town, and are only separated by a short interval.

It seems to me that, from this incident, the site of Laurentum may be deduced with some probability. The town was situated in the plain, but close to the mountain; close enough to the shore for the sea to be visible, yet so near the hills that one came upon it on issuing from the forests and the heights. Neither Tor Paterno nor Capocotta seem to me quite to fulfil these conditions. The first of these two places is too near the sea and too far from the hills. If it is where Laurentum stood, we no longer understand the manœuvre of Æneas, and to go round the mountain in order to reach it is a ridiculously circuitous proceeding. The other, being in the mountain itself, and situated a little above Pratica, is somewhat too far from the shore. Strabo, relating that Æneas left Laurentum for Lavinium, says that he plunged into the country. If we place Laurentum at Capocotta, the expression is no longer accurate, since, on the contrary, from Capocotta to Lavinium one descends for several miles. Thus Capocotta no more satisfies those who would find the ancient town of Lavinium than does Tor Paterno.[1]

But where could it have been, then? Of course there is no question here of exactly designating its site and pointing out its ruins. It is very probable that,

---

[1] The map in Gell's *Topography of Rome* gives Capocotta quite an inexact position.

in the words of the poet, "even those ruins have perished"; and, in any case, if they still lie hid under some heap of rubbish, a passing traveller cannot flatter himself that he will discover them; but he may get relatively near them. Let us try to do so, and, at the risk of tiring the reader, start again, for the purpose of approximatively settling the situation of the town. Just now, it will be remembered, we left Ostia and skirted the coast. Let us this time take a new road. Virgil's account, which we have just read, proves that we shall not do wrong to ascend a little towards the heights. In going from Rome to Tor Paterno, we pass through three regions that have not the same character. First there is the vast undulating plain called the Campagna, by which Rome is surrounded on all sides; then a series of hills covered with woods; and, lastly, the plain beginning again and extending uninterruptedly to the sea. The intermediate zone is the one that most strikes the traveller. It begins at Decimo, a kind of fortified farm, recalling the days when in this land one could only sleep behind strong walls. There the ground rises, the aspect of the country changes, and one enters what remains of the wood of Laurentum. I went through it in the month of May, when all the bushes were in flower; and what in my eyes made this journey most charming, was that at every step the incidents of the way awakened in me some memory of the *Æneid*. Passing beneath the shadow of the great trees, I recollected that hither the Trojans and the Latins had come after the battle to cut wood for the funeral pyres. "In virtue of the truce," says the poet, "they start for the forest and walk about the mountains together. The ash resounds under the blows of the axe ; they fell the pines, whose head touched the sky ; the wedges cease not to rend the oak and the sweet-smelling juniper ; and the waggons groan beneath the weight of the young elms."[1]   As in the time of Virgil, the road is still bordered by ashes,. elms, oaks, and pines. The savage-looking woodcutters and charcoal-burners, whom I from time to time saw issue from some dark alley, reminded me that Æneas already met robust peasants there, armed with knotty sticks, and I felt as if, at some turn of the road, I was about to see the terrible Tyrrhus, " emitting cries of fury, and brandishing his hatchet against those who passed."[2]   As we get deeper into the wood, the road becomes more varied, rising and falling continually, and hills succeeding hills, cut sharply by somewhat deep valleys. It is the only spot where the ambuscade of Turnus can be placed with some probability. Æneas doubtless got there by following the bottom of the valley, and upon one of these summits covered with trees his enemy silently awaited him. The landscape, I own, is less gloomy and terrible than Virgil represents it, but in poets one must overlook a few exaggerations. It is natural, too, that on quitting the monotonous plains of the Campagna the least hills should appear mountains and the smallest valleys assume the proportions of veritable precipices. Here we are then, about to leave what Virgil calls " the deep forests." At this moment we come upon Castel Porziano, a handsome château, formerly belonging to a noble Roman family, which the

---

[1] *Æn.*, XI. 134.   [2] *Ibid.*, VII. 509.

King of Italy has repaired and much embellished, and turned into a hunting-box. This château, in its present state, resembles a little village. Besides the King's house, which is of modest appearance, it contains dwellings for the servants, barracks for the soldiers, an *osteria*, and a *sali e tabacci* store. It is so placed as to offer good views from all sides. A few minutes ere getting there, while following the avenue of pines, we have before us, on turning round, the mass of the Alban Hills, and in the immense plain, bounded by Soracte and the Sabine mountains, Rome, with a multitude of towns and villages bearing glorious names. Directly on leaving it we catch sight of the sea, including a vast extent of coast. While I stop to enjoy this sight a memory of Virgil occurs to my mind. It is doubtless along these last heights that Queen Amata must have taken refuge when, in order to withdraw her daughter from Æneas, she called the women of Laurentum to celebrate the orgies of Bacchus with her. From below, their savage cries must have been heard, and they must have been seen passing through the trees with bare shoulders and floating hair, waving their thyrses crowned with vine, or furiously shaking their blazing torches. From Castel Porziano the descent becomes rapid, and the plain is soon reached.

It is at the place of egress, at the foot of the hills, two or three kilomètres from the sea, a little lower than Capocotta, a little higher than Tor Paterno, and about half-way between Ostia and Pratica, that I should be inclined to locate Laurentum. The place quite agrees with the descriptions of the *Æneid*, and Virgil seems to take us by the hand and lead us thither.

IV.

THE PALACE OF LATINUS — HOW VIRGIL COMPOSES HIS
DESCRIPTIONS — WHY HE DOES NOT EXACTLY RE-
PRODUCE THOSE OF HOMER—MIXTURE OF DIFFERENT
EPOCHS—UNITY OF THE WHOLE.

It is not the only service he renders us, for, after pointing out the site of the town, he helps our imagination to
reconstruct it. He depicts it, not as it was in his time,
half deserted and ruined, but as he supposes it must
have been in the days of good King Latinus.

It will be remembered that scarcely had Æneas
landed in Italy when he sent deputies to solicit the
friendship of the Latins, and whom we followed some
time in the beginning of their journey. After marching
along the sea, they turn to the left, and arrive at Laurentum. Here Virgil describes the sight depicted before
them. In a large plain, before the ramparts, all the
youth are assembled. "The lads, and those in the
prime of life, are engaged in breaking a horse, and
guiding a chariot through the dust. Others are striving
to bend a resisting bow, launch with nervous arms
flexible javelins, or contend together in speed or
strength."[1] The town is situated near a large marsh
and defended by strong walls. Upon a height rises the
King's palace. This edifice, majestic and immense, is
supported by a hundred columns, and surrounded by a
gloomy wood, which has from all times inspired the

---

[1] *Æn.*, VII. 160.

Latins with a religious awe.   It is a temple as well as
a palace.   Assemblies of the Senate are held there, and
on festivals the chiefs of the nation come thither to sit
down to solemn repasts.   It is there the kings receive the
sceptre on their accession, and the fasces are borne before
them for the first time.   In the vestibule rich statues
of cedar-wood represent the king's ancestors.   Each is
in its place : Italus ; the venerable Sabinus, who planted
the vine, still holding his bent sickle; and Saturnus ;
Janus with the double face; and all the kings since
the beginning of the nation, and the warriors who
received glorious wounds fighting for the fatherland.
There are also seen, hanging from the roofs of the
sacred porticoes, the arms and chariots of the vanquished,
axes, casques, the gates of conquered towns, shields, and
beaks taken from ships.   Picus himself—King Picus,
tamer of horses—is seated, covered with the trabant,
bearing in his hand the augur's wand, and in the other
the slanting shield of the Salian priests. " [1]

This is the idea which Virgil gives us of the palace of
Latinus.   Could it have been quite thus, and is the
poet's description of a nature entirely to satisfy a rigorous historian and antiquary ?   In order to ascertain
this, let us consult the curious book just published by
Dr Helbig, in which he seeks to elucidate Homer's epic
by means of monuments.[2]   We have, in fact, to-day,
two means of going back to those remote times.   The
first consists of the faithful picture drawn of them in the

---

[1] *Æn.*, VII. 170.

[2] The exact title of Dr Helbig's book is : *Das Homerische Epos aus
den Denkmälern erläutert.*

Homeric poems. Antiquity lives in them, and in order
to live in it, we might be content to read them; but the
excavations undertaken in late years in Greece and
Italy furnish an additional source of information not to
be despised. After exhausting the first layers of the
soil, the explorers of our day decided to go lower. The
depths they penetrated to will probably never yield us
many masterpieces; but they preserve the memory of
very ancient epochs, and from time to time they give
us a few remains of them. These are arms of stone, of
bronze, or of iron, pottery with rough designs, and, sometimes, in tombs rather more modern, jewellery, metal
coffers, rough paintings representing battles or feasts—
those two pleasures of young nations. Dr Helbig
thinks that these remains, nearly contemporary with
Homer, may serve as a commentary and an illustration
to his verses. They bring into relief what is often
masked by the charm of his poetry, namely, that he
lived in the midst of a barbarous society. From the
very first this society had in Greece attained perfection
in poetry, but the other arts did not proceed so quickly.
In reading the *Iliad* or the *Odyssey*, we are tempted to
think that but little way remained for it to make; but
on seeing the arms and utensils it used, we soon recognise that it was still making its first steps.

Virgil, in composing the *Æneid*, found himself in a
difficulty unknown to Homer. He could not, like his
predecessor, give the heroes of his poem the manners of
the people of his time. Had the Trojans of Æneas and
the Latins of Turnus quite resembled the people of the
court of Augustus, he would have been laughed at. He
was therefore obliged to age them, and, as far as possible,

carry them back to their epoch. He could, it is true, lighten this work by being content to copy Homer, and this he has often done ; but he has also not unfrequently departed from his model. It is patent, for example, that the palace of Latinus, of which we have just read the description, is more majestic and more sumptuous than the dwellings of the kings of the *Iliad* or of the *Odyssey.* Homer, speaking of the house of Ulysses, tells us that it is the finest in Ithaca, and that it first attracts all eyes, because it possesses a court surrounded by walls with folding gates, which shut well ! This is the magnificence that distinguished it from others ! In the royal houses there is no question of statues filling the vestibule, and of columns supporting the roof, as in that of Latinus. It is much if the façade is ornamented with great polished and shining stones, on which the king comes to sit and administer justice to his people. Manners, we see, are very simple, and we are at the beginning of a civilization. What proves it still better are certain details drawn by Dr Helbig from the Homeric poems, and which depict the time. In those great apartments, where the suitors of Penelope and the flower of the Achæan nobility feast all day, the remains of the repast bestrew the floor, and sheep or ox bones lie about, which the revellers sometimes fling at each other's heads. The hall where they eat is the same in which the feast was prepared, and it is much that a small hole has been left in the roof to let out the smoke. The smell of broiled meat, however, does not seem to have been thought unpleasant in those days. On the contrary, for the people of the period, a good house was one where the grease was smelt (κνυσσῆεν δῶμα), and one's opulence was even gauged by the intensity of this smell. Let us add that before the palace of Ulysses a heap of dung was spread, which served the poor dog Argus as a bed, and that some is also found in the court of Priam's house. "Here is quite enough," says Dr Helbig, "to prove that the atmosphere then breathed in royal dwellings would have singularly irritated the nerves of our exquisites."

To-day, when we like crude colours and expressive details, these are, perhaps, the traits which an author would choose in preference, in order to give an idea of life in ancient times. If Virgil has neglected them, the timidity of his taste is not solely to blame, since he has occasionally risked bold delineations which to some fastidious critics have seemed gross. It has been complained that in describing battles he is seen to insist with too much complacency upon the brains that gush out, or the blood and pus which flow from the wounds; and when he describes to us the gulpings of an old pilot who has fallen into the sea and vomits salt water, Heyne gets angry with him, and reproaches his testamentary executors, Varius and Tucca, with not having had the courage to suppress these unpleasant lines. Nor must it be thought that if Virgil usually gives his lines a more modern air, it was because he had no understanding and love for antiquity. No one among his contemporaries loved it more or understood it better. Not only did he not shrink from exactly reproducing the manners of Homeric times—he has even, now and then, gone further back. Vestiges are found in him of a more distant past than the age of the *Iliad*. When Æneas goes to visit King Evander in his little townlet on the Palatine, he is shown, on the sides of the Janiculum and the Palatine hill, masses of fallen wall covering the soil. These are the remains of the towns of Janus and Saturn. So there were ruins, already, in the time of the Trojan War. In these towns which have been destroyed, there lived a generation of men now vanished, and of whom Virgil tells us. He speaks of this primitive race, " born of oak trunks, and as hard, who had neither customs nor laws." He tells us that they knew neither how to harness oxen, to cultivate the fields, nor how to gather the wealth of the earth ; that they thought not of the morrow, but lived from day to day, shaking the trees to gather their fruits, or pursuing the beasts in the forests.[1] Of these first 'inhabitants of Italy we have now recovered the trace. The depths of the soil, the waters of the lakes, have given us back their arms of stone or bronze, their utensils of clay or wood, and even the remains of their food ; but we may say that Virgil, who knew them not, divined, and was intuitively conscious of them. We see, in M. Bréal's study on the legend of Cacus, how, under his hand, this fable has reassumed its antique air. He has restored to it its first aspect, and made it live again, " like those springs which for a moment give back to dried flowers their brilliancy and brightness—he has rejuvenated it, yet not for a moment, but for all ages." It is above all in the short invocation of the Salian priests, by which the narrative ends, that he seems to have found again the tone of the poetry of the first ages. M. Bréal shows that nothing can give a more exact idea of the poetry

---

[1] *Æn.*, VIII. 314.

of the Vedas than this short passage, and that there is
not a line in it that cannot be connected with certain
verses drawn from them. "Is it not interesting," he
adds, "to find in the masterpiece of learned poetry,
a fragment that would hold its place among the creations
of the most spontaneous poetry that has ever existed?
It is the privilege of genius. It can re-awaken echoes
that have slumbered for centuries."[1]

It is certain, then, that Virgil could at times go
back to the most remote antiquity, but the end he had
in view in his work did not allow him to remain there
long. Let us remember that he did not write solely for
the pleasure of the curious. He had other pretensions
than to satisfy a few pedants who would have liked
to hold him strictly to Homer. He addressed all, and
desired to find readers for whom his poem was a living
work, as low down as letters could descend. Instead,
then, of losing himself in the distance of the ages,
whither few persons would have followed him, and con-
structing at great pains an archæological creation that
would have only interested a few scholars, he strove to
put before the eyes of his contemporaries a world in
which they should feel at home. In carefully studying
his last books, where the action takes place on Italic
soil, it will be seen that he almost everywhere introduces the usages of his country and of his period.[2]
Those who read the *Æneid* were charmed to come

---

[1] Bréal, *Mélanges de Mythologie*, p. 145, *et seq.*

[2] Thus, to cite but a single example, the Latins, before beginning
the war with Æneas, solemnly open the Temple of Janus (VII. 601),
and take care to raise a large standard, as was done on the Capitol at
Rome in similar circumstances (VIII. 1). Nor do they fail to ad-

across customs familiar to them, and they felt themselves brought nearer to these characters whom they
saw in action round about them. Thus the poet was
enabled to reach that deep mass of readers who only
take an interest in what touches them, and do not easily
risk themselves in a land which they would find quite
new. Virgil's work, then, is not one of those air-built
constructions that float in a vacuum. In it the narration of the past rests upon the present, and imagination
leans upon reality. These fables, stepping every moment into history, give the reader an illusion of truth
and life.

To this advantage was joined another, not less
precious to Virgil. Like his friend Horace, and all the
other poets of that time, he had made himself the
collaborator of Augustus. He worked with ardour at
the strengthening of his dynasty and the durability of
his reforms, thinking this the best means of serving his
country. Augustus was at this moment carrying out a
difficult undertaking. He was endeavouring, as far as
possible, to reconcile the present with the past; and it
was a point with him to retain as much of the government which he had just destroyed as could suit with
the order of things he had founded. In order to save
the ancient institutions from the ruin with which they
were threatened, it was useful to show that they were
of ancient date. With a people conservative by nature

---

minister an oath to those who present themselves to take up arms,
while new soldiers, in order to give themselves courage, strike with
their swords upon their shields (VIII. 2, 5). This is a usage still
practised in the Roman army in the time of Ammianus Marcellinus.

like the Romans, to have existed long was a reason to exist for ever. By ageing them, Virgil rendered them more venerable and sacred. This was especially his aim in representing the young people of Laurentum practising in the management of chariots, in throwing javelins, in running, in contending together round the town. Custom imposed these occupations on the Roman youth, and the wise attached great importance to them. It seemed to them that they could not be neglected without risking a loss of vigour, bodily and mental. Horace, who in his verses always puts himself on the side of virtue and the ancient customs, harshly reproaches Lydia with inspiring a young man with a mad passion that makes him forget his duties. " Tell me, in the name of the gods, Lydia, why thou burnest so to cause his ruin ? How comes it that he shuns the labours of the field of Mars, and can no more bear the dust and sun ? Why leaves he his companions when they tame a stubborn horse ? Why fears he now to plunge in the Tiber's yellow waves, nor longer proudly shows us his arms, all blackened with the bruises of the the disk ? " [1] Evidently there were then many young Romans who, instead of going to the field of Mars, passed the morning with Lydia. Horace wishes to shame them out of their softness. Virgil attains the same result by a roundabout way. He ages these customs in order to give them more authority, and render those who abandon them more criminal. How dare to discard exercises respected by so many centuries, and practised in the time of King Latinus ?

---

[1] Horace, *Carm.*, I. 8.

Unfortunately it was not an easy task thus to bring together the present and the past. Virgil had great difficulties to contend with in placing the usages of his time in the *Æneid*. What figure would the usages of a recent epoch make transferred to such ancient ages? Did he not, in introducing them, expose himself to displeasing inconsistencies; and could he hope to give to such a patchwork production an appearance of unity? He succeeded in doing so by a very simple process. With a view to mingling ancient and modern, he rejuvenates the one and ages the other, so that they end by meeting half-way. He has thus managed to create a sort of medium antiquity, where fable and fact, legend and history, the ancient and the modern, may live together side by side without our being shocked by the mixture.

In order that the poet's skill may impress as it deserves to do, and full justice be done him, his work must be viewed very closely. At a certain distance, a uniform tint envelops his narratives, all seems of a piece and flows like a stream; but on approaching one becomes conscious of the touching-up, and we can count the diverse details and incidents that concur to form this beautiful whole. This is a critical work which may sometimes appear trivial, but has the advantage of making us better understand the divine art of Virgil. Only to mention the town of Laurentum and the palace of Latinus, with which we are at this moment busied: of how many distinct elements is not this learned picture formed? How many different ages meet in it! The palace is supported by columns, like a Roman edifice of the imperial epoch; but at the same time it is surrounded by a thick wood, like a Druidic dolmen.[1] The vestibule is decorated with statues of cedar-wood [2]—a grave anachronism, since we know from Varro that Rome remained more than two centuries without raising any in her temples. Is it credible that such existed at Laurentum three hundred years before the foundation of Rome? Virgil, it is true, tries to give his statues a Roman look and an air of antiquity. It is Janus with his two faces, Picus in the costume of an augur, the curved wand in his hand, as •Romulus was represented. In these costumes one is less shocked at seeing them in the house of Latinus. But here we go back further still. In the middle of the *atrium*, a few steps from these statues, is found what preceded the statues themselves in the veneration of the nations —one of those large trees which were honoured as the image of the gods ere men had learned to give the divinity a human form. It is a laurel, with its sacred foliage respected by all, and which causes a sort of superstitious fear to those who pass beneath its shadow.[3]

The religion of Latinus is somewhat like his palace, being composed of practices borrowed from different epochs and countries. When he desires to consult an oracle on the subject of his daughter's marriage, he retires to the vicinity of an Albanian spring, " whence exhale pestiferous vapours,"[4] immolates a hundred sheep, and, lying on their fleeces, waits for the god to make his will known in the course of the night. This is a species of divination very celebrated among the Greeks, and was still used in the time of Aristophanes.

---

[1] *Æn.*, VII. 170-3.　　　[2] *Ibid.*, 177.
[3] *Ibid.*, 59.　　　[4] *Ibid.*, 81.

But Latinus also practises the most ancient rites of the Roman religion. He has his daughter to serve him at the altar when he sacrifices, as the vestal serves the pontiff,[1] and a voice issuing from the depths of the forests instructs him what he is to do, " the voice that speaks "—*aius locutius*, as the old Romans called it. The figure of the king at first sight appears a copy of that of Nestor ; and, like him, he is fond of old stories and likes to relate them.[2] Yet Virgil had given him a physiognomy of his own. Certain touches make us feel that he is a Latin, and that he reigns over this people, " virtuous by nature and needing not the laws to force it to be just."[3] There is in his character something more honest, more gentle, and more pacific. He is not a despot who decides alone and takes nobody's advice : he has his council, which he assembles on grave occasions.[4] However, so does Agamemnon, who omits not to consult the Greek chiefs, whenever an important decision is to be come to. In these assemblies there is a good deal of talking, and the Greek and Latin heroes, like those of our own *chansons de geste*, are inexhaustible orators. As Homer says, " they have been bred to be speakers of words and doers of deeds." There are among them some who support authority and others who oppose it. In the *Iliad*, the opposition is represented by Thersites. Homer, who loves the kings, sons of the gods, has drawn a very unflattering portrait of this rebel : " Of all the warriors assembled under the walls of Troy, there was none more frightful. He

---

[1] *Æn.*, VII. 72.   [2] *Ibid.*, 95.
[3] *Ibid.*, 203.   [4] *Ibid.*, XI. 234.

was bandy-legged, and with one foot he limped. His high shoulders contracted his chest, and on his pointed head floated a few scattered hairs."[1] Clearly, a man thus moulded must have a grudge against the entire human race for his ugliness. Drances, Virgil's Thersites, has quite another look. He is a rich, important man, a good speaker whom people like to listen to, and who knows how to cloak his personal resentments with the finest pretexts. As Thersites detests Agamemnon, so he is the mortal enemy of Turnus. His motives for disliking him are of those that are not pardoned. He is old, and the other is young; he is accused of faint-heartedness in battle, and naturally loves not those who have a reputation for bravery; he possesses fortune, but not consideration, for although connected by his mother with the greatest houses, his father's family is unknown. He belongs, then, to the category of people whom we now call *déclassés*, from whom malcontents are usually recruited. I cannot help finding that this portrait has a modern appearance. A person like Drances can only be imagined and made to speak well if we have lived under a free rule, and have found out by experience what importance jealous mediocrities can assume, and the means they use in order to lower brilliant merit. In creating this type, Virgil surely thought of the obscure struggles and base discords in which the last years of the Republic were worn away.[2]

We see that many loans have here been made from different epochs and societies; but they are guessed at

---

[1] Homer, *Iliad*, II. 217.   [2] *Æn.*, XI. 336.

rather than clearly discernable. In order to bring
out the various tints of which this picture is formed, I
have been obliged to exaggerate them. In reality, they
blend into a uniform colouring. The marvel is that
they could have been so well united that the joining is
scarcely distinguishable. Virgil has succeeded in this
nearly throughout, and if we except a few passages
where the mixing is less skilful and the joins more
apparent, it may be said that, taking the poem
altogether, the component parts are so ingeniously put
together that they end by making an harmonious whole.
The elements composing the work are taken a little
from everywhere, but the poet only owes to himself the
connecting-band which holds them together, and the
medium in which he has placed them. This is his true
originality. In order to frame his stories and group his
personages, he has created a conventional antiquity, at
once broad and elastic, a sort of twilight age in which
men and things of all times may meet without surprise,
and has succeeded in giving to his creation an astonishing appearance of truth and life. This is what other
writers of his time did not always manage to do. Many
of those about him who professed to love antiquity
scarcely understood it, and he almost alone of his age
possessed understanding and taste for it. Varro the
elder, so enamoured of the past; Titus Livius, whose
mind, as he says, felt so much pleasure in making itself
antique—when they tried to write the history of those
primitive times, could not make them live again. On
the other hand, pictures which Virgil has traced of
them, although often fancy ones, have taken forcible
possession of all memories; and whatever discoveries

Archæology may have in store for us, I think it may be positively asserted that the imagination of the learned will always picture Laurentum and the palace of Latinus as he has drawn them for us.

V.

COMBAT OF ÆNEAS AND TURNUS — ARTIFICES USED BY VIRGIL TO DEFER IT — THE BATTLE-FIELD — DIFFERENCE BETWEEN THE FIGHT OF ÆNEAS WITH TURNUS AND THAT OF ACHILLES AND HECTOR.

But if we would assist at the last scene of the *Æneid*, we must leave Laurentum and this palace, where it will perhaps be found that we have tarried too long. The concluding drama of the poem takes place outside the town, in the plain extending from the mountains to the sea.

The fight between Æneas and Turnus is announced in advance and prepared with care. Æneas first suggests to the Latin envoys, who come to ask a truce of him, this easy means of quite terminating the difference.[1] Drances, one of them, hastens to report to Turnus his enemy's challenge, and the latter has too much courage not to accept it at once. But the gods who watch over his days take care to retard as much as in them lies a struggle in which he must succumb, and protect him more than he would have them to do. In the first combat, which takes place about the Trojan camp, as Turnus seeks Æneas with

---

[1] *Æn* , XI. 115.

fury, and the latter does not fly him, one might think the meeting inevitable. Yet Juno finds a means to separate them. "She forms of a light vapour a shadow without consistence, resembling Æneas; she clothes it in Trojan arms, lends it vain words, sounds without ideas, and gives it the bearing of the hero. Such, they say, are the phantoms that flit about after death, such the dreams which sport with our drowsy senses."[1] Turnus, deceived by the resemblance, pursues the false Æneas to a ship, in which he takes refuge. As soon as he is in it, the goddess breaks the cable which attached the vessel to the shore, and the poor champion, in spite of his prayers, is carried by the waves far from the field of battle where his companions seek, and his enemy awaits him. Another time, circumstances seem more grave and more pressing yet. All is ready for the single combat, and the final conditions are about to be arranged. An altar rises in the midst of the plain, on which Æneas and King Latinus agree, by solemn vows, to respect what has been agreed on, and the two armies are assembled to assist at the decisive struggle of their chiefs. At this moment, Juturna, sister of Turnus, who has been beloved by Jupiter and in exchange received immortality, excites the Rutules not to let their king expose himself for them. Pity seizes them when they see this young man measure himself against an adversary who appears to them more redoubtable, and it occurs to them to avoid by all means a struggle whose issue they foresee. An arrow, suddenly let fly from their ranks, strikes one of the

---

[1] *Æn.*, X. 636.

Trojan chiefs, and the *melée* begins afresh.[1] This unfore-seen and improvised combat is certainly one of the most original in all the *Æneid.* Both sides are carried away by fury, and use as weapons anything that comes to hand. They fight around the altar which they have just sworn to respect, and one of the combatants even seizes a flaming brand used in the sacrifice, and hurls it in the face of an advancing foe. "His long beard catches fire," says the poet, "and the odour it exhales in burning is smelt from far."[2] These various incidents not only serve to delay the end of the poem, and allow it to attain a proper length; they are very skilfully handled so as to increase our impatience. When this combat, so often expected and so many times deferred, at last takes place, all minds will be excited by ex-pectation, and will follow its varying fortunes with a more passionate interest.

Virgil gives this great struggle a setting worthy of it. Let us imagine in this now deserted plain, on one side Laurentum with its high walls, and on the other the Trojan camp, with its gates and its retrenchments. On the ramparts of the town and on the tops of the towers press women, country people, and children, looking on. The two armies surround the field of battle, each keeping its ranks, as if from one moment to another they might be forced to resume the interrupted struggle. Meanwhile the spears, for the moment useless, are stuck into the ground, and the shields rest against them. The chiefs flit about in the midst of the soldiers, resplendent with gold and purple. All eyes

---

[1] *Æn.*, XII. 216, *et seq.*   [2] *Ibid.*, 300.

are stretched towards that empty space, where the fate of the two peoples is about to be staked. Heaven is not less intent than earth on this great spectacle. Juno, in order to be nearer to it, has alighted on the heights of Mount Albanus, whence the town of Latinus and the two armies may plainly be seen, while Jupiter, in his heavenly abode, holds in his hands the scales in which he weighs the destinies of mortals.

The account of this combat is one of the most dramatic and engrossing descriptions in the *Æneid*. In reading it, one well sees that the poet was not exhausted by his long journey. He arrives at the end of his work with his mind as vigorous and his talent as fresh and youthful as when he began it. Death took him by surprise at the age of fifty-one, in the full possession of his genius. Had he continued to live, not only would he have given the finishing touches to the *Æneid*, and left it more perfect, but we should doubtless also have possessed that philosophic poem of which it is said he thought in the leisure moments left him by the composition of his epic, and which was to have been the ripened and serene work of his last years.

I think it needless to resume and analyse this beautiful narrative here. All readers of Virgil have it before their eyes. Let it, then, suffice me to point out in a few words what seems to me its distinguishing characteristic. The last combat of Achilles and Hector in the *Iliad* has certainly a very great importance, and one feels very well that it is to decide the fate of Troy; but after all, the fall of the town is not its immediate consequence, and it survives the death of its staunchest defender for some time. Nor can it be said that the combat is premeditated : the two opponents do not seek each other, and they encounter merely by chance. After a defeat of his side, Hector would not flee like them, but stopped before the gate to await the enemy. In reality, he is so little resolved to fight with Achilles, that he takes to flight on perceiving him. In Virgil, on the contrary, everything is perfectly arranged and decided beforehand. Turnus has taken leave of Amata and Lavinia, and Æneas has bidden adieu to his son, while judges have chosen and prepared the spot where they are to encounter. It is a large plain, smooth and bare, and in order to leave no advantage of which the one might profit to the detriment of the other, any few trees that grew there have been levelled. A solemn sacrifice precedes the signal of the struggle. While the priests immolate a young swine and a white sheep, the chiefs of the two armies turn toward the rising sun, whose first rays colour the mountain tops, and, holding in their hands cakes of salted flour, invoke all the gods, and engage to respect the issue of the combat as a decree of Destiny. According as Æneas or Turnus shall win the victory, the Trojans or the Latins will be definitively masters, and the fate of the two peoples is bound up in the fortune of their champions. A sort of judgment of God is therefore in preparation, and it is impossible to follow Virgil in all the details of this fight in the lists without thinking of similar narratives found in old *chansons de geste*. There, too, knights engage in combat in the presence of an assembled people, and before fighting we see them worshipping relics, taking solemn oaths, and giving gages of battle. What completes the illusion is that here, as in many tournaments of chivalry, a woman is the pretext and prize of the struggle. "In this arena," Turnus proudly says, "we must win the hand of Lavinia." [1]

" Illo quæratur conjux Lavinia campo."

However great the emotion we feel in reading the combat between Achilles and Hector in the *Iliad*, it contains certain incidents at which we cannot help feeling somewhat surprised. For example, the sight of Hector flying when he sees Achilles, "like a trembling pigeon before the hawk," and his only deciding to fight when he has no other means of escape, grates upon us. Of course we are wrong, and nothing is more natural and more true than these sudden timidities and momentary hesitations in the face of a great peril; but in spite of all, in the present day they seem to us out of place in a hero. We are therefore grateful to Virgil for having spared us them. Of course Turnus flees, like Hector, but only when the weapon he is using is broken in his hand, and he remains without defence. "Then he runs hither and thither, and makes a thousand uncertain turns"; [2] he approaches his soldiers, whom terror renders motionless; he calls them by their names, and urgently begs them to give him his sword, and the moment he receives it, bravely recommences the struggle. What also shocks us in the narrative of Homer is the part the gods take in the fight. In reality, the victory is theirs. Minerva never wavers in

---

[1] *Æn.*, XII. 80.

[2] *Ibid.*, 743.

her aid to Achilles, who is the stronger, and brings him back his javelin, which he has flung unsuccessfully, and she basely deceives Hector, who is the weaker, by making him think that his brother Deiphobus is going to fight at his side. It is only when the struggle has begun, and Hector wants his brother's help, that he perceives he is alone, and that the pretended Deiphobus has disappeared. In Virgil, the gods neutralise each other by dividing. If Juturna gives Turnus back his sword, Venus allows Æneas to draw out his javelin, which has stuck in the trunk of a wild olive. Thus the intervention of divinity does not annul the merit of the men; the victory is their personal work, and the final success is decided by their own valour. It is also curious to note that between the date of the two poems the sentiment of honour has become refined, and that Virgil already knows and respects certain delicacies, or, if you will, certain prejudices still prevailing among us at the present time.

His personages, when compared with those of Homer, give rise to the same observations. Although Æneas plays nearly the same part as Achilles, and the poet at moments has chosen to lend him his character, he nevertheless differs from him very widely. In his combat with Turnus, he pushes respect for plighted faith to excess. When the Latins, violently breaking the truce, begin the struggle again, he does not at first think that their perjury authorises him to break his vow. Unarmed and bareheaded, he would stay his people, who are trying to defend themselves; and while preventing them from returning the enemy's blows, is himself wounded. More remarkable yet, the poet has managed to make him keep his humanity and gentleness, even in the bloody scene at the end. There, especially, we remark the difference between his character and that of Achilles. In reading the *Iliad* our hearts fails us at the last violences of the Greek hero. Not only does he slay Hector without ruth, but he replies to his touching supplications merely by regretting that "he cannot eat his quivering flesh." Pious Æneas, on the contrary, allows himself to be softened by the prayers of Turnus. He is even about to forgive him, when he perceives the baldrick of his young friend Pallas, whom Turnus did not spare, in spite of his youth, and whose spoils he has appropriated. We understand that his anger should be stirred up again at this sight, and we forgive him for giving way to a just resentment. It is not Æneas, but Pallas, who avenges, and strikes Turnus by the hand of a friend.

> " *Pallas te, hoc vulnere, Pallas*
> *Immolat.*" [1]

Turnus resembles Homer's heroes more nearly, and is made upon their model. Yet he has certain features of his own, and which are stamped with the epoch of Virgil. Above all, he seems sensitive to what we call the point of honour. When, deceived by his sister, who would save him at all costs, he has followed the false Æneas, and the ship into which he has imprudently thrown himself carries him far from the battle, his grief is intense, and nothing is more touching than his laments. "Mighty Jupiter!" he exclaims, "have you then found

---

[1] *Æn.*, XII. 948.

me worthy of such infamy? What will all those brave men say of me, who have followed me, and whom I have delivered up to death without accompanying them? What is to be done? What abyss deep enough will open itself under my feet? You, at least, O winds, have pity on me. Carry this bark against the cliffs. Turnus himself conjures you. Break it on these rocks, where the reproaches of my friends and the cry of my remorse may reach me never more!"[1] Do we not seem to hear certain heroes of our *chansons de geste?* It is the same generous ring, the same chivalric ardour, the same scrupulous care for honour. Turnus is concerned, above all things, for his reputation; does not wish any one to be able to accuse him of disloyalty, and would willingly have taken his device from the words of Roland:

" Que mauveise chançun de nus chantet ne seit ! "

If I have made a point of dwelling on the resemblances observable between the *Æneid* and the poems of the Middle Ages, it is because they seem to me to have some importance. It is useful to show how Virgil, who loves to connect himself with the past, sometimes stretches out a hand to the future. When we know what is ancient and what modern in him, we better understand the part he has played in the history of letters. Placed at the meeting-point of two ages, and by a happy chance partaking of both, he has served as an intermediary between them. It is through him that we reach Antiquity; it is he who opens it up to us, he who

---

[1] *Æn.,* X. 668.

leads and guides us to it. Between it and us he forms a kind of connecting-link, and in this sense Baillet was right in saying that "he is the centre point of all the poets who came before and after him."

Such are the reflections that forced themselves upon me while trying to picture to myself the combat of Æneas and Turnus in the plain of Laurentum. I fear they have carried me very far. My readers will doubtless find that I have kept them too long on that desert shore, searching for lost towns of which no trace remains. But travelling with Virgil, one delights to linger by the way, and he is a companion from whom 'tis hard to part.

THE END.